WANTED
GREENER GRASS

a novel about love, envy, and a crazy kind of courage

LILIANE GRACE

Published by Grace Productions
Ferntree Gully, Victoria, Australia

https://lilianegrace.com

A catalogue record for this book is available from the National Library of Australia

Also available in Kindle and Apple iBooks formats.

Cover art by Mira Ktajraatmadja

Typeset in 11pt Minion Pro Condensed

Print on Demand by Ingram Sparks, Australia

For Derek

How readers are responding to *Wanted: Greener Grass*

*'What a spellbinding story! I was so entranced, I read it in one sitting
- seven hours straight through - not even stopping for food! It felt like
the characters were real people and 'reality' next day was quite unreal
by comparison! I love it when I am so engaged that I start yelling at
the page (or screen), "Nooooo!" or "You go girl!" or "Yes!" etc. The
excitement even carried into the next day- I wasn't tired even after only
three hours sleep! Buzzing! Can't wait for the sequel!'*

- Cecilia Whiting

*'Thought-provoking and I love how you wove the Hero's Journey
through it, and how relationships are our best teachers.'*
   - Dr Rosemary McCallum, counsellor and Doctor of Metaphysics

*'I loved it and couldn't put it down! Both the characters' frustration
with a long-term relationship was well written and I could fully relate
to Mia's feelings, wanting time on her own, wanting something more,
wondering if she wanted to continue the relationship or get out. I'll
recommend it to my friends.'* - Tania

*'I absolutely loved it and cried at the end. I thoroughly enjoyed the
higher wisdom and insights you wove into the story line.'*

- Jenny Rawson

*'I loved it! It was easy to read and the story kept me very interested
right through. I read it in just three days, which is unusual for me as
I normally only get a maximum of around an hour a day to read for
pleasure.'* - David Grau

*'The refreshingly honest characters and twists of the story make this
book an intriguing read. I thoroughly enjoyed exploring the unexpected
intricacies of these human beings and the lives they lead.'*

- Joelie Atkinson

*'Liliane has a way of captivating you through her storytelling. Principles
about life, relationships and love woven elegantly throughout help you
understand these areas at a deeper level and break traditional beliefs
around relationships so that you can live a more aware and empowered
life that is right for you. Beautifully written.'*

- Tanya Cross, Counsellor

'Now is the winter of our discontent.'

– *William Shakespeare*

◇◇◇◇◇◇◇◇◇◇◇◇◇◇◇◇◇◇

'We have met the enemy
and he is us.'

– *Pogo*
(Cartoon character created by Walt Kelly)

1

John was the one making this trip across the world but she was the one not yet ready to leave the house.

Mia hit send on that last email and dashed to the loo, calling, 'I'm coming!' even though she was now sitting there with bare knees, skirt up around her waist, feet perched on the loo stool. She could just imagine him, waiting patiently by the front door, neatly packed case at his feet, checking his watch... She breathed in to zip up and washed her hands to the noise of the toilet flushing, then snapped off a piece of floss and began to work it through her teeth as she hurried from the bathroom to find her shoes. Curses! Not beside the bed! Wardrobe doors slammed as she searched.

'They're down here, next to the couch,' John called. She heard him walking to the living room to retrieve them for her and flew to meet him, breathless. A muttered 'sorry' as she pushed her feet into the damn shoes. Bag. Keys – shit! Where –? John held them up, the big jangling bundle, and she made a thank you/apologetic face and headed for the door, pulling her green jacket on. John squatted beside Bitsy for a moment, scratching their Papillon's big, feathery ears and murmuring, 'Good dog... goodbye... look after Mia...'

Bitsy wagged her tail and gave one short sharp bark when they closed the door; then they heard her running for the window to watch them leave.

Sitting in the car while it warmed up, she turned to him to ask, again, 'How are you feeling?'

He gave a very small shrug.

Was anything else coming? Any other comment? Was he going to suddenly share some deeper feelings? No... Right. She turned back to the wheel, checked her mirrors (little frown puckering her forehead, brown hair looking as boring as ever), and reversed.

'I really hope you get there in time,' she said, when they stood idling in traffic, a stream of cars ahead of them and behind them.

He looked at her in surprise. 'We won't miss the flight. I've allowed plenty of time.'

'I mean –'

'Oh.' He gave a tiny nod and let silence pervade the car once more.

He was locked up in himself, even more so than usual. It was no wonder they hadn't made love last night. Although also partly her fault, she thought with a flush of guilt and an abrupt flick of the indicator to get out of this bloody, going-nowhere lane. If she hadn't stayed on the phone so long talking to Sheryl while he was packing, and if he'd bloody well said something to her like, 'I'm going to bed now', some sort of clue so she would have known to wind up her call but no, that would be 'Communication', which was not John's 'thing'.

Someone was finally going to let her through. She merged, waving thanks, and they moved a few metres before coming to a stop and watching the lane she'd been in begin to flow past. Fuck. Glanced at John. He was still gazing ahead with that distant, closed expression.

Her waistband was cutting her in half. Really wrong choice for a long drive to the airport when you've put on so much weight, but she did love this multi-coloured skirt and it went so well with the jacket. She reached behind her with both hands to release the button, and just then her lane began to move.

Music. That would help with this silence. She flipped between her favourite stations but there was mostly news and talkback radio. Revolting time to have to drive to the airport but this was the first flight John had been able to book at short notice.

'Don't forget to get that paperwork to Matt,' he said suddenly.

'I know.' Mental note to self: *Paperwork. Matt.* She glanced at John's profile. Would he notice if she scribbled herself a little reminder?

Finally they were on the freeway and moving. She reached out suddenly, put a hand on his thigh, and he gave her a brief smile and covered her hand with his. They continued without speaking, the radio filling the gaps.

Short-term Parking was chockers, as ever. They wound up and down the aisles looking for a space, not wanting to believe the little red 'taken' lights, and finally found one.

'Yellow, Level One, Column F,' John said as they began the hurried walk to the terminal. Her smile was a mixture of gratitude and resentment.

'Coffee?' she asked as they stood waiting to check his luggage in.

'Thanks.'

And then she waited in another queue, eyeing the muffins and telling herself no. A tall man with very short sandy hair at the back and sides but a profusion of curls on top came to stand beside her. Broad-shouldered. Suit. Little diamanté stud... Interesting. He caught her looking and smiled, and in the blink of an eye he had said something and she had laughed and he had whisked her away on some romantic life together, and it was lovely. Then the waitress said, 'Next,' and it was her turn. She ordered a standard latté for John and a chai for herself and took the number she was proffered. The man stepped into the space she had left and ordered an iced coffee. He took his number and came to hover beside her.

'Travelling?' he asked.

'No. My...' *Spit it out, girl.* 'Husband.' Was he losing interest immediately? There was no ring on 'that' finger, although a big gold one gleamed on his pinkie. Sandy hairs on the backs of his hands... 'You?' she asked.

'United Arab Emirates. Business.

'Ah. What...?'

'Architect. Hotels.'

She could just see the floods of money pouring into his bank account. Checked his shoes. Smart, probably expensive. Not that she knew much about shoes.

'Business or pleasure?' he was asking. 'Your husband.'

'Oh. Neither. His father is...' How did you put it without sounding clichéd? She gave up. 'On his deathbed. He had a stroke a couple of days ago. Doesn't look like he's going to make it. So it's the farewell visit and then probably a funeral, and helping his mother tidy things up.'

'You're not going?'

She made a little face. 'I don't really know his folks. I've only met his parents once. And I've got a conference starting on Friday. I'm PA to the people who are hosting the event – it's all resting on my shoulders! And we have a dog.' A shrug, a helpless laugh that hopefully didn't sound too guilty.

'Twelve,' the girl behind the counter called, and she stepped forward, wondering what Mr Sandy-Curls-Handsome-Architect was making of her story. Was she a bitch for not ditching the conference to go to the UK with her husband and deal with his mother's pain and loss and resentment of Mia for whipping her son away so many years ago? Or a coward? Or just realistic? Did she really need to inject her controversial presence into the family grief? Did she and John really need the extra expense and the extra loss of income? And besides, the thought of having a few precious weeks to herself felt like sheer magic. A gift from heaven. A reprieve. A chance to think, reflect, feel her feelings and make some new choices. It wasn't as if going to England together would be an opportunity for them to reconnect and holiday; he'd be helping his mother wind up his father's affairs and they'd be choosing headstones and planning funerals and selling the house and getting his mother ready for her move into the retirement village. He'd be responsible for most of this since younger brother Jake was apparently useless at anything practical. So John would be in big brother, eldest son mode, managing stuff, and she'd be in the way, restless, lonely... Better that he be fully present there without worrying about how his wife was fitting in and occupying herself, and she be fully here, free, unchained...

'All the best then,' Sandy-Hair said, tall frothing glass in hand.

'Thanks,' she replied, a paper cup in each of hers. 'You too.'

He flashed the gorgeous smile and she basked in one last romantic image of the two of them in Abu Dhabi, walking down busy streets among head-scarved women… and then gave it up and headed back to John.

He was at the counter. She wove through the aisle toward him with the two steaming cups, reaching him as his case jerked away on the conveyor belt and he thanked the check-in attendant and stepped away. They had another few minutes before he had to pass through the final doors, so they hovered, sipping their drinks, watching people walk past or gather in knots to talk. A large Indian family had stopped nearby and she admired the women's saris. A couple of twenty-somethings wearing backpacks strolled past. She nudged John.

'Bring back memories?'

He followed her gaze and nodded.

'Seems so long ago now. An age,' she mused.

'It was,' he said.

There was a truckload of significance in those two words. A cavernous space opened up and their nine years together toppled into it, dragging her doubts and questions with them. A happy age? A worthwhile age? Or a big mistake? She teetered back and forth between those options herself. No relationship was only happy, of course; you'd be stupid to expect that, but there had been so much doubt, especially lately. So much frustration – on both sides, she guessed, although he didn't talk much about what he was feeling. She had to comb her memories to find the happy, contented moments these days; they were becoming increasingly lost in the tangle of… what? Regret? Disappointment?

She remembered that day in Spain when they'd had to say goodbye and had clung together, making promises to stay in touch because the connection had been so exactly right, like two puzzle pieces fitting together with a little click of confirmation… And then he had followed her to Australia, turning up out of the blue with that beam, those beautiful hazel eyes shining – surprise! I couldn't get you out of my mind. I love you. I want to be with you. Let me share the rest of your life.

And it wasn't as if she had anyone else, and definitely there was something between them, some real, genuine love and friendship, and it's no small thing to have someone follow you across the world declaring their love... She couldn't say she agreed to marry just because she was flattered – that wouldn't be true, but there was an element of it...

'I'd better go,' John said, crushing the empty cup in his hand and reaching for hers.

He'd already spied a bin. She watched as he walked to it and tossed the cups in. That walk. The slim frame, the erect head, the slightly turned-out feet... Going home to England for three weeks... She couldn't deny the rush of delight that recurred at this thought. Space! Freedom! Relief from constant heaviness as they bumped up against each other's frustration.

And then they were facing each other, and his hands were encircling her upper arms as he regarded her steadily. 'I'm sorry,' he said, 'I haven't been much fun lately.'

She conceded this with a little sign of assent.

'Lots on my mind,' he said.

'I know,' she said. 'Me too.'

'Lots to talk about when I get back. I just need to get this over with.'

'Yes.'

He bent down and kissed her softly on the lips. Put one hand against the side of her face, cradling it. She melted a little.

'Take care, Mia. I do love you.'

Tears pricked her eyes; she hugged him. 'I know. I love you too.' *But geez, it would help if we were having some fun,* she didn't say. *Instead of all this same old, same old, and seriousness and nothing new or fresh.*

John released her gradually, letting her hands go last, his gaze drinking her in, as if to form an impression that would stay with him for the next three weeks. Then he picked up the satchel with his book and laptop and walked to the International Departures doorway, turned back to smile and wave, and then continued on through it.

Mia stood there for a moment, almost to check that this was real and he wouldn't be coming back out, and then she headed off to find the car. Yellow,

Level One, Column F. Thank God he'd noticed. She would have walked out of the terminal and arrived at the car park and been suffused by panic at the number of floors and vast expanse of vehicles, and had no frigging idea where she'd parked. Instead, as she made her way through the travelling crowds and along the covered walkway toward her Holden Cruise, a smile was blossoming on her face.

When she had heard the news of John's father's imminent death she had been shocked by the immediate sense of relief – dare she say it, even delight – that had rushed through her. He would go to England for the funeral and she would stay here. He would have to be there for a while to help his mother adjust. The sense of space and freedom and possibility that this disloyal thought unleashed in her had been troubling in the extreme, and now it declared itself, full-frontal.

2

The buzz in the office was at maximum volume when Mia arrived. With the conference beginning the next day, boxes of registration kits were now being carried by staff out of their Board Room to be transported to the venue. Susan was co-ordinating this traffic, clipboard tucked in the crook of her arm, the usual sour expression on her heavily made-up face. She caught Mia's eye and beckoned her over.

'Thank God you're here! Interstate and international guests are arriving and already phoning in with problems and requests, the gala dinner magician's been struck down with laryngitis, and there are dramas with the hotel kitchen. Reynald's been dragged out of a meeting with Paula to find something for them and she's fuming. It is All Hands On Deck.'

'Right,' Mia said. Susan would have taken great pleasure in dumping that list of problems on her. She quickened her pace and found her boss sitting at her desk, his broad back hunched as he combed through her files.

'Can I help?' Mia asked, looking over his shoulder.

'You're back!' Reynald swivelled in her chair with an expression of utter relief. 'Where's the list of dietary requirements for the speakers? The hotel kitchen reckons they never received it.'

Mia frowned and reached past him to her keyboard. 'I definitely...' she began, clicking through her files.

'I'll get out of your way,' he said, lifting his bulk out of her chair. 'I'm supposed to be in a meeting with Paula but they were stressing about it so much that I ducked out. When you've found it, catch up on all the other fires that need to be put out, will you?'

Mia half-smiled, shrugging off the green jacket and settling into her pre-warmed seat.

'Hubby get off all right?' he added as an after-thought, turning back.

'Yes thanks. On his way to the motherland.'

'Good.' He took a few steps toward his office and then turned back again. 'Thanks for staying. I suppose you should have gone with.'

'It's fine,' she said, focused on her screen. 'Here it is. I'll send it through again.' 'Again', because she was sure she had, although she was a little afraid to check her sent mail…

How Mia had lasted so long in a PA job was anyone's guess. Having followed her parents' pointed finger toward secretarial college after leaving school, she'd bounced from one office to the next, winning friends wherever she went but eventually meeting her limit for administrative tasks. John joked that she had a split personality: at home she was chaotic and prone to losing things; at work she seemed able to keep track of details quite efficiently – up to a point. And that point was eroding. She was becoming more and more distracted, ten-plus years into this career, and more and more restless. Unlike Sheryl, who had been bossing people around since her playground years, Mia had had no idea what she wanted to do when she grew up; she had just kept following the path of least resistance. But now her inner resistance was rising. She wanted to find her own thing, something that would light her up and fill her days with joy rather than busyness, and perhaps she was finally on the cusp of doing that. This latest job for ACCAT, a counselling and coaching organisation, had exposed her to a whole new possibility.

Her attention was captured by the glossy conference schedule on her desk. Eight speakers and another four presenters running workshops over two and a half days. The topics were fascinating – much more interesting than the conferences for the manufacturing company where she'd worked last – techniques for 'stress resilience', for simultaneously healing the client and the practitioner, for reading non-verbal signals… play therapy for refugees… mindfulness for dealing with compassion fatigue and burnout… a paper on securing client information in the digital age and another on ethics and setting industry standards… a workshop on 'fulfilment through conscious living instead of unconscious eating'… and something called 'the Hero's Journey' for helping clients find their life purpose and manage life transitions… Madeleine Spottie was leading the fulfilment workshop. She was blonde and svelte – not someone who looked as if she'd ever had an eating issue; Mia hoped she'd be able to sit in on that one. The other topic attracting her interest was the 'hero's journey' presentation. The speaker was Bernard McFafe. Quite handsome in a mature, older-man kind of way. She wondered what a hero's journey was, and if heroines were eligible too. But now was not the time; Mia had fires to put out.

She slid the brochure out of the way and picked up her phone.

Mia arrived at Sheryl's at Crazy Hour. The front door was unlocked so she let herself in to the sound of Talia bawling, and found Sheryl in the smart lilac pant suit pacing the kitchen with the baby on her shoulder, jiggling her and patting her back, and an array of vegetables spread out on the kitchen bench, some sliced and others still waiting. A pot of water bubbled on the stove, steaming up the windows.

'It's my fault,' Sheryl grimaced. 'I went out for lunch today and had a latté. The cow's milk's given her a bellyache. I feel so bad: half an hour of pleasure for me and two hours of misery for Tahls.'

'Oh, poor baby,' Mia said, putting a hand gently on Talia's stiff little back. 'You too, Mummy.' She planted a kiss on her friend's cheek, pulled her jacket off and draped it over the back of a chair. 'What can I do? Hold Talia or chop the veg?'

Sheryl held out her crying, hiccupping daughter. 'You try. I'm too stressed now. Who woulda thought a little tiny creature like this could bring a big grown woman to pieces?'

Mia cuddled the damp-faced baby against her shoulder, patting her bottom and swaying back and forth while Sheryl returned to the stove and emptied a packet of rice noodles into the boiling water.

'Honestly,' she said, turning back to the bench and picking up her knife. 'I am the owner of a major event management company. I can solve problems in the blink of an eye – big problems, like pallets of stock being delivered to the wrong venue on the set-up day of an expo, and staff all falling sick at once, and important people expecting display stands who haven't ordered them, but one crying baby and my stomach is in knots… I think I've mentioned this before.'

'Several times,' Mia murmured, her cheek against Talia's wet one, breathing in her delicious fragrance.

'Forgive me, it's cathartic,' Sheryl said, chopping.

Talia gave a loud burp.

Her mother looked up and beamed. 'That magic sound.'

Mia wandered around the kitchen, swaying and stroking while Talia snuffled against her chest and Sheryl powered through the vegies, adding the regular thud of her knife to the gentle bubbling in the background. This was divine, Mia thought, relishing the naturalness of Talia's little body in her arms. She so ached for a baby of her own. She and John had tried for the last couple of years, and Sheryl and Alec had pulled it off in only a few months.

'You have the touch,' Sheryl remarked into the quiet. 'She's settling.'

'Probably just exhausted from crying.'

'Don't bump it away; I complimented you.'

'Thank you,' Mia said automatically. She came to rest by the bench and picked a piece of carrot out of the pile. 'Your hair looks nice.'

'I straightened it for the lunch. Haven't done anything just for me in ages.' Sheryl turned back to the stove, lifted the wok off a hook and placed it on a burner. 'Alec wasn't in a hurry this morning so he looked after Tahls while I indulged.'

'I complimented you,' Mia pointed out.

'Oh. Thank you.'

Talia's eyes were closing. Mia moved away from the stove so she wouldn't wake when Sheryl dropped the vegies into the hot oil. 'A social lunch or a business lunch?' she asked from the other side of the kitchen table.

'Bit of both: potential work. But enough about me! How are you feeling with John gone?'

'Free. And guilty.'

Sheryl paused with her chopping board of vegies poised over the wok. 'So what are you going to do?'

'What do you mean?'

'Kick up your heels while he's away?'

'Sheryl!'

'I'm serious. You've been down in the mouth for ages about this relationship. Maybe a little playfulness on the side will help.'

'Terrific. My best friend advises adultery.'

'Your best friend advises being more spontaneous and following your heart for a while instead of being all tied up in knots about constantly doing the right thing – and being miserable while you're at it. Remember what Osho says: 'Life is not a problem to be solved. It is a mystery to be lived.' A dramatic flourish of her knife accompanied these words, and then Sheryl tipped the vegetables into the wok; they sizzled loudly.

Mia checked Talia but her delicate eyelids remained closed and her breathing was steady. 'That sounds good in theory but in practice…? I don't do secrets well and John doesn't deserve that. It might be awful at the moment but I don't want to cheat on him.'

'So don't go all the way. Just play a bit.'

'He would still be hurt.' Mia adjusted Talia's position so that she lay tucked in the crook of her arm, and sank gently onto the kitchen sofa with the sleeping baby.

'Not if he doesn't know. Why tell? Just give yourself a break. Stop taking everything so seriously. And anyway, who knows what *he* might get up to over there! '

'I don't think so! Not John.'

'Don't be so sure. Underneath that sensible conservative exterior there could be a wild boy waiting to be unleashed.'

Mia smiled. 'I think I met the wild boy when we first crossed paths in Spain. Not so wild, Shez. More of a nice, caring, responsible boy.'

'I thought you said he let his hair down when he got onto the grappa?'

'He gets so sick afterward that it hardly ever happens.'

The garage door in the laundry opened and a moment later Alec appeared in the kitchen with a bottle of wine in one hand and his brief case in the other. Whenever she saw him, Mia had to repress a pang of envy. Not that she wanted Alec *per se*, but the romance of how he had bided his time, watching Sheryl move through brief relationship after brief relationship while he was summoning the courage to ask her out, repeatedly being foiled at the last moment when she revealed yet another new crush and it wasn't him... And, actually, envying their romance wasn't the whole truth either because the beginning of Mia's relationship with John had been huge on romance – Sheryl had been utterly green that this man had followed her half-way across the world with a proposal of marriage – but then it had all settled into boringness whereas Alec was still, apparently, madly in love with Sheryl and utterly besotted with Talia.

Mia watched him kiss the side of Sheryl's neck as she stood at the wok stirring, and then wrap his arms around her. They were both tall – you kind of got the Jack Spratt-and-wife image because she was so large beside him in both size and character, and because they complemented each other so beautifully.

Sheryl made a little noise to let him know they were not alone, and Alec lifted his balding head from where he was nuzzling her to meet Mia's eyes. He gave a small self-conscious smile.

Later, as they sat with the remains of their meal on the table and Talia snuggled against Alec's chest, Sheryl picked up the conversation. 'I've been telling Mia she should get out while John's away,' she said. 'Play around a bit.'

Alec raised his brows.

Mia raised hers in a 'See? Crazy idea!' but Sheryl charged on. 'I don't mean an affair, exactly,' she said. 'Just the odd date to have a bit of fun and get some sort of perspective –'

'What kind of perspective will that give her?' Alec demanded. 'That an unattached flirtation is more fun than a committed relationship?'

Sheryl threw her hands up in the air. 'Okay! All right! Maybe I'm being the child around here, but Mia needs some fun and John needs a wake-up, and maybe something a little edgy will help shake up the status quo… It was just an idea.'

'You two have a committed relationship and you're still having fun,' Mia objected, pointing her wine glass at them.

'Three years against your nine,' Sheryl reminded her. 'We're still in the honeymoon phase.' But the smile they gave each other was drenched in 'forever'.

Waiting for her car to warm up, Mia checked her phone but there was still no message from John. He'd be at Gangzhou Airport, she imagined, walking around to stretch out before the next leg of his trip, or sleeping on the floor somewhere. These little airports often had dodgy Wi-Fi.

She pulled away from Sheryl and Alec's home and headed toward her own quiet, dark, empty house, and Bitsy, her baby, who would be lying on the bed with her nose on her paws, mournful because Mia had rushed in after work to feed and walk her, and then disappeared again and left her all alone.

3

D ay One of the conference proceeded much more smoothly than any of
  them had expected given the dramas of the previous day. The venue
looked excellent, the hum in the foyer as enthusiastic participants gathered
set the tone for the rest of the day, the scheduled speakers turned up on time
and delivered thought-provoking papers and workshops, and the logistics
team managed all the behind-the-scenes stuff without a hitch. They were
busy – they were run off their feet, in fact – but no dramas. Sheryl texted Mia
several times through the day since it was her event management company at
the helm. For a woman on maternity leave, she sure did have trouble letting
go of her work.

Back at home at the end of the day, Mia switched on the lights, nudged
the door closed behind her, and bent to scratch a euphoric Bitsy behind the
ears. Then she kicked off her shoes and headed straight for the heater with
the mail. Only three: all bills. She put them aside and went back to cuddling
Bitsy. When the chill in the air was finally giving way to warmth, she ventured
into the kitchen to make herself a cup of tea, and her phone pinged. It was
John.

> Here at last. Horrible flight. Jake late to pick me up –
> nothing new there. On our way to the hospital. Dad
> in a coma so I'm probably too late. :(How are you?

> Fine thanks. 1st day of conf done – going well.
> Crossing my fingers for you.

There was no reply to this. She hovered for a while, waiting, then put her phone aside and settled on the couch with her tea and a banana and an episode of *Mad Men* to unwind before bed. Really she should be going straight to bed, and she would probably nod off here on the couch, but she still felt wired. Bitsy leapt up beside her, turned around in a circle, and settled against her thigh.

In the middle of the night there was another ping. She heard it from a great distance, and swam toward the sound lazily, thinking, *I should get up… John…* but each stroke she took through the ocean of her dreams seemed to draw her further away… and it wasn't until some time later that she finally surfaced, after being harassed by thoughts of him that kept cutting through the deliciousness of sleep, thoughts and images of babies – her baby about to be born only no one can find the father and the baby won't come until he is present.

Suddenly she was wide awake, feeling shocked and tender at the same time. So close. She had been so close to holding her own child. The disappointment was like a bad taste in her mouth. She sat up in bed, dragging the covers to her chin and wondering why she had to get up, and then the memory of the phone returned, and she emerged into the cold air, stepping into slippers and scooping her dressing gown off the hook as she passed out of the bedroom and headed for the kitchen where her phone was on charge. This was her rule: no phones in the bedroom, but maybe she would need to keep it closer while he was overseas. She heard Bitsy's toenails on the hallway boards behind her.

The kitchen light was harsh and sudden; she stood in the doorway, shielding her eyes for a moment, and then padded to the bench where her phone lay. Two messages from John:

12.15 a.m.

Dad's been in a coma all day. They reckon he'll go any minute. So no chance for a final conversation for me. :(Jake reckons he had a good chat a few days ago. Mum the walking dead…

2.30 a.m.

He's passed

She sat with the phone at the kitchen table, wondering what to say.

So sorry :(

What else?

Give my love to your mum and Jake

Would they want her love? The distant, apparently uncaring wife of the runaway son? She sighed, deleting, and wrote instead:

Wish you'd had a chance to speak to him

He had hoped for that; she knew he'd wanted to somehow repair the pain caused by his apparent abandonment and distance. His parents were not the sort to take to Skype or other internet communications, and their interactions over the years had been reduced to occasional letters and phone calls. She hoped her message would feel like genuine empathy and not just rub salt in the wound… In a moment of insight, she added,

Looks to me like he was waiting for you to get there…

then worried that he might not take that as she meant it. Waited, but there was still no reply. She really should say something about his mother and brother. She picked up her phone again.

Give my love to your mum and Jake ?

Would the question mark convey her tentativeness? Would he understand what she meant? Surely. She hit send and moments later his response appeared:

Thanks. You still up?

> Woke up, heard the phone

> Sorry, didn't mean to wake you

> It's ok. It's important. I feel bad that I'm not there with you

There was a long pause. She saw that he was typing but nothing came. The ellipsis-in-a-bubble disappeared and she waited, trying to imagine what was happening over there. His mother, usually so strong and bustling, now grey and pinched… The shadowy brother whom she hadn't met: the unreliable Jake who'd nonetheless managed to be at his father's side for the deathbed conversation and had pushed John out of the way yet again…

She was jolted out of her daydream by the light on her screen as more words appeared:

> Maybe you can come later? If it works

She frowned as a mess of feelings and images showed up: disappointment at the end of freedom, packing and flying all that way, leaving work behind and Reynald's troubled face, trying to find a kennel or a minder for Bitsy, arriving in England where everyone was depressed and it drizzled constantly, meeting a stream of grave relatives, dealing with John's grieving mother…

> Yes

hoping no with all her heart.

> Play it by ear…

Mia woke seconds before her alarm blared. She silenced it and fell back against the pillow feeling exhausted. All those midnight interactions had disturbed her sleep. She'd taken ages to settle again, her mind ticking over the question of where she should be: here in Melbourne or over there in London with John? She had sorted her feelings into little piles: the guilt about not wanting to go went into that pile, the shame about wanting her freedom went there, the guilt about her growing interest in other men went here, her hopes for a fresh start with John went there… Some of the piles were much bigger than others.

Dragging herself out of bed, she went to shower and transform her bleary-eyed face into the bright smiling visage she would need to show up with and wear for the whole day.

Madeleine Spottie's workshop was scheduled for today. It was after lunch and Mia had arranged to be on the back tables so that she could listen in. It turned out that Madeleine had been plagued with bulimia. She was so elegant and calm up there on the stage; it was difficult to believe she had ever stuffed food into her mouth, watching the door in case someone came in and caught her, and even more difficult to believe that she had ever knelt by a toilet, puking. But clearly she was speaking from personal experience, and her description of feeling empty, of constantly thinking about her next meal and taking pleasure from food because the rest of her life seemed so colourless… all of that Mia could relate to easily. She hadn't resorted to making herself vomit but she completely understood the bewitching magic of food.

When the urge came for her to go to the toilet, she whispered to Susan that she'd be back shortly and slipped out of the room, through the main area where all the speakers had their displays set up, and into the Ladies. And there she sat. And sat. This was probably the greatest bane of *her* life: constipation. The times she could just go quickly and easily and completely felt like heavenly gifts; for too many years she had struggled to empty her bowels, and then struggled to find ways of concealing how long she'd spent in the toilet. She remembered going to the loo one time at the family home of her first boyfriend. They'd all been playing cards, and when she returned, hoping to slip unnoticed into her seat, her boyfriend's father said, 'Glad you're back, love. We thought you'd fallen in!' and they'd all looked at her, and she'd wished she had fallen in. At seventeen the embarrassment had been lethal.

When Mia finally flushed and washed her hands and crept back into the room, the participants were gathered in small groups talking to each other, and the logistics team was preparing some handouts. She couldn't ask what she'd missed because she didn't want to draw attention to her absence, so she joined the staff in counting papers, snatching a look at the headings, which were about recording memories, associations to foods, and moments of mindfulness. After these small-group conversations Madeleine led everyone through a meditation about connecting with their bodily wisdom and releasing self-judgement. Mia was just feeling the stirring of compassion for herself when someone gave her shoulder a little shake and a voice hissed, 'Now'. Opening her eyes, she saw Susan and the others standing with armfuls of handouts, and picked up her pile to help distribute them to the closed-eyed participants. Quite a few had tear-stained faces, she noticed, as she walked quietly around her segment of the room placing sheets on tables.

She had an opportunity to apply the snippets she had gleaned at the gala dinner that evening. Sitting in front of her plate of fish and vegetables, she closed her eyes for a moment, placed a hand on her stomach, and tuned in. How was she feeling right now? Relaxed, she concluded. Hungry. Ready to eat and looking forward to it but not in that desperate way. She opened her eyes and the woman opposite leaned forward and said, 'Madeleine's conscious eating? Going to enjoy every bite?' They both laughed and tucked in.

Bernard McFafe's presentation was scheduled on Sunday morning. She had seen him floating around the venue chatting with people and signing books at his stand, and was looking forward to hearing what he had to say. He was quite attractive, she reflected, as he stepped onto the stage. Not an absolute dish like Hugh Jackman, or a hunk like Gerard Butler, but there was something strong and kind and 'deep' about him.

The Hero's Journey, he told them, came from the work of psychologist Carl Jung and a mythologist called Joseph Campbell who had studied cultures around the world and discovered that each one had a set of myths or legends that conveyed lessons or principles for living. He rattled off a list of Hollywood films that had deliberately incorporated those very messages: *Star Wars, Lion King, Finding Nemo, The Matrix…* a long list of films about individuals who grappled, in their own ways, with life's big questions and experiences.

'So we shouldn't view these myths in a theoretical or abstract way,' he said, looking at them over his rimless spectacles, 'and we shouldn't view these films as pure entertainment. When we recognise the patterns they are showing us, we can all apply them to our lives because the patterns track the human evolutionary story; they explore the art of being human.'

His slides threw up compelling images of people from around the world going through various rites of passage. Pictures flashed of indigenous and third world and first world peoples all engaged in the same kinds of events: births, coming of age, marriages, deaths. Certain elements accompanied each life event, he said: a 'Call to Adventure' that summoned us to face a fear or develop a skill or transform stuckness and move on from our 'Ordinary World'... 'Threshold Guardians' – those people who stopped us and made us question our path, allies who encouraged us, mentors who guided us, enemies who confronted us... Along the way obstacles would become more challenging until finally we were in 'The Abyss, the Cave', grappling with the dark night of the soul –

'Mia,' Susan hissed.

Mia looked up.

'Reynald needs you. He's in the logistics room.'

Reluctantly, Mia rose. Reynald met her in the doorway to the logistics room. Someone was sick. A sweaty, pale-faced participant sat in a chair, head resting back against the wall. An ambulance was on its way. Mia was to sit with him until it arrived.

'Sorry,' the man murmured. 'Nuisance...'

'Nonsense,' she said, patting his hand. This was patently untrue, but what else could she say? He couldn't help being sick. She was sure he would rather be in the conference room than sitting here, about to be trucked off to hospital. But then again, maybe this was a pattern for him – maybe being sick was his way of avoiding something he didn't want to face. If you thought about yourself as the hero of your own life story, as someone going through meaningful rites of passage rather than someone just having random experiences, then you had to examine and question everything that happened. Life would be a whole lot more interesting but also a whole lot more confronting. The stakes were raised when you lived consciously.

She looked at the man more closely. He was fiftyish, plain, thick around the middle, wearing a brown woollen jumper and brown suede pants. There was a wedding ring on the hand that hung listlessly at his side. A name tag that said 'Alf Lesser'. 'Lesser'... Probably a German name that meant something else but if you grew up with a name like that, how could you ever feel 'greater'?

Her quandary about her relationship with John was the rite of passage she was going through right now. John's trip to Europe flung choices in her face, pushing her to stop marking time and make a decision. Sheryl was clearly a threshold guardian – tempting her to stray, or perhaps inciting her to stop sabotaging her life and live more fully. Osho was a mentor along her path, although his advice could be unsettling. Mia had come across an old, dog-eared copy of his book *Intimacy* at a yoga class, and he'd become their shared inspiration. She wondered what kind of cave or abyss she might be heading toward.

The other issue was her job. She was really over this administrative stuff. Since coming to work for ACCAT – Australian Counselling, Coaching And Training – the idea had been dawning to train as a counsellor and be one of the participants at these conferences instead of one of the logistical team. She wanted to walk away from filing cabinets and computers and instead sit opposite real people and listen to their stories and go hunting for the meaning with them. She wanted to be the wise one, the guide, the supporter...

Voices and noises outside the room heralded the arrival of the ambulance officers. The door opened and Reynald led two blue-clad men in; they wheeled a stretcher between them. Mia hovered, hoping to return to the conference room, but then Reynald needed her for something else and so the next time she got to see Bernard was that evening during the closing drinks and networking, when she found herself standing beside him against the glass wall overlooking the lit-up city, drinks in hand. It was dim inside, so your eye was drawn outside, to that glittering night scene below.

Bernard was quiet, clearly tired now that the event was winding down. Most of the interstate and overseas guests would be leaving in the next few days, having allowed time for sightseeing, but he had an early flight. There was a hum of conversation all around them in the room, and a quietness between them, like the still surface of a lake. She tussled with herself, wanting to dive in and speak to him and unsure what to say. He stood, swirling the ice in his glass absently, rimless specs tucked into the top pocket of his jacket.

'I really enjoyed your presentation,' she said abruptly, and he looked up at the splash her voice made. 'The part of it I heard, anyway. I just wish it was as easy to recognise our own hero's journey as the ones in movies and books.'

'It's not too difficult,' he said. 'The more you look, the more you see.'

She thought of her same-old, same-old with John and said, 'The Ordinary World is easy enough, but interpreting your Call to Action... I mean, it's not always straightforward, is it?'

Leave John? Was that her call? The idea of it shimmered invitingly. Or somehow make it better with him? The sparkle dimmed. Or take Sheryl's advice and play around? That set up a flash of colour that died out and resurged and died out...

Bernard regarded her thoughtfully. His skin looked tanned and weathered, unless it was just that the room was so dark, but she could imagine him spending as much time outside as he could, taking long walks or fixing things, building things – something that took him outside. He had a practical, capable look about him despite the specs that suggested hours at a desk... Two deep lines formed brackets on either side of his mouth. For a moment she imagined kissing that mouth, feeling the softness of those lips, and then banished the thought in a wave of embarrassment, relieved that he couldn't see her face more clearly, or read her thoughts.

'You can't take the wrong journey,' Bernard said, and she laughed because that made so much sense, but then fell back into silence, wondering again which way the arrow was pointing.

A waitress came by with a platter of pumpkin and sage arancini balls. They both took a napkin and dipped a golden ball into the little dish of bush-tomato chutney.

'Because, you see,' Bernard said when she had moved on, as if they had not been interrupted, 'you are not in the wrong life.'

'Do I give you that impression?' she asked lightly, 'that I think I'm living the wrong life?'

'Yes,' he said, watching her and chewing slowly.

She laughed again, and knew it was a nervous tension laugh, the laugh she gave when she felt seen and didn't know where to go.

'How old are you?' he asked, and for a ridiculous moment she wondered if he was wondering if she was too young for him, and then told herself off sharply and said, 'Twenty-nine.'

'Ah, the Saturn Return. One of your biggest challenges is in the wings – or already on stage, perhaps?'

She nodded. Life with Bernard would not be trite. She could imagine sitting with him over breakfast and discussing deep, important things, not just who was picking up the dry-cleaning.

'Well, my dear, be true to yourself. If you feel that you're making the same mistakes over and over, make them with gusto or do your darnedest to figure out what the message is.'

'I'm just on the admin staff here,' she began.

'You're not 'just' anything,' he corrected.

'What I mean is, I'm not a counsellor like the conference participants. I should probably get myself one! I'm facing some big decisions and I'm probably going to need someone who can warn me of dangers and point out the right path.'

'No one will do that for you.' He looked around for somewhere to put the used napkin and, not seeing anything, tucked it into his pocket. 'But life itself will deliver all the guides you need if you're paying attention. And listen, dear, stop 'should-ing' on yourself. You don't necessarily even need a counsellor – although don't tell anyone here I said that.'

'Really? I've been thinking of training as a counsellor myself. What you people do seems so great, so helpful...'

'If it calls you, do it. But the main thing is: pay attention to your feelings and keep navigating by what's in your heart.'

'It's not always easy to know,' she said. 'I've got mixed feelings...'

'You're human. That's the human condition.' He put a hand on her shoulder. 'I'm in a Saturn Return period too. It comes again age fifty-eight, sixty: a cycle called Atonement. So that will give you an idea of what I'm dealing with.'

'You're not sixty!' she exclaimed. 'I would never have guessed. You're very well preserved.' That was the wine talking. She blushed.

He smiled and inclined his head, then drained his glass. 'Well, my dear, I think it's time we oldies hit the sack.'

'Honestly, I don't believe you're sixty – or that you'd have anything to atone for.'

'Check my bio,' he told her, and gave her arm a little farewell squeeze. 'It was nice talking to you, Mia. And don't worry so much; trust the journey.'

There was an email from John waiting for her when she arrived home. She sat at the computer with Bitsy in her lap, stroking the dog's warm back and reading.

A date had been set for the funeral. His mother was grim but coping. They were writing notices for the paper and meeting with the minister and finalising headstones. There would be a reading of the will soon. His father had been very organised so there wasn't all that much to do; his 'affairs were in order' and John's mother had already found the retirement village she wanted to buy into when the sale of the family home went through. John wished he could speak to her about more than just the practical details but she was as taciturn as ever, and he stood outside the closed door of his father's life, unable to enter or even peek through a peephole. Jake was dealing with a couple of dramas of his own and so not helping much, but that was to be expected.

Jake had always been this way, Mia gathered – a spendthrift, gambling, partying type who lived a promiscuous lifestyle and had no sense of responsibility. As a child he would take John's stuff, use it, break it and discard it… Apparently he had ex-girlfriends and kids all over the place. But also – and it fit the stereotype – he was a charismatic guy who was loved by everyone and even had old ladies flirting with him. John had left the UK all those years ago partly in order to stop living in the shadow of his more gregarious younger brother. It was mainly to be with her but there was also a sense of him needing to find his own space where he wasn't constantly competing for attention; and his escape was a 'so there' to his parents, who were charmed by their youngest and only set high expectations for their eldest. Over the years Mia and John had heard snippets about Jake's foray into theatre and his stuttering career as an actor, his various failed business ventures, his passionate love affairs that never ended in a wedding, to his mother's disappointment. And yet, despite all the disasters, he was still the apple of their eye.

Mia knew what that was like. She had her own wound: an older sister who had died before she was born, draining her mother of colour and life, so that when Mia finally came along a year and a half later, she was alternately smothered and neglected. Sharing stories over sangria and tapas in a musky Spanish tavern, she and John had recognised each other's wounds, and their puzzle pieces had locked together like a healing.

4

From: John Hartington
Thursday 24th June at 6.46 a.m.
Subject: news
To: Mia Hartington

Hi honey

How are things your end? The funeral was okay. Masses of people I haven't seen in ages. Jake and I shared the eulogy, and he got everyone laughing, of course, with little stories about Dad's life and their relationship, while I did the more serious chronological stuff. Did I ever tell you Dad was painting? He and Mum used to call it his 'dabbling' – I never paid much attention to it because they didn't seem to take it seriously, but Jake reckons he was really good. Could have shown his work, apparently. I'm going to have to dig some of those paintings out of the attic and have a look.

Mum is holding it together. She's the stiff upper lip expert, as you know. She hasn't said a word about you not coming, other than, 'Is Mia well?' when I arrived, but it would be great to have you here. What do you think? Fancy a trip across the world? It is summer here, remember, your favourite season…

I ran into Melissa Penn at the funeral. Do you remember me telling you about her? She's an old flame from uni years. We came close to marrying back then but I got cold feet and then I met you and you stole my heart... She was at the funeral. Turns out she's stayed in touch with Mum and Dad over the years. They always got on – her folks are friends of my folks. She ended up marrying a lawyer and has a couple of kids but they got divorced a year or so ago, and now she's doing the single mum thing.

What did Matt say about the option on those shares? It looks like a good investment to me but he's the expert.

Glad your conference went well. Signed up for that counselling course yet? ;)

Give Bitsy a scratch for me. I bet she's taken over my side of the bed...

Miss you
xo J

From: John Hartington
Monday 28th June at 2 a.m.
Subject: Re: news
To: Mia Hartington

Hi honey

So no answer from Matt yet? Unusual. Stay on his case, okay? That window will close soon.

The reading of the will was pretty much as could be expected. A bit of cash for me and Jake and some shares each, but the rest of it will come after Mum passes. No major surprises. He donated some money to a charity for motor neurone disease. Apparently he met a woman on the Tube whose husband has developed the disease. They've got a little kid and she's dealing with all this heartbreak watching the love of her life deteriorate in front of her eyes. The guy was already in a nursing home when Dad met her. Mum says Dad went to visit him and stayed in touch with the wife for a couple of years. Seems so out of character for him to me! Life is full of surprises.

Mum's been having little breakdowns. I'll find her standing in the kitchen with tears pouring down her face but not making a sound, and then she won't say a word about how she's feeling. It's quite troubling. Jake seems to know how to deal with it. She'll give him a hug when he comes over but not me. Usually that would piss me off no end but Jake and I are - extraordinarily - getting on better than ever. We had a great old chat the other day. A real honest heart-to-heart. First ever, I reckon. He confided in me about a few big challenges he's got on his plate - some debt and a dodgy real estate deal that he's trying to get out of, and an affair he's been having with the wife of a theatre director. So what's new, eh? But he seems genuinely troubled.

Remember those paintings of Dad's? I dug them out and had a look, and honestly, Mia, they are brilliant. I don't know what planet you'd have to be on to call them 'dabbling'. He had the touch. It's criminal that he didn't do anything with them. I sat up there in the attic for hours just looking at canvas after canvas. Jake and I are thinking of putting on a posthumous exhibition - a belated tribute to Dad. Wondering if we can pull it off before I have to leave. I might extend a week or so.

Are you coming over???

xo J

From: John Hartington
Tuesday 29th June at 4.20 a.m.
Subject: Re: news
To: Mia Hartington

Hi honey

Thanks for the update from Matt. Sounds okay. Just go along with whatever he suggests. I'll have to sign docs from here though. Sounds like the party at Sheryl's will be fun. A shadow theme, you reckon? What are you going to go as? I'm sorry I missed your call the other day.

I've been doing lots of thinking. I know I said we'd talk when I got back but just wanted to let you know that I'm seriously considering making some major changes when I get back. It's all churning around inside me at the moment so none of this will sound clear but I'm pretty definitely going to resign. I feel like my life is in a rut – as you know. You've told me often enough… :/

I don't have any great talents like Dad or Jake but seeing all that brilliance go to waste has really affected me. Mum reckons he didn't have any ambitions but I wonder about that. I wonder if she just kept putting him down – she's good at that… Maybe he did have dreams and couldn't say. If so, they died with him. Makes me wonder if there's something more to me that I'll never know about if I just keep doing the same old. I feel as if I want to take a leap into the unknown and discover if there is something more to me than just accountancy. Scary stuff…

We've found a café that promotes artists' work where we're going to put on an exhibition for Dad if we don't find anything bigger – still looking; we'd prefer a gallery so we can show some of the big pieces – so I am going to extend my trip a couple of weeks. I don't think I could live with myself if we didn't give Dad's art some kind of public recognition, even if it's just to family and friends and the odd passer-by.

So there you go. You can be confident that I'll be coming back a changed man. I want to embrace life, Mia! No more boring John for you. I'm going to be the man you've always wanted.

Love you, can't wait to make love to you.

xox J

From: John Hartington
Friday 2nd July at 7.15 a.m.
Subject: Re: news
To: Mia Hartington

Hi honey

Well, it's all happening! We found a gallery on the outskirts of London that had an exhibition unexpectedly cancel. They took one look at some pics of Dad's work and threw open the doors. Seriously, Jake and I could be managing our father's posthumous career! Anyway, I'll be flying back in another three weeks or so – after the exhibition, which kicks off next week. Mum thinks we're making too much of it but we'll show her! Will send exact arrival date when I've confirmed the flights.

I thought I'd treat myself to a few days in Paris while I'm here. Be a bit spontaneous... See, no more stuffy old John! The times, they are a-changing. Speaking of which, I've been in touch with work and sent in my resignation. I know what you're thinking: what about all my talk about the longer I stay with Buxton the more shares I receive? Well, I'm forcing myself out of my comfort zone. (I haven't totally taken leave of my senses. I'm getting paid bereavement leave and then I'll be paid out in full with no penalties, despite the lack of notice.) Still, talk about burning my bridges… I'll be coming back to nothing – and the possibility of everything.

Love to you and Bitsy,
xo J

Mia sat perched on the kitchen bar stool eating toast and reading the course guide with a pen in hand.

'Do you like helping people?

Are you a good listener?

Do people seem to pour their troubles out to you?

Are you fascinated by human behaviour?

Are you patient and empathetic?'

Yes, yes, yes, yes, not very… Well, not very patient but fairly empathetic, Mia thought. She'd been putting big ticks next to the first few questions but in all honesty the patience one called for a question mark. Would that mean she wouldn't make a good counsellor?

She took another crunching bite out of her toast and read on through the specialisations that a counsellor might choose to focus on: relationship counselling, stress management, children and young adults, crisis and trauma, addictions, grief and loss, career counselling… Relationship counselling was the one that leapt out at her, irony of ironies. How could she possibly advise other people when her own marriage was on the rocks? Surely you'd have to have your own act together!

Bitsy was sitting at the foot of her stool, gazing up at her. If anyone had patience around here, it was her pup. She broke off a tiny crust of vegemite toast and dropped it; Bitsy snapped it up, crunched, and swallowed. Mia stroked the little dog's chest with her toe absently. The other problem was time and money. Did she sign up for a full-time three-year bachelor or drag it out over six years so she could keep working? Or do one of those shorter diploma courses so she could start sooner and see if this really was what she wanted?

The big issue, of course, was: what was going to happen when John got back? If he wanted to change careers too – and the horse had bolted on that one now that he'd resigned – they couldn't both not be earning! That would be too hard… She wasn't sure if she felt irritated with him for upsetting her process or happy because he was finally climbing out of his rut.

Piano riff. She glanced at her phone. John. Mia touched the green 'accept' button and chewed her last mouthful more rapidly.

'Mia?' he said, all the way from London.

She swallowed. 'Hi honey.'

'Can you talk?'

'Just for a few minutes. The traffic was epic yesterday. Lots of rain here.'

'I thought this might be bad timing. I just wanted to say hello before I hit the sack. I've been thinking about you. Missing you…'

That was nice. Heart-warming… But had she been missing him? Not exactly…

'Me too,' she said into the silence. She wished she could think of something more honest but caring to say. She wished she actually felt the missing. She wondered if she should talk about the work issue since he'd rung at such an amazingly synchronistic moment, but she should stay conscious of what was happening at his end. After all, if they didn't stay together everything would change anyway.

'How are things over there?' she asked. 'How's your mum? How's the exhibition coming along?'

'All good. Mum's the same but less of that crying now. She's started packing the house – partly to keep busy, since she doesn't move for another couple of months, and partly because I don't think she knows what to make of all the fuss about Dad's art.'

'That's kind of sad,' Mia said. She hit loudspeaker so she could put the phone down and slipped off the stool. 'Keep talking. I'm going to wash my plate.'

'Okay,' he said, and there was a little pause. Maybe he was waiting.

She flicked the tap on quickly and ran water over her plate. Left it in the sink with her knife. 'What?'

'I said the exhibition is a whole new learning curve. We've been creating a brochure and catalogue and taking pictures of all the paintings. Big job.'

'The pics you sent were impressive. You're right, he's good.' *Was* good, she corrected in her mind, as she walked to the bathroom.

'I'll bring one home for us.'

'Perfect.' She stood in front of the bathroom mirror. Her eyebrows needed plucking – 'tweezing', her mother would say.

'You sound distracted.'

'Sorry. Got to brush my teeth. So do you think your mum will be okay? Does she have friends?'

'The Bridge Club. But I don't think she talks to them about her feelings.'

'It's just as well we're growing past all those inhibitions, isn't it?' she said, squeezing paste onto her toothbrush. 'Like, evolutionarily.'

He was silent for a moment. There was a slight rustling sound. Then he said, in a very English accent, 'You mean that people are talking about their feelings more these days? Yes, but, my dear, not in Britain.'

She smiled, watching the lines around her eyes deepen. 'You can bring that accent back with you. You've been losing it. I like it.'

'All right,' he said. 'Smashing! Will do.'

'I really have to go.' The brush was poised in her hand.

'Have a lovely day.'

'You too,' she said. 'I mean, sleep well.'

'Love you.'

She kissed into the phone and a moment later the call cut off.

Mia's mother rang as she was walking Bitsy after work. It was so rare for her to call that Mia answered immediately.

'Hello Mum. Everything all right?'

'Well, that's why I'm ringing you, dear. Your father and I are a bit worried.'

'What about?' Mia paused as Bitsy squatted to pee. The woman with the greyhound was approaching. Bitsy was watching them as she peed, eager, anticipating their meeting.

'Well… are you sure he hasn't just taken off?' her mother asked tentatively.

'Who – John? Of course not! Why would he do that?'

'He just arrived out of the blue,' her mother said. 'You hardly know his family, and he's been gone much longer than planned…'

'It's because of this show they're putting on for his dad. He left everything here, Mum, and he's in touch with me regularly.' Bitsy took off, jerking her arm. The woman with the greyhound turned onto another path, heading away from them.

'All right then, dear,' her mother said. 'Don't get cross with me. I'm just asking. We're just looking out for you.'

'I thought you liked John.'

'We do, dear. We like him very much. And of course he's much too stable to just disappear on you but things happen. We really think you should have gone with him.'

'Why? To stop him running away? If he wanted to leave me then going with him wouldn't necessarily help.'

'Oh, darling! Of course it would. Husbands know when their wives aren't showing interest in them.'

Mia shook her head in amazement. So that was where this was going! She was getting a 'how to be a better wife' lecture! She took a deep breath, calming the prickles of irritation. 'John is not planning on leaving me. He loves me.' *I'm thinking about leaving him,* she didn't say, *but he hasn't given any sign of wanting to leave me.*

'We know he loves you,' her mother said. 'It's just that it was all so sudden…'

'His father had a stroke. That sort of thing happens suddenly. He wanted to see him before he died.'

'Of course. And you couldn't go. You had that…'

'Conference.'

'Yes.'

'And the dog.'

'Did the conference go well?'

'Very well.'

'So it was worth staying?'

'Yes.'

'I see… Give him our best when you speak to him. You are speaking to him, aren't you?'

'Emails and text messages mostly so far. It's been hard to co-ordinate our times.'

'All right, then. Take care, dear.'

'I will.'

5

Mia gazed at her reflection in the mirror with excitement and fear in equal portions. She really was losing weight! If Sheryl hadn't encouraged her to try on this figure-hugging outfit at the Party Hire shop she would have walked right past it. She'd taken one look at the stunning dress in crimson velvet on the stiff, barbie-shaped model, and had laughed aloud.

'No, come on,' Sheryl had said, one hand jiggling the pram and the other hand flapping a piece of the skirt at her.

'You must be joking,' Mia had said. 'It looks great on that mannequin but on me! I won't even be able to do it up.'

'Humour me,' Sheryl had said with that 'you're not going to talk me out of this' look on her face. So Mia had stripped off in the changing room and amazed herself when she could actually do up the black, laced bodice. Not entirely all the way, but if she really was going to do this, if she really was going to this party as her shadow tarty self, then a neckline that gaped open a fraction more than it should would hardly be a problem. She had stared at the expanse of breast she was revealing and wondered if she had the gall to wear something like this. It was so not her! Usually she wore black, something that reduced her backside and smoothed out some of the lumps. But now they weren't showing! Turning from side to side she'd had to acknowledge to herself that while she still couldn't be called thin, she looked curvaceous rather than fat.

She'd peeked through the changing room curtain and Sheryl, who was sitting on a bench breastfeeding Talia, had gestured for her to come out so she could see. And had gasped and said how sexy she looked and she was absolutely hiring this dress, no discussing, no excuses, no two ways about it.

So here she was, on the night of Sheryl's fortieth birthday, dressed up like a royal tart, boobs almost totally exposed, waist looking smaller than in ages, face flushed with excitement and nervousness. She'd upped the ante on the make-up too: more mascara and eyeliner than she'd usually wear, and a bold red lippie… Meet Mia, the tart. Bending down, she lifted the skirts to reveal her fishnet tights and pinned some of the fabric to her left hip with the brooch that had come with the dress for that purpose. When she stood up to survey the full effect, she felt a delicious tremor of fear…

Ye gods. Did she dare? What would John think if he saw her now? For all his talk of lashing out he was so conservative that he'd totally disapprove of this. He'd think she was being cheap. His idea of being spontaneous was a weekend in Paris – so what? He'd done that before. But revealing herself like this – this was a major risk. This was dangerous. This was playing with the dark side…

On a sudden impulse, she twisted her wedding ring off and dropped it into the crystal bowl on her chest of drawers.

Sheryl's place was still quiet when she arrived, although the fairy lights outside signalled that a party was imminent. Mia had offered to help set up but Sheryl had refused. 'What for? I'll have my own staff here to cater and serve, and I want you to make the grand entrance.'

But Mia wasn't quite up for that. She didn't know many of Sheryl's friends, and arriving when they were all already there felt a little scary. She wanted to assert her friendship rights by being there when *they* arrived, and helping take coats or pass nibblies around would give her something to do. The last thing she wanted was to be a showpiece. It was confronting enough just wearing this outfit.

Alec opened the door, completely taking her by surprise in his bikie get-up. He'd sprouted a great bushy beard and was wearing leathers, boots, and a singlet that covered some sort of fake tattoo.

'Wow,' she said, 'this is your shadow self?'

'I think the 'wow' is mine,' he replied. 'You look… fantastic. John would be…'

'Shocked,' she said, blushing already. 'Is it too much? Do I look like –'

'A tart?' he asked. 'Yes. A very tempting, tantalising –'

'Keep your hands off her,' Sheryl ordered in ringing tones. Alec swung around and Mia blushed again. A large, white-clad Florence Nightingale was mock-glowering at them. 'I'm starting to regret wearing this,' the nurse said. 'You're going to have so much more fun than me.'

'You still haven't told me,' Mia began, closing the door behind her and moving toward the living room with them. There were tea light candles in holders of different heights and shapes on the floor around the entrance and down the hallway. 'Why a nurse?'

'Because it's the gentle, caring, selfless side of me that doesn't get much of a look-in,' Sheryl said. 'Champers?'

'You're joking! Your gentle caring side is alive and well.'

'You see it. Alec sees it. But not many other people. I'm usually really brusque and bossy and controlling. And it's all about me; there is barely a selfless bone in my body.'

'Yeah, I see that too,' Mia said, and ducked as a cushion flew in her direction. 'Just kidding! You drop everything if I need you.'

'But I'm massively ambitious,' Sheryl said, passing her a glass of champagne. 'There's another event company that's in financial trouble at the moment, or so I've heard on the grapevine. So here I am, breastfeeding a babe, and already thinking about takeovers.'

'Where is the babe?' Mia asked, looking around.

'Sleeping, by some miracle. She will probably wake and freak out at everyone being here –'

'To say nothing of her father in a beard,' Alec said. 'If she freaks, the beard goes. Just warning you.'

'Of course.'

'I'll help with Tahls,' Mia said.

'No way. You're on task tonight: you've got men to seduce. Plus, if she cops a look at your boobs she'll get confused.'

Mia laughed, and looked around at the living room decorations. Sheryl and Alec's home was classy, modern, simple. Now masses of candles flickered and glowed from every horizontal surface, and large displays of flowers injected colour and fun into the sparsely furnished space. A big, 'Happy 40th Birthday, Sheryl!' had been scrawled on the mirror above the mantelpiece in pink lipstick.

That reminded her. She reached into her bag – 'Prezzie!' – and drew out a small box: a pair of Swarovski earrings that Sheryl had admired when they were out shopping together, and a note offering unlimited babysitting.

'You remembered!' Sheryl exclaimed, giving her a warm hug. 'Thank you. Gorgeous! I'll put them on right now. And of course you'll be babysitting – at least until you have yours. That *will* be happening, of course.'

Mia smiled her nice smile; actually it was her mother's smile – the close-lipped one she kept for strangers when she didn't want to reveal her true feelings.

Sheryl was fastening the earrings at the mirror and hadn't seen the smile, but Alec had. He gave Mia's arm a squeeze as he passed, saying, 'I'll check on progress in the kitchen,' but at that moment the doorbell rang so he changed trajectory and went to receive their first guests, and Mia took refuge in the kitchen where Sheryl's staff were busy laying platters and putting trays in the oven. Her offer to help was politely declined, so she drifted out of there back toward the living room, which suddenly felt quite full. Three people had arrived: a clown, a musketeer, and a cowboy, and they were already taking turns standing against a ceiling-to-floor white screen with a spotlight behind it that cast a giant shadow of themselves onto the screen. There was lots of laughter.

A dress-up party is the best sort to attend when you don't know anyone, Mia reflected later that evening. She'd already had interesting conversations with a number of people who had all shared quite openly about their shadow selves. Many had asked her about the tart, and she'd confessed to usually being fairly quiet and demure, and that she was actually feeling totally out of her depth in this outfit. She supposed she should be flirting with everyone and dancing on the coffee table, but she was hard pressed just to wear the flaming dress without running for a scarf to cover up her chest...

'Oh don't do that!' all the men would say, their eyes roving, taking the opportunity to sidle up and put an arm around her shoulders for a better perv.

Sheryl was making sure that her glass remained topped up so that she could sustain at least part of her act, Mia noticed. Whenever one of the waiting staff tinkled a little more champagne into her glass, she'd look up and see Sheryl smiling at her or winking from the other side of the room. If she had Talia in her arms, and was surrounded by a cooing group of women, Mia was not allowed near; instead, Sheryl would wave her away and mouth words at her like 'Go flirt', and send intense messages with her eyes.

It was fortunate that there was a steady stream of finger food or she'd be off her face by now. But all that champagne also meant that she kept needing to go to the loo. Mia squeezed her way through the crowded living room and headed for the guest toilet. An Indian yogi and a trapeze artist were hovering outside the door, deep in conversation. 'Is this a queue?' she asked, and they nodded, so she made her way to the toilet in the laundry – not many people would know about this one.

She was right. It was empty, so she ducked straight in and bunched up the great armfuls of crimson velvet, and struggled to lower the black tights without ripping them so that she could sit and release a now urgent stream of fluid... She sat there for an extra moment, enjoying the relief from strangers and the constant noise and chatter, then stood up to grapple once again with the tights and skirt. Someone was in the laundry. She could hear glass and ice clinking, and remembered that there were drinks in the trough. She flushed the toilet and stepped out, and there, cracking open a dripping stubby of beer, was a tall handsome stranger in jeans and a t-shirt that stretched across a broad chest and well-rounded biceps.

'Not in costume!' she said in mock accusation, to cover her embarrassment at emerging from the toilet.

'I *am* my shadow,' he said, with a brief incline of his head, and toasting her with the stubby. 'I like yours.'

She blushed. 'Most of the guys do. But really, come on. That's a cop-out. If I've got to wear something like this, how can you get away with that?'

'The shadow is your dark side, right?' he said. He had a lovely voice, deep, calming. 'I'm a journo specialising in crime and with a special interest in government and corporate evil-doing. I delve into political strife and expose it – I deal in darkness.'

'Ah, but the shadow includes admirable qualities as well, not just the evil ones,' she countered. 'Didn't you read Sheryl's invitation?'

"Help me celebrate my 40th by coming dressed as your shadow self", he quoted. "Your repressed darkness or your disowned magnificence".

'Exactly,' she agreed, impressed. 'So what is this then?' indicating the everyday clothes.

'Okay,' he acknowledged. 'You've nailed me. I'm so caught up in society's dark side that I've lost track of my personal shadow. Perhaps you can help me find it...'

'You're a little drunk,' she said. His magnificence, on the other hand, was perfectly clear to her. She was fighting an urge to touch his arm, run her hand over that hard muscle...

'So tell me about yours,' he was saying. 'I don't want to put a foot wrong by identifying you incorrectly but... a hooker?'

'A tart. I'm expressing my inner temptress.'

'You're not doing a very good job of it,' he said. 'You're coming across like a librarian. Or a kid playing dress-ups.'

Mia stiffened. 'Really?' she said, unable to trust herself with more words than that, and wishing she had not paused to chat.

'Really,' he said, holding her gaze. 'I want a smoke. Care to join me in the greater darkness?' He jerked his head toward the laundry door.

'That leads into the garage,' she hedged.

'I know. I've used it a few times already. But there's a backyard you can get to as well, with a deck and seats. And it's quiet.'

Mia knew that route and deck quite well. She knew the love seat too. 'I...' she said.

'I won't eat you. Or ask you to act out your act,' he added.

Screw the man. 'All right,' she said.

'Do you have a drink? Can I get you something?'

'Oh just... what's in there?' peering past him into the trough.

'A bit of everything. How about...' He pulled out a clinking bottle of vodka lime.

'All right,' she agreed. 'Thanks.'

'Need a glass?'

'No, that's all right.'

'Okay.' He unscrewed the lid, passed her the bottle, and opened the door, giving it a push so that she could pass through first.

Mia stepped out into the darkness of the garage and made her way cautiously between Alec's BMW and the shelves that held an array of tools and camping gear and storage boxes, toward the back door. The bloke – she still didn't know his name – got there first and opened it for her.

'Thank you,' she murmured, and they stepped through onto the deck. It was cold out here. Mia wished she'd thought of bringing a jacket. They looked at the love seat, sitting motionless, and at the iron seats that would be freezing, and instead leaned against the wooden railing, where they both placed their drinks. He pulled out a packet of cigarettes, put one between his lips and lit up, throwing his rugged face into light for a moment.

'I'm Mia,' she said, crossing her arms for warmth, and then dropping them quickly when she realised that action would press her breasts together and push them up even more.

He blew smoke out of the side of his mouth and extended a hand. 'Nick.'

His hand was warm and hard, the skin dry, the handclasp strong. 'So who do you know?' Mia asked, when he didn't let go. 'Sheryl or Alec?'

He let go. 'Alec initially; now both. You?'

'Sheryl initially. We're long-time friends.'

'She strong-armed me into introducing her to some of my reporter buddies,' he said, and drew on the cigarette again. 'Knows her mind, that one.'

'She certainly does. This,' gesturing the dress, 'was her idea. She thinks I need to… kick up my heels a bit more.'

'I'd go along with that,' Nick said. 'Go on, tell me more about it. Why the tart? *Are* you a librarian?'

'No! I'm a PA…' Equally boring, perhaps. 'I work for a counselling and coaching organisation.'

'So was the shadow thing your idea?'

'It was a throw-away idea that Sheryl loved. I'm really interested in this idea that we have a shadow side but I was joking when I suggested it for her party. Shez grabbed it and ran with it. She's like that. But come on, I want to know what your real shadow is.'

'I asked first,' he said. 'Why the tart?'

Mia looked out into the dark garden for a moment, and then back at him. *'You've* nailed *me*,' she admitted. 'I'm not comfortable being… seductive, I guess. I'm more conservative than I'd like to admit.' John flashed into her mind. She always accused him of being boring and conservative, but really, she was just as bad.

'So you judge your conformity and repress the part of you that wants to be wild and sexy.'

She took a big sip of her drink. 'That's about right.'

'You are very luscious,' he said. 'I'm controlling my urges right now – just thought you should know.'

Mia gave an embarrassed, hiccupy laugh. 'Oh! 'Scuze me… I get the hiccups when I drink sometimes… It's your turn for 'true confessions'.'

Nick dew on his cigarette again and flicked ash into the garden bed below. 'Positive shadow: creative; I'm writing a novel. Negative shadow: I'm the sort of guy who has a girl in every port. Can't commit – I get bored and easily distracted. I love women.'

'So I *am* in great danger here,' she said lightly, rubbing one bare arm discreetly. It was really cold out here.

'Great danger,' he agreed. 'Or great opportunity. It depends how you look at it.' He reached for her left hand and rolled his thumb across her fingers. 'No wedding ring. Are you single or just doing the costume?'

'Doing the costume,' she said reluctantly.

'I assume he's not here.'

'Overseas.'

'And Sheryl suggested you dress like that… I'd say she's putting you up to something.'

He still hadn't released her hand. 'You could be right,' she allowed.

'Not happy with him?'

'We're kind of… stuck… at the moment. In a rut.'

'Exactly why I keep leaving,' he said. 'Can't stand it when it gets boring.' He released her hand and indicated the love seat. 'You're cold. Want to sit down?'

'Okay…'

He stepped on his cigarette and kicked it off the deck, and they settled onto the seat, which squeaked and wobbled, and was also very cold, and put their drinks on the timber decking at their feet.

'Come on,' he said, drawing her close. 'I'll be good… if you want me to… Let me warm you up.' His arm around her shoulders was deliciously toasty.

'How come you're not freezing – out here in a T-shirt in mid-winter!' she exclaimed.

'I don't know,' he said, and his mouth was close to her hair. 'I just run hot… Always have.'

'Now you're being deliberately provocative,' she said, holding herself apart but wanting to melt into him.

'Playing *your* role. Aren't you meant to be doing that?'

'Oh I'm out on the skinny branches right now, don't you worry,' she said. 'I'm a hotbed of anxiety.'

'Relax,' he soothed. 'I'm not going to compromise your virtue, little tartlet. I only go ahead if the girl gives me a definite signal.'

And it was true. He was holding her close against his body to warm her up, but not trying anything. For some silly reason, Mia felt like crying. She held the tears back, pressing her lips together and staring out into the darkness.

'It's really very difficult to know what to do, sometimes, isn't it?' she said at last. 'You want to be good and honour your vows and all that, and yet there's a part of you that wants to be free…'

"An alive person, or an alive relationship, or anything that is alive has to be unpredictable. What is going to happen in the next moment cannot be forecast," he said.

'Oh my God! That's Osho!' Mia exclaimed, turning to look at Nick. 'Are you quoting him? Was that an exact quote?'

'I believe so,' Nick said. 'I've got one of those memories – photographic. Very helpful at work.'

'I bet. It's a great quote. Confronting.'

'So why is your guy overseas? Working?'

'His father passed away. But he's doing this big self-examination thing at the moment too. He reckons he's going to come back different.'

'Unpredictable,' Nick murmured, drawing her close again. 'That should be good for the marriage.'

'Yes…' she agreed, sinking against his chest. She was nestled close to him now. His smoky breath was hot against her ear.

It began to rain, a quiet steady downpour. They sat together in silence, rocking slightly in the love seat. Mia struggled with herself. Her body was straining toward him, and her mind was dragging her backward, like a desperate horseman trying to control his runaway steed…

Suddenly the hum of noises and music from the house grew louder as a door opened, throwing a slanted rectangle of light onto the deck not far from where they sat. A woman said, 'Oh poo. It's raining,' and the door closed again, muffling the sounds and extinguishing the light.

As if by silent consensus Mia turned toward Nick and he lifted her chin and kissed her gently on the lips. She was throbbing. Her hand fell into his lap, and she felt the heat in his crotch, and he kissed her again, more purposefully. This was so lovely... Was it wrong? Her lips parted a little and their tongues met, and the hand on his far side came to rest against her belly, and moved up slowly, toward her breasts...

'It's working,' he murmured between kisses.

'What?' she gasped. His hand was on the side of her breast now, and his thumb was rotating, just a tiny distance from her nipple.

'The costume. You're connecting with that shadow side... Owning your whole self...'

And then three things happened one after another: she came, right there and then, in a brief and mild but definite shudder; he drew her close more roughly, kissing her hard and lifting her into his lap in a great rocking of the love seat; and the door opened again and Sheryl's voice called, 'Mia?'

6

Mia surveyed the piles of clothes on her bed with a set jaw. Nothing was going back into the wardrobe unless it fit well and made her feel great. She was especially not keeping any of her 'fat clothes'. Now that she was looking trimmer, she was determined to keep the door firmly closed on those extra kilos – they would not be allowed to return!

She wondered how quickly John would notice her new figure. And wondered how it had happened... She hadn't dieted at all. Just feeling happier, she sensed – she hadn't felt like having as many extra serves as she used to, and hadn't snacked on chocolate as constantly as before. Less need to get pleasure from food because life itself was feeling better. (She did not want to think too much about *why* life was feeling better – surely her marriage hadn't been that bad!)

Bitsy, who was sitting smack-bang in her way on the floor between the wardrobe and the bed, sat up suddenly and began to bark. A moment later the doorbell rang. Mia headed for the front door, a wispy apricot blouse in her hand. She loved the colour but the fabric was so thin and clingy that it really wasn't very complimentary. Keep it?

She opened the front door and Bitsy exploded through the gap, yapping and fawning at the feet of a delivery man who was holding a bouquet of flowers.

The man stepped backward off the doormat, looking down at Mia's frenzied dog with distaste. 'Does it bite?'

'No,' she said, bending to grab Bitsy's collar. 'She's just excited. She loves visitors – she loves anyone, in fact.' As soon as Mia had revealed this, she heard John's voice in her mind: *Don't tell strangers that Bitsy loves them. You're putting the welcome mat out for uninvited guests.*

'Sign here,' he said, keeping a wary eye on the dog as she restrained Bitsy between her ankles and straightened up to take the scanner.

He gave her the flowers – a striking bunch of lemon-coloured oriental lilies – and hurried away. She retreated inside, sniffing their spicy scent and looking for a note. Who…? There it was. A little card tucked in deep. She drew it out and flicked it open, and immediately recognised Sheryl's handwriting.

You can do this.

Do what?

Mia laid the lilies on the sink and brought down a vase. Greet John with a smile at the airport? Pretend that she was happy to see him? Talk to him about how frustrated she'd been? Reveal her indiscretion with Nick? A deep flush rose in her face, from its roots in her belly, or even lower, at this thought… Every time she remembered that kiss on the love seat and her body's hungry response…

'I'm the sort of guy who is very bad for you… for your marriage,' Nick had said, out by the car.

Sheryl had backed off, apologising, as soon as she saw them on the seat, but for Mia the moment was broken and already tainted with embarrassment and guilt. She'd told Nick she had to go, even though Sheryl had come to tell them they were about to do the birthday cake, and Nick had followed her out to the car and then refused to let her rush away, holding her in a long, firm hug while tears filled her eyes; breathing steadily into her neck while her breath came in little gasps against his chest.

'You're not a bad person,' he had said, as if he knew exactly which demon she was battling. 'But I'm not going to pretend. If you want to let that beautiful seductress out again…' he took her hand and produced a pen from his pocket.

'You carry a pen?' she asked, shivering in the cold as he withdrew the shelter of his body and wrote a number on the back of her hand.

'I'm a journo. And I can't stand texting.' He had kissed her fingers and then her mouth, and had pressed her into the chilly car, saying, 'Ciao, bella. Good luck. I won't hold my breath but I'll be around – for a while. I head overseas again soon.'

Sheryl had rung first thing the following morning and Mia had apologised for not being there for the cake, a regret that Sheryl had brushed away with a snort. She was totally pissed off with herself for ruining Mia's moment. She'd been hunting the house for her missing friend, wondering if Mia had run away out of embarrassment about wearing the dress, only to find Mia 'seizing the moment' with Alec's drop-dead gorgeous-looking old friend – and to then totally ruin the moment for her.

They'd talked about it, a little, and Sheryl had agreed that pursuing Nick wasn't, necessarily, her best next step but that her feelings, her desire for fun and pleasure, were not to be suppressed any longer. She was to confront John when he got back. She was to ask for what she wanted. (What *did* she want? Mia wished it were clear...) At any rate, she was to not settle for boringness any more.

Mia had sat there on the phone, looking at the number that was still scrawled on the back of her hand. Wash it off? Copy it somewhere? Commit it to memory? She had already looked at it so often by then that she knew the number by heart. And besides, she could always get it again from Alec.

Standing in the shower after talking to Sheryl she had scrubbed at those blue slanted figures until only the faintest smudge remained. Then she had taken the crimson dress back to the Party Hire place, feeling as if she was surrendering something precious when the salesperson took the plastic-wrapped gown out of her hand. She'd almost forgotten to let go, and they'd had a brief tug-of-war – the saleswoman turning toward the rack behind her to hang it up, and then having to turn back because the gown wasn't going with her... Mia had apologised, letting go immediately with an embarrassed laugh.

And then she had walked through the park, zipped up to her chin against the cold, hands deep in her pockets, thinking about everything. It was getting hard to remember that she loved John. He'd been away for five weeks at that point, and her memories of him and of their relationship before he left were so drab that the golden moments seemed very long ago... She knew that she *had* loved him. She knew they had lots in common and often made love beautifully, but it was as if this information was recorded on a file somewhere, and not something alive in the cells of her being.

She had stood in front of the creek, gazing at the still brown water, and remembered Bernard's comment about being on the right journey, and that it wasn't so hard to recognise your opportunity if you looked for it, but she felt as baffled as ever. What *was* her 'Call To Action'? Was she supposed to break off with John and make a fresh start? She seemed to be giving every decent-looking man her very serious consideration, as though she'd walk out of her marriage into something new at the drop of a hat. Surely she wasn't that fickle!

Or was this an opportunity to shake their marriage up and turn it into exactly what they both wanted? After all, John had been declaring in all his latest emails and messages that he was a new man; he'd be coming back different. And he'd actually resigned from his job! That had taken her by surprise. Wow. That he'd actually done it and not just talked about it! He'd said he was thinking of maybe doing gardening in the meantime, or something more physical for a change. Her John! How bizarre. If that really happened, then things were definitely going to change. She felt a little surge of hope, and an unsettling twist of disappointment.

The thought of a new journey together was wonderful! She should be feeling happy, not feeling like this – as if she'd just lost some great opportunity... There would have been nothing in her future if she'd left John for Nick; he was clearly not the monogamous type. There was no point hanging her hopes on him, as deliciously romantic as that moment had been when they'd made their way past the awkwardness and before she had lost control so completely...

Mia arranged the flowers in her vase. Sheryl was a treasure. Despite the difference in their ages, she considered Mia to be her best friend, and even though she was often pushy and confronting, she'd always been there for her. Mia could feel Sheryl's genuine good wishes in this gift. With a sigh, she left the kitchen and returned to the chaos in her bedroom. She had only four hours before it would be time to leave for the airport. Four hours in which to cast off the clothes that no longer fit, bag them up for the op shop, and do another quick clean so that the place would look as sparkling as it always did when she returned from a trip and John was the one waiting at home.

Mia stood among the knots of people at Arrivals, all heads craning up towards the screens that revealed passengers emerging from doors at either end of a long wall. Out they came, pushing laden trolleys and looking tired or harassed or eager. She watched as person after person emerged, her attention wandering when it seemed as if the flow of arrivals had dried up, and then focusing again when the doors re-opened. Asian businessmen, brisk and impassive, pulling neat black cases. Young couples with lots of luggage and small children dragging their own cute bags on wheels. A large man in a wheelchair being pushed by an elegant hostess in heels. (How did they manage on those heels for so many hours?) A Japanese student with dyed red hair and a garish pink jumper with pompoms, texting on a big pink smartphone as she walked. Twenty-somethings with their backpacks and dreadlocks, eschewing trolleys, strolling through the doors as if they hadn't been travelling for ten-plus hours and carrying those things for months beforehand…

And then there he was. Coming slowly through the entrance and pushing a trolley that bore his case and another few bags – probably some extra stuff from shopping or things his father had left him – and looking around for her.

She waved, threading her way through the crowd, and he caught sight of her and smiled and waved and gave his trolley a spurt of energy toward her.

That beautiful smile. Some of her anxiety dissolved. She reached him and they hugged, and she breathed in the familiar aftershave and kissed the side of his neck and then his cheek, and then their lips met in a long, gentle, kiss. Nothing probing – John wouldn't do that in a public place. But tender, like he'd really missed her. She felt tears coming to her eyes and blinked, smiling up at him.

'It's good to see you,' he said.

'And you.' She snaked her arm around his waist and he wrapped his arm around her shoulders and drove the trolley with one hand as they walked toward the exit. 'How was the flight?' she asked.

'You know. Long. The inevitable crying baby. Someone farting in the row behind me.'

She laughed and he smiled, and as the automatic doors opened in front of them, she said, 'Get ready for the cold. It's bitter today. You actually look brown, you rotter.'

'What do you expect? Six weeks of summer...'

'I don't want to think about it... So, tell me. How was your mum when you left?'

He took his arm away from her shoulders to steer the trolley across the road and said, 'As well as can be expected. Getting used to being alone. Jake is going to help her settle into the new place.'

'Jake will stick around long enough to do that?'

'I think so,' he said, concentrating on negotiating the curb.

They found the car quickly. 'Yellow, F?' he had asked in a teasing tone, knowing that she would have instinctively followed a similar route to the last time she'd been to the airport. Her ability to become lost was legendary, and so she stuck to the known. It was kind of bizarre, this combination of sticking to similar routes (which suggested she remembered where she was going), and frequently becoming disoriented. 'Geographically embarrassed', her first boyfriend had said.

John stowed his luggage, returned the trolley to a collection zone, and climbed into the passenger seat beside her. Then, before she could start the engine, he leaned across and turned her face toward him, and kissed her deeply.

'Well...' she breathed, when he released her. He was looking at her as if... like... as if he hadn't seen her in ages, which was true... like he was seeing her properly for the first time... so maybe he really had changed...

'I've been looking forward to doing that all the flight home,' John said. 'And for weeks before that. And, of course, I'm looking forward to doing everything else that we're going to do as soon as we get home.'

'Are we?' she asked, and couldn't deny the little thrill, the flutter of delight and anticipation at his purposefulness.

'My word,' he said, and turned back to the front, but left one hand on her thigh.

They were quiet during the drive home. John was gazing around at the usual old scene: freeway, cityscape, the streets approaching their inner suburban home. At one point she had asked about his father's exhibition, even though he had already emailed pictures and a long enthusiastic description of the event. Yes, Jake would be following up with the gallery and the sales and the various art critics who had shown up and shown interest. It was such a pity that there would be no more paintings. But this limited range guaranteed good prices and a bit of a splash in the arts pages – and the potential to create prints of their father's work to extend its life. Not to be too commercial about it, but there would be a decent influx of funds... Mind you, they'd direct a fair proportion of the funds to that charity he'd favoured. Or perhaps establish their own charity in their father's name – something for artists who got started late in life, perhaps...? He and Jake would look into it.

Mia turned into their street and John said, 'It's good to be home.' She unlocked the garage with the remote; as they pulled in they could hear Bitsy going nuts inside.

John lifted his case out of the boot and gave her a couple of plastic bags to carry in. One of the packages still lying in the boot was a big square, bubble-wrapped thing – 'some of Dad's pics,' he said. 'Had to keep a few of them for us.'

She unlocked the door and they both stooped to fondle Bitsy, who was beside herself with excitement. There was never any point carrying shopping or anything in until you'd said hello to her. Nothing could be done until her head had been scratched and she had rolled onto her back and looked up at them with her dainty legs jerking in the air and her tail brushing the floor, intent on having her stomach rubbed. This ritual performed, she sprang to her feet and darted around them as they brought his luggage inside. Watching John carry his case to the bedroom, those turned-out feet bringing back more memories, Mia had a brief disloyal flash of Nick, so masculine and strong beside her husband; she reminded herself that she had no intention of being one girl in one port.

John was taking off his jacket and hanging it up and then turning to face her with an expression that she hadn't seen in a long time, if ever. 'Come here,' he said, and she came slowly – shy, for some ridiculous reason.

'You know, your accent is much stronger again,' she said. 'You sound like a real English boy.'

He didn't reply to this; just concentrated on undoing her jacket and peeling it off.

'I like it though,' she said. 'You know me: I'm an accents girl. I probably fell in love with your accent in the first place.'

He was undoing the buttons on her blouse now. She wondered what he'd say when he saw her new, slimmer body. Not that it was that different – just a few kilos, but surely he'd notice. He'd teased her about her spare tyre often enough…

'I'll make sure I keep it then,' he said, and paused to look at her body without the blouse, but didn't speak. He leaned forward and kissed her neck gently, and turned her around so that he could undo the catch on her bra, then drew the straps down, his hands moving slowly on the bare skin of her arms. Her bra fell to the floor and his hands skimmed up her stomach to her breasts, cupping them.

She leaned back against his chest, breathing, feeling herself grow warm and wet.

One of his hands travelled back down her stomach to the button on her jeans, which he undid, kneeling to pull them down her legs. She tottered, unbalanced, with the fabric bunched at her ankles, and fell, laughing, onto the bed. He grinned and yanked her pants past her inconvenient feet. 'So unromantic,' he said. 'I was doing well before that, don't you think?'

He ripped off his t-shirt and she couldn't help noticing that he was a little thicker around the middle; when he lay down beside her she gave his flesh a bit of a squeeze, teasing, 'What happened here?'

'Mum's cooking. Traditional English, very stodgy,' he murmured. 'Not much choice.' Still no comment about her slimmer waist but he was all over her now, relishing the aroma of her skin, rolling her onto his chest and massaging her back... holding her close and kissing her, kissing her... He felt bigger against her leg than she remembered, but she was more receptive than she had been in a long time... She was moaning with pleasure at the touch of his fingers on her inner thigh... She wanted to bring him inside but he stopped her. 'Wait... there's no rush... let's draw this out...' And it was almost two hours later before they finally stopped, locked together, sated, and drifted into dreams.

7

Someone was moving around in the bedroom. Mia fought the urge to stay asleep and opened her eyes.

John's side of the bed was empty, the covers turned back where he'd climbed out. She looked around groggily. The light was on in the ensuite. Was it already morning? If so, that had felt like a very short night. She lifted herself up on one elbow and squinted at the clock. Its green, luminous figures read 3.02 a.m. Sighing in relief, she let her head fall back to the pillow.

The ensuite door opened and John emerged.

'Okay?' she mumbled, shielding her eyes against the light.

'Can't sleep. It's the bloody jet lag,' he said. 'Sorry if I woke you.' The light snapped off as he closed the door and lovely soft darkness returned.

'S'okay...' Her eyes were closing again.

'Go back to sleep,' he said. 'I'll go... do something for a bit and then hopefully get sleepy again.'

She was already drifting, but slept lightly, aware of occasional sounds from the rest of the house: doors closing, the kettle coming to the boil and clicking off, Bitsy's claws on the floorboards...

When she finally woke, John was fast asleep beside her, lying on his stomach, face partly buried in the pillow, and making a little snoring noise. She sat for a moment, looking at him. There were a few grey hairs near his temples. She hadn't noticed those before. Perhaps the stress of his father dying was ageing him… Being rejected by his mother wouldn't be helping much either – she knew what that felt like.

Mia put a hand lightly on his back, feeling the vibration as he breathed and snored. She wondered how he'd feel when she said they'd been invited to her parents' place for an early dinner. She'd given him an out, telling them that he might not be up for it after the flight, but she knew he would do his duty and come along.

She was just throwing back the covers to climb out of bed when he rolled over, his face coming to rest against her thigh, his left arm slinging over her legs, capturing her there. She looked down at him. Eyes closed, still breathing as if he was asleep. But his left hand was slipping down into the warm space between her legs… his fingers were slowly kneading the flesh of her inner thigh. She caught her breath, watching and waiting… And then the fingers relaxed, the little snore started up again; he was sliding back into sleep.

She lifted his hand gently and shifted her leg, put his arm back on the bed, pulled the covers up to his neck. Then she bent and placed a light kiss on his stubbly cheek and went to the kitchen to get some breakfast.

It was later than she'd realised. Waiting for the kettle to boil she went to the iPad that was stationed on the bench and tapped through to her mother's station. The cheery tones of Steve Lawrence and Eydie Gorme burst into sound: '*I don't know what's a-comin' tomorrow, Maybe it's trouble and sorrow…*'

Mia joined in as she filled the kettle: 'But we'll travel the road, sharing our load, side by side…'

Usually she was out and about on a Saturday morning before her mother's community radio program started, and she rarely heard the show, but today she would actually listen and be able to comment on it when they went for dinner. 'Have you been listening to your mother on the radio?' her father would always ask, as if his wife's involvement in local radio was one of the seven wonders of the world. 'Yes, Dad, I have!' she'd be able to answer, and would win some points.

The dog-door banged as Bitsy scampered inside and came to sniff around her feet. 'Hungry, pooch?' she asked. Stupid question. She took the packet of dog food out of the pantry and rattled some of it into Bitsy's bowl. Bitsy licked her hand in thanks and began to crunch.

'*When they've all had their quarrels and parted,*' the duo sang, '*We'll be the same as we started, Just travelling along, Singing a song...*'

'Side by side,' Mia chimed in. Her phone pinged and she glanced at it. Sheryl.

> Welcome home to Johnnie. How does it feel to have him back?

Mia put a chai tea bag in her mug. What to say? She took her phone and sat at the table.

> Pretty nice, actually. So far, so good

> Ooh! I read 'sex'

> We'll have you two over for dinner soon

She sent a 'thumbs up' in response to this. The song finished and her mother's very correct voice said, 'Well, that was 'Side by Side', the classic Harry Woods song, and it was sung by Eydie Gorme and Steve Lawrence for you on Golden Oldies Community Radio, now streaming to the whole world.'

Compared to the other volunteer announcers, who sounded like characters from down the pub or the retirement village and often played the wrong song or cut it off before it had finished or forgot to raise the volume, creating the dreaded 'dead air' effect, her mother always sounded elegant and professional, and her segment ran without a hitch. She'd clearly missed a great vocation as a radio announcer, but coming from the old thinking that women stayed at home to raise their children, she'd never pursued her interests – or even appeared to have any – until this unexpected foray into radio just a few years ago.

The kettle clicked off. Mia poured the steaming liquid into her mug. Her mother was starting on her community announcements.

'… and the Green Thumbs Azalea Club cordially invites you to join them for a fascinating talk about caring for your plants. Meetings are delightfully informal and there's a delicious supper afterward. No need for you to feel left out or lonely. Just call Colleen to book in on triple seven, two five four zero. And thank you to Phillip for ringing in to tell us how much you're enjoying the program. Thank you to Joan who is also enjoying the program. And Martin, it's lovely to hear from you again, thank you ever so much. We're always pleased to hear from our listeners. We do appreciate you calling in. And thank you to all our sponsors and thank you to our members. We sincerely appreciate your support. So please, if you have any requests just call the studio on seven five seven zero nine two nine eight and we'll be delighted to play them for you…'

Mia smiled. If there was anyone who could overdo gratitude, it was her mother.

'Ah,' said John, from the doorway. 'Mum is in fine form.' He was tying his dressing gown belt.

'Yes… Could you bear dinner there tonight? We've been invited.'

'I suppose so…' he said, and came to wrap arms that were still warm from bed around her.

'Not going for a ride?' she asked.

He nuzzled the side of her neck. 'Not today. I'll pick it up again tomorrow.'

'That's very slack of you…'

'Well, I have had some exercise already,' he murmured, 'and perhaps, if you feel you need some more…'

She laughed. 'You never go back to bed once you're up! I don't believe you.'

'I'm changing,' he said. 'I told you I was coming back a changed man.'

Mia twisted around to look at him, but he was kissing the back of her neck. 'Are you serious?'

'Dead serious,' he said, and began to lick her ear.

She squirmed. 'You know I don't like that!'

'Just checking… I'm rediscovering you. Things change, right?' He was moving her mug away from the edge of the table and drawing her up, his hands under her arms.

'We should send you away more often,' she said, as he guided her back to the bedroom.

It was after midday by the time they had showered and dressed. 'It feels like we're on holiday,' Mia said, as she dropped two pieces of bread in the toaster. 'Or back in our early days when we stayed in bed for hours.'

It had been amazing. Long and slow and luscious. She felt deeply relaxed, deeply content. It was extraordinary to her that all those months of frustration and resentment and daydreaming about leaving and other men could be dissolved in two lovemaking experiences. Probably it wouldn't last, if she was realistic about it, but John's intense desire for her was bringing back feelings of love for him that had long lain dormant. They said that absence made the heart grow fonder, but she hadn't known that it also made desire so much more acute; he had never been so attentive, so patient, so focused on her pleasure. It was probably the best sex they had ever had.

'We've been in a rut,' he said simply, opening the pantry to bring out the spreads. 'And that's all going to change.'

'Bring it on,' she said.

When they'd eaten, he called her into the living room, where he was unpacking the large bubble-wrapped paintings. 'I brought two for us,' he said. 'Tell me what you think.'

She sat on the arm of an armchair, watching as the wrapping fell away and he set the painting on the sofa then stepped out of the way.

A street scene, observed from inside a house. Light, spotted curtains hung on either side of a big window, but one's gaze was drawn to the street, to the houses and people walking along the pavement: an elderly man with his dog on a lead, a teenager dribbling a soccer ball while carrying a plastic bottle of milk in one hand and a loaf of bread in the other, a child in a tree…

'It's stunning,' she said. 'You didn't send me a picture of this one.'

'Keeping it for us – as a surprise,' he said. 'This is the view from Mum and Dad's living room.'

Mia went closer to examine the detail. 'It's so realistic and yet… not. Something unusual about it…'

'That's his style. A kind of blend.' John began unwrapping another package, slightly smaller. 'Go back again.'

She retreated to the armchair and he moved the window scene and replaced it with the second picture: a couple standing by the Thames, holding hands loosely. The girl had red hair in a ponytail. She was gazing across the water, her other hand stuffed into the pocket of her jeans. The guy was looking at her with an expression of longing and loss… there was something poignant about it.

'It's beautiful,' Mia said. 'He's definitely got the ability to bring scenes to life. They're amazing.'

"Just dabbling," John said, in a parody of his mother.

Mia shook her head. 'That is so sad.'

'I think she was starting to wake up to how good they were by the end of the exhibition.'

'I would hope so!' Mia exclaimed. 'Where will we put them?'

'You can decide.' John went back to unwrapping.

'There's more?'

'I brought one for your folks. What do you think?' He held up a small square picture of a child kneeling by a garden bed watering a plant with a little red plastic can.

Mia leaned closer. 'Is that…?'

'Yes.'

'Oh, how sweet.' The plant was not growing; it had been picked or found and then pressed into the soil by the child, who was holding its limp stem up with one dirt-encrusted hand while he sprinkled water on it with the other. 'Simple, everyday scenes,' Mia said, 'painted with such love and sympathy. I wish I'd known your dad.'

It was quiet between them for a moment.

'You didn't come over,' John said.

Mia sat back on her heels and then turned to face him. 'No. I... didn't want to. I felt... I wanted some space. Everything between us was so... dead.'

He nodded. 'I know. I didn't really expect you to come.'

An image of Nick flashed into her mind and receded just as quickly. The attraction and longing and confusion were fading.

'Last ones,' John said, unwrapping yet another boxy package. He brought out a set of three sketches drawn on a train. In one, a businessman sat reading the paper next to a large, black-clad Italian woman who was eating a mandarin; in another, a woman listened to something on her iPhone, eyes closed, while the two people on either side of her sat hunched over their phones, texting; in the third, a number of passengers stood pressed together, swaying and falling into each other as the train moved through a tunnel. The drawings were not quite finished but utterly life-like and compelling.

'For Sheryl or for us; it's up to you,' John said.

'Sheryl would love them,' Mia said at once, 'but I don't know if I want to let them go.'

'We can get prints, remember? Jake is looking into that.'

'Yes... They're all wonderful. I hope you sell lots of prints.'

'So do we. Seems like the least we can do for the old man.'

Mia wrapped her arms around her knees, still gazing from one picture to the next. 'What are you going to do today?'

'Unpack and some washing. You?'

'I was thinking I'd duck out to an open day at a college that offers a counselling course I've been considering.'

'Good plan. Are you narrowing the field?'

'Mmm... not very successfully yet. Have to decide how serious I am. You know, degree, diploma, short course...? It kind of depends on what you're going to do, too.' She looked at him pointedly.

John glanced at her and then away. He began to gather up the bubble wrap. 'You mean work-wise? If we can afford to both be starting afresh?'

'Yes.'

'You can't study part-time?'

She felt a little flash of anger. 'Sure. But that might stretch it out to six years if I do the degree. I don't think I'm patient enough for that... And what are you going to do, anyway? Did you really resign while you were in England? Weren't they pissed with you?'

'I'd been kind of hinting before I left. It's not bad timing because they're restructuring again. A few people were getting retrenched. They didn't especially want me to go but I decided it was time to make the break. If I didn't do it while I was feeling inspired to change my life I'd come back and fall into old habits. You know what I'm like.'

'So what are you going to do?'

'I'm thinking about gardening,' he said, and she stared at him.

'I thought you were joking! You don't know anything about plants.'

'Not landscaping,' he said. 'Mowing lawns.'

'That's going to be a bit of a crash in income, isn't it? And in satisfaction?' She couldn't imagine being satisfied crunching numbers but that was what John had always loved, whereas he would push a lawn mower only when he had to.

'I think I need to use my body more,' he said. 'Back in a sec.' He was heading for the door with the armful of bubble wrap.

'You're not going to throw that out, are you?' she called after him. 'I'll take it to work.'

He hesitated and then came back. 'Silly me. Where do you want me to put it?'

'In the laundry, I suppose. I'll bag it up.' She followed him. 'You were saying?'

'I've been sedentary for too long.' He looked around the laundry and then dumped the bubble wrap on the washing machine.'

'I wouldn't leave it there,' she said. 'You're about to do a wash.'

'Oh. Yes.' He looked around again.

'Here,' she held out her hands. 'I might as well put it straight in the boot. But finish that sentence before I go.'

'It's no big deal. Having all that time away from the screen has just made me reluctant to lock myself to a desk too quickly… I think it will be good for me to use my body for a bit. Not that I'm thinking of gardening as my next big career but just for a break while I think about it.'

'Okay…' she said, still surprised, automatically folding the bubble wrap into a more compact size. 'You'll need equipment though.'

'Our mower is good enough to start. We've got an edger. I might have to get a blower.'

'But you drive a Commodore. You're going to need a wagon… or a ute.'

'Barry's probably going to lend me something. I'll follow up with him this week. If not, I'll just hire a trailer to begin with.'

'Wow. Okay. You've really thought it through.'

'Just as a 'for now'.'

'So you'll be mowing lawns and I'll be studying.'

'If you ever decide. You've been talking about it for ages.'

She made a face at him. 'I'm getting closer. The conference helped – hearing all those counsellors talk about what they do. It was fascinating. Especially – have you ever heard of The Hero's Journey?'

'Nope. What's that?'

'This kind of universal human story that shows up in all cultures about… just… whatever people do, all their life challenges and stuff. It's kind of a pattern for living and how we deal with problems. Films like *Star Wars* and *The Matrix* were modelled on it, so people everywhere relate to the film because they recognise the pattern. Am I making sense?'

'Not much,' he said gravely.

She grinned. 'Oh well. Anyway, it's really interesting. I want to learn more about it.'

'Well, if I'm throwing caution to the winds, you have to as well. Deal?' he asked, holding out a hand.

'It's not going to give us much security,' she said. 'Security' was John's top value.

He looked at her, pained. 'Are you trying to stop me from taking a risk and getting out of the rut?'

'No!'

'Then don't talk like that. You know it will make me start doubting.'

'I promise,' she said, shaking his hand. 'We'll live on the edge for a while. Right on the skinny branches.'

'That's better. Honestly, Mia, you're going to have to help me with this. I don't know how powerfully...' he made a sucking noise.

She smiled and grabbed his arm. 'I'll hold you. I won't let you fall back into the old habits.'

'Thank you,' he said, and moved closer, until his lips rested against hers in a lingering kiss.

Taking the bubble wrap out to the car a few minutes later, she found herself singing, '*We'll be the same as we started,*

Just travelling along,

Singing a song,

Side by side...'

8

It was a thirty-minute drive to her parents' place. Mia talked a little about the open day as she drove, and the conversations she'd had there with people who had been through the course.

'It looks quite good but they don't help you get any practical placement whereas I reckon ACCAT would, so I'm veering in that direction. If you do the course online, you have to be videoed counselling people and submit the videos – scary! I suppose I would need you to video me... Don't know who I'd counsel – who do you think?'

'Hm?' John murmured.

She glanced across at him and saw that he was reading something on his phone. 'Have I just been talking to myself?'

'Sorry, no.' He closed whatever he'd been reading and put the phone back in the console. 'I was listening. Just missed that last part.'

She repeated what she'd said and he agreed that her current place of employment would probably be a good place to study, especially since her boss was fond of her, and yes, of course he would video her. It would be fun! And Sheryl would surely agree to a mock counselling session.

Arriving at her parents' place with its neat front yard and beautiful garden beds, ('Just travelling along, singing a song, side by side,' she hummed), Mia pulled into the driveway behind her mother's Mazda. She switched off the engine and looked at John. His eyes were closed, although he was sitting upright. She touched his thigh. 'We're here.'

The eyes opened immediately; they were bloodshot. 'It's catching up with me,' he said.

'We won't stay long,' she promised.

'S'all right. I needed to get myself into this time zone by staying awake all day. Nearly made it.'

Her mother answered the doorbell almost immediately. They heard her steps, slightly muffled by the thin hallway rug, and then the door opened and she stood there with a spotless apron over her white shirt and navy pants.

'Welcome home, John,' she said, and stepped back to let them in. Their cheeks met in an air kiss.

Something smells good,' Mia said.

'Does it? That's good. Now,' leading the way through their tidy house to the kitchen, where Frank Sinatra was playing in the background, 'how was England? How is your mother?'

'Mum's as well as can be expected,' John said. He was carrying the painting, now gift-wrapped. 'I've got something for you both. A little memento from Dad. Is Lionel around?'

'He's on the porch, cooking the chicken. He can probably leave it for a moment.'

'I'll get him,' Mia said.

She could see her father on the other side of the glass sliding door, standing at the barbecue and moving food around with tongs. She walked past the family room table, which was set with orange napkins in fans at each place and a big bowl of salad in the centre, and opened the door.

'Hello, Dad.'

Lionel looked up and smiled. 'Hello, love. I didn't hear you arrive.'

'Just this minute,' she said. 'Smells good.'

'Your mother's marinade,' he replied, poking at a piece of meat, which sizzled.

'Can you come in for a mo?'

'Of course.' He put the tongs down and came to give her a brief hug, then followed her in. 'The traveller is back!'

John shook his hand. 'I've got something for the two of you.'

'You didn't need to do that.'

'It's not a souvenir from England,' Mia said. 'It's –'

John shushed her. 'My limelight.'

'Oh, excuse me!' she smiled, pulling a seat away from the table and sitting on it.

'I don't know if I've ever told you,' John said to his in-laws, 'but Dad was a bit of a painter in his later years. Mum used to say he was just dabbling but really he's quite good. We had a, uh, exhibition of his work before I left, which is why I was delayed.'

'Mia told us,' his mother-in-law said.

'Good. Well, so I thought I'd bring you two a painting of his.' He picked up the parcel and held it out to her.

Glenys quickly wiped her hands on the apron and received it, then sat with it in her lap, knees and feet neatly together, while she loosened the sticky tape.

'Your mother all right?' Lionel asked as they all watched her hands moving around the package.

'As good as can be expected under the circumstances,' John said.

'She's moving into a retirement village?'

'That's right. It was on the cards for both of them but then Dad passed. We got started with putting the house on the market before I left, and of course she'll get a packing company to help her with the move.' John was watching his mother-in-law. She was sitting with the painting propped up in her lap on its discarded wrapping, gazing at the picture with a faraway expression.

'You going to show me?' Lionel asked, and she stirred herself and turned the picture around for him.

He nodded, lips thrust out a little in a thoughtful, 'that's good' expression. 'Very nice. Very impressive.'

'Mum?' Mia asked.

'He's an excellent artist,' her mother said, rising and taking the painting to a place on the wall. 'What do you think? Here?'

'Wherever you think, Glenys,' Lionel said. 'You're the decorator.'

'Here. I can look at it while I'm cooking.'

'Shall I mark the wall?'

'We'll remember,' she said. 'You'd better check the meat.'

Out he went. Glenys stood the painting up on the bench against the wall and beside the telephone.

'Anything I can do, Mum?' Mia asked, helping herself to a carrot stick from the salad.

'It's all done. I'll just get the vegetables out of the oven.'

Mia met John's eyes and gave a little shrug. It was strange how her mother could be so appreciative of strangers ringing in to thank her for songs played on the radio, and yet so reserved about expressing her thanks for a personal gift. Perhaps personal gifts made her feel obliged, in debt. It couldn't be that the picture of the child was bringing back memories of Rita, surely? Their firstborn had died as a baby, just a few days old; she, Mia, was the infant who had made it into toddlerhood and then beyond. She was the one who would have done those touching childhood things like trying to revive a dead plant. Her mother couldn't be still mourning the fact that Rita had not lived long enough to do any of that – surely!

Glenys was standing in the middle of the kitchen, a little frown puckering her forehead, and looking around.

'What have you lost?'

'The Myer catalogue. I saw a throw rug in it that I thought you might like...' Her face cleared up. 'I remember. I was looking at it in the living room.'

'I'll get it,' John offered.

Glenys brought a dish of green beans to the table and then returned for the casserole of roast vegetables. 'See if your father's ready, would you?'

Mia opened the glass sliding door again and poked her head outside.

'All ready,' her father said. He was placing the last piece of chicken on a dish.

They took their seats. John hadn't come back. 'What's taking him?' Mia wondered aloud. 'I'll grab him – we don't want this delicious meal to get cold.'

He was standing in the dim living room with the catalogue in his hand and gazing at the Rita tribute above the mantelpiece, the print of Rita's tiny baby hands and feet, captured just after she had died, on either side of the photograph of her tiny face with its delicate closed eyes. Mia hesitated just inside the room. She hadn't properly looked at that picture for ages. Having grown up in the shadow of a child who never was (in her world, at least), she'd been resentful and guilty in turns of this ghostly big sister. She hadn't wanted to have a child of her own at first, probably out of some unconscious fear that it would die on her. But then she had changed her mind, as the idea of loving and cherishing her own baby, of making it feel as loved and wanted as she never had, took hold. And then Talia had been born, utterly winning her over to the idea. She remembered John saying they would talk about everything when he got back; a baby was one of those things.

John turned around and caught her looking at him. Neither spoke. He came toward her and picked up her hand and turned her around toward the doorway. There was something very gentle about the way he had picked up her hand, as if to communicate: *I know how you feel about all this. We're going to do something about it.*

Glenys took the catalogue from John and handed it to Mia. 'I thought these might suit, dear. But you just take it home and look in your own time. I don't need it back.'

Mia looked at the two her mother had circled. 'Thanks, Mum. They're nice.'

During dinner Mia trotted out the proud fact that she had listened to her mother on the radio that morning.

'Sounding good, Glenys,' John had agreed. 'You're a catch for that radio station.'

'Thank you, dear,' Mia's mother said. Peggy Lee was singing in the background now.

'You're not wrong.' Lionel sliced a green bean into short pieces and then speared them all in turn to eat with his last piece of chicken. 'Your mother has a very nice voice for radio.'

'Thank you, dear,' Glenys said. 'Anyone for more potatoes?'

John held up his plate and she scooped another serve out for him. 'And you're a catch for us,' he said. 'These are delicious.'

'You've already won them over with the painting,' Mia said. 'You don't have to go over your carb ratio as well.' She was teasing him since he usually strictly managed his taste for spuds, but for just a moment he looked trapped. Then he laughed, saying that all would come back to normal tomorrow when he started cycling again.

'Your mother *is* a catch,' Lionel was agreeing. 'Beautiful, caring mother, excellent cook, charming radio host...'

'Goodness,' said Glenys, and she changed the subject.

'Dad still tiptoes around Mum all these years later,' Mia said as she reversed out of her parents' driveway later that evening. 'You'd think it would be over by now but no...'

'Well, she fell apart pretty dramatically back then, didn't she?'

'Yes.'

'What's the age difference between the two of you again?'

'Two and a half years.'

'So she was still grieving...'

'Yes. The old 'have another baby asap and you'll get over it'... But that was crap advice. She was fearful all the way through the pregnancy that I'd die too, and massively over-protective when I was growing up. It was a funny childhood – I was smothered *and* neglected. She'd disappear into these daydreams... But you know all this. Fuck! I should stop harping on about it.'

'Not if it still bothers you,' he said sleepily. 'Anyway, they named you 'Mia', so surely they were pretty clear about wanting you, even if it was an accident.'

Mia. 'Mine.' Her parents' unconscious attempt to hold her, claim her, possess her after losing their first-born? 'Maybe. But then why did I grow up feeling so neglected and rejected and inadequate, and like she was never fully there?'

'Because she wasn't,' he said simply. 'She was still lost in the grief.'

'Even though she had a live, cute, gorgeous new child.'

'It makes no sense. People are strange. Complex…' His head was leaning back against the headrest, eyes closed. 'You'll carry me in when we get home, right?'

'You'll sleep in the car,' she said tartly.

He smiled, eyes still closed, and put a hand on her thigh. Mia drove through the dark streets with a smile on her own lips. Somehow, for some reason, she felt as if John had come back more open to having a child. She'd begun to think that perhaps he couldn't, physically, and that they should both get checked out, but perhaps it had been some emotional resistance that was now evaporating…

9

When she opened her eyes on Monday morning, it was to see John propped up on one elbow next to her, looking at her with an expression of wonder.

Something caught in her heart, a sense of being wanted and valued... It burst open like a delicate flower, overwhelming her with its perfect scent. She felt as if a much-needed vitamin that had been missing from her body for years had suddenly been provided.

No words passed between them. He leaned forward and kissed her gently on the lips, then rested on his elbow again, stroking the side of her face, brushing hair away from her eyes, just gazing at her. The magnitude of his attention was almost overwhelming. She felt torn between a desire to run away and a desire to let this feeling grow, to not move or disturb it, so that it could send strong roots deep into the earth of her. She felt breathless.

The moment was shattered when her alarm went off, and they both jumped and laughed, and he reached across her to switch it off. And then bent over her with another kiss.

'Good morning.'

'Good morning,' she answered, lifting one hand to touch his cheek. 'That was a beautiful way to wake up.'

He smiled, turning his face to kiss the tips of her fingers, and then said, 'Well, time to get the routine happening again. I've lolled around for long enough.'

While she headed for the shower, he changed into his cycling gear and when she came out, hair in a turban, he'd left. She moved around the house getting breakfast, gathering bits and pieces, tidying up here and there, and was sitting in the car, warming the engine, when he rode back up the driveway, fluorescent orange helmet hanging from the handlebars. He slowed down beside her and she wound the window down. There was a sheen of sweat on his flushed face and his breath was coming hard.

'Good ride?' she asked, shivering at the chill coming in through the open window.

'Yes… although I'm very out of shape… Phew!' He wiped a hand across his forehead.

'Oh well. It will come back. What are you doing today?'

'Thought I'd drop in at work and say hi, bye. Make the farewell a little more personal than a call and email from the UK.'

'Good idea.'

'And I'll follow up with Barry about that ute.'

'It's really all happening,' she marvelled.

'I did warn you,' he said, and threw one leg over the bike to wheel it back into the garage. 'Have a good one, honey.'

'Thanks.' She blew him a kiss and wound up the window, feeling relief as the cold air was locked outside and her car heater could get on with its job.

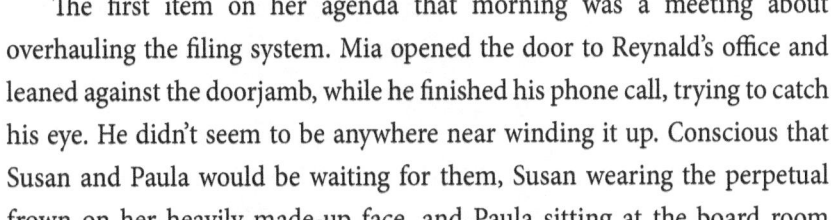

The first item on her agenda that morning was a meeting about overhauling the filing system. Mia opened the door to Reynald's office and leaned against the doorjamb, while he finished his phone call, trying to catch his eye. He didn't seem to be anywhere near winding it up. Conscious that Susan and Paula would be waiting for them, Susan wearing the perpetual frown on her heavily made-up face, and Paula sitting at the board room table in her smart pencil skirt and tailored jacket, and tapping away at her keyboard, never wasting a minute, always working, Mia took a few steps toward Reynald and when he looked up, she raised her brows at him, pointing at her wrist. Not that she wore a watch but that was surely a universal signal.

He nodded, and returned to his call, and she stood there battling anxiety, feeling Susan's 'get in here!' lasso whistling through the air toward them to scoop them up. Finally he said goodbye and rose, grabbing the manila folder she'd already left on his desk, and hurried with her toward the boardroom.

They were a pair, she and Reynald. He was an ex-therapist who had somehow found himself managing a national counselling body and, she suspected, only wanted to return to the field and lock himself in a cosy office with clients and listen to their tales; she was a PA who had learnt her trade like a good kid and now found herself restless, pulling away, realising she had been cast in the wrong role. By comparison, Paula was the epitome of an excellent executive – she was constantly coming up with brilliant ideas for expanding the business and she ate problems for breakfast. And Susan, for all her grouchy personality, was efficiency personified. Mia and Reynald were like a pair of phonies – they kind of knew what they were doing and did it reasonably well but they would both rather be somewhere else.

Paula started talking as they took their seats. She wanted the office to go paperless. If they were going to lead the way into the future, they had to look at their office systems as well as at their organisational practices. Susan and Mia would be in charge of evaluating the current situation and coming up with simple systems that everyone in the office could implement that would reduce the company's paper usage to as close to zero as they could manage.

No one could object to this given environment issues, but Mia knew that Reynald would be hurting. He was an old-fashioned paper kind of guy, and she completely understood. Your eyes got so sore doing everything on a screen. And you could get lost in a profusion of open documents on the computer, whereas when they were laid out on your desk you could see where everything was at once… But the times, they were a-changing… Mia tried not to look at Reynald, who was frowning and hunching in his chair, and instead took notes (oops, on paper), while Paula buzzed through her list of warnings and reminders and suggestions before cutting her and Susan loose to manage the job.

She would let Susan lead the way, Mia thought. That would make both of them happy. The little battle she'd had with Susan for supremacy ever since joining the company was no longer important to her; she was just marking time now until she left.

Sheryl texted her at lunchtime when she was sitting in the café downstairs from her office, eating a wrap.

> Dinner Saturday night?

Mia opened her calendar to check

> All clear

> Great. Couple of other people coming as well. Okay?

> Sure

As soon as this message had gone, she had an image of Nick, and texted back:

> Not Nick, right?

> No def not

She took another bite of her wrap and sent a message to John.

> Dinner at Sheryl and Alec's this Sat night. Ok?

There was no reply. She added:

> Howdyou go at work?

And this time she saw that he was replying.

> Ok. Good

She sent a smiley face and went back to her lunch, psyching herself up for the beginning of the horrible task.

By the end of the week there was a faded blue ute in the driveway. Barry, whom Mia had never met, was an older work colleague of John's who'd recently had a heart attack and was now taking it slow. He and his wife had had to sell the property he was doing up in the country, and the sight of the ute was a too painful reminder of abandoned dreams.

John had produced a little flyer, with Mia's input, and they'd walked the streets together dropping it into letterboxes. There had been one almost immediate phone booking, and tomorrow he'd be heading over to this person's place to do their lawns. He was loading the gear into the back of the vehicle when Mia arrived home on Friday evening.

She parked in the street and sat watching him for a moment. He'd let down the tailgate, propped some old timber planks against it for a ramp, and was now pushing the mower up into the tray. Aside from his regular morning bike ride and cutting their grass once a month or so, John had rarely ever done anything physical. He dressed in a suit and headed out to his corporate accounting job in the morning, coming back in the evening as neat as when he'd left. But watching him now, she reflected that there was something satisfying about a man useing his muscles and grunting. Something satisfying in a primal sort of way.

After a few moments she climbed out of the car, calling, 'Wow, it's all happening! Need a hand?'

He gave the mower a last shove and it thudded into the tray. Mia joined him at the ute. A whippersnipper, some secateurs and a lawnmower, and he was ready to go into business.

'I still can't believe you're actually doing this.'

'I can't either,' he said. 'To be perfectly honest. I'm a little in shock.'

They both gazed at the equipment, and then a fierce gust of wind blew her hair into her face and she dragged it out of her eyes and said, 'Hope the weather holds for you,' and he looked at the sky grimly and slid the timber ramp into the back of the ute.

'What shall we do for dinner tonight?' she asked.

'I'll cook,' he said. 'I've been here all day while you've been working. I picked up some fish.'

'Okay.'

'How are you?'

'Brain dead.'

Mia walked Bitsy while John cooked. It was bitterly cold and already quite dark. She walked briskly, watched her pup scampering at the end of the lead, darting from one dog's do to another, sniffing, and tugging at the lead again as she scooted off to examine a tree or a lamp post or a fence. They hurried through the wind down one side of the block and then the other, and through the little reserve among the trees, and past others who were walking their dogs and were also zipped up against the cold.

She wondered when it would be appropriate to initiate The Conversation... They'd had drinks at work today for Isabelle, who was going on maternity leave, so the whole baby thing was throbbingly present for Mia. She'd been off the pill for the last couple of years at least, and had been surprised when month after month her period turned up with depressing regularity – by comparison with Sheryl and Alec, who'd been pregnant within minutes of abandoning contraception. You heard about plenty of couples who couldn't conceive for ages and then did right after they adopted, so there was obviously some sort of weird emotional factor that could block conception. Was it stress? Fear? Resistance to becoming a parent? If so, now that things were so much better between her and John that block was probably melting away. She hoped so, but if nothing happened soon, they'd both have to go and get checked out. It was not a conversation she fancied having.

The house felt very warm when she got back, and the aromas from John's dinner preparations were enticing. Bitsy dashed straight into the kitchen, claws tapping. John was chopping parsley for the fish and quartering a lemon. The vegetables were steaming and a salad was ready to go. His usual menu. This and Chicken Chasseur. And trifle – he made a great trifle.

They ate dinner to the sounds of Rod Stewart. John had turned out the lights and put candles on the table, which meant that she could hardly see her meal, but it was nice. Flickering golden pools of light. She sat opposite him, legs stretched out under the table, feet in his lap.

'It's not dress-up tomorrow, is it?' he asked suddenly.

'At Sheryl's? No. Just a dinner party.'

'You never told me what you wore to her birthday.'

'Oh.' An image of herself in that low-cut crimson dress brought another image with it: Nick. His hands on her. The kiss. Her body's hungry response... She concentrated on her plate, hoping her face wasn't as flushed as it felt. 'Didn't I?' Stalling for time...

'No.' He was looking at her now, kind of penetratingly. 'Are you embarrassed? What did you wear?'

'Oh God. Sheryl put me up to it.' Her mind was racing, leaping ahead of what she was about to say to check his response and find out if it was safe or not. 'We were in this party hire place and we saw this dress on a mannequin that was pretty... lovely... and she made me try it on.'

'Why do I feel as if there's something you're not telling me?' he asked. He'd stopped eating. He was just looking at her, appraising her, almost...

'Well,' she flustered, 'it was... kind of an out-there dress for me... A bit saucy.'

He raised his brows. 'Saucy? And you didn't send me a pic?'

'I didn't think of it. You know me and photos. And I was too self-conscious.' Oh God. She'd said too much.

'You are turning me on,' he said, and pressed her feet against his crotch where she could feel the evidence. 'I'm imagining you in a mini skirt with lots of cleavage showing...'

She gave a little burst of laughter. 'It wasn't a mini.'

'But the cleavage?'

'There was a bit...'

'Why don't you dress like that when I'm here?'

'You...' She stopped. Why? Because she didn't feel that he was interested in how she looked. Because she was hiding the rolls… 'I don't know,' she said.

'Tomorrow night, then,' he said. 'Wear it tomorrow night.'

'I can't!' she laughed again, and tossed down a mouthful of wine. 'It was a dress-up – fancy – inappropriate for a dinner party! It would be over the top.'

'I don't care,' he said. He was massaging her foot with one hand now.

'Well, I do! But…' she rifled mentally through the dresses in her wardrobe. 'I'll wear something –'

'Hot,' he instructed. 'Something hot.'

Hot. Had John ever before wanted her to wear something hot? She searched her memory. 'I can't believe this is you talking,' she said.

He looked away for a moment and then focused on her again. 'It's Dad dying. I just… sitting there next to his body and thinking about all those years of his life as a shipping clerk, having Mum run him down, thinking he was nothing special… It really affected me. I don't want to go to my grave feeling I lived a half-life. And I know I've let you down for years now. I haven't made you feel like the beautiful, loved woman you are. I want to change that.' He reached across the table and took her hand. 'I want you to know how gorgeous you are and how much you mean to me every single day.'

She sat gazing at him, melting, tears in her eyes, breathless with love.

10

John had trundled out of the driveway on Saturday morning to drive the few streets to his first mowing job. He'd already been out cycling before breakfast and seemed to be getting his old fitness back – he wasn't quite as puffed anymore when he returned.

Mia ripped the shopping list off the pad, gave Bitsy a pat, and headed out herself. She had the usual things on the list, plus more flour – John reckoned he was going to make her a Yorkshire pudding on Sunday night. And she needed to pick up a gift for Sheryl and Alec. Chocolates, wine...? She would see what grabbed her.

On the way back, she spontaneously took a detour, driving slowly through unfamiliar streets, looking for John's mowing address. The image of him cutting someone's lawn instead of sitting at his corporate desk totting up numbers was so strange that she had to see it for herself.

She caught a glimpse of the blue ute out the front of the place as she turned into the street, and approached slowly, ready to smile and wave. He was standing in the front yard, sleeves rolled up, leaning on the mower and talking to a woman with short auburn hair. Mia cruised towards them. The woman turned and pointed ahead up the street and John looked in the direction she was pointing. He said something and she turned back and laughed and he laughed, and it all looked very friendly but Mia had an unsettled feeling in her stomach. Was he flirting? Not John, surely! But...

Mia picked up a little speed and drove more purposefully toward them.

She slowed down again as she approached and yes, the woman was blushing and laughing and John was smiling and winking... Mia rolled down her car window and leaned across the passenger seat. John looked up and smiled, and the woman turned around as Mia said, 'Thought I'd –' *come by and check on you* *didn't sound good.* 'Just wondering if you'll be home for lunch?' she asked instead.

He glanced across at the lawn and back to her. 'Should be. Nearly finished here.'

Mia looked at the woman, who was looking from her to him.

'Oh,' John said. 'My wife, Mia. And this is... Sandra?'

The woman nodded. She was pretty.

'Sandra's booked me to do her lawn tomorrow. She lives up the street here.' He pointed.

'I was just walking past on my way back from the milk bar.' Sandra indicated the plastic bag in her hand.

'Great,' Mia said. 'Well... I'll see you at home soon, sweetheart.'

He saluted, and she wondered, as she drove away, if the woman would think he was hen-pecked. And how would John feel, having her breathing over his shoulder like this? Over-thinking! she scolded herself.

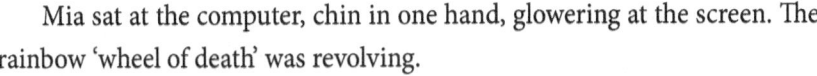

Mia sat at the computer, chin in one hand, glowering at the screen. The rainbow 'wheel of death' was revolving.

'John!' she yelled. 'Can you help?'

No answer. She walked around the house, checking rooms, knocking on the bathroom door. Nowhere. Went to the back door and peered outside into their pocket-handkerchief garden. Not there either. Returned to the front of the house, calling again, and saw him through the living room window. He was leaning against the letterbox, talking to someone on the phone. Why you'd go outside to chat she had no idea. The sky might be a clear sunny blue today but it was icy out there. But then, men did seem to run hotter than women. She remembered Nick in his T-shirt on Sheryl's deck that midwinter night…

Mia returned to the computer and tried again but struck the same problem. Maybe they needed to upgrade or get more RAM or something. She stood up, frustrated, and went into the kitchen to make a cup of tea. John came in as the kettle was boiling.

'Tea?' she asked.

'Love one,' he said.

'You were out there for a while. Weren't you cold?'

'Not at first. Talking to Jake about the prints we're producing of Dad's work.'

'Oh. Good. Could you help me? I've got the bloody wheel of death.'

'Did you force quit the program?'

'Yes but it just came back again.'

'Okay. I'll have a look.'

'Thanks.' She took another cup out of the cupboard and dropped bags into each one. John preferred making tea properly, in a pot – English boy that he was – but she couldn't taste the difference. She tipped a little milk into their cups and carried them into the living room. He was sitting at the computer reading a message on his phone. He flipped the cover and slid it out of the way to make room on the table for their cups.

'Ta.'

'Have you figured it out?'

'I think we need a restart.'

She tutted. 'I've already done that once today. This is so frustrating!'

'Don't they teach you how to solve your computer problems at work?'

'Of course. We're on a different system there. This old thing… maybe it's time to upgrade.'

'Maybe it is,' he said. 'But you can't just buy a new toy every time the old one isn't working.' Typical John. The irrepressible 'save money' accountant gene.

'Yes but this is so *frustrating*.'

'Well, if I can throw off old habits and totally change my career you can do a computer course or something to find out how to solve this sort of thing yourself. You can't always be dependent on me.'

She looked at him sulkily. 'You know I would hate that.'

'Poor thing.' John leaned toward her, the corners of his eyes crinkling with laughter. 'Poor baby.' He kissed the side of her mouth. She turned her head a little and kissed him back properly.

Mia sat in the loo, feet perched on the loo stool, reading the novel she kept in there for occasions like this.

John knocked on the door. 'You going to be much longer?'

'Use the other one,' she called.

'I don't need to go,' he said; 'we need to go.'

'Oh. What time is it?'

'Six-thirty.'

'Okay.'

She heard him move away and made a face at herself in the mirror. A sarcastic, at-the-end-of-her-tether face. Not that it helped. Making faces at yourself when you were constipated did not help to get things moving but it did relieve some of the frustration. Straining didn't help either. Waiting was the only thing that worked. Hence the novel. She'd just become used to waiting for her body to realise that she was sitting in here expecting it to perform. And sometimes it did, like magic. Sometimes it didn't and she stormed out of there, irritated with her own bowel for not doing what it was designed to do. Sometimes she got a sort of half result – 'poodle poo', one naturopath she'd been to had described it. They'd ruled out allergies, and changing her diet didn't seem to make any difference. One day a certain food seemed to clog her up and the next day she ate heaps of it and went to the toilet three times satisfactorily. It was the fucking mystery of her life.

She looked up from her novel and closed her eyes, tuning in. Yes! Action!

John was dressing when she flushed and emerged. He was trying to do up a pair of pants.

She paused in the doorway, watching him struggle with the button. 'Still a few British-food kilos to lose, I see.'

'Mm,' he grunted.

'Those pants were always too small for you,' she reminded him, going toward her own wardrobe. 'If you want to wear those you'll have to leave the button undone or you won't be able to eat.'

'Any other suggestions?' he asked, unzipping with a little out-breath of relief.

'Sure.' She rattled through his hangers and pulled out another pair. 'You haven't worn these in ages. They should be fine.'

'Forgot about those,' he said, taking the hanger from her. 'What are you wearing? This is your seduce-your-husband night, remember?'

'Oh… yes…' She was smiling but biting her lip as she turned back to her own choice bank. *What to wear?* She didn't have anything particular saucy. This was Conservative-Mia's Wardrobe, after all; the crimson dress had been her escape from the prison of normality. One brief excursion, quickly suppressed.

She pulled out the requisite little black dress. Not low-cut. Not particularly sexy but short and elegant with a kind of lace overlay. She always felt smart wearing it. The thing was: would she be over-dressed for a home dinner? The little black dress kind of said cocktails, not an at-home dinner with Talia hopefully in her lap…

John came to stand behind her. 'That looks good.'

'Yes, but too formal…'

'What about…?' he moved items along, taking dresses out that would be hopelessly inappropriate, realising, and putting them back.

'I know!' she said. 'What about my jeans and that white gypsy top? It's pretty low-cut, Mr Husband. You've always liked it.'

'Show me.'

She pulled it out and held it up.

John regarded it appraisingly. 'You're right. I like it. But jeans? No legs on display? I don't think so.'

She shook her head and laughed. 'Honestly, what are they putting in your water over there? Since when do you care what I wear?'

'Since I felt jealous that you wore a saucy dress for a whole lot of other men,' he said. 'And since I'm changing – embracing life – getting out of the rut.' He held out the black dress. 'I think it's this one tonight, and then I take you shopping.'

'Yeah, right,' she said, pulling her top over her head.

When they arrived at Sheryl and Alec's, the other couple were climbing out of their car. Mia squinted at them in the dark. Did she recognise them?

'Do we know them?' John asked, also looking in their direction.

'I don't think so.'

'Do we know who they are?'

'Sheryl said a colleague of Alec's and his wife. Can't remember their names.'

'Okay. Good.'

'Why is that good?' she asked as they emerged from their car and she reached back in for the wine and chockies and gift.

He shrugged, taking the bottle from her. 'No particular reason.'

The others were still in the hallway, taking coats off and chatting, when they reached the open front door. Alec had Talia in his arms. She was wearing a pink gro-suit that made her look supremely huggable, and was observing everyone with bright eyes. The woman was gushing about how gorgeous she was. Mia wanted to reach right past her and assert best friend rights; she restrained herself, just placing a little kiss on the baby's soft, warm cheek.

'Good to see you, mate,' Alec said, shaking hands with John. 'Glad to hear there was a happy side to a sad event.'

'Thanks.'

He introduced everyone as they moved into the living room. The guy, Paul, was an insurance broker and an old buddy from school days. His wife Jacinta, who wore an expensive, close-fitting burgundy silk dress, was on all sorts of charity boards. The Very Rich, Mia concluded, thanking the gods that she hadn't worn her jeans. But what was Sheryl thinking? What would they have to say to people like this? She felt a little surge of irritation. It would have been much nicer to have had dinner just the four of them.

They gathered around the coffee table for drinks and she sensed Sheryl watching her as glasses of sherry were handed around; she checked that her visitor smile was on. They toasted each other and then Alec took her glass from her and put it down and handed Talia to her, and Mia nestled the baby close, breathing her divine scent. Sheryl leaned in to tweak her daughter's collar, and murmured, 'Trust me.'

'Got a gift for you,' John was saying. He reached inside a crackling plastic bag and drew out the three gift-wrapped sketches.

'You didn't need –' Sheryl began.

'Just open it,' Mia urged, swaying from side to side with Talia.

And then they were all admiring the pictures, and Jacinta's eyes had narrowed and she was examining them with more than a casual interest. It turned out that she was also on the board of an art gallery.

Sheryl raised her brows at Mia. *See?* 'I hadn't guessed you'd be bringing a sample of your father's work, John,' she said, 'to say nothing of giving it to us, but I thought Jacinta might be interested given what Mia has said about the response in the UK.'

'Definitely interested,' Jacinta said, and she began to ask him all sorts of questions, keeping it up as they moved into the dining room, and taking the seat next to him.

Mia settled opposite, Talia still in her lap, Paul beside her.

'Do you have children?' he asked. He had a slightly mournful face.

'Not yet. You?

'Two. Seventeen.'

'And?'

'Twins,' he said.

Well, Jacinta had done a good job of restoring her figure in that case. Mia would have to first achieve the figure in order to restore it, but would there be any point if she were about to lose it? – she hoped.

Sheryl placed prawn cocktails in front of them and reached out for Talia.

'I'm happy to hold her,' Mia protested.

'Sure?'

'Of course.'

She caught John watching her with the baby, and every pore of her body responded with: *'See? I'm good at this. I'm supposed to be having a baby around now. It will be good for us.'*

He smiled at her from across the table, and she felt as if the message had been received, and relaxed a little. Another problem they would have to deal with would be income. If she wanted a baby and he wanted to cut grass... would that work? She had an idyllic vision of herself studying counselling while her baby snoozed in the pram next to her and John arrived home, sweaty and suntanned, bulkier than ever in the shoulders from all that hard labour...

'Jacinta, you're monopolising John. I'd like to hear about what he does,' Paul said.

'Did,' John said. 'Financial Accountant for Buxton Petrochemicals, but I recently gave notice. I'm doing something of a midlife change of direction.'

'What's the new focus?' Paul asked with interest.

'Gardening at the moment,' John said.

Paul's eyes widened in surprise. 'That's some change of direction!'

'Yes. I'm a numbers man at heart,' John said, 'but your father dying does strange things to you. Made me wonder what else there is to me that I'm not even aware of. The gardening is just in the short-term – almost to shake up the status quo while I figure out what I want to do next.'

'I can imagine that being one of, what, one hundred accountants all doing highly specialised work, the same thing over and over –' Alec began.

'One twenty-eight.' John injected.

'Is it? I can imagine that would grow tiring after a while. But surely a more stimulating numbers job...?'

'Maybe I'll come back to something like that but in the meantime I'm forcing myself out of my comfort zone. We accountants are very rigid, as you know. Don't like change. Value stability above all else... I decided to see what else there might be to me and to life before I petrify...'

'All sorts of things have changed since he's been back,' Mia said. 'We were getting stale, as a couple, and now it's as if there's a whole new breath of life in our relationship. I'd hate to say you need a parent to die for things to change but it's certainly made a big difference to us.'

Jacinta murmured, 'How lovely for you,' and Mia realised that she had deliberately said this to Paul's elegant wife, who was sitting a little closer to John than she really needed to.

'Yes,' Mia continued boldly, 'it feels as if we're falling in love with each other all over again.'

John smiled at her, another warm, tender smile, and she felt as if she was drowning in happiness. For him to cherish her like this and actually show it, for their love-making to be so much more fulfilling – and so much more frequent, for him to know that she wanted a baby and not shy away from it, for him to finally crack the conservative mould and climb out of his staid habits – what wasn't there to be happy about?

When Talia had fallen asleep in her arms, Mia offered to put her to bed so Sheryl could serve the mains and Alec could entertain Paul. She carried the drowsing child upstairs, enjoying the little snuffling noise she was making, and placed her gently in the crib, tucking her in and rocking it, one hand on the infant's tummy, just firmly enough to make her feel that she was not alone until she had settled into a deeper sleep... She stayed there for a while, gazing down at the child, and around the room at all the paraphernalia: change table, cot for when she was bigger, fluffy toys, nappy bag... She couldn't believe how powerful this nesting instinct was becoming.

A door opened to one of the rooms outside Talia's, and then closed again. 'Mia?' John's voice asked quietly.

'In here,' she called softly.

He appeared in the doorway. 'Dinner is served, madam.'

'All right.' She was reluctant to leave the crib.

He came to stand beside her, one arm around her shoulders, and they breathed in the beautiful sight together. And then his hand was on the back of her head, stroking her hair, and he was turning her to face him and kissing her lips. 'Did you really mean that?' he asked, 'about falling in love again?'

She nodded, and he kissed her, deeply this time, and she felt her body respond, and kissed back urgently. His hand roamed down her back and she had to pull herself away, hushing them both and leading him out of the room by the hand.

They returned to find plates of apricot-glazed ham, sweet potato mash and roasted asparagus spears at their places. Sheryl thanked Mia for putting Talia down, and said it with a particularly meaningful expression that made Mia look away, blushing.

Jacinta continued to show an inordinate interest in John's father's art, and since none of Paul's questions about his work drew John out, Paul settled into a conversation with Alec about boats and golf and financial something or others. John was drinking a little more than usual, Mia noticed. She gave his leg a little kick under the table when Alec next topped up his glass, but he didn't seem to pick up the message.

When Sheryl was clearing the mains, Jacinta excused herself to have a smoke outside and John offered to keep her company. Carrying dishes into the kitchen, Mia could hear the muffled sound of their voices; she found herself remembering the last time she had been on the back deck.

Sheryl picked up the thread of her thought. 'Did you ever call Nick?' she asked, flicking the tap on and rinsing a dish.

'No!' Mia exclaimed, taking the dish from her and stacking it in the machine.

'Not needed anymore anyway, I gather.'

'That's right.' She couldn't have prevented the instant, happy smile if she'd wanted to.

'I'm so glad for you,' Sheryl said bluntly. 'I've been worried.'

'I know. We all were.'

Sheryl took a tray of small crème brûlée pots out of the fridge. 'Call them in, would you?' she asked, nodding toward the back yard.

Mia walked around to the door and opened it. John and Jacinta were standing by the railing, almost exactly where she and Nick had stood that night. Jacinta was smoking and naming outlets that might be interested in selling his father's reproductions.

'Dessert is being served,' Mia said.

Jacinta butted out her cigarette. 'So do take your time getting that bit right,' she said. 'It will pay in the long run,' and then came through the door that Mia held open. A faint cloud of smoke came with them. John caught her hand as he went past and gave it a little squeeze.

'You're going to have such a hangover tomorrow morning,' she said as they drove home. She was driving; he was snaking one hand over her thigh. She gave the back of his hand a gentle slap.

'You think I drank too much?' he asked. 'More than usual?'

She laughed. 'I'd say so!'

'You know, I think my problem with alcohol is stress,' he said. 'When I'm stressed I don't deal well with it, but when I'm relaxed...' The hand began to move again.

'We'll see,' she said, giving it another little slap. 'You're being such a teenager!'

'I can see how much you're hating it,' he said.

They fell into bed giggling and undoing buttons and zips. He wanted her to leave the sheer black panty hose on, and the lacy black bra, which was fun at first but only got in the way. John had always been a courteous lover, always stimulating her to orgasm first, but all this extra interest and attention was drawing their love-making out much longer than ever before… and he was more creative than ever – changing what he was doing just as she was about to fall off the edge into an abyss of pleasure, and keeping her hanging on, desperate for release, until he finally let her come.

'I love you,' she said as they drifted off to sleep.

He looked at her almost gravely, and drew her close.

11

Coming into the kitchen for breakfast Mia found John sitting at the table in his cycling gear, the phone to his ear. 'Only ten per cent?' he asked, glancing at her then concentrating again on what the other person was saying. 'So we need to apply for government grants... Well, for sure. I'll look into the legal and accounting side of it and you can explore crowdfunding and make a start on that documentation about the aims of the organisation. We won't get anywhere if we don't have a very realistic plan.'

Ah, he was talking to Jake about the charity idea. She took a grapefruit from the bowl and stood over the sink, peeling it.

John was silent again, listening. She could just imagine how difficult it must be for a methodical person like him to organise a scattered artistic brother on the other side of the world in doing his fare share.

'Mel should be able to help with all the marketing stuff,' John said. 'That's right up her alley...'

It was a delicious grapefruit. Very juicy. She leant over the sink, chin dripping. Outside it was raining steadily. Mia gazed at the downpour as she chewed, half listening as John carried on his conversation.

'I think we need to do a stack more research before we get to that... I know... Well, somehow we need to flush them out...'

He listened for a while longer and then said, 'I think a gallery is the best way. Something small to begin with, but we can charge entrance fees and then we've got a space to display the work of our beneficiaries... Promote into retirement villages? Absolutely.'

Mia rinsed her hands and patted them dry on a tea towel. She opened the fridge to get the container of leftover roast vegies that she was taking to work for lunch.

'All right. Talk soon. Give my love to Mum.' John put his phone down.

'Getting the charity idea moving?' she asked.

'Trying to,' he said. He sat, drumming his fingers on the table, gazing outside at the rain.

'You been for a ride?'

'Not yet. It was pouring and then Jake rang.'

'It's still pouring. Who's Mel?' Mia asked, standing in front of the bread bin and wondering if she wanted toast as well.

'Melissa Penn. Remember that old flame of mine I told you about? The one who stayed in touch with Mum and Dad after I left England?'

'That's a bit weird, isn't it?'

'Not really. Her folks are old friends with mine and she always got on with Mum and Dad. I think Mum has come to rely on her quite a bit since I wasn't around and Jake was always hard to contact.'

'Oh.' Mia wondered if she should feel guilty about this. 'So what does Melissa do that she can help with the charity?'

'Marketing. She's the media manager for a pet food company, so she knows her way around Pinterest and Facebook and all that.'

'Aha.' One toast, Mia decided. She opened the bag and looked for a thin slice. 'So how will you raise funds for it? Your dad didn't leave you that much money.'

'No. We've both agreed to put in a few grand from our inheritance to get it started, and we'll apply for grants. The government should be up for it given the ageing population. And we'll approach some of the larger philanthropic organisations, although they rarely provide more than about ten per cent.'

'Hence the crowdfunding idea and the entrance fees.'

'Yes.'

'Sounds like you're going to have a lot on your plate getting all of that organised from here.'

'Yes,' he said again, absently.

The dog door rattled and a wet Bitsy shot through and shook herself, sending droplets around the kitchen.

'Agh!' John exclaimed, standing up and moving out of her range. 'Manners, puppy!'

'But you don't get your inheritance till your mother passes, do you?' Mia asked, scraping butter onto her toast.

'There's a small amount now and the rest when she goes,' he said. 'Didn't I email you about that after the reading of the will?'

She thought. 'Yes, maybe you did. Have you fed Bitsy?'

Before starting the conversion to a paperless office there was the inevitable 'Mandatory Training Course'. Mia plugged her earphones in and hit the start arrow on the video. Smiling, immaculate office staff began their presentation about the benefits of a paperless office for the company and the environment while a 'calming', monotonous tune played in the background. Clean desks! No overflowing recycling bins! Airy offices without walls of filing cabinets! Instant access to information at the touch of a button! Trees growing unimpeded...

It all sounded lovely and very sensible and benevolent but she could just imagine the scary moment when they condemned their final hard copy to the shredder. This might be the brave new world of business management, Mia thought, watching the shredder in the video presentation destroy 'important documents', but was it truly reliable? There was something much more comforting about a piece of paper you could hold in your hands than mere scans of those documents. What if they corrupted or were accidentally deleted? What if you summoned your urgent, confidential document back from 'the Cloud' and it didn't come? Soft copies were supposed to be forever but they seemed so delicate and ethereal, not nearly as real as hard copy. And yet this was how things were going.

She wondered how life might be in a future world where everything was virtual – even your relationships. Virtual, unreal... just images you were somehow able to interact with, like in *The Matrix*. She shuddered. There was something really discomfiting about interacting with someone who wasn't really there. It was going to be a very strange new world in the near future... But she should stop daydreaming. She could see Susan at her desk, also plugged in. Mia glanced at the video length indicator on her screen – she was going to be here for hours. *Come on. Concentrate. Get it over with.*

First step, the cheery woman announced: working on an electronic filing system that matches the older paper filing system. Important question: 'Where would I find this if I were looking for it in six months' time?'

Second step: scanning all hard copies.

Third step: shredding them to go paperless. Some companies have their own industrial shredders, some have a contract with a secure shredding company, others will have to find one, in which case: research, locate, call and discuss if they rent bins by the month, etc. Get prices. Compare companies. Get sign-off from her boss. Order the bins and await their arrival.

Mia was halfway through the training course when Reynald poked his head around the partition and asked her to plug some budget details into a spreadsheet. 'Don't tell Paula I interrupted you,' he added with a grimace.

'She just pulled Susan out to do something.'

'Good.' He gave a relieved smile and disappeared.

Mia paused the video and opened the email Reynald had sent her with the information he needed organised. Spreadsheets. Ugh. Her private bugbear. She was frowning over formulas that weren't working when Susan turned up in front of her.

'What are you doing?'

'Reynald needs some budget figures.'

'Hmph.' Susan said. Or something like that. She was wearing a hot pink eye shadow today to accompany a hot pink suit. On that scowling almost rectangular face with the heavy brows it was not a pretty look. Susan pursed the hot pink glossy lips. 'Well, can you get that done over lunch so we can finish the training the minute we get back? Making a start on this new filing system is the priority job now, you know.'

'Sure,' Mia smiled nicely and made a face to Susan's back as she turned away. *'The minute we get back!'* *You mean you, since you're not letting me go out for lunch...* She sighed, opened her drawer and scrabbled around to find the muesli bars she left in there for emergencies like this. There were two: yoghurt-covered apricot and a coconut almond one. She might need both – comfort food for a nasty job.

She switched back and forth between the attachments Reynald had sent her and the spreadsheet she'd opened, chewing and filling in the fields, then frowned when they didn't add up properly.

Reynald was working over lunch too. She could hear him on the phone. He'd probably be able to figure this out but she didn't want to bother him. John. She'd ask John. She flipped her phone open and called.

Hello. This is John Hartington. I'm not able to take your call right now. Please leave a message...

'Honey, can you call me? Quick question. Thanks.'

She went back to frowning at the screen, trying this and then that, double-checking everything, wondering why nothing was working. No answer from John but surely he was on lunch now too? He had quite a few gardens to mow already but she knew he always stopped for lunch. He was predictable like that.

Mia tried a text but there was no reply. She grabbed Milenko as he was returning from lunch to get some help with it, and he settled into her seat for a few minutes, a toothpick between his lips, but was soon stumped too. Seeing Susan come back into the office amongst a gaggle of staff, she flicked back to the video, thinking she'd carry on with the training and come back to the spreadsheet later – hopefully when she'd heard from John.

A reply came when she was churning through the task of researching shredding companies later that afternoon:

Sorry I missed yr call. What's the problem?

She rolled her eyes. So why didn't he just ring her to get the information he needed and then tell her what to do on the spot? She called again, and again got his voicemail. Reynald would be needing that spreadsheet by close of business and she didn't want to ask Susan. Maybe this was a sign. Maybe this horrible day of mind-numbing video presentations and going cross-eyed over spreadsheets was her Call to Action to get out of this job once and for all. And really, she was much better placed now to be a counsellor. Now that things between her and John were so much better. She'd be able to sit in front of clients with confidence, understanding their angst since she'd been there too, and yet gently able to lead them out of the pain back into love...

A little voice at the back of her mind said, *'But you didn't do anything different. He came back different. You were just lucky.'*

Mia frowned more deeply. That was true. John was the one who had changed. The staid, stuck John had changed. She'd been dreaming about other men and even... Nick's face swam back into view, bringing a sudden heat to her body. She flushed at the thought, and it was a combination of remembered pleasure, shame, and guilt that she'd been contemplating affairs and even leaving John, and all the while he'd been accepting his Call to Action and stepping up like a bloody knight while she was doing nothing but being a miserable, envious complainer.

His father's death had launched him on a journey to transform his life and he was actually doing it. *He was actually doing it...* Whereas what had she done differently or better? One party in a tarty outfit. Big fucking deal. What kind of a risk or change was that? If she wanted her life to change, if she wanted John to change, she had to be prepared to change too. It was only fair.

Maybe she should give notice too? The thought was exhilarating, like the feeling of freedom she'd had when John had walked through that International Departures door... She wondered if that was how he'd felt when he'd sent 'the' email from England to Buxton Pharmaceuticals. Somehow she couldn't imagine him excited; she could imagine an inner tussle, a daring-himself voice balanced by his usual measured tones of logic and reason... She could imagine the moment when the daring voice won and he reached forward and hit 'send', and then sat back and broke out in a cold sweat at what he'd done...

So was *she* up for it? She hadn't yet even decided if she would do a diploma or a degree or just a taster short course, and she didn't like abandoning Reynald. He'd always been good to her. She valued that sense of camaraderie they had, as if it was 'you and me against the world' – or as least against big institutions and the efficiency of people like Paula and Susan. But she couldn't carry on doing this job forever – she was completely over it.

Another message flashed through from John:

Flat out. Can you send more info?

It would be so much easier if she could just talk to him for a moment. She couldn't send him a screenshot because that would be a breach of confidentiality and he'd be way shocked if she did anything as rule-breaking as that, even though neither of them would have the slightest interest in doing anything with the information. She'd ring. If Susan looked in her direction, she wouldn't know who Mia was speaking to since she was supposed to be on the phone anyway, calling shredding companies.

Mia picked up her phone and got his frigging voicemail again. Did her best to describe the problem, reading formulas out quietly with frequent glances over her shoulder. Then she went back to her fun job finding and renting secure bins while she waited for an answer.

Her pocket buzzed an hour later when she was in the tearoom. There was a long message from John with a few suggestions to be tried in the precise sequence he was giving. She went back to her desk and tried the first one. Nada. But the second worked and all the numbers fell into place like magic. The guy really was worth his weight.

'You know, we haven't done this in years,' Mia said, as John pulled into a bay in the shopping centre car park and switched off the engine.

'Done what?' he asked, taking his wallet out of the console.

'Gone shopping together for clothes for me. I think the last time was… in our first or second year together when you bought me that lingerie…'

He stopped, with one hand on the car door, to look at her. 'Where is that lingerie? Why don't you wear it?'

'You put it through the wash without using the delicates bag.'

'Oh. I remember. My bad…'

They walked toward the entrance hand-in-hand, and in through the automatic doors. It was warm inside, and noisy. People of all ages and nationalities hurried and dawdled around them. They passed a café, its seductive aroma of coffee enveloping them. She caught a glimpse of pastries in the glass case at the counter. She'd have wanted to buy one in her frustrated, unhappy days, but now that she was feeling so much more content, she didn't even give them a thought. The multi-coloured skirt sat lightly around her waist without those extra kilos.

'Where do you think?' he asked.

'Um…' She looked up and down at the fashion boutiques on either side of them. 'Let's try that one.' There was a very glam dress in the window that she'd admired a few times and had not dared try on. She suspected that the price was going to be out there too, but this was the day. She pointed it out as they walked in and he agreed that it was a must-have, going straight to a salesgirl and asking if his wife could try on the dress on the mannequin.

The girl, a young thing with caked-on foundation and mascara so thick she might have been wearing false lashes, stalked toward a rack on her stilettos saying, 'What size, please?' She pulled out a couple of hangers and pointed Mia in the direction of the fitting rooms.

John hovered outside for a diplomatic moment and then, when no one was looking, switched the curtain aside and slipped in with her.

'There isn't room in here,' she whispered, stifling a giggle as he immediately began 'helping' her remove her top and skirt.

'I'll be the judge of that,' he murmured, planting a kiss between her breasts.

'John!'

'All right, all right!' he stood back, the half-step there was room for, and leaned against the wall. 'No touching, just looking.'

She slipped the dress off the hanger and lifted it over her head, half-expecting to feel his hands on her skin again while she was trapped inside the fabric, but instead he helped to lower the dress around her body, smoothing it against her waist and legs with an approving sound.

'Don't count your chickens,' she said. 'I haven't done it up yet.'

He swivelled her around and raised the zip slowly. She held her breath – would it fit?

They got three-quarters of the way up and then it stopped.

'Bugger,' Mia said.

'So close. Breathe in.'

'I am.'

'If you're talking, you're not.'

'I have to be able to breathe and talk while I'm wearing it!'

'Just teasing,' he said, and his hands snaked around to cup her breasts. 'It's these beautiful things. They're taking up all the space.'

'Oh dear.'

The salesgirl called from the other side of the curtain. 'How are we going in there? Need any help?'

Mia and John made eyes at each other. 'We'! Was that the royal 'we' or had she heard him in there?

'Fine thanks,' Mia called. 'It's a little too small.'

'I gave you the bigger size as well,' the girl said in a bored tone.

'But this is the colour I like. Do you have the bigger size in the same colour?'

'I don't think so. I'll go check.'

'Okay, off with it.' John unzipped her and the dress fell into a soft pile at her feet. 'Where's the other one?'

'Behind you.'

He twisted around for it while she squatted, as straight-backed as she could in the cramped space, to pick up the abandoned dress, and then they swapped garments. This time they could do it up but it was a little loose around the waist.

'What do you think?' she asked, gazing in the mirror and turning slightly from side to side. 'I could have it taken in a little there.'

'It's got potential. I don't mind this colour, either. But let's keep looking for something perfect.'

In the end they spent two hours wandering through boutiques trying on dresses and did finally find the perfect one: a low-cut dress in a colour she loved with a slit that worked for her shape beautifully. Then they looked at the price tag. 'Oh God. Forget about that!' she said, stamping on her disappointment as she took it off.

'Why?' he demanded. He took the outfit out of her hands. 'How often do you treat yourself like this? Come on, Mia, lash out.'

'*You're* telling *me* to lash out!' she laughed.

'We had a deal,' he said. 'No more boringness. Time to take some risks.'

'Yeah... but I don't even have an occasion to wear this! We're just buying for... fun! It feels so extravagant.'

'No buts. You deserve it. I'll go pay.' And he was out of there, sliding the fitting room door shut behind him and leaving her alone with her almost naked body and a pile of rejected dresses. The mirror reflected a delighted smile on a flushed face.

When she emerged, John was standing near the counter with a plastic bag in hand talking to a plain, worn-looking woman who was examining the dresses on a nearby rack. The woman was saying, 'I don't think I'd get away with this,' and John was telling her, 'If you want it, make the world love you in it. Don't let anyone else make you feel inadequate.'

The woman smiled at him as Mia joined them. 'That's the nicest thing anyone has said to me in a long time,' she said. She waved the dress at Mia. 'What do you think?'

'Definitely try it on,' Mia agreed. 'There's no harm doing that.'

'I think I will!' she declared. 'Even if the only fun I have is in that change room.'

They walked out together, and Mia pulled lightly on John's hand as they emerged, bringing him to a halt so she could plant a kiss on his lips. 'Thank you. I feel very special.'

'You *are* special.' He returned the kiss and then they moved out of the doorway, merging with the people passing by along the mall. 'You'll have to wear it somewhere now. We'll have to go somewhere special.'

'If we can afford to go anywhere after spending that amount on a dress!'

'Even if it's just a candlelit dinner at home,' he said.

They headed toward the supermarket to pick up some groceries, but before going in he ducked away to use the loo and while she waited, wandering toward a pop-up store of smart phone covers, she heard her name being called and turned to see that Asian guy from Buxton Petrochemicals walking towards her.

'Hey! How are you?' she smiled in response. 'Long time no see.' *Name, name!* she instructed herself urgently.

'Ages,' he said, stopping in front of her. 'So I gather that John resigned.'

'That's right. You didn't see him when he dropped in?'

'Did he? When was that?'

'A few weeks ago. Just after he got back from the UK.'

The guy – Tony! His name was Tony! – shook his head. 'No. Must have been out when he was there.'

'Oh. Well, he's here if you want to say hi – just went to the loo.'

Tony looked at his watch. 'I've got to keep moving, but tell me: what's he doing now? He was thinking about applying for a Management Accountant role at one of the big banks last time we spoke.'

'Yeah? Well, right now he's gardening.'

'No shit!'

'No shit.'

'Man.' Tony stood there for a moment, almost gaping. 'Like, landscape gardening? That's a bit out of left field, isn't it?'

'Mowing lawns.'

'No shit!'

'No shit. It's only temporary. Just wanted to use his body a bit before it decayed from lack of use...' Mia looked in the direction of the toilets. Surely he'd have finished by now? John didn't share her problem.

'Okay. Whatever,' Tony said, still looking amazed. 'So looks like we've lost both of you now.'

'Yes,' with an 'oh well', expression, and *yay!* she cheered mentally. Buxton Petrochemicals hadn't been her favourite place to work but when John had first arrived in Australia she'd been able to let him know there was a position going for an accountant. He'd applied and been there ever since, while she'd moved on and had had three different positions since then – or was it four? But he was a stayer.

'Well, better keep moving!' Tony said. 'Give him my best. Geez, lawn mowing,' he was marvelling as he walked away.

John turned up at her elbow a few moments later.

'You just missed Tony,' she said.

'Tony?'

'You know, from work. He was gob-smacked that you're mowing lawns.'

'Ah! Yes, he would be.'

'Said he missed you when you dropped in that day.'

'Yeah, a few of them were out. So what are we getting now?'

'You've got the list.'

He pulled out his wallet and found the bit of notepaper. 'We'd better add something delicious to this list and have that candlelit dinner tonight. I want to see you in that dress.'

12

'**I** 'll bring you up some lunch,' Mia mimed.

Reynald nodded, still listening to whoever was on the phone. She gave him a stern, 'wind it up' expression, and withdrew.

There were an abundance of salads in the downstairs café but he usually preferred a wrap or a sandwich – something less messy. Standing in the queue, she peered between the shoulders of the two people in front of her to catch a glimpse of the labels on the salad bowls in case there was something new. If not, she'd go that delicious quinoa and sweet potato and spinach salad. Reynald would have his usual chicken and avocado combination.

The woman in front of her was dabbing at her eyes with a hankie. 'Honestly,' she said, 'it was so moving. I mean, they started sessions sitting on the couch as far away from each other as they possible could, and they finished up last night snuggled as close together as they possibly could.'

'Makes you know you're in the right business, doesn't it?' her companion replied.

Mia recognised the two women as members of ACCAT. The coaches and counsellors mostly worked from their own premises but showed up regularly for meetings and supervision and personal development events. It was comments like this that had first captured her attention, planting the seed that there might be something more rewarding for her than filing and typing correspondence and managing her boss's diary.

The queue shuffled forward a tad and she wondered about interrupting them: *'Excuse me. I couldn't help overhearing. It sounds so rewarding. Have you always done this? Would you recommend it for me? I'd really like to do something to help people but I don't know if I'd be good at it...'*

'Did you hear those latest stats on suicide?' the other woman was saying.

'No.'

'Eight per day.'

'That's awful.'

'It's the highest Australia has ever had.'

Their conversation cut off as they reached the counter and ordered their meals.

Eight a day. Mia imagined eight families discovering a body where a live person had been; eight ambulances arriving; eight lives cut off because eight people a day had decided that life wasn't worth living. Eight people abandoning their Hero's Journey, perhaps because they hadn't found enough allies and mentors along the way...

Reynald was off the phone and texting a message when she returned with his lunch. *Do it now. Do it now,* she instructed herself. *Do It Now.* She put the package on the desk in front of him and said, 'Do you have a moment?'

He nodded, still texting.

'This is not official notice,' she began, and he looked straight up at her and put his phone down.

'All right, you have my full attention.' He indicated the chair and she drew it closer and perched in it.

'Since coming here –' she hesitated, palms sweaty, hunting for the right words. 'This has truly been the best job I've ever had because... because the work you people do is so inspiring.'

He nodded, contemplating her with those grey-green eyes. She liked this about Reynald – he never over-reacted, never blew off steam; always just listened first. *Come on, Mia,* she urged herself. *Spit it out.*

'I've been thinking for a while now that I'd like to train as a counsellor myself.'

He gave her a slow smile.

'I don't know if I'd be any good but...'

'Don't give that another thought. If it's in your heart, that's what you need to do. I trust you'll be studying with us!' He regarded her sternly, with the expression of mock seriousness that had caught her out a few times when she'd started working for him before she realised he was joking or teasing.

'Of course,' she said at once, a little guiltily.

'No, you go and check out other courses as well. You've got to end up doing the one that's right for you whether it's here or somewhere else. Have you got a particular focus in mind?'

'Relationships,' she said. 'Or maybe vocational guidance – helping people to sort out what they want to do so their lives are more fulfilling. It's really sad that so many people hate their jobs...' It was really ironic to hear herself saying that right now.

Susan and Paula walked past his office, their voices carrying through as they passed: Susan's strident tones and Paula's clipped, efficient responses.

'So you're going to abandon me to this lot, are you?' he asked.

'I'm not ready yet –'

He patted her hand. 'Jump,' he said. 'Choose the course and make your move. Don't put it off if it's what you want. But you don't need to leave us, you know. We can arrange to release you from work a couple of days a week for study, and cover the cost of the course for you, so long as you agree to keep working here for, say, the next couple of years.'

'That would be awesome!' She could just hear Accountant-John's approving voice: 'You saved us ten grand? (Or whatever the course cost.) Go, Mia!'

Reynald picked up his phone to finish his text message.

'Remember your lunch,' she said from the door, and he gave her a brief smile.

'I did it,' Mia said, before she'd even put her bag down or unbuttoned her coat, Bitsy still going nuts at her feet.

'Did what?' John asked. He was standing at the kitchen bench in front of a chaos of ingredients, chopping onions.

'Told Reynald I'm thinking of quitting to study. What *are* you doing?'

'Cooking, of course. Good for you! I'd hug you, but...' he held up onion hands.

'I mean what are you making? This doesn't look like fish or chasseur. Have you broken the mould on your dinners too?'

He looked slightly offended. 'I'm allowed to try something new.'

'I'm not complaining! I'm just surprised.' She began the unbuttoning. 'So what are you making?'

'A curry. How did he take it?'

'Oh, Reynald! He's always nice. I think he's sad that I'll be going but he was very supportive and encouraging.'

'Well, a new dinner to celebrate a new beginning,' John said with a flourish of the knife.

'Want some help?'

'No. You walk Bitsy. I'm right. But don't go into the living room, okay? There's a surprise in there for after.'

Mia glanced at the door, which was usually open, registering that it was now firmly closed.

'Okay...' She began to re-button her coat. 'Walkies, Bits!'

The curry was so delicious that Mia forgot she was usually cautious about eating too much onion or cauliflower.

'Do you like this shiraz?' John asked, holding his glass up.

'Yes, not bad.'

'Very cheap, you'll be glad to hear. I found it at Aldi but I think it's pretty good.'

'It is.' She looked toward the closed living room doors. 'I'm dying of curiosity.'

'All right. Let's stick these in the machine and then all will be revealed.'

His phone buzzed as he was carrying their dishes to the sink. A message from Jake.

'It's your brother.'

'Okay.' He dumped the things on the bench and came straight back, reaching for the phone with a wry smile. 'So much to discuss with this charity. I'll tell him I'll call him back later.'

Her phone pinged while John was texting and she was stacking the dishwasher. Sheryl.

> Early walk tomorrow?

> Okay

John slipped his phone into his back pocket and put the wine away. She gathered up leftover vegetables and returned them to the fridge. He wiped the bench.

'You're slipping,' she said, pointing to a patch he'd missed.

He made a face at her, cleaned the spot industriously, and tossed the sponge into the sink. Wiped his hands on the back of his pants. Then led her to the closed doors. 'Are you ready?'

'Sure… Do I have to shut my eyes? Are you going to turn me around three times?'

'That's an excellent idea,' he said, and she obediently closed her eyes, smiling, as he turned her around by her shoulders three times. Then she heard the doorknob turning and said, 'Can I open now?' and opened her eyes, slightly dizzy, to see him giving the door a little push. It swung open, revealing a brand new flat screen TV – a big one!

She gasped. 'John!'

'I know. A little extravagant, but…'

'A little extravagant!'

'We have things to celebrate… New beginnings, new directions…'

'Yeah, but we can't keep buying new things if we're both on reduced incomes! I think you must have left your accountant's brain behind at Buxton when you left.'

'Maybe I did,' he said.

'I wonder what your dad would think of how much his death has changed you,' she murmured, moving into the room. 'I didn't think it was possible for a person to change so much.' She picked up the new remote that stood on the coffee table and switched the huge TV on. It burst into colour in front them, the people's faces big and bold.

'He'd – who knows?' John said, following her in. 'But don't they say that people on their deathbed don't regret the risks they took? They regret the stuff they *didn't* do; they regret staying safe and small.'

She pushed the sound-up button and the presenter/newsreader on the screen suddenly boomed out at deafening volume: 'Twin study that reveals –'

'Yikes! Too loud!' John grabbed the remote out of her hand and muted the sound. He switched to another channel and brought the volume up again very slowly. 'My father went through his whole life doing the same tedious job every day for forty-plus years,' he said. 'Do you reckon that would be good for the soul?'

'He *was* painting.'

'Yes. When Mum let him off tasks...'

'So we're doing these new things because they're good for our souls. I like that.' She kicked off her shoes. 'Let's watch something.'

John threw himself onto the couch, landing with a thump, and patted the seat next to him. 'Come on.'

She laughed and sat down. He raised his arm dramatically, pointing the remote at the screen and navigating through the viewing options. He paused on *Bridget Jones' Baby*.

'We saw that one not long ago, remember? But it was fun. I don't mind seeing it again. Especially on this scale.'

'So you like?'

'It's amazing. It feels like we're at the cinema.' Mia snuggled next to him, and he clicked start. Then said, 'Wait. Do you want another wine?'

'Um… okay. But three reds for you? Isn't that a recipe for a hangover?'

'I was okay after that night at Sheryl's, remember?'

She thought back. 'Yes… You were…'

'Less stressed these days. That'll be the reason.'

Having seen the movie already this time she was not so caught up in the story. She found herself thinking about that Hero's Journey idea again. Bridget Jones was stuck in singledom, wanting a man she could love and who would love her but perpetually ending up alone. Until her Call to Action: the pregnancy that brought two men closer, unleashing ridiculous moments and touching moments and a choice between the long-time, sometimes-lover Mark and the new, almost too-good-to-be-true Jack. She remembered wondering, when she first saw the film, what she would do in that position: who would she choose? Mark and Jack each came with a clear set of pros and cons, as per real life. It seemed that mostly it was impossible to get a man who offered everything you wanted, although John seemed to be turning into that man…

He was massaging the back of her neck absently as they watched. She made a little sound of appreciation.

Somehow she'd really scored… She had the good-hearted, stable, devoted husband who was responsible and committed and good with money, and who was now finally loosening up his rigid nature as well and bringing more spontaneity and fun into their marriage. With this little touch of unpredictability to spice up their lives her roving eye no longer needed to check out the rest of the field… She sent a prayer of thanks to his father, wherever he now was.

'You're so tense,' John said, working on the knots in her shoulders. He shifted away a little on the couch for a better angle and began to work his way down the muscles on either side of her spine. She murmured with pleasure as the story unfolded and they watched handsome Jack produce takeaway food and his symbolic apology-flowers and the Ikea table that would test the mettle of his and Bridget's relationship.

'Do you think the sound is okay in this room?' John asked. 'Maybe one day we'll convert the spare room into a home theatre.'

As if, she thought dreamily. *You wouldn't make changes that didn't add value to the house...*

He was lifting her top off now, and encouraging her to lie on the couch. He was producing a towel and unscrewing a little bottle of something aromatic... and then his warm hands were spreading oil on her back and he was really getting into the massage, working on her back more thoroughly than he ever had before.

'You were planning this...' she breathed, face turned toward the screen but barely watching anymore.

His strong hands were circling her shoulder blades and driving deep into her lower back. She was drifting... luxuriating in pleasure... His hand slipped under her belly and fumbled with the button and zip of her jeans. He worked them over her bottom and down her legs and off her feet, and began to massage her calves and thighs and buttocks...

'So good...' Her eyes were closing now, all the better to focus on his hands and the delicious sensations...

'I don't know why she chooses that dull Mark character,' John said, and she drifted back a little.

'He's been there for her forever...'

'Yes but he's such a – so colourless. Bland.'

'They're just saying that loyalty counts for something. Loyalty and friendship...'

'Of course. But look at Jack, what he's offering her: love and romance and commitment and financial security and fun...'

'True...' she lifted a hand to wipe a trickle of spit from the corner of her mouth. 'But he's also a bit corny, don't you think? With that algorithm book about relationships. And he's kind of controlling – the smoothie and the 'no toxic thinking'! And he might not hang around if he finds that the baby isn't his...'

'But he's big enough to apologise when he does the wrong thing and he just wears it when she humiliates him in public...'

'Mark says he'll love her and be there no matter whose the baby is.'

'I'm sure Jack would too,' John said. He gave her buttocks a gentle pinch. 'Time to turn over.'

She swivelled around on the couch and looked up at him, somehow suddenly feeling self-conscious as he gazed down at her exposed breasts and belly. His warm hands began to stroke her chest and down her sides to her stomach, and then up and around her breasts... And before long he was ripping his pants off and they were making love on the couch, and it was so good. Bridget fussed in the background while John leaned over Mia, thrusting, jolting the crown of her head into the armrest as her fingers kneaded the flesh on his back until he collapsed onto her and she lay squashed and breathless, head crooked, pressing light kisses onto his prickly cheek.

They fell asleep there, vaguely aware of the film unfolding its story, the last scenes infiltrating their dreams, until Mia became aware of a phone singing somewhere... John lifted his heaviness off her and suddenly she felt light and cold. She snuggled into the towel, wrapping it around her and trying to block out the noise so she could go back to sleep. The singing stopped and she could hear his voice quietly from afar. She wanted to drift right back to sleep but she had a pain in her belly now, and she was very cold. She rolled onto her side, digging into the backrest of the couch for warmth but it was no use. Dragging herself up, she pulled the towel close around her shoulders and padded toward the bedroom.

'Don't give me this shit,' John was saying in a low, angry voice as she entered. He was sitting on the edge of the bed with his back to her. She hesitated. He was silent for a moment, and then his voice bit into the quiet again: 'Fuck off. Don't you come the parent with me!'

Mia came slowly into the room, awake now, wondering what was going on. She dropped the towel on the floor beside the bed and slid in between the cold sheets, pulling the covers over her and shivering. John reacted as the mattress sank under her weight, swivelling around quickly. He looked furious. She sent him an inquiring expression and in a flash he was calming down, giving a little shake of his head to say it was nothing, go back to sleep, smiling at her, reaching over to give her shoulder a quick squeeze, then standing up and moving out of the room with the phone still clamped to his ear.

She lay wondering, waiting to warm up, glad when Bitsy leapt onto the bed and settled into the crook of her legs. The pain in her belly was still there, a cramp that she recognised. She pressed deep into her abdomen, massaging in big circular movements, hoping for relief.

When she was finally drifting back into sleep, John returned. The bed creaked a little as he lifted the covers and settled beside her.

'Everything okay?'

'It's fine.'

'It didn't sound fine.'

'Just Jake... pissing me off. Talk about it tomorrow.'

'Okay.'

He moved closer, seeking her warmth, shifting Bitsy with his legs so he could spoon her back. She felt Bitsy's small feet tread on her thighs as the dog climbed over her and found a new position against her belly, which was good; the pressure on her stomach was like a hot water bottle, soothing. They slept.

13

The alarm clock summoned Mia back from dreams about John in England. He was helping his father paint the house and his mother was suggesting that they run away… Mia bumped the alarm button to cut the horrible noise off and dragged hair out of her eyes. She still had that ache in her belly. Bitsy was gone and John had rolled onto his back and was snoring lightly. She lay with the shreds of her dream dissolving around her, psyching herself up to get moving.

John turned towards her sleepily, and came to nuzzle. Then, 'Oh poo!' he said.

'What?' she asked, flushing already.

'You stinky little thing!' He burrowed his face into her neck.

Mia felt hot with embarrassment. They usually never mentioned if one of them farted – a silent mutual consent that mentioning such a thing would be far too embarrassing. Now John had broken the code. She lurched away from him out of the bed and went into the ensuite, closing the door.

His voice followed her: 'You all right, honey?'

Mia sat on the loo, feet up on the stool, arms crossed and leaning on her thighs, cursing her body. It was the bloody onions and cauliflower. She'd known that was a risky combination.

'Honey?' His voice was closer now, right outside the door.

'I'm all right. I'm embarrassed, you jerk.'

'I don't know why,' he said. 'It's perfectly normal.'

He really had changed. She wasn't sure if she liked this aspect of the new John. It was almost too direct, too open… 'I don't want to talk about it,' she said. Frowning. Childish.

It was quiet for a moment. Then he said, 'All right,' and she heard him move away from the door and open his wardrobe. When she emerged he'd left to go cycling. The covers were still in a heap halfway down the bed. She pulled them up, straightening them, then dug around in her own drawers for a tracksuit.

Sheryl's Lexus SUV was already parked outside the large, treed reserve where they liked to walk. Mia pulled in behind her and switched off the engine. Sheryl's door opened and she climbed out and gave a little wave, then opened her boot to lift out the pram. Mia scooped Bitsy up from the passenger seat and clipped her lead onto her collar, freeing the lovely feathered ears. Bitsy scampered as soon as her feet touched the ground, tugging at the lead.

'Not too freezing.' Sheryl was struggling to lock the pram into position. 'I hate this pram but I'm not allowed to kick it. Will you get Tahls?'

'Love to.' Mia dropped the lead, stepping on it to keep Bitsy close, and opened the back passenger door. Talia was sitting in her baby capsule, straining forward in an attempt to get out. She beamed at her rescuer, raising short arms toward her. Mia released the catch on her seat belt and lifted the pink-cheeked child out and into her arms.

Once Talia was in her pram and swathed in blankets against the morning chill, the two women set off at a brisk pace along the gravel path, Bitsy leaping and cavorting at their feet.

'Nick dropped in last night,' Sheryl said. Straight to the punch. 'He asked about you.'

Mia felt her colour rise. 'He did?'

'I think he was quite taken by you.'

'I don't believe that.'

'Why not? You're very pretty and you looked fucking amazing that night.'

'John was mad with me that I didn't send him a photo. He took me shopping for a new sexy dress – did I tell you that?'

'No! Describe it.'

Mia did, and then circled back. 'So… what did he say?'

'Nick? Not much. Just a very casual enquiry, very off-hand.'

'What? What did he say?'

Sheryl steered the pram around a puddle. 'Can you have another party and invite that sexy wench again?'

'He did not!'

Sheryl grinned at her. 'Okay, not exactly that. More like, 'How's Mia?"

'Oh.'

'Don't sound so disappointed. What would you expect him to say? At least he was showing he hadn't forgotten you.'

'So what did you say?'

'Deeply in love with her husband again who's come back totally transformed by the death of his father.'

'Did you really!'

'Well, kind of. I mean, that's true, isn't it? From what you've been telling me.'

'Yeah.'

'Look, he's not the kind of guy to be put off by a husband. If you were interested, he'd clearly be interested.'

'No, I'm not interested. Well, I'm interested but I'm not going there.'

'Things are much better between you and John, right?'

'Hugely much better,' Mia said. She thought about the awkward exchange in the bedroom that morning. 'You're not wrong about totally transformed. He's, like, a new person.'

'I was going to tell you – remember Maryann who used to work for me and always had a bit of a mouth on her?'

'Short, wiry, cropped hair? We thought she might be gay?'

'That's the one. Who thought she was gay? She's married with three kids.'

Mia shrugged, pulling Bitsy away from a particularly revolting-looking pile of dog poo.

'*Was* married, I should say,' Sheryl said. 'Her father died a few months ago and she has gone off. The. Rails. Like, totally.'

'What do you mean?'

They entered the lovely grove of trees where birds seemed to sing more frequently. Mia took in a deep breath of fresh air.

'She left hubby and kids and went back to her childhood Christian stuff.'

'Wow. I thought she'd rejected all that.'

'She had. To the max. Was totally critical of it. And now she's right back into it apparently.'

'That's massive.'

'I know. I wanted to tell you because I know you're a bit shocked by how much John has changed. So there you go. It must be some real psychological thing that happens. Kind of unhinges them out of their usual personality.'

'Yeah... She left her kids?'

'Just walked out one day.'

'I don't know how someone can do that. Leave a husband I get, especially if it's not working, but your kids...'

'Thing is, it wasn't not working. They were fine, he reckons.'

'How do you know all this?'

'I ran into him up the street the other day. The guy is still rocked by it. He can't understand what's got into her. She reckons that he seduced her away from her family values and she's just woken up to it.'

'That's crazy! What about her own family – their kids?'

Sheryl shrugged. 'Don't ask me. Makes no sense.'

A young woman was jogging toward them, white cords trailing from her ears and a kelpie trotting beside her.

'I wonder if all this new tech is going to morph us into some new strange-looking kind of creature,' Mia remarked.

'Sure to.'

'It's the one thing that makes me wary of having kids – that they're coming into a world that's going to be so strange and different.'

'And marvellous.'

'Yes. But, you know, virtual… Like, AI-everything. A push-button, ask-for-what-you-want-and-it-appears world.'

'You're ten years younger than me. You're supposed to be the one embracing all this magic.'

'Some aspects of it. Some of it's unsettling.'

'That's life, I guess. The good and the bad.'

They paused at a fork. 'Which way?' Mia asked.

'How much time have you got?'

Mia checked her phone. There was a message from John that she hadn't heard come through.

> Sorry. Love you xx

'I can do the long one,' she said, putting the phone back into her pocket.

'Okay?' Sheryl asked, watching her.

'Yeah. He's not the only one changing, you know. I've kind of given notice.'

'Really? Woohoo!'

'Just sort of advance warning.'

'How did the boss take it?'

'Totally fine. I knew he would be. So now I've got to follow through.'

'I'll stay on your case.'

'Thanks.'

'Does the bitch know?'

'Susan? Not yet. No one knows. Just Reynald and John and now you.'

'So I'll be able to come to you for counselling.'

'My arse.'

Sheryl grinned and waved to an old couple walking their Labrador on a parallel track on the other side of the creek.

'Anyway, what do you need counselling for?' Mia demanded. 'You have the perfect life: a husband who adores you, the most adorable baby in the world, a business that's going gangbusters even when you're not there…'

'Don't you believe it. I've got problems too.'

'Like what? Where to have lunch today?'

Sheryl gave her arm a gentle punch. 'I have a sick mother and a bossy set of in-laws and a big decision to make about whether we buy that other events company. And the biz might be going gangbusters but not exactly without me. They must call or text about fifteen times a day, I reckon. And Tahls is teething at the moment, which is exhausting. I was up for about three hours last night. I nearly cancelled on you this morning I was so wiped.'

'You could have. I'd have understood,' Mia said, humbled.

'Eh! The babe was awake and Alec had already left so I wasn't going to get any more sleep anyway. And I am bloody determined to lose some of this pregnancy weight. Big is beautiful but I'm sick of feeling so heavy and not being able to wear my more fabulous clothes. Is that enough trials and tribulations for you?'

'I sincerely apologise.'

'Apology accepted. You should take a moment to count *your* blessings, girlie. Husband who adores you, boss who values you, about to leap into new more fulfilling career, and slimmer than I've seen you in years. Bitch.'

'You're right. I do have a very good life.'

'You do.'

They walked in silence for a bit. Talia began to grizzle.

'More blossoms,' Mia said, pointing. 'Spring is nigh! Yay. Can't wait.'

'I've hardly noticed winter this year.' Sheryl began to jiggle the pram.

'You've been somewhat preoccupied.'

'You've had an interesting winter yourself.'

'Yes…'

'I'm really glad things are better for you. I was worried.'

'I know.'

'And guilty about being so happy with Alec. Thank Christ I can stop feeling guilty!'

'He is a bit of a god.'

'A bald-headed, shy, awkward god,' Sheryl agreed.

'Do you believe in soulmates?'

'As a 'truth'?' Sheryl asked, sketching quotation marks in the air with one hand. 'No. At least, I don't think there's one Mr Right you're destined to be with that the gods have chosen for you. I reckon we can be happy with all sorts of people if we work at it.'

'But you said Alec was 'the one'. And you had tried quite a few, by memory.'

'You having a go at me?'

Talia was crying now. Sheryl stopped the pram, unclipped her and lifted her out.

'No, 'course not! But what made it work with him and not the others?'

'I don't know,' Sheryl said, lying Talia on her shoulder and patting the little bottom.

Mia took over the pram so they could keep walking. 'You said it felt more right with him than anyone else you'd been with; more comfortable, natural, easy. That sounds like a soulmate to me.'

'Hm.'

They were on the home stretch now and Mia's stomach was rumbling, ready for breakfast.

'There are a couple of women who work for me who left their husbands for 'the soulmate',' Sheryl said, switching Talia to her other shoulder. 'One walked out on hubby and kids, the other one was having an affair for ages… Neither of them is still with Mr Soulmate but they've both lost the hubby too. One of them reckons she made an awful mistake but it's too late: he's remarried and apparently he's happier. The other one is still glad the marriage is over but the affair's over too. End of dream, dawn of reality. The two of them catch up every second weekend in bars and commiserate.'

'I'm not sure what you're telling me.'

'I'm not either,' Sheryl grinned. 'Maybe just that I stopped looking for unreasonable things. I mean, I'd always known Alec was keen on me; I put him off for years… Feels so cruel now. But I just thought, 'this gawky, bald loser – who needs him?' I was constantly chasing those dashing, dangerous types, and then licking my wounds. You remember. I even did drugs to attract one of those dropkicks, for Christ's sake! When I finally went out with Alec it was like I could stop trying and drop the act and just be myself.'

'But maybe that is a soulmate?'

'So how did you feel when you met John?'

Mia cast her mind back to that yacht in the Mediterranean. The unexpected meeting during someone's party, both of them there as ring-ins. John's gorgeous English accent and his courtesy and attentiveness. Those beautiful eyes. Looking after her when she nearly drowned – dragging her out of the water while she coughed and spat, and then sitting with her for the rest of that day and talking about their childhoods. Him drinking too much and being incredibly romantic and gregarious, and then chucking for hours the next day while she looked after him… And the spontaneous detour they'd both taken to Spain. A week of delicious food and sex and lying on beaches and sex and that fabulous Gaudi architecture and sex…

'It was special,' Mia said. 'But once I got back home it sort of faded from memory. And when he turned up I was taken aback. I don't think I'd thought of him as 'the one'. Just a really nice guy.'

'I was so envious of you when we met and you told me that story about how you and John hooked up!'

'I know.'

'To be chased instead of doing the chasing… *mama mia!*'

'And all along you had Alec chasing you and you were acting like he was a big nuisance.'

'Well he didn't cross the world for me like John did. He just kept popping up with little invitations for dinner. I thought he was annoying.'

Mia shook her head. 'Biggest mis-read of all time!'

'I know! And there I am, Madam Relationships-Advisor with all my friends and staff. God, what an idiot!' Sheryl's pace slowed down and her voice lowered. 'Is she asleep?'

Mia stepped behind Sheryl and peered at Talia's little face. 'Eyes still open, just, but she looks very sleepy.'

'Good.'

'You know, when we first got together it was just like you described with Alec. Very comfortable, very easy. It was just the fun part that gradually died out.'

'Working for that Buxton company would do it to you,' Sheryl said darkly. 'That was soul-destroying busy-work. I was glad you got out and I'm glad John's out now.'

'Yes. The prognosis is good.'

'The thing that worried me when I met John was that I wasn't seeing the guy you had talked about meeting in Europe.'

'So who is the real John?' Mia asked. 'The romantic guy I met on the boat, the conservative man I married, or the full-of-surprises guy he is now?'

'Paging The Real John!' Sheryl declared in her best exhibition centre announcement voice. 'Would the real John please step forward!'

Mia grinned. They had reached their cars.

'I suppose I'll wake her up putting her in the capsule,' Sheryl muttered, feeling in the hood of the pram for her keys. 'And she'll cry all the way home.'

It was hot in the car after that long walk. Mia rolled her window down and buckled herself in. She could see Sheryl sitting in the backseat of the Lexus breastfeeding Talia. She waved as she passed, then turned onto the main road. They really should do this more often – she felt great. Alive and awake! She would arrive home around the time she was usually getting out of bed and into the shower. It was difficult to believe that most mornings she slept through this special first-light-of-day time. It felt like such a waste! No wonder John always came home from his ride refreshed and glowing.

She had to slow down for a forty zone and that was when she saw his bike. It was locked in a bike stand outside a coffee shop called 'The Golden Cup'. She recognised his fluorescent orange helmet strapped to the handlebars. Her head whipped around because she was already nearly past it and she just caught a snap of him sitting at a table in the window, mug in front of him, phone to his ear.

14

Mia was reversing out of the driveway for work when John came cycling home. She braked and wound down her window. 'Not too puffed, I see. Getting fit!'

'Yes.' John slowed, then stopped, still perched on the bike, resting his weight on his right foot. He looked troubled, distant.

'Or maybe it was the coffee break?' she teased. He was always so perfect, so fit, so organised beside her plump, chaotic, constipated self. It was kind of fun to bring him down a peg...

'What?' He looked at her properly, focusing.

'Here I am, thinking you're out there doing laps of the surrounds and you're sitting in a café on the phone! Sprung bad, Johnno!' She was grinning, but he was still frowning.

'Oh,' he said. 'You saw me at The Golden Cup. I just pulled in there to take a call from Jake. He'd been texting me the whole ride so I figured it must be important.'

'Was it?'

'He needed an urgent answer for a form he's submitting about the charity. The deadline is in a couple of hours so...'

'Oh. Right. Is that all going okay?'

He shrugged. 'You know, tricky managing it from here. A lot of paperwork and that's not his forté...'

'Is it going to be worth it?'

'We're getting masses of interest. You scratch the surface on late-blooming artists and you find so many people in little art groups here and there doing tremendous stuff. If we can pull it together, it could be huge.'

'That's great, honey.'

He nodded. 'We're planning a national annual prize... John's found someone in government who's helping –'

'You mean Jake.'

He looked confused. 'What did I say?'

'John.'

'Oh. The stress is getting to me! Don't know who I am anymore.' He smiled, but the usual light wasn't in his eyes. He did look stressed.

'Take it easy,' she said. 'Your dad wouldn't want you to get all knotted up about it.'

'This admin stuff is just a temporary stage. It will pass. Anyway, I have to...' he glanced toward the house.

'Geez! I've got to go too!' Mia said with a start. What was she doing chatting in the driveway when peak hour traffic was building up! She put the car back into reverse. 'Have a good one, honey.'

'You too.'

Usually he would lean in and kiss her goodbye, but that frown was still puckering his forehead. She reached out and covered the hand that was within reach on the handlebar, hoping to convey tenderness. She hadn't enjoyed the little rift that had opened up between them this morning, and she didn't like this feeling of distance from him now – wanted to plug the gap before it widened. She knew how quickly little cracks could turn into giant chasms.

But he nodded in a distracted kind of way and pushed off toward the garage. Her hand trailed away.

Today's Mandatory Trainings were: 'How To Conduct Paperless Meetings

– no printing out of presentations or reports!' – and 'How To Conduct Your Day Without Notepads'. A handsome smiling man in a suit showed how easy it was to use your laptop or phone or device to create absolutely anything you needed and keep track of it and display it for others. All you had to do was remember to take your computer with you to every meeting. So instead of picking up a pad and pencil when you need to quickly see the boss with a question, you just disconnect your laptop from its security cable, unplug the power cable and the second screen cable, take the laptop and mouse (unless you're lucky enough to have a touch screen laptop), and make your way to your boss's office. Then you can refer to your notes and make notes about his responses, etcetera. You'll be used to the new routine in no time at all!

Mia stifled a yawn. She could see Susan staring at her screen intently and wondered where she was up to. She'd probably finished the whole training already and had loved every dreary minute of it. Susan relished systems and methods; she could see through a forest of details to the most efficient pathway in the blink of an eye. It was infuriating. Not that Mia wanted to be Ms SuperPA but she hated always feeling less, inadequate, inefficient. It would be good to be out of this…

The counselling organisations were open in tabs on her browser. With another glance at Susan, she tabbed across, scanning the course options again. She wanted to start helping people as soon as possible, rather than spending years on theory first, so Psychology was out. Most counselling courses, she had discovered, were designed to be hands-on right from the start with students even counselling each other in the very first class. Doing something so completely different from filing and admin was an exhilarating thought; spending her day talking about what she so often thought about was becoming more and more appealing.

She wondered whether she would want to study here. It would be good to stay in touch with Reynald and a few of the others, and fun to stroll in through the glass doors and then turn left for the meeting rooms and an interesting class with other students rather than right toward the admin area and a desk and tasks. But it would also be good to not have to see Susan's disapproving frown ever again. Enrolling somewhere else would give her a completely fresh start. Then again, Reynald's offer to cover the fee was pretty damn compelling.

With a sigh, she tabbed away from the course information back to the training video.

John was late home that evening. The ute was usually already there when she arrived, and he'd be in the shower or watching something on his prize TV – more films these days, probably because the screen was so cinematic. Or he'd be making a start on the evening meal. But tonight when Mia let herself in and dropped her keys into the bowl by the door, the place was quiet and still, aside from Bitsy fawning at her feet.

She stepped out of her shoes and went to switch the heater on, but the place felt stuffy after being shut up all day, so instead she opened windows and made herself a cup of tea. She sat at the kitchen bench gazing outside and wondering what to cook for dinner. The days were growing longer now that they were so close to spring, but darkness was already falling so he couldn't still be working. She flipped her phone open and sent a quick text:

> You be home soon?

Bitsy began leaping up at her legs so she slid off the stool. 'No, Bits. You'll make my tights run. I know we usually walk now but we went this morning, remember? Big long walk with Sheryl and Talia? That's right...' She sat by the table, scooping the little dog into her lap and stroking her. Bitsy looked up at her with adoring eyes, licking her hand whenever it came within reach. 'How's my baby?' she cooed, which reminded her that she should check her dates. She was pretty sure that she should have had her period by now but was avoiding going back through the diary so as not to be disappointed again.

Six forty-five and still no reply and no sign of him, and it was growing cold. She tipped Bitsy off her lap and went to close windows, switch the heater on, and tackle dinner. Pasta. She tried to minimise pasta but there wasn't much in the fridge. Waiting for the water to boil she scrolled through her Facebook notifications. The usual photos of happy family gatherings and posts about job successes and requests for healing blessings for someone who was sick and silly quizzes... Sheryl had posted a gorgeous picture of Talia laughing. Mia 'liked' it, smiling at the pink-cheeked child who was sitting in Alec's lap and waving her hands. So happy. The simple things: feeling loved, warm, safe. So much to laugh about...

She put her phone down and rinsed some basil. Tossed a handful of pine nuts into the blender and dropped the basil on top. Pressed some garlic. Drizzled olive oil around the top, round and round. While it was blending she took the grated parmesan cheese out of the fridge and put two bowls and forks on the bench. Chopped up some tomato and sprinkled it with pink Himalayan salt and cracked pepper.

Seven p.m.

Maybe he'd told her he had some errand to do and she'd forgotten about it? Nothing came to mind.

The water boiled and she tipped the pasta into the pot. Back to Facebook. On an impulse she clicked on Alec's name and looked through his friends until she saw Nick: a picture of him standing on a bridge at sunset in some Asian city – there were people on rickshaws behind him. Clicked on the picture and went through to his profile. Nick Reece, investigative journalist. There was very little information. The latest post was five days ago: a picture of refugees and a link to an article he'd written about them. Seventy people had liked the link and there were a few comments like, 'Great article, Nicko' and 'Why are people so cruel to each other?' and some random ones like, 'Hey Nick, when will you be back in Sydney?' or 'Perth' or 'Singapore'. Those comments were always from women...

She studied his face in the pictures. So good-looking. Remembered the hard muscle under that T-shirt, his hands on her body... She felt calmer when she thought about it now – less guilty. She had been lonely and he had given her some attention, it was as simple as that. The fact that her body had responded so strongly... well, that was an indication of exactly how lonely she had been feeling. And how frustrated... Those feelings seemed so long ago now. Love and desire had been reignited since John had returned home. Actually, she was surprised that the renewed sexual connection with him was lasting so long. She'd expected some degree of revival when he returned, at least for the first few nights, but it had been close to a month now and he still wanted to make love most nights. Perhaps it was as Sheryl had said: Buxton had drained him, been bad for his soul. And now he was coming back to life – although the thought of him mowing lawns still amazed her. His father dying had clearly had a profound effect on him, making him want to seize life with both hands rather than just let it tick past.

The timer rang and she stood up to drain the fettuccine.

Seven twenty-five. She stirred the pesto sauce into the pasta. Her stomach was feeling growly now and she wanted to eat. Checked her phone in case a message had popped through without her hearing. Nothing. Sent:

> Dinner's ready. What's your ETA?

It was completely dark outside now. She took her bowl to the pot and served herself and then carried her dinner into the living room and switched on the grand TV. At eight-fifteen a message popped through from John:

> Sorry. On my way

She heard him coming into the laundry at half past eight. Stood up, stretching her legs. Bitsy was already barking at the door. She could hear him taking his boots off, grunting, and then two thuds as they fell onto the floor. She opened the door and Bitsy burst through, yapping. 'Hey Bits,' he said, bending to pat the dog. He sounded tired.

'Everything okay?' she asked.

He shrugged. She couldn't see his face properly in the dim laundry, but as he came toward her into the kitchen she caught a whiff of smoke and alcohol.

'Where have you been?'

'The pub.'

'The pub!'

She moved closer, empty pasta bowl still in one hand, putting the other arm around him and reaching up to kiss the stubbly cheek. He wasn't nearly as thorough about shaving now that he didn't have to toe the corporate line.

There was a moment, a hesitation before he kissed her back. Then he forced a smile and said, 'Sorry 'bout disappearing on you.'

'You've been smoking!' she said in surprise. 'Since when do you smoke?'

He let out a long, deep breath and moved away from her into the kitchen. 'Got some bad news today from the UK. A friend died. It shook me up a bit. Dinner ready? I'm starving.'

She pointed to the pot, taking her own dish to the sink. He stood at the stove with his bowl, staring into the saucepan.

'You might want to warm it up a bit.'

'It's fine like this.' He began to scoop spoonfuls into the bowl.

'Someone you were close to?'

'Yes. Years ago… It was just a shock because he's young – my age. I cancelled my afternoon job and went for a long walk. Needed some time alone. And then wound up at the pub. I lost track of the time.'

'Do you want to talk about it?' she asked. So much of his life in England was a mystery to her. He'd never wanted to talk much about it. The odd comment about his younger brother Jake who always stole the limelight and left him feeling inadequate; the odd comments about the parents she had met once, his very controlling mother and his hen-pecked father; the odd comment about the climate or a job he'd had years ago or something at uni or holidays they'd taken in Brighton; but not much.

He shook his head, and stood with his back to the stove, eating.

'Was it an accident or was he sick?'

'Suicide.'

'Oh, John.' *Eight suicides a day…*

Suddenly he put his bowl on the bench and dug a hand into his pocket, bringing out a handkerchief and sneezing loudly at the same time. He blew his nose.

'Bless you,' she said automatically.

'Thanks. Hay fever.' He sniffed, replaced the hankie and picked up his bowl again. 'Thanks for this. It's good.'

'Even cold?'

He nodded slowly, chewing. Then, 'I'd like – if you don't mind – to be alone a little longer.'

'Sure,' she said. She went back into the living room and curled up on the couch. She heard him move from the kitchen a little later and into their bedroom; picked up the faint sound of water running. At nine-thirty she switched the TV off and went looking for him. He was already in bed, lying in the dark, soundless.

Mia undressed and climbed in beside him. He raised an arm to let her close and she rested her head on his shoulder, one hand on his chest. This was very early for them to be going to bed; she didn't think either of them would sleep. Lay there wondering about the pub. John wasn't the sort to drown his sorrows in the pub. Maybe Sheryl was right. Maybe he had kind of snapped, like Maryann. Maybe that was what explained all the changes.

To her surprise, she drifted off to sleep, lulled by the sound of his steady breathing.

John was gone when she woke up the next morning. She looked at the bedside clock and was amazed by how long she had slept. Went into the kitchen and flicked the radio on to her mother's program while she was waiting for the kettle to boil. A man was announcing the songs instead of her mother. Perhaps they had changed slots? But no; after the next song he said, 'I'd like to thank you all for turning me on this morning,' which made her laugh aloud, and then, 'I've been replacing Glenys who's caught the horrid cold that's going around at the moment, so we wish her well and a speedy recovery. At least we spring into spring this week, so things are looking up.'

She muted him and called her parents' place. Lionel answered after several rings.

'I gather Mum's not well,' she said.

'That's right. She's had a cold for the last week but it's gone to her chest and she's got no voice now.'

'Do you want me to come over?'

'Oh no, love, that's all right. I'm making her soup.'

'I can come over. Do you need anything picked up?'

'Well, if you're in the area you can drop in but don't make a special trip. We know how much you full-time workers need your weekend.'

'Weekend is also for family,' she reminded him, feeling irritated. Why did she always feel as if she had to make an appointment to visit her own parents?

She made her shopping list and headed out to get it done, adding a gourmet fruit juice and some herbal cough lollies to her purchases, and coming home via her parents'. Lionel let her in, surprised to see her. Her mother was dressed but sitting on the couch under a blanket, eyes closed but upright. The community radio station was on low, though her segment was now over.

Mia sat beside her and placed the cough lollies in her lap; she opened her eyes and gave a tiny smile of thanks, and put the packet on the coffee table. Mia chatted for a little, but her mother had no voice and, it seemed, nothing to say, so eventually she gave up the one-sided conversation.

Found herself looking up at the picture of her big sister, eyes shut in her forever sleep, and then saying, "How old were you when you had Rita?'

Her mother followed her line of sight. 'Twenty-three,' she said in a croaky voice.

'So twenty-five when you had me.'

Glenys nodded.

'I don't think I've told you, but John and I have decided to have a baby,' Mia said, and it felt to her as if someone else had spoken, as if that was not her voice.

Her mother said nothing.

'I think it will be really good for us.'

Glenys blew her nose and dabbed at her eyes.

'I didn't want to, our first few years together, because I felt so plugged in about babies… It's probably silly but I always felt like I was an intruder, like you just had me to make up for losing Rita and you didn't really want me…' Why was she saying – blurting all this? She felt prickly, on edge.

Her mother made a sudden movement and then pressed her fist to her mouth, looking away, across the room, at the old fringed lamp that stood by Lionel's favourite armchair.

'And then I decided that it was ridiculous for me to not have children just because I felt hurt. That was just punishing *us*.' It was as if she had been fed truth serum. Maybe it was all this thinking about counselling that was making her so keen to get to the truth of things and heal old hurts.

Her mother cleared her throat and turned red eyes towards Mia. 'Of course we loved you,' she whispered. 'What made you think we didn't love you?'

Mia traced her memories, following threads of images and words: her mother gazing at the picture of Rita while she tugged at her skirt, trying to get her attention… her mother telling Aunt Claire that all the joy went out of life when Rita died… her father saying, 'Don't trouble your mother now, pet'… Words and images that stood out from the fog of her memories like hints and clues.

The door opened and, as if on cue, Lionel stood there, looking at them both anxiously.

'It was a very shocking experience,' Glenys whispered. 'You'll understand when you have yours.'

'But then you had me!' Mia said, in a low voice to match. 'Didn't that help? Didn't that –'

'Mia, love,' Lionel began and Glenys reached out and grabbed her wrist and, holding it tightly, she said, 'You can't replace a child. They told me to have you to replace Rita but it doesn't work like that.' She coughed a thick mucousy cough and pressed the tissue to her mouth.

'Don't –' Lionel began again, and Mia interrupted him. 'It's all right, Dad, I'm going. I just needed...' *to talk to Mum*, she was going to say. But that didn't seem right because really it had been a one-sided conversation; her mother hadn't had the voice to say much. Maybe she'd dumped all that on her mother now because she could, because her mother's bright, controlled persona had come a little undone and she wasn't able to deflect...

Mia leaned forward and kissed her mother on the cheek. Not an air kiss; a real kiss that made contact with her mother's soft skin. 'Get better,' she said.

The tears started on the way home, and she didn't understand why she was crying.

The ute was in the drive when she arrived and John was on his laptop at the table. Mia avoided his eye. She was still sniffing a little as she opened the fridge door and stowed her shopping away. Luckily there wasn't much freezer food, given the extra time it had all waited in the car.

'What are you doing?' she asked John, under cover of the noise she was making as she bundled carrots and zucchini and broccoli into the crisper.

'Emails,' he said, concentrating. 'Have a look at this. Jake's had the prints made and they look fabulous.'

She closed the fridge door and stepped over the shopping bags on her way to the table where he sat. There was an email from jake hartington and a series of images of their father's artwork, beautifully reproduced and ready for distribution.

'They're great. What's the plan? Is he going to door knock gift shops?'

'Some, but Melissa's helping us develop a marketing plan. Internet mostly, of course.' He glanced up then looked back at her more closely.

'You okay?'

'Just had a cry in the car.' She wiped an eye. 'I don't know why. I feel a bit out of sorts.'

He picked up her hand and held it against his chest. She could feel his heart making its steady beat in there.

'I've been at Mum's. I told her we want to have a baby – that's the first time I've said anything about it. And I told her how I feel about Rita.'

'What did she say?'

'That I'll understand when I have one.'

'You're really ready, aren't you?'

She nodded. 'As ready as you can be, I suppose.'

He took a deep breath and drew her down to sit on his knee, saying, 'In for a penny, in for a pound.'

'Why do you say that?' she asked, but he shook his head with a little smile and shrug, and directed her attention back to the screen, pointing out a realistic picture of the postie bending at his father's front gate to deposit some mail.

15

Mia pushed the vacuum cleaner forwards and backwards, forwards and backwards, music pouring into her ears via her earphones. She was singing along to Michael Jackson, who produced good cleaning music.

'*Gonna make a change for once in my life...*'

She moved from the hallway into the bedroom and drew up short; looked back over her shoulder. The machine was stuck at the doorpost, whining away like a stubborn child. She gave the hose an impatient jerk so that it would clear the wall and follow her through the doorway. Actually she was the child when it came to vacuuming: she acted as if she expected the vacuum cleaner to be an intelligent creature capable of following her sensibly around the house while she cleaned, rather than a blind thing that needed to be constantly guided. Maybe she could be persuaded into buying one of those intelligent robot type of vacuum cleaners... The squat little thing cleared the corner, still whining, and she moved on into the bedroom, singing away with Michael.

'*I'm looking at the man in the mirror. I'm asking him to change his ways...*'

The spider dropped suddenly from somewhere horribly close – surely not her hair! – and onto the floor at her feet before scuttling under the bed. She gave a little screech, heart racing.

'John!'

Thumps and thuds from somewhere in the house where he was cleaning.

'John, quick!'

'What?'

He appeared in the doorway, sleeves rolled up, and sneezed. 'Geez!' Blew his nose. 'What?'

'Spider. Under the bed. I thought I saw red on its back...'

'Shit.' He didn't like spiders. It was one of the things he'd told her when he first arrived from England and discovered how many creatures in Australia could kill you. He still wouldn't swim in the ocean – scared of sharks.

'We can't leave it there,' she said. 'Imagine being fast asleep and it crawls up in the middle of the night...'

'Stop!' he said, raising a hand. 'I've got the picture.'

They both kneeled and peered under the bed warily.

'Can you see it?' she asked.

'Nope.'

'Shit. I won't be able to sleep in here till we find it.' She crawled along the side of the bed and looked under it again from another vantage point.

'*You* won't!' he exclaimed, standing up. 'You're the native. You're used to these – fuck!' he leapt backwards as the thing scuttled out from under the bed near his feet.

'Have you found it?' She stood up hurriedly, scanning the floor.

'There.' He pointed.

She looked at him.

'What?'

'Are you going to get it?'

'Seriously? You want me to engage with that...'

'Okay. I'll get it then, my knight. Keep an eye on it.'

She returned to the vacuum cleaner, picking up the handle again and switching it on.

'Quick,' he said. 'It's moving toward the dresser. If it goes behind...'

She plunged at the spider with the head of the cleaner. 'Did I get it?'

'I don't know. Don't think so.'

'Damn.' She pulled the head of the vacuum back cautiously and they both looked at the carpet. Nothing. 'So does no spider mean I got it or it escaped?'

He was shaking his head slowly. 'You think it was a redback?'

'I don't know. I thought I saw red but...'

'We've got to find it.'

'It could be anywhere.'

They both stood, looking at the place where the spider had been.

'Come on,' she said. 'Let's be reasonable. They're not super-creatures. It's probably just hiding somewhere, scared.'

'Right,' he said, then cooed, 'Come on, spider-ider! Out you come. No need to be – fuck! Shit!'

A mottled and hairy spider with a leg span of some ten centimetres had appeared from behind the curtain and was making its rapid, crab-like way across the wall.

'Fuck me dead!' John exclaimed, clutching his chest.

Mia looked up from her search. 'That's a huntsman. They're pretty harmless, remember?'

'With a name like that? And what do you mean by 'pretty' harmless?'

'They're not deadly. You might have a little sore spot if they bit you. I told you about those when you first came out.'

'It looks like one of those man-eating South American tarantulas. Are you sure it's safe? I mean, one hundred per cent? You're not mixing it up with anything else, are you?'

'Totally sure. We Aussies grew up with those babies. They eat cockroaches, so we're fond of them.'

John's eyes widened. 'Oh. Lovely! Fond of the huntsman. Which is clearly more attractive than the lowly cockroach. Now there's an insect we all love to hate!'

'Stay focused,' Mia frowned, scanning the carpet in ever-widening circles. 'We're looking for a redback: tiny, red flash on its back, evil. They're the real danger.'

'What *is* this?' John demanded, searching with her in quick, short glances while keeping a wary eye on the huntsman, which was, fortunately, heading away in a diagonal, up-the-wall direction. 'Spiders-come-out-to-play Day?'

'There it is.'

'Where?' He swung around.

'Near the architrave this side of the dresser. Ssh.' She was unscrewing the wide end of the cleaner so she could use the nozzle.

'Good luck,' he said.

'Switch it on for me.'

He pressed the button and she moved in slowly, pointing the nozzle at the spider, ready to suck. She jabbed; it ran.

'Did you get it?'

'No. It's gone behind the dresser.'

'Fuck.'

'But I got a good look at it this time. It's not a redback.'

'So I should relax?'

'Yeah.'

'Great.' He blew his nose.

She looked at him sympathetically. 'Poor you. So scary.'

'Hey!' he objected, wiping red, teary eyes. 'I'm the one fearing for my life every day in gardens. Whenever I have to move rocks or get under overhanging bushes...'

'Poor baby.'

'Between all the grass and pollen making me sick and the possibility of death at any moment –'

Mia laughed.

'No, I'm serious! I'm rethinking this little career path.'

'Well, it was never going to be permanent. Have you had any other ideas?'

He nodded. 'Working on something. I'll tell you about it soon...'

'Speaking of soon,' she said. 'What time are we supposed to be at Cooney Avenue?'

'Two.'

'We'd better get a move on then.'

'So nice to drive a decent car again after doing battle with Barry's ute all week,' John remarked as he parked the Commodore outside the block of flats. 'It always takes about three goes to start up and then whenever you're idling at lights it starts to shudder and I'm certain it's going to die any moment.'

The agent was waiting for them on the front steps in his black suit and lime-coloured shirt and slicked-back hair. 'What about real estate?' Mia murmured as they approached, smiling.

John made a suppressed choking sound.

'Phillip Marsden,' the agent said briskly, extending a hand. He was in his twenties and had that earnest, good-boy look about him that made Mia instantly wary.

'It's not the best news, I'm afraid,' he said, unlocking the security door and holding it open for them. 'They've left a bit of a mess.'

'So Alison told us.'

They clattered up the stairs to the second floor and around the landing to number three. He unlocked the front door and gave it a little push with his shoulder. 'Jamming,' he said briefly.

There was a strange odour inside. Mia puckered her nose. 'What *is* that?'

The agent gave a little cough. 'I'm not sure. Something they've spilt... If you'll come through here.'

Their tenants had left belongings in every room: tins of food and tomato sauce in the pantry, clothing hanging over the backs of chairs, an old hair dryer on the bathroom sink, sheets and quilt in a twisted mess on the bed...

'There was even an unfinished pizza on the coffee table when we got here after they advised us that they'd left,' Phillip informed them, trailing after them as they looked into each room in turn. 'But as you can see... things still in the cupboards, there are stains on the carpet, a big scratch on the wall in the hallway... Someone has been letting the shower drip and there's water damage on the floor in the bathroom and on the carpet just outside... Could be a mould problem starting up…'

In one of the bedrooms, he opened a wardrobe door and pointed, silently. Mia looked inside and gave a little shriek. A blood-spattered axe stood leaning against the wall.

'Oh my God! Were they murderers or what?'

John squatted for a closer look. He reached for it and Mia grabbed his shoulder, 'Maybe you shouldn't touch it! We should probably send it somewhere for testing – just in case.'

He ignored her and took it out of the cupboard. He touched the bright red stains thoughtfully. 'That's paint. It's probably just a prop from a performance of some kind.'

'An axe!'

'It's a tomahawk.'

'Well, they've definitely forfeited their bond!' Mia declared, hands on her hips. 'It's going to take us ages to clean this lot up.'

John looked up at her for a moment, with an inscrutable expression.

She sighed, swinging around to look at the venetian blinds, which had been half-closed at a crooked angle so that they bunched tightly at one end and spread out at the other. 'I suppose we'd better come back tomorrow and get into it.'

'Yes,' he agreed, standing up. 'The sooner we get another tenant in here, the better. I don't like the thought of the place standing empty and costing us.'

Mia dug her phone out of her bag to check the time. 'When does that show start tonight? Maybe we can do a bit this afternoon.'

'Eight o'clock. I suppose so.'

John had decided he quite liked the pub where he'd drowned his sorrows after his friend died. He'd taken Mia there to hear a live band the previous night. She'd been surprised by how many people seemed to know him as he steered her toward a table.

'It's the Pom!' someone had called drunkenly.

John had laughed and waved and settled her at the table before going to order their drinks at the bar.

'You know these people?' she asked when he returned with two beers.

'These people,' he said, sitting opposite her and putting their drinks on the table, 'are resident at *every* bar. They are standard issue.'

'But they seem to know you.'

'They *think* they know me. They see a face once and decide you're a mate for life.'

The band was good and it had been fun to be out, hearing live music, instead of same-old, same-old at home. But then they'd noticed flyers on their tables for a new up-and-coming theatre group that presented edgy, thought-provoking shows about current issues. John had suggested they go tonight, opening night.

Mia hummed as she changed out of her dusty cleaning gear and into a short skirt and top. It was still a bit cold for warm-weather clothes but the sky had been blue and the sun shining this first day of spring. She pulled tights on and zipped up her boots.

John whistled. 'Looking hot, honey.'

She glowed.

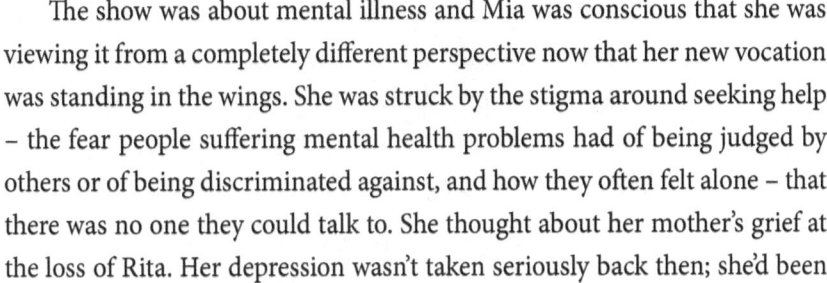

The show was about mental illness and Mia was conscious that she was viewing it from a completely different perspective now that her new vocation was standing in the wings. She was struck by the stigma around seeking help – the fear people suffering mental health problems had of being judged by others or of being discriminated against, and how they often felt alone – that there was no one they could talk to. She thought about her mother's grief at the loss of Rita. Her depression wasn't taken seriously back then; she'd been told to get over it and move on...

John wasn't in a hurry to leave when the play had finished, so she ducked to the toilet while he hovered in the foyer with audience and emerging cast and crew members. When she returned, he was deep in conversation with a man she gathered was the director of the show. Mia listened for a while as they talked about the statement the show was making, then drifted away to look at the big black-and-white photos of the cast and to read their bios.

'Well hello,' said a voice at her shoulder.

She swung around, heart thumping.

Nick stood there, still tall and handsome, a glass of champagne in his hand.

Her face reddened as she remembered. 'Hello.'

'How's the unpredictability coming along?' he asked.

Geez! She gave a flustered laugh. 'Quite well, actually.'

He was looking at her hands. 'I see you're owning him now.'

The wedding ring. 'I hadn't exactly disowned him... It was the role I was playing...'

'Of course,' he agreed. 'No such thing as a tarty wife.'

'How's your novel coming along?' she shot back.

'It's coming,' he said. She sensed he was suppressing a smile.

She looked away. John was still talking to the director. What would he have to talk to a director about for so long?

Nick followed her gaze. 'That hubby?'

'The one in the grey jumper,' she said.

'So I'd better not invite you out onto the deck.'

She gave a strangled laugh, and he leaned in and said quietly, 'I was sorry that you never rang, but I'm glad things are better for you now. Anyway, the number still works.' And then he moved on. She stared after him, watching as he weaved his way through the crowd and was absorbed into a small knot of people on the other side of the room. Her whole body was pulsing.

'Who was that?' John. Standing beside her and looking in the same direction.

'Just someone I met at Sheryl's party. A friend of Alec's.'

'The party I missed where you were dressed up to kill? No wonder he was looking at you like that.'

'Like what?' she flushed.

He grinned. 'Don't worry, I'm not threatened. It does something for a man to know other men desire his wife.' He banged his chest. 'Makes me feel like the alpha male.'

She laughed, relieved. So she wouldn't have to confess all... 'And you? What were you talking about for so long with the director of the show – doing his books?'

'Good idea,' he said thoughtfully. 'That hadn't occurred to me. No, smart arse. I was interested in the theme. The point they were making. Weren't you, Ms Counsellor-In-The-Making?'

'Of course. But you weren't talking about that when I was there. You were talking about liking his interpretation of the play. Have you seen it before?'

'Oh, years ago,' he said vaguely. 'Back at home.'

'Really? I'd have thought it was quite a current piece – quite contemporary, with that mental illness aspect.'

'Yes, well, out here in the colonies...'

She gave him a light punch in the arm. 'Seriously. I thought you were saying something about always wanting to do it the way he did it.'

'To see it *done* the way he did it,' John corrected her.

'Oh...' She hesitated, trying to recall his exact words.

'You have to start by feeding their egos about their show or they won't give you the time of day,' John explained. 'Did you notice how he was when I first started the conversation? Restless – he wanted to get away. So I was showing him that I really appreciated his take on it. Ah, the things I've learnt from my theatrical bro.'

'Mm.' She glanced away and saw the Director talking to a young woman who was scribbling in a notebook.

'But, as Jake would say, who are we to him but plebs?' John continued. 'The unwashed unartistic. What would we know?' He took her arm. 'Shall we go?'

'Sure.' They headed for the door and she schooled herself to not look back for a last glimpse of Nick. *Just walk. Eyes straight ahead, girl. You're going home for wild sex with your husband.*

Skirting puddles in the dark car park she said, 'It's a pity your friend didn't get to see a show like this. Maybe it would have helped.'

'Which friend?' he asked, unlocking the car doors.

'The one who suicided. Do you think his problem was just not having people to talk to?'

'Oh. I sure that was part of it.' He held the door open for her and she perched on the seat. As she swung her legs in, he added: 'But also people not knowing what to say – how to communicate with someone who's depressed. This production did a superb job of showing that, don't you think?'

'Yes.' She waited while John closed the door, walked around the bonnet of the car and climbed in beside her. 'All those broken conversations and missed opportunities. It was painful to watch.'

'That's the beauty of theatre,' he said. And sighed. 'So much to offer.'

She pondered that comment as he started the car and the engine warmed up. Then touched his knee. 'We should do this more often. It was great. Thanks for organising it – getting us out.'

His smile was almost tender. 'You're welcome.'

They bumped their way out of the gloomy, rutted car park and turned onto the road.

'You know,' John said, 'Jim Carrey reckons his father could have been a great comedian but he didn't think it would work out for him so he opted for a nice, safe job as… drum roll… an accountant.'

'Really?'

'Really. And when Jim was twelve or fourteen or something, his dad lost the nice, safe job and the whole family was on skid row.'

'How sad.'

'It was one of the big life lessons he learnt from his father: if you can fail at what you don't want, you might as well take a chance on doing what you love.'

'Kind of relevant for us at the moment, isn't it?' she reflected.

'Supremely relevant,' he said.

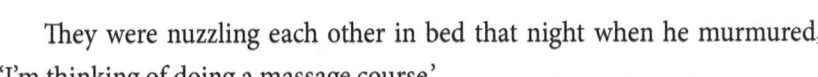

They were nuzzling each other in bed that night when he murmured, 'I'm thinking of doing a massage course.'

She pulled back and looked at him, stunned. 'What?'

'Massage. You know...' he gave her shoulder a brief, magnificent squeeze with one hand.

'I know! But –'

'I can't take the gardening anymore, Mia. All that pollen... I haven't been this affected by hay fever since I came out here.'

'But massage...?'

'I'm a natural, don't you think?'

'You're amazing. But I want this new skill for myself. I don't want you touching other women like that.'

'I don't – wouldn't be massaging breasts and pussies,' he murmured, beginning to massage hers.

She held his hands to stop him. 'Are you really serious?'

'Sure. Why not? Lots of men do massage. I might specialise in remedial. No happy endings, I promise.'

'Well... It's so...' She shook her head. 'So out of left field!'

'More so than gardening?'

'They're both in that field.' She wished she could see his face more clearly. There was only the faintest light coming in through the window. 'Aren't you missing numbers? Don't you want to get back into something you're really good at? I mean, I don't care. If it makes you happy and pays the bills it's all good, but...'

'Sure,' he said vaguely. And then, 'I'm doing some number crunching for the charity and the gallery and sorting out how to market Dad's artwork, remember? Jake keeps asking me to quote different sized bundles of the prints and figure out how much it's going to cost to run the charity. So I'm keeping my hand in and getting that numbers buzz. Scratching that itch... But until I find a paying job that really lights me up, I want to keep trying new things.'

'Wow...' He was a bag of tricks since that trip to the UK. 'I want to start my course soon,' she reminded him, not willing to miss out on the blessings being stirred up by the winds of change. 'So we've got to be careful about how we manage our funds.' Ridiculous that she was the one saying this! It was usually John's lecture.

'Of course,' he agreed. 'But we're fine for now. We're cruising. We don't want to be like Jim Carrey's dad, do we?' And he silenced her with a long, deep kiss.

16

It was almost balmy this morning. Mia had spontaneously woken early and taken Bitsy for a walk around the block before work. They arrived back home as John cycled in.

She whistled. 'Got the legs out, I see!'

He climbed off his bike and posed. 'The spring cycling fashions are taking the world by storm. Little old ladies faint by the roadside as strapping cyclists ride past, their bare legs flashing in the sun.'

Mia laughed. 'Talk about taking your cue!'

He curtsied. 'I haven't been learning my lines for nothing.'

Mia unclipped Bitsy and John walked his bike into the garage. She sat on the laundry step to pull off her muddy shoes and he waited for her, Bitsy in his arms, stroking the Papillon's feathery ears.

'It's finally fading,' she said, looking at his knee as her second shoe plopped onto the ground.

'What is?'

'Your scar. You can't even see it anymore.'

John bent down and let Bitsy leap from his hands. 'Which scar?'

'You know,' Mia said, 'the one you got when Jake was pushing you too fast in the go-kart and you ran into the tree? You had a long jagged line on your knee from where that piece of broken wood went in and ripped your flesh. Seven stitches, wasn't it?'

John examined his knee. 'You're right,' he said. 'I thought that would never heal. My evil brother… I think he ran me into the tree on purpose. *Eleven* stitches, I'll have you know. Plus a tetanus injection. But I got lots of ice cream and a gameboy.'

'Lucky you.' She heaved herself off the step and they went into the kitchen for breakfast.

'Speaking of the evil brother,' he said, opening the fridge, 'he wants to come out for a visit.'

'Yeah?' Mia unscrewed the coffee jar and put two spoonfuls into the plunger. 'It would be great to meet him at last. Seems absurd that I have still never met your brother.'

John shook his head. 'You're better off not meeting him and definitely not hosting him. He's a spendthrift. Moves in and takes over. No sense of responsibility…'

'I've heard all this before – he's still your brother. And it will make it much easier for the two of you to sort out all your dad biz if he's here instead of all these early morning, late night conversations.'

'That's true,' John said. 'But I'd still rather he stayed over there. The whole point of me coming out here was to get some breathing space from him.'

'I thought it was to marry me,' Mia said.

'*And* that,' John said. 'Definitely that.'

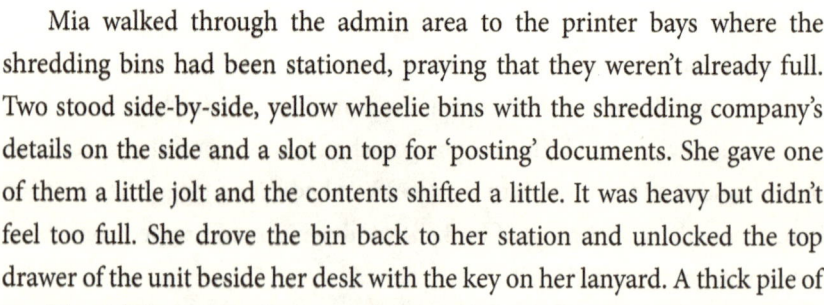

Mia walked through the admin area to the printer bays where the shredding bins had been stationed, praying that they weren't already full. Two stood side-by-side, yellow wheelie bins with the shredding company's details on the side and a slot on top for 'posting' documents. She gave one of them a little jolt and the contents shifted a little. It was heavy but didn't feel too full. She drove the bin back to her station and unlocked the top drawer of the unit beside her desk with the key on her lanyard. A thick pile of confidential documents lay in here, destined for demise. She lifted them out and then stood in front of the bin, posting them, one after another. This was 'it'. Once it disappeared through that slot for shredding, there was no longer a single hard copy of that document in the office. There was something very final about that.

It was peaceful in here today. Susan was off sick and Paula was away at a conference. Mia stood posting and dreaming. A slanted rectangle of sunshine lay on the floor, from the part of the window that wasn't shaded by other tall city buildings. She could see Reynald across the office sitting on the edge of someone's desk. He was much more relaxed when Paula was away; it was as if the real Reynald came out to play. She heard him laughing.

Beyond him the glass doors opened and some students entered and turned left toward the training rooms. She wished she was going with them. Reynald looked up and noticed them walking through, and caught her eye as he returned to his conversation. He wiggled his brows at her and winked.

Mia smiled back. She had submitted her application to study here. Reynald had pretty much promised to approve her request for study leave, and she'd continue working at ACCAT while she was studying, training up a replacement for when she'd completed her course and was finally ready to leave.

The bin was very heavy when she'd finished and had to wheel it back to the printer bays.

John was at the computer when Mia arrived home. She dropped her bag onto a chair and came to look over his shoulder. 'So you're doing it.'

'I think this one.' He was on a website promoting massage courses, his cursor pointing to start dates. 'They're one of the only colleges that has a new intake in spring, and I'd like to get started straight away.'

'So you're just going to drop the whole gardening biz?'

'Not yet. I'll keep it going for a while longer – we can do with the cash.

And then I'll aim to convert them: 'Ladies and gentlemen, let your gardens grow! I can now offer you a phenomenal relaxation and remedial massage service instead!"

Mia flashed on an image of Sandra lying on a table naked under a towel while John worked aromatic oils into her neck and shoulders, making the short auburn hair slick at the ends… She frowned. 'It's very old-fashioned of me, but –'

John pulled her onto his knee. 'I know. You're jealous as hell. You're worried about me diving under the towel with all the pretty women…'

'Well you are much more flirtatious these days,' she said defensively, in her little girl voice. 'The old John would never have flirted the way you do now. It unsettles me. Makes me wonder if I can trust you…'

'Because you'd never flirt, would you?' he teased. 'You'd never flash your cleavage at tall handsome strangers…'

She started to get up and he held her more tightly. 'Hm? Come, come. What's good for the goose…'

'What! You saying you *are* intending to flirt with them?'

'No!' He put those hands on her shoulders and began to rub. 'Relax… I'm just saying, watch your judgements. You've got a tendency to be one-eyed – to blame other people for things you do too.'

'Like what?' she flashed, but memories were coming back to her: criticising her friend Hannah for cheating on a test when she, Mia, had 'accidentally' copied Rowan's work… silently disapproving of Sheryl for being cruel to the patiently waiting Alec when she herself had cut John short multiple times… ignoring her mother to pay her back for all the times that she hadn't been fully present…

'Well, us, for instance,' John said. 'Blaming me for a boring old marriage; but *you* weren't doing much to put more fun into it, were you?'

That stung. She tried to get up again and he held her down.

'It takes two to tango, Mia-mine.' His arms were wrapping around her, drawing her close against his chest. 'Massage is a perfectly respectable profession. I've – I'll be doing an official accredited course and I'll be supervised and evaluated all the way down the line. There's nothing for you to worry about. I love *this* body,' pressing a hand against her belly, 'and I won't be touching anything that's off limits. I promise.'

She melted a little, her gruffness and guilt losing their sharp edges.

'Do you trust me?' She felt his breath brushing her ear.

'All right...' She positioned one of his hands over a breast and one over her pussy. 'So long as you remember who is a client and who is a wife...'

Encouraged by Mia's enthusiasm about their night at community theatre, John had suggested they see a play at the Malthouse.

'We'll invite Sheryl and Alec too!' she had said. So now here they were: the two women sitting together at the end of the sixth row with Alec and John on either side of them. Seats were gradually filling up, the noise of voices and activity giving Mia a childlike thrill. A large 'mature' woman settled herself into the row in front of them; when she turned to face the nondescript man beside her, Mia caught a glimpse of a very powdered face and a whiff of perfume, and heard the woman ask in a perfectly modulated voice, 'Did you bring the barley sugar?' An excited child behind them was saying, 'Peter's in this, isn't he? Isn't he, Dad?' And from somewhere above them they could hear thuds and footsteps.

'Shocking acoustics,' John remarked, glancing upward. 'This could be dodgy.'

'Someone must be in the upstairs offices,' Alec said. 'They'll stop when the show starts.'

Mia leaned toward Sheryl, who was loosening her scarf and freeing a profusion of blonde ringlets. 'Who did you say is looking after Tahls?'

'Alec's mother.' Sheryl made her eyes starey to convey barely-controlled alarm. 'Which is why I have a medium-sized knot in my stomach, and why we're sitting on the end of a row in case we need to make a hasty get-away.

Alec has assured me she doesn't eat little children for dinner, but...'

The play was *Some Girls*, a dark comedy about a man who meets up with four ex-lovers before his upcoming wedding, seeking completion or insights or perhaps even an escape.... John read the brief summary of the show aloud from the program to Sheryl and Alec, who had agreed to come without knowing what it was about.

'Should be a few laughs in this,' Sheryl said. 'For those of us who haven't been out in months to play with grown-ups, it's all very exciting.'

'So how's the grass-cutting business going?' Alec asked, leaning forward from the other side of Sheryl. 'Do you do much gardening as well, or just lawns?'

'I'm strictly a 'Mow, Blow and Go' man,' John said gravely.

Mia gave a little snort. 'That sounds terrible!'

'It's building up nicely but I'm doing battle with hay fever at the moment, so I'm thinking it's almost time to exit stage left.'

'That was a very brief career!' Sheryl dug Mia in the ribs and whispered. 'Lots of change and unpredictability now! Can you keep up?'

'From what I gather it's potentially quite lucrative.' Alec was looking at John with a slight frown, as if something didn't add up. It was not surprising, Mia thought; he and John had always had plenty to talk about when John was working at Buxton. Being in management, Alec had a fair grasp of the financial side of the business and they would fall into conversations about things like the effect of staff and legislation on profit whenever their paths crossed. Now that John appeared to have turned his back on that old world, Alec had been cast adrift. Actually, they were all watching John, wondering what he'd do next. It was almost dizzying... She hadn't yet told Sheryl about the massage course he'd already signed up for. Sheryl would be amazed.

The lights flickered and the child behind them called out in an excited voice, 'It's starting!'

They were both sitting and frowning at their screens: John on his laptop working on spreadsheets for the charity or projections of print sales or something, and Mia psyching herself up to make that final course commitment. She'd been accepted and just had to pay the deposit, especially if she wanted to take advantage of the spring intake, which started in a few days. It would be nice to be starting her new course at the same time as John started his… But she had to commit right now. The deadline was today. She dithered for another few minutes and then hit 'submit'.

'I've done it,' she said.

'What?' John asked, distracted.

'Signed up for the course. So we'll both be students now. Students with part-time jobs and part-time incomes and your student loan.'

'That's great,' he said. He was obviously still concentrating on whatever he was doing.

The thought of their income taking a further dive was unsettling. She clicked her online banking tab and typed in her password. She'd been expecting it, but their joint account balance gave her a little jolt of alarm. The loss of rental income wouldn't be affecting them yet – those tenants had only been a month behind before doing the bunk, and John's payout from Buxton had been quite nice, so why…? She began to scroll down the entries. Groceries, rent, gas, internet, Tarocash… $197.

'You been buying clothes?' she asked.

John looked up. 'Yeah. New shirt. New pair of pants. Why?'

She focused back on the screen and kept scrolling. There was a payment to the JHFLBA Charity – the 'John Hartington Foundation For Late-Blooming Artists'. $800. She wasn't too bothered about this. They'd reimburse themselves once the boys' inheritances came through and once they had proper funding in place for the charity. John had opened accounts for the charity and the sales of his father's prints, but both had been set up in the UK, of course, so she had no idea what funds were being deposited.

She scrolled down further. Another $800. And another… each about a week apart.

John's phone rang and he answered. 'No,' he said at once, and something in his tone of voice caught her attention. She glanced up but he was pressing the lid of his laptop shut and standing and moving toward the door.

She kept scrolling. There weren't many payments recorded for his lawn mowing work since most of it was cash. 'Beth $40' and 'Jo $70' must be for lawns, though. There was another $800 going out to the UK account. And back in July, at the end of the month before he'd come back home, $2000… Her forehead puckered in a frown. She'd have to ask him – this was a lot of their money going out when they were about to be earning much less… She couldn't hear him anymore – he was probably standing in front of the calendar in the kitchen booking a garden. Although that hadn't sounded like his 'clients' voice: too curt.

A door closed and a moment later she saw him outside, still on the phone. He looked like he was arguing with someone. Probably Jake. And if the bugger was spending their money inappropriately, she was right with him!

Mia logged out of banking and stretched and yawned. She hadn't felt like eating much today – a bit queasy. But now she was hungry. She ran a mental check of the contents of the fridge and pantry, wondering what to make. What she really felt like was Mexican: beans and cheese and sour cream and avocado and burritos, but that was a sure recipe for an unsettled stomach…

Abandoning her computer, she headed into the kitchen. Opened the fridge and stood there gazing inside, seeking inspiration.

The front door slammed and John strode into the kitchen. 'Jake's on his way.'

'What?' She closed the fridge and turned to face him. 'Now?'

'He rang from Heathrow. He's boarding in ten minutes.'

'My God! No more notice than that?'

'I told you. He's a pushy git. Once he gets an idea in his head…'

'Oh well… It'll be all right. When does he arrive?'

'Tuesday night. Nine p.m.'

'God. That's awkward timing. Both our courses start on Wednesday…

Oh well. I'll get the spare room ready. Have to confess I'm curious to meet this badass.'

John said nothing, arms crossed, mouth tightly shut. She could see a pulse ticking in his jaw.

'You're not that upset, are you?'

'You don't understand!' he muttered. And stormed out of the room.

17

On Monday night after work Mia rolled up her sleeves to tackle the paraphernalia that had collected in the guest room. There were four empty cardboard boxes already in the room, one that had recently contained a flat screen TV… She labelled them *'Donate', 'Fix/Action', 'Put somewhere else???'* and *'Recycle'* and then stood the boxes in the hallway outside the guest room with a rubbish bin and the laundry basket. Bitsy came nosing around, sniffing everything she moved.

John poked his head around the door. 'Can I help?' And sneezed.

'I'll call out if I need you,' she said. 'There isn't room in here for two – three, including Bits. But I do need to know what you want to do about all that old paperwork.'

'Mm.' He frowned, following her pointed finger to the stacked archive boxes.

'I know you like to keep old records, but really, this is ridiculous. Surely everything older than seven years can go?'

'You're right,' he said, in a moment of decisiveness that took her completely by surprise. 'Toss them.'

'You don't want to store them in the garage?' she called after him, doubt edging in.

'Toss them!' he called back, sneezing again as he retreated.

'What about the exercise bike?' she shouted. That thing took up so much space and was completely redundant now that he went out cycling every day.

'It goes!' he called.

Wow. That was easy. So much for old habits and sentimental value. She turned back to the room, taking a measure of the mess that remained, and put the timer on for fifteen minutes. Not that she was allowed out of here till she'd finished, but it felt less overwhelming in small chunks.

The ironing pile (which included some of John's shirts from before his trip to England...) was easy. She carried it into the living room and set the iron and board up next to the sofa where John was sitting and reading something on his laptop.

Mia tapped him on the shoulder. 'You can iron these. That would help.'

He looked up in mild alarm but said, 'Sure.'

Back in the guest room, Mia surveyed the piles of stuff lying on the couch-bed and in the open wardrobe and reminded herself sternly to do the big stuff first. No looking through papers and photos yet or she'd never finish. So... Bitsy's dog crate – the garage or up in the top of the wardrobe? The suitcase needed to go back up there too – it had been on the floor since John's return. She called him back in for help to lift those big things up the top, and he handed down long dusty rolls of Christmas wrapping paper and bags of decorations that had been pushed to the back.

'Can't they stay up there?'

'You're the boss.' He shoved the dog crate and suitcases to the back and replaced the Christmas stuff.

'But near the front so we can see them and remember they're there.'

He saluted. 'Done.' And climbed off the stepladder.

There were no less than five bags and briefcases that he'd received at various conferences. 'Before you go,' she said. 'What about these?'

He looked at them blankly.

'Pick the one you think you'll use and I'll op shop the rest.'

'Okay. That one.'

'Do you think so?' She picked up the brief case with the least obnoxious branding and the most sections. 'I reckon you'd get more use out of this one.'

He looked at her. 'Well, if you know better, you decide.'

'It's up to you – they're yours. I just don't remember you ever using that one whereas you've used this one a few times.'

'You're right,' he said. 'That one.' And withdrew. A moment later he put his head back around the door. 'No, actually, I think I'd like to go with my original decision.' And disappeared again.

Hm. O-kay. She put the rejected bags and briefcases into the 'Donate' box and put the chosen one in the 'Move' box, to be parked in his wardrobe where he'd be reminded to use it. The exercise bike was in the hallway with a mental 'eBay' note.

There were board games in here that they'd never played and others they hadn't played in years. She sat on the edge of the bed for a moment contemplating their abandoned intention: games, jigsaw puzzles and interaction instead of TV. What had become of that plan? And, more importantly, now what? Resurrect the old intention or be realistic and give up on it? Maybe they'd play a few games with Jake? Something to break the tension between the boys if it got uncomfortable... She put the games in the 'Move' box. Maybe she'd be able to arrange them in the living room in an attractive kind of way. After all, out of sight, out of mind; in view, they might remember to play them.

The timer went off so she formally congratulated herself on what had been achieved thus far – fighting a brief fight about rewarding herself with chocolate, and managing to resist – and programmed the timer for another fifteen.

Their big winter coats were stored in the spare room wardrobe, and so were some of John's best suits, in their protective bags, and the dress she'd worn to Sheryl's wedding as matron of honour. She carried them into the bedroom and opened the wardrobe doors. Having sorted through her clothes before John got back she actually had a little more room in here – enough to squeeze the dress and a couple of coats... John's side was pretty full but she pushed everything along and managed to fit all but a bulky jacket that went back into the spare room wardrobe.

Wedding gifts were the next thing. They stood on the wardrobe shelves, still in their boxes. Duplicate items and big crystal dishes they never used and odd little gifts from family and friends that they didn't want to give away but didn't want to keep either... What had that decluttering expert recommended? You hold each item in your hand and ask yourself, *'Do I love this? Do I use it? Does it make me feel good?'* If yes, you keep it; if no, it goes. Immediately. No argument.

But what about items that John valued, like the tartan lampshade his aunt Meredith had posted from Scotland that had sat in here ever since it had arrived? She parked it in the 'Donate' box, ready to have it out with him when he saw it there. *'Do you love it?'* she'd ask him, hands on hips. *'Do you use it? Does it make you feel good?'*

Back in the guest room she contemplated the collection of hiking boots and old soccer balls and tennis balls and cricket bats that lay in the dust at the bottom of the wardrobe. More ancient intentions that had gone to ruin... But maybe one day when their kids were old enough...

Kids.

Pregnancy.

Period.

She stopped, thinking. What was the date? When had she last...? Went quickly to the computer, barely aware of John standing at the ironing board in front of the TV, and checked her diary. Last period: 2nd - 7th August. Today was the 12th September. She was late. She was late!!! A thrill of delight rushed through her. She glanced at John, his arm automatically moving back and forth along the ironing board as he watched some action movie. Would she say? Not yet. Not yet. Wait a little longer. Wait until she was sure.

She quit out of her calendar and went back to the guest room, unable to stop smiling. Now that the horrible big 'clean-out-the-guest-room' job was almost done, when Jake left they'd get rid of the uncomfortable couch-bed (she hoped he'd sleep okay; she and John hated it), and replace it with a crib. Talia's nursery flashed into her mind. She remembered shopping for baby things with Sheryl; this time, Sheryl would come with her.

'Stop. Don't count your chickens,' she told herself sternly. And forced herself back to the job at hand. Bats and balls. Right. Where should they go? The garage! She carried them out to the 'Move' box, dropping a tennis ball on her way that Bitsy leapt on and immediately began to worry, butting it away with her nose and then leaping on it with a shrill bark.

'Out, Bits,' she said firmly, closing the door. 'You can't do that in here.'

It was time to face the big plastic storage box full of old birthday cards and letters and theatre programs and craft supplies and memorabilia. She set the timer again, placed the lid of the tub on the bed beside her, and looked at the mess inside. The main thing filling up this box was her old journals and diaries. She counted them: fourteen. It seemed ridiculous to keep so many but she had never yet been able to turf any of them. She opened one at random, and read a snatch of her teenage thoughts in a big looping script:

'... instead of the party. Michelle was sitting in the front with Chris, of course, so I was stuck in the back with Matthew, who kept trying to pull me over for a kiss and there is no way on this earth –'

The memory of it made Mia smile and yet she still felt the shadow of a knot in her stomach from the anxiety of keeping someone at bay who didn't interest her, and pretending disinterest in the one who did. Ridiculous that she should still feel tension at the memory, even if it was very slight. Another diary caught her eye – her travel journal. She flicked through it, moments of those weeks in Europe coming back to mind as she saw postcards and tickets and read the odd entry.

Met a very cute English guy... Not like the rest of the crowd on this party cruise. He's quiet, a bit shy, a thinker. He pulled me out of the water when I missed my footing on the ramp, being a bit tipsy... and sat with me for hours while the others were getting wasted, as usual. I think I coughed up half the ocean and he was totally lovely about it. Usually I'd be so embarrassed about being such a klutz but he distracted me with stories about life in England, laying on the accent till I had a stitch from laughing...

She flicked through the journal pages and read again:

John booked us rooms in a gorgeous villa in Spain and we had an absolutely magic time exploring and making love – mostly making love... I bought a *travel guide and he's been showing off his amazing ability to read upside down. Apparently it's an accountant's skill from all the times they have to talk a client through a presentation, usually sitting opposite.*

As she turned the page, a bundle of envelopes fell out into her lap. Lifting the flap on the top one she remembered, instantly, John's love letters from England during the period they'd been apart. She pulled a thin sheet of paper out, unfolding it and smoothing the wrinkled page against her lap.

> *Dear Mia,*
>
> *I can't stop thinking about you. I'm sitting here at my desk in the offices of Kirkwood and Underling, CPAs, and daydreaming about you. I'm supposed to be entering the numbers of a client's income and expenses, and all I can think about are numbers to do with you:*
>
> *The number of days we spent together in Spain: eight, all wonderful.*
>
> *The number of nights: nine, magnificent.*
>
> *The number of touristy things we did: four – one walking tour, one cathedral, one palace, one volcano. So special sharing them with you…*
>
> *The number of your hostel room in London when I picked you up to meet my folks: 317.*
>
> *I don't want to disturb you so I won't share the other numbers that are coming to mind other than this one: The number of days I want to spend without you: zero.*

She sat with the letters in her hand, remembering her mixed feelings reading them. His intense interest in her had been both exciting and unsettling; he had forced her hand when it came to committing, which was probably a good thing since she had a habit of procrastinating and delaying until she was absolutely certain. She'd been glad of his certainty and leadership – she'd gone with the flow without having to decide for herself.

She'd felt hugely special, and they'd had lots of fun times together at first. But then… what? What had gone wrong? When had it all become boring and tedious? Just gradually, over time, as the newness faded and his accountant personality came to the fore? Was it as simple as that? She was fascinated by these changes in his character from the entertaining tourist-lover to the work-obsessed husband, and now, in the wake of his father's death, to the man with a renewed appetite for life and love…

The timer went off, making her jump. There was no way she was getting rid of any of this memorabilia. She put the letters and journals back in the box and carried it out to their bedroom, tripping over Bitsy as she went and stepping wildly into the rubbish box as she tried to regain her balance. She leaned against the wall while the prickles of adrenalin in her fingers faded away, then stepped out of the rubbish box and carried the plastic tub into the bedroom. She'd just sit it on the floor next to the dresser for now.

Back in the guest room she took a moment to admire the spaciousness. All that remained were a couch-bed and a bedside table and a chair. She'd make the bed tomorrow before they headed out for the airport. And she'd get a pregnancy kit tomorrow.

The traffic was horrendous on Tuesday for some reason. Mia arrived home to an empty house at six forty-five, still stressed from time spent inching forward along jam-packed streets. There must have been an incident somewhere. She took Bitsy for a hurried walk, then whirled through the house making Jake's bed and laying a clean towel and washer on the end of it, then tidying the bathroom while a freezer meal warmed up in the oven.

John arrived from his first day at the massage course at seven-thirty. When she asked how it had gone he said 'Good', and nothing else. He was on edge, restless, frowning. He didn't finish his meal. Mia was preoccupied herself; she hadn't had a chance to pick up a pregnancy kit yet, and the precious secret was burning away inside her. She kept hosing the flames, afraid the fire would leap out of control and she'd say something prematurely or get too excited…

They locked up and headed back out at eight p.m. It was drizzling.

'Well, he'll feel right at home with this dreary weather,' she remarked, as John turned the Commodore onto the main road.

No reply. His jaw was locked; that pulse was ticking.

'So who is going to entertain this brother of yours since we're both working and studying?' she asked. It was crazy timing for them to be hosting a guest!

'He'll just have to amuse himself.' John's hands were gripping the steering wheel so tightly that the skin was smooth across the backs of his hands. He was staring ahead with a fierce concentration.

Mia watched the rear of the car in front of them for a while. A lit-up screen was showing a movie for the passengers in the back.

'I'll pick up a few touristy brochures for him tomorrow,' she said. 'Didn't have a chance today. He should be able to do some sightseeing – if the weather picks up.'

No reply.

The traffic was still moving so slowly.

'And I guess he'll only stay with us for a couple of weeks and then go travelling. Don't you think?'

Silence. Jaw tense. Hands locked on the wheel.

'It'll be fine, John,' she said, giving his thigh a gentle squeeze.

He grunted, not moving to cover her hand with his as he usually would.

To be honest, Mia was intrigued by this charismatic brother who would make such an impulsive decision. She couldn't imagine inviting herself to visit someone halfway across the world with so little notice. But still, why was John so stressed? They'd seemed to be getting on so much better lately. Why all this tension?

She leaned her head back against the headrest and gazed at the wet black roads and shadowy interiors of vehicles passing on her left. The traffic on the freeway was finally beginning to speed up.

'Did I ever tell you,' John said suddenly, 'that he's my twin?'

Mia swivelled to look at him, taken aback. 'No! I thought twins were close –'

'Not all twins,' he said grimly.

'Why did it never come up? Why did you never tell me?'

'You know!' He changed lanes with an unexpectedness that made her look around in alarm to make sure they weren't about to hit anyone or be hit. 'I was always in his shadow. I was sick of him – sick of being compared. If we'd had kids – twins – it would have come up. But it was just such a relief to get away and find myself and not be constantly compared. You wouldn't understand.'

'Well… try me,' she said, exasperated. 'You always said he was your *younger* brother.'

'He is: by eight minutes.'

Silly question. Of course, they couldn't be born simultaneously. But still, why the secrecy? Surely he could have confided in her, his wife?

'I don't get it,' she said. 'It wouldn't have mattered to me. I don't get why you didn't tell me.'

'I was cutting him off. It was symbolic.'

'Yes, but you could have told *me*.'

'I told you you wouldn't understand!'

'Oh. Right.' She set her own jaw, and turned back to look outside the passenger window.

After a moment John reached out and put his hand on her thigh. 'I'm sorry. It's bringing up a heap of stuff for me. It's this bloody barging-in pattern of his.'

She gave a curt nod, saying nothing. But his hand was on her thigh just near her own clasped hands. The impulse to reconnect made her right hand move a little, until it was touching his.

'Imagine Rita coming to life,' he said. 'Turning up out of the blue. How would you feel?'

'That's completely different. Rita was never *in* my life and Jake was closer to you than the average sibling. You can't compare them.'

'Not those relationships, exactly,' he acknowledged, 'but the comparing was there from the beginning for both of us. Oh, never mind!'

He merged with the traffic that was entering the airport and following the arrows to short-term parking. When he'd parked, he exhaled, resting back against the seat with eyes closed for a moment, then turned to face her. 'Sorry. I've been a shit.'

'You two seem to have been getting on so much better lately – apart from the odd quarrel. I thought things were going well.'

He bit his lip. Leaned across and kissed her gently. 'Yeah. It's okay. Just childhood stuff, I suppose. You'll be able to analyse me about it soon, and sort it all out for me.'

She smiled, and kissed him back, one hand on the side of his face. 'Sure, honey. We'll sort you out.'

She was not prepared, when they stood waiting at Arrivals, for the brother emerging from the doors with his trolley and big old tattered backpack, to be an identical twin. A replica of John. His absolute spitting image.

18

She clutched John's arm. 'He's an identical twin?'

'Yes.'

'Why didn't you tell me!'

'I thought...' John took a step forward and waved to his brother, who had hesitated and was scanning the waiting crowd.

They both watched as Jake smiled, waved, and headed toward them. The same smile. He had the same beautiful smile.

Mia felt frozen with shock. She watched her husband's replica weave his way through the crowds and then come out from behind his trolley to shake hands with John. He turned to face her. Same hazel eyes. Same build. Same smile. She held out her hand automatically and felt absurdly as if she were shaking hands with her own husband. The formality felt all wrong – she wanted to hug him. As if he'd read her mind, he leaned in and wrapped his arms around her, saying, 'We are family, right?' in that very English accent, and held her for longer than you would hug a stranger, but this was Jake, right? The womaniser...

'How was the trip?' John, breaking in, an edge to his voice.

'Not bad.' Jake, finally letting her go. Something... intense... in those hazel eyes as he held her gaze before she broke away, flushing.

'My God,' Mia said. 'You two... you're so alike!' Looking from one to the other in amazement. 'You could switch on me and I'd never know.'

They both laughed. Jake returned to his trolley – he had the same pointing-outwards feet! – and John took her hand in his, with an almost possessive firmness. She found herself looking from one to the other in wonder.

As they walked toward the exit she asked, 'Did you guys ever do those twin pranks – swapping places at school to test people?'

'No,' John said at once. 'We weren't that close when we were kids. We were very competitive.'

'Yes, we did,' Jake contradicted. 'Don't you remember, John? The time you did that test for me, for instance?'

John darted an unreadable look at his brother. His comments about the many years of tension between them now made more sense to Mia, but she was entranced by this new development. There was a 'Don't Touch' sign around their 'twinness', but she felt irresistibly drawn to reach out with a gentle, exploratory finger... Another question bubbled out of her before she could stop it: 'What's it like, having a double?'

'We're very different,' they both said, almost in unison, and then John added, 'That's probably one of the questions that made us the most furious about being twins,' and Jake asked over the top of him, 'Hasn't John ever told you that he has an identical twin?'

'No,' she said. 'The bugger. He held out on me! I gather you two have had a... tumultuous relationship.'

'You could say that,' Jake said.

'Is that normal for twins?'

'Not all twins but many have a difficult relationship.'

They'd emerged into the night air. Not drizzling now. John led the way toward short-term car parking.

'You'll have to forgive me if I ask a whole lot of stupid questions,' Mia enthused, 'but I'm so intrigued! I don't know any other identical twins and, of course, I wasn't prepared for this,' shooting an expression of mock irritation at John. 'So tell me, why does that question make you so furious?'

'Because we're not doubles,' John said patiently, as if speaking to a child. 'We're two individuals who happen to share the same genes.'

'But doesn't that make you very alike? You certainly look alike. I mean, tastes, habits, interests –?'

'An accountant and an actor,' Jake broke in. 'Very different.'

'There are lots of differences,' John added curtly. 'You'll find out over the next couple of weeks.'

'All right, last question and then I'll shut up: do you have a psychic connection? Do you know each other's thoughts, or when something has happened to the other one?'

They'd arrived at the car. John made a deal of unlocking it with the remote and lifting Jake's backpack off the trolley and into the boot; Jake moved in quickly to help. 'Not exactly a psychic connection,' he said, placing a box beside the backpack. 'I think you have to be close for that, and we're not. But when we're living together we do tend to finish each other's sentences. And we often know what the other is thinking.'

'It's so fascinating!'

'Mm,' said John, shutting the boot with a little bang. He came around to the side of the car and opened the passenger door for her and the back door for Jake.

Mia swivelled in her seat to face Jake as well as she could from the front as John drove out of the airport precinct. Jake was looking around with interest, almost avoiding her eye. She could see John's rigid expression in profile. She sighed and turned back to the front. This was not going to be an effortless experience…

Part way home she said, remembering, 'I'm so impressed with your father's artwork, Jake. It's just stunning.'

'Yes. The old man was much better than we realised. He'd always been good at sketching but the painting was something he got into after we left home, so we didn't know much about that until he died and we found all those canvases in the attic.'

'Not even you, living in the U.K.?'

The brothers exchanged glances in the rear view mirror.

'I was aware that he was painting and I did encourage him,' Jake said, 'but

I was often away and Mum was a bit of a wet blanket about it, so he never acted on the encouragement, This charity idea is an act of atonement; it's our way of giving others like him what he should have received.'

'I think it's a great idea,' she said warmly. 'I really do.'

'Thanks.'

'Have you found a gallery yet? A home for his work and the charity itself?'

'We're close,' he said. 'I'm looking at a few that are promising.'

Bitsy went even more berserk than usual when they arrived. Mia would have loved to know what her dog-nose was discovering about these identical twins. She leapt up at Jake repeatedly, even after he had squatted to give her a good, long, greeting rub.

'You've got a lovely place,' he remarked as they showed him through to the guest room.

'Thank you,' she said, and felt honour-bound to warn him about the bed. 'Hope you sleep okay. It's a couch bed and it's not the best. There's a hard sort of ridge...'

'It'll be fine,' he said, his back to her as he laid his box on the floor beside the curtained window.

'Cup of tea?' she asked, hovering in the doorway.

'Thank you. That would be lovely.'

'Are you hungry?'

'No. Thanks.'

'Honestly,' she whispered to John in the kitchen as they boiled the kettle and collected cups. 'I am flabbergasted.'

'Do you forgive me?' he asked, taking her arm and turning her towards him. 'For holding out on you?'

'I'm still too shocked to know what I think. I thought I knew you... I thought you'd shared your life with me as honestly as I've shared mine. I'm...'

Bitsy was giving excited little yaps; they moved apart, sensing footsteps and movement in the doorway. John released her arm and opened the fridge for milk as Jake entered.

'I won't keep you people up late,' Jake said. 'I know you've got work tomorrow.' He was holding the box out toward Mia. 'Just a little gift for you as thanks for accepting this gate-crashing stranger...'

'A *little* gift!' She received the box and took it to the table. John opened the utensils drawer and passed her some scissors. 'You didn't have to,' she said. 'Family...'

'It was very short notice. I'm an impulsive kind of guy.'

'So I've heard,' she said, slicing through the tape and releasing the tabs on the box. 'Oh my goodness! There's a whole hamper in here.'

John came to stand at her elbow as she opened the lid and lifted out a cute brown bear dressed as a Queen's Guard.

'It's gorgeous. But...' looking in the box again, the bear cuddled to her chest, 'there's so much more! You didn't need to..."

John went back to pouring tea and Jake helped himself to a seat at the table while Mia took item after item out of the box. 'Assorted toffees and fudge... a set of preserves packed in an English phone box – how cute! An Eton mess pudding – what's that?'

'It's mostly meringue,' John said, putting their cups on the table and picking the package up to read the ingredients. 'Flippin' 'eck, bro!'

'Shortbread...' Mia continued. 'English breakfast tea... and the royal coat-of-arms packaging – of course! A lavender-scented candle... A tea towel of a London scene...'

'May I see?' John took it from her and shook it out. 'That's Dad's!'

'Prototype. What do you think?' Jake asked.

John nodded. 'Looks good. We can definitely sell those.'

'So this is the first one?' Mia asked, admiring her father-in-law's sketch imprinted on the cloth.

'This and a couple I had made for Mum,' Jake replied.

Mia lifted out the now empty, wicker basket. 'Thank you, Jake. It's all utterly lovely. Let's eat something now!'

'There's more,' he said.

She looked back into the box in surprise, and found, folded at the bottom, a beautiful blue knotted throw rug. 'Oh my God! Jake, you shouldn't have.' The fabric was lovely to touch; it would not have been cheap. 'You must have known!' she burbled. 'We've been needing a throw rug for the sofa. I'm going to see –'

She carried it into the lounge room, unfolding it as she went and then tossing it over the back of the sofa. 'It's gorgeous! Come and see, John!'

The boys followed her in.

'Very nice,' John said, a little stiffly.

'Wow,' Jake remarked. 'That's some TV...'

'I'm feeling very treated lately,' Mia beamed. 'All of this you've just given us, and yes, John surprised me with the big TV a couple of weeks ago, and he bought me a gorgeous dress... I'm feeling very spoilt.'

'Good times,' Jake murmured. 'The throw suits the room, don't you think? A lucky stab.'

'As if it was designed for it,' Mia said admiringly.

'What do you want to open?' John asked over his shoulder as he returned to the kitchen. 'The shortbreads?'

'Perfect,' she called back, giving the rug a last stroke and straightening its edge. Jake was looking at her, that same intense look as at the airport.

'Thank you,' she said. This was so bizarre. She felt as if she could so easily just go up and give him a big hug. She felt as if she'd known him for years! Appearances were obviously very powerful when it came to creating a sense of affinity. What a trip this was! Jake took a small step toward her.

'Tea's getting cold!' John called from the kitchen.

Suddenly Mia felt uncomfortable. Awkward. Feigning a light-hearted smile, she beckoned to Jake to follow her and rejoined John in the kitchen, where he was tipping shortbreads onto a plate.

They toasted Jake's trip with the tea and crunched through a few of the butter-soft shortbreads in the silence that was emerging between them.

'Now, in the morning,' Mia said, to break it, 'we'll try not to wake you up. There's plenty of breakfast food in the fridge and pantry, so just help yourself; and cups and plates up in those cupboards'.

Jake was watching her rather than where she was pointing. 'Don't worry about waking me,' he said. 'I'll be doing the sleep of the dead, probably. My problem is going to be getting to sleep tonight. So if you hear me walking around...'

'That's fine. Feel free to watch something...' gesturing in the direction of the TV.

'Thanks. I'll keep it quiet if I do.'

'I'll find you some tourist info tomorrow so you can do some exploring,' she went on.

'That'd be great.'

'Actually, you can give me a hand with some of the lawn mowing,' John cut in. 'Earn your keep.'

He was smiling easily; Jake regarded him with a slightly set jaw. Mia looked from one to the other. It was as if there was some challenge or test going on between them – she couldn't tell what.

'Sure,' Jake agreed. 'What time do you start? I'll be ready.'

'Not tomorrow, surely!' she objected. 'Let the guy sleep in after his long trip.'

'I'm not working tomorrow anyway,' John replied. 'I'm at the massage course.'

'You and me both,' she grinned, remembering with a burst of excitement. 'I'm starting a counselling course tomorrow,' she told Jake. 'I've been thinking about it for ages and finally bit the bullet. As for this stranger,' indicating John, 'he came back from England a changed man! Left the company where he's worked as an accountant for the last ten years to start gardening – and now massage! But I'm sure you know all this.'

'Yes.' Jake leaned back in his seat, eyes on John. 'I was amazed. My stuffy older brother suddenly breaking the mould and having some fun.'

'I wouldn't exactly call cutting grass 'fun', John returned. 'But I'm definitely enjoying being out of… petrochemicals.'

'Not that you were ever really in them,' Jake said. 'Just the numbers, right?'

'Right.' John drained his cup. 'Well, I'm ready for bed. Mia?'

The tension between the brothers was palpable. She was fascinated. The counsellor-to-be in her was itching to uncover what had happened in their childhoods to set them against each other like this. Was it normal for twins? She'd do some research… She drank the last of her tea and rose.

John took her cup and placed it in the sink with his. He looped an arm around her shoulders and said to Jake, 'Sleep well, bro.'

Jake sat up a little, meeting John's eye and avoiding hers. 'Thanks. You too.'

On an impulse, Mia reached forward and picked up the London bear from where it was sitting on the table, leaning against the Eton pudding. 'I'm taking my bear to bed with me! I'll have to think of a name for him. The only one I can think of right now is Paddington.' She laughed at her own silliness; neither brother laughed with her.

It was strange undressing with someone else in the house, someone who looked so like her husband. John drew her close as soon as she lay down, one hand roaming down her back, circling her hip, cupping her buttocks… 'I don't think I can,' she whispered. 'I feel too self-conscious.'

He made a little sound, as if his breath was catching in his throat, and contented himself with stroking her hair. They lay together in the quiet house, listening as Jake rinsed out his cup and pushed chairs in around the kitchen table, and walked back to the guest room. They heard him moving around in there, and then he went to the bathroom, and they could hear the low rumble of his voice talking to Bitsy, who hadn't followed them into the bedroom as she usually did. They'd closed the door, of course, so she'd have to get up later to let Bitsy in or listen to scratching all night. That was her last blurry thought as she drifted off to sleep in her husband's arms.

19

The door to the guest room was closed when Mia and John rose in the morning. He'd slept in too late to go cycling so they breakfasted together and left the house together, he for the second day of the massage course and she for the first day of her counselling course.

'Bit of an unwelcome to a new country,' she said, car door open, one foot on the sill as John commanded the garage door to rise with the remote.

'Serves him right for giving us so little notice.'

'Yes, true. But don't be too hard on him. He's here now, so we've just got to get on with it.' She folded her arms on the top of the door frame and looked at him across the roof of the car. 'To be honest, I'm really happy about this chance to get to know you better as well. Having him here opens up your whole family to me. I've been thinking about this ever since you said he'd be coming over. I haven't shown nearly enough interest in your family... I suppose that's because you never wanted to talk about them but I could have shown more interest and drawn you out! I feel really bad about that now.'

'Don't feel bad. It's not your fault. I set it up like that.'

'I know, but... I've been really self-absorbed too.'

He regarded her with an inscrutable expression. 'Well, I guess everything will be different now.'

'Yes.'

'Have a great day.' He came around to her driver's door and, holding her face on either side, kissed her tenderly. 'Enjoy the course. I love you, Mia.'

Stunning how just the littlest bit of tenderness broke her up. She could feel tears already pricking her eyes. 'I love you too, John Hartington.' Kissed him back, ran her fingers through his hair and down the side of his face. 'Enjoy your course, you master-massager. And be good!'

'Good or good at it?' He was grinning now, lines crinkling the skin around his eyes, winking at her.

She laughed and batted him away. *'Good!'* And on reflection: *'And* good at it – but just with me.'

'Oh! Right! So you're going to clip my wings, are you!'

She flapped little constrained chicken wings at him and he laughed and returned to his car.

Mia drove out of the garage and John followed a moment later, and they left his sleeping identical twin brother alone in their home to amuse himself for a whole day.

It was as exhilarating to walk through the doors at ACCAT and turn left toward the training rooms as Mia had expected. She glimpsed Susan in the admin area, open laptop in her arms as she read something to Milenko – perhaps her clipboard had been shredded now that they were paperless? Milenko was hovering beside her and pointing to the screen, and they appeared to be arguing.

Mia smiled and strolled in the opposite direction, following a woman in her 50s with straggling blonde-grey hair piled in a loose knot on top of her head, and a girl who might have just finished school a few days ago, who was wearing a short summer dress over bare legs (despite the fact that it was still quite cold) and a pair of chunky black ankle boots. A tattoo that looked like ivy snaked up the calf of her right leg. There was already a young man in the room, rocking back in his chair and chatting to Reynald, who was setting up his Powerpoint.

Mia took a central seat, and Reynald gave her a warm smile. She sat there, excited, nervous, watching as the door opened and new students entered, listening to the young man who was confident and relaxed and giving his opinions about who should be selected to play in the approaching footy Grand Final. A man in his 40s entered, phone to his ear, and took a seat at the side of the room by the windows, turning away from the rest of them to finish his call. They were a smallish group – just eight. That would mean lots of personal attention, which would be both good and bad…

Right on the knocker of nine a.m. Reynald cleared his throat and welcomed them. He acknowledged their desire to be of service to others and shared how much this vocation meant to him. Then he invited them to introduce themselves, and Mia settled into enjoying a peek into stranger's lives. The man by the window was a drugs and alcohol support worker who wanted to upskill, she discovered. The girl who looked like she was straight out of school was actually twenty-eight; she was very intense about wanting to 'help people', explaining that she was a hairdresser whose clients and friends always came to her for advice. Many of them had told her she should be a psychologist and she'd thought about that but a one-year course compared to four or more years was much more appealing to begin with so that was why she was here. The woman with straggly hair was an interior decorator now seeking a new vocation; she observed clients gaining a new lease on life by successfully changing their physical surroundings and wanted to now work with people on their inner life – true interior design, she quipped, laughing at her own joke. The young man was a support worker for an AIDS organisation who was also upskilling. A plump woman in black had experienced trauma of some kind – she didn't say what – and wanted to help those in similar circumstances. A smartly-dressed woman in her 30s said that she had no desire to work as a counsellor but just wanted to do the course for her own interest and growth. And a very tattooed young man who had arrived late told them he was an ex-drug user on parole, now learning what he could to help others. Mia felt very ordinary beside them.

When everyone had been introduced, Reynald walked around to sit on the edge of his desk. He looked from student to student, making eye contact with everyone in turn. 'So… how many of you have been told that you're very intuitive or you give great advice?'

A few hands waved. Mia glanced involuntarily at the tattooed hairdresser; she was listening intently.

'Feels good, huh?'

Some nods, some comments of affirmation.

'All right. So now just let that go. You're not training to be a counsellor to give advice. If you want to do that, we suggest you go work for the Citizen's Advice Bureau.'

A few people tittered at this comment. He smiled.

'As counsellors we're here to *listen*, to reflect back to our clients so *they* can resolve their own problems. We are not here to solve their problems for them or to tell them what to do or to show how clever we are.'

There was a little silence in the room as he looked from one to the other again. Tattooed Hairdresser was still staring at Reynald intently.

'This path is not about imposing your beliefs on others. It's not about imposing your experiences or your solutions on others. If you've had some trauma in your life – and most of us have; and if you've managed to transform that so that it doesn't hamper you, *well done*. But your solution, what worked for you, might not be appropriate for someone else, so just put that aside. This is no longer about you; it's about the client. Our position, here at ACCAT, is that we are not the expert. The client is the expert in their own life; your expertise is going to be in assisting them in resolving their issues. You'll be standing side-by-side with them, looking at their problems as a colleague, rather than assuming you have the answers.'

Mia sensed a ripple of surprise from some of the students seated around her. She was quite glad about this 'anti-expert' position: she knew so little herself that she couldn't possibly advise anyone else on how to resolve their issues – it was the irony of all time that she was even sitting here! Learning how to guide others in finding their own answers felt like much safer ground than being the font of wisdom.

She wondered if this course would give her insights into how she and John had gone from in love to bored to back in love. And was she always just living in reaction to him – falling in love because he was in love with her? Agreeing to marry because he wanted to marry her? Losing interest in their relationship because he had? Falling in love again because he had returned with a renewed passion? She didn't like this image of herself as merely reactive, but she couldn't deny the evidence.

And now there was Jake in the mix: an opportunity to learn more about her husband as his twin brother slotted jigsaw pieces into the gappy puzzle that was 'John Hartington'… She remembered his comment the other night: 'The whole point of me coming out here was to get some breathing space from Jake.' 'I thought it was to marry me,' she had said. '*And* that,' John had replied. *'And that.'*

But perhaps she had never been the first thing on John's mind. Perhaps he hadn't been coming to Australia for her but to escape Jake. She had an unsettled feeling at the thought, but again her truth-telling conscience squatted on her shoulder and hissed in her ear, 'But you didn't entirely want him either. You weren't sure. You *both* had mixed feelings.'

The elegant woman sitting beside Mia was asking a question. Mia jerked herself back to full concentration on the class. There would be time to analyse herself later.

There was a text message from Sheryl when she checked her phone at lunchtime in the Ladies:

> How goes the new course? And how are things with The Brother?

> So far so good with the course. The Brother is an IDENTICAL TWIN!!!

She wondered how Jake was doing, rattling around their strange house on his own. Watching TV? Reading? Would an actor be interested in business texts (John's) or romance novels and self-help books (hers)? They'd left the fridge pretty full so he could make himself a meal, but their home was in suburbia and they hadn't had time to explain the public transport system to him. Oh well, he was a grown man. And he had Google. She presumed he'd brought a smartphone with him.

No answer from Sheryl. She dropped her phone back into her bag, flushed, and exited the loo. Susan was in the bathroom washing her hands very thoroughly and staring at her reflection. Her lips were pursed, forehead furrowed. Mia would not have liked being at the receiving end of that severe expression. For a moment she wondered what it would be like inside Susan's head: not pleasant, she sensed.

'Hi.' Mia joined her co-PA at the sink.

Susan's eyes shifted sideways to take her image in. 'It's the new recruit. Enjoying the course?'

'Loving it!'

Susan nodded, and went back to washing her hands. She finished, shook them vigorously, switched both taps off at once, and turned to the dryer.

Mia's phone rang. She wiped her hands on her bum and searched around in her bag for it. Sheryl. Tried to swipe 'accept call' and nothing happened. Wiped her hand again and tried swiping again. The call cut off. Phones! *You have a missed call from…'* Damn. She was just navigating back to her Favourites for Sheryl's number when Sheryl rang again, and this time she was able to answer. Susan was leaving the bathroom now, so Mia stayed put.

'He's an identical *twin*?' Sheryl hissed. 'Got to be quiet – Tahls is asleep in my arms. Give *all*. What the fuck!'

'I know.'

'He's never told you? John's never told you that?'

'Never.'

'That is, like…'

'I know.'

'A bit sick. Or sad. Or something.'

'I know.'

'Stop saying you know. How do you feel about it?'

'Shocked.'

The bathroom door opened and two women from the course entered: Ms Straggly-Hair and Ms Elegant. Mia slung her bag over her shoulder, smiled at them, and headed out, phone still pressed to her ear.

'And betrayed, I would think,' Sheryl said.

'Yes, a bit of that.'

'There was always something about John...' she said. 'Something... hidden...'

'You've never said that before.'

'I just figured it out now. There was always something... but I couldn't put my finger on it.'

'That's not all,' Mia said, suddenly unable to hold the news back. But she'd arrived at the lifts, and workers and students from her floor were collecting beside her, everyone waiting for a ride down to the café.

'What?' Sheryl demanded. Madam Impatience.

'Hang on... Tell me your news for a minute.'

'Can't talk?'

'Not just now.'

The lift pinged, the door opened, people emerged and those waiting entered, Mia moving in with them.

'Okay. Let me see...' Sheryl continued in a low voice. Mia could imagine Talia tucked into her arm, delicate little eyelids closed and flickering as she slept. 'I'm in conversation with this other events company I was telling you about – the one that's in trouble. They specialise in entertainment and managing local council events like concerts in the park and community days. They've got a pretty extensive database of performers. I'm pretty close to buying the company.'

'That's awesome! Wow. But why are they in trouble?'

'Just bad management. Nothing that can't be sorted, and it will be a great way for me to cut out the middle man when I need an entertainer. Can you talk now?'

'Almost.' Mia angled herself away from the other passengers in the lift and spoke as quietly as she could. 'So you'll be a mega events management company with a branch that deals with entertainment as well as conferences. Is it biting off too much?'

'Alec's looking at it with me, and we've got my accountant on the job. Don't worry – I won't leap unless I know I'm going to land.'

'Good. After all, you're a mother now. You've got to be there for Tahls. You can't go sticking Talia into childcare all day.' *And be there for me, when I have my baby,* she thought. *I want us to be mothering together.*

There was a moment of silence, during which the lift doors opened at the ground floor and Mia emerged with the others.

'No.' Another little silence. 'Mia –'

'I'm out now. I can tell you my news.'

'Good! What is it?'

Mia moved through the automatic glass doors into the weak spring sunshine. The air was cold. She found a sheltered spot on the sunny side of one of the big marble columns at the entrance, conscious that she must hurry up if she was going to order and eat her salad and get to a pharmacy and walk the three blocks to the Visitor Information Centre for some brochures for Jake before the lunch break was over.

'I think I'm pregnant,' she whispered.

For a moment there was no reply, and then Sheryl exclaimed, 'Oh my God that's great! Congratulations. Does John know?'

'Don't congratulate me yet. I've still got to do the test. But I'm late, which is unusual for me. I'm on my way to get a kit now.'

'There. You see? I told you you'd be having your own baby!'

'You did. I'm so excited about doing this with you! I'll still be studying and having to work part-time, I guess, after maternity leave, but eventually I'll leave ACCAT altogether and just be a mum and a counsellor.' The thought of it was thrilling; Mia couldn't keep the smile off her face.

'September, October, November, December,' Sheryl was mumbling. 'January, February, March, April, May – you're going to have a May baby. A lovely autumn baby. But... Mia, I hate to say this, honey, but I'll be back at work full-time by then.'

Now Mia was silent. She cast a glance at the café and saw that the queue still reached out to the door. Go to the Pharmacy first? She began walking down the street, battling disappointment.

'Mia?'

'I'm here.'

'I'm sorry, honey. I just... I'm already going a bit crazy being at home all the time.'

'Even with work calling you every half hour?'

'Even.'

She should be using her earphones, Mia thought. She shouldn't have the phone to her head for so long. Who knew how safe these mobile devices were? Especially if she were now carrying a child – she should be looking after herself.

'I'm going to hire a nanny,' Sheryl was saying, 'until Tahls is old enough to rule the joint at a childcare centre.'

Mia grinned, despite herself.

'So I'll have Talia in at work whenever I feel like seeing her. And can you imagine how much fun for Talia when she's older – having any type of entertainment at the snap of her fingers?'

'Don't you dare spoil her,' Mia threatened. 'She's too perfect.'

'You're right. Don't let me spoil her,' Sheryl said humbly. 'My God, what times of change! You having a baby, discovering John has an identical twin, me buying another company...'

'It's outrageous,' Mia agreed. She had reached the pharmacy. 'Where do they keep pregnancy kits?'

'With the condoms.'

'Where are they?'

'Ha ha. Good luck when you do it. Ring me the minute you know,' Sheryl instructed.

'I will. Of course.'

'Do you think John will be happy about it?'

'Yes,' Mia said instantly, remembering that moment in Talia's bedroom when he had stood with her looking into the crib… the moment at her parents' after he'd turned away from Rita's picture and found her watching him…

'I'm so glad.' Sheryl's voice was warm. 'You deserve it, honey. You've had a long time in the wilderness in that marriage. You deserve all the happiness.'

'Thank you.'

'And I'm sure him not telling you about Jake being a twin, I'm sure that's no big deal… Just usual family crap.'

'I always knew he'd left England partly to escape the shadow of the bro, so I guess that's why I'm not overly shocked. It makes more sense now. Just… just disappointed that he never told me the whole story.'

'Yes… Well, never mind. All people are screwed in some way. That's his.'

'What's yours?'

'You know mine! Going through every eligible bachelor in Melbourne while the perfect one was standing on my doorstep.'

'And mine?' Mia checked the time. She really should keep moving or she'd miss out on lunch. It was already probably too late to walk to the Visitor Centre.

'Yours? Yours is settling for less when you can have more. Which is why I'm glad you're finally getting off your bum and doing this course instead of staying in a job you hate. And why I'm glad that self-absorbed husband of yours is finally giving you some love.'

Mia hovered by the shelf with the pregnancy kits. 'Is that how you'd describe him? 'Self-absorbed'?' She'd described herself that way just that morning. To John. In the garage.

'Not always, I'm sure, but too much for too long. It was that evil Buxton empire, sapping his spirit. He's coming back to life now, which is brilliant.'

There was a little squawk at Sheryl's end of the line, and rustling noises, and murmuring. Talia had woken up.

'Give Tahls a kiss for me,' Mia said. 'I've got to get lunch.'

Sheryl made a loud kissing noise. 'Done.'

Mia smiled. 'And I will call you the minute I know.'

'You'd better, girl.'

Pregnancy kit in her bag, Mia legged it back to the café at speed. So her version of being screwed up was always settling for less, in Sheryl's opinion. Which wasn't too far off the truth. Although, as her little voice of conscience never hesitated to remind her, it was always partly her fault: she didn't take action on what she wanted, she just went with the flow... Well, actually, that was what Sheryl had said: *'you're finally getting off your bum and doing this course'*. So mostly her fault... But, yes. She finally was. She was getting off her bum and things were finally going her way.

She walked into the café and straight up to the counter. There was no one else in the queue.

20

John was already home when Mia arrived that evening. He and Jake were sitting at the kitchen table with cups of tea and his laptop open, talking about the gallery.

'If we take the space in Browns Lane,' Jake was saying, 'we'll be able to stick a board on the main road and even by the Thames to direct people to us, so it might be out of the way but it'll be easy to find. There's – hi Mia.'

'Hi.' She scooped Bitsy up for a pat. 'How was your day? Not too boring, I hope.'

'No. Fine, thanks. I slept pretty late and went for a walk. Got my bearings… How was the first day of your course?'

John swivelled in his chair to face Mia, a slightly irritated expression on his face, as if he'd wanted to be first with that question.

'Yeah, good,' she said. 'It's going to be great. How was yours, honey?' moving closer to John for a greeting kiss, Bitsy still squirming in her arms.

'Fine, thanks.' John slung an arm around her hips, drawing her closer. Jake turned back to the screen.

Mia ruffled John's hair and then moved away to let Bitsy leap from her hands. 'Anyone hungry? I'm ravenous. What shall we do for dinner – go out?'

'Sure. You walking Bitsy first?'

'Yes. Want to come?'

'We've still got a bit to do here…'

'Okay. I won't be long – too hungry.'

Mia left them talking about the little room that could be used as an office at Browns Lane. She passed the guest room and saw the bed neatly made and nothing else in sight. Very tidy. She'd expected to see chaos from this actor brother. Perhaps he was on his best behaviour, being a guest.

She sat on the side of her bed and dug around in her bag for the pregnancy test. Read the packet, feeling an anticipatory whorl of delight in her belly, then slipped the box into the top drawer of her bedside table. She'd do that first thing in the morning. She unzipped her boots and peeled off her skirt and panty hose. Changed into comfy pants and flat boots, and swapped her office jacket for a casual one.

The boys were talking about gardening together tomorrow when she returned. Jake was being very accommodating about this plan to leave at seven a.m. and mow six gardens together, taking turns at edging and tidying and cutting grass. She felt unsure about this – it seemed rude to expect a guest to work, even if he was a brother.

'Don't you want to do touristy things?' she asked. And then, 'Oh shit! I'm sorry – I didn't have a chance to pick up those maps and brochures for you.'

Jake shrugged. 'Internet is fine. I don't mind helping out with the lawns. It's only one day a week. Leaves plenty of time to look around.'

'It's your holiday! Walkies, Bits!'

◯

She'd stepped in dog poo somewhere along the line, so when she arrived home, she stood by the back door scraping at the sole of her boot with a twig, nose screwed up against the smell. Bitsy kept coming in for a sniff and she had to push her away, wobbling.

She could hear the boys inside. One of them was speaking very loudly. She caught the phrase, 'Like hell I will!' and shook her head. It would be very disappointing if they were going to constantly argue. And uncomfortable for her. Being a single child, she'd watched her friends squabble with their siblings whenever she went over to visit and had always felt uneasy around the fighting and bantering. There were definitely benefits in not having to deal with sibling contrariness. But she'd also been envious of the camaraderie and joking around the dinner table, and the bodies sprawled around games on the living room floor; her childhood had always been so quiet and tidy and solitary by comparison. If these two could only appreciate the good side of what they had!

She limped to the garden tap and ran water over the sole of her boot, then brushed it on the grass and left both shoes on the back step. She entered the laundry in her socks.

'That is *not* happening,' one of them was saying in a hard tone. She hesitated for a moment, wondering which of them it was. Crazy how alike their voices were! Oh right, it was John.

Then Jake said, 'Be reasonable,' and she hesitated. Or was that John?

And one of them – no, that was John! – said, 'We had a deal,' and she gave up and walked into the house.

They were standing on either side of the dining table, tension crackling in the air between them.

'Come on, boys,' Mia teased. 'Break it up!'

John, who was facing her, gave a short laugh and Jake turned and smiled also, though it was a strained smile.

Bitsy darted in, having finished her exploration of Mia's boots. She ran from one brother to the next, back and forth excitedly.

'Ready to go eat?' Mia asked. 'I'll just get better shoes. Ssh, Bitsy! On your mat!'

John's phone rang and he answered it, walking toward the living room. Mia felt Jake's eyes on her as she left for the bedroom. The little bear he'd given her was sitting on the bed. The pregnancy kit was in the drawer. A baby was possibly growing right now in her belly. Mia smiled.

She returned to the dining room. Jake was sitting at the table, staring into the distance, his expression... sad... He rose as she came in, and seemed about to say something but didn't, held it back. She was about to ask when

John entered, looking from one to the other as if checking on what had happened in his absence. Mia felt irritated. They could bloody well keep their fights to themselves! She wasn't getting involved.

'You know what I'm going to call my bear?' she said brightly. 'Jayjay – for the two of you!'

The brothers gave her identical tight smiles.

They took Jake to a favourite Thai restaurant where the owner and his staff marvelled at the alikeness of John's twin, and talked over dinner about life in Australia versus life in England, about their father's art and the charity and the gallery, about gardening and massage and counselling, never sticking with any subject for long, always drifting away or skirting it as if it might be dangerous.

'Tell me about your life as an actor!' Mia asked, in a flash of inspiration after their meals had been served. 'Do you work mostly in theatre or film or TV?'

'Mostly theatre. The occasional bit part or extra work in a film or a series, or in a TV commercial.'

'It must be so interesting! So different to our lives – just filing and boring bookish kind of stuff. You've got the glamour of the stage and film crews and going backstage and meeting famous people and fans wanting your autograph!'

Jake laughed. John drank.

'And auditions when you don't get called back,' Jake said, picking up where she had left off. 'And auditoriums with no heating where you freeze, night after night. And tin roofs, so that no one can hear a word on stage whenever it rains. And opening to a handful of people in the audience who are mostly friends and family. And helping to build sets and paint and sew and bump in and bump out… all unpaid…'

'Oh. That sounds tough.' She remembered, now, John's remarks from time to time about his brother's unfortunate career...

'Jake's downfall has been 'profit-sharing jobs' where there's no profit,' John put in. Mr Accountant would be keeping track of that.

'Sad but true,' Jake said, turning his wine glass in his hand and watching the pale liquid swirl inside. 'They tell you they're sure the show will go to Singapore or Dublin or Berlin, but it never happens. It dies right where it is and you're back on your agent's doorstep, knocking, looking for the next thing.' He took a sip of his wine and put the glass down. 'That's the actor's fatal flaw: hope. You're always dreaming about the next role, sure you're about to land your big break, but mostly it's just a hard slog and the good jobs pass you by. It's a very competitive industry.'

'That must be so difficult,' she sympathised. 'If it's the thing you most love to do.'

'Yes...' He picked up his fork and twirled some noodles onto it.

A group of women who'd just entered the restaurant were guided their way by a waiter and now settled noisily into seats at a nearby table.

'Only a handful of actors ever make it big,' John said, over the scraping chairs and bright voices. 'That's the harsh reality. Only a few can live off their earnings. Most have to do other jobs as well.'

'So what do you do?' Mia asked Jake.

'Work in a mate's pizza shop. Help out in a friend's café. Do a little m–' he stopped to cough, suddenly coughing almost violently, as if something was stuck in his throat.

'Are you all right?' she asked in alarm, half-standing.

John reached across and slapped him on the back.

Jake spluttered and drank some water. 'Thanks. Swallowed the wrong way.' He drank again.

'It's a tough gig, acting,' John remarked. 'From what I've seen of Jake's journey, anyway. He's had this dream of fame and fortune since he was a kid in the school play. But it's been a road of constant rejection and disappointment.'

Mia covered John's hand, touched by his empathy for his brother.

'So it's time to grow up a bit,' Jake declared. 'Move on! Accept that I'm not likely to make the big time and look for something else.'

'Like what?' Mia asked through a mouthful of stir-fry. 'You're so artistic and creative. You'd never be happy as a bookkeeper or salesperson. Will you go into hospitality?'

'Actually this charity might be my saviour. It gives me a chance to do something that will make a difference for artists in general rather than just playing little roles that never take me out of the backwaters.' He speared another mouthful and then put his fork down. 'There was a moment in one of my last roles that perfectly sums up my experiences as an actor: I was working alongside a couple of big names. It was a hospital scene and I was playing a doctor. I had to walk up to within twenty paces of the stars and say, 'I'm sorry,' and then exit stage left. I wanted to get closer to them and put more into the role but the Director cut me off. He said, 'Just the two words, thanks.' So that was my acting career in a nutshell: get close to the real action… but exit stage left before you have a chance to do anything with it.'

It must have been very difficult for him to confess all this in front of his successful accountant brother. Mia glanced at John. He was watching Jake with a strange expression, a mixture of anger and admiration, if she had to name it, but that made no sense. Jake was concentrating on his meal now. She wasn't sure which of them was more tense…

'So… the charity is a good thing for both of you,' she said. 'John wanted to get out of petrochemicals and do something more… less…' This was a landmine. 'How would you put it, honey?'

'More interesting, less boring, right?' he asked her.

'Well, I'd put it like that but I can't stand number crunching…'

'That will do,' he said. 'Dad inspired me to find what else might interest me instead of just doing same-old, same-old. Jake knows.'

'And you think this gallery and charity could become a going concern, right?'

'I do,' he said.

'And if it works for you as well,' to Jake, 'that's a bonus.'

'Working with John does mean I won't screw up my finances anymore,' Jake acknowledged. 'He'll be managing that side of things and I can stay on the people side of things.'

John reached for the bottle of wine and topped up their glasses. Mia put a hand over hers and he looked a little surprised but didn't remark. Instead he said: 'Yep. Jake's had a tendency to invest in dodgy schemes that look great in the brochure but aren't very sound.'

Jake agreed with a shrug. 'Not very good at reading the small print.'

'So this way he can do something interesting and useful without going down the gurgler in the process.'

'A perfect win/win,' Mia beamed. 'So long as you two can work together without killing each other.'

That might have been the wrong thing to say; she sensed the tension rising again. It felt as if they were constantly on thin ice! Fortunately a waiter paused at their table just then to ask how their meal was going, and the tension dissipated. When he'd gone, Mia said, 'I know you don't like to talk about it but can you just get over yourselves and help me out? I need to understand, partly as John's wife and partly as a counsellor-to-be. What is this strain between you all about?'

There was a moment of silence. Then John said, 'Just sibling rivalry. It's more intense for twins because you're constantly being compared.'

'And always comparing yourself,' Jake added. 'If John did better on a test I'd feel left behind but he'd feel bad for getting ahead of me; if I beat him at sport he'd feel left behind and I'd feel bad.'

John shook his head. 'Complex, tricky childhood...'

'Then when your parents give you birthday or Christmas presents,' Jake continued, 'you've always got one eye on what your twin got, to see if it's fair, if the gifts are balanced.'

'So in the end they give you the same stuff because they can't stand the fights. Which means I got books about theatre and Jake got books about birds.'

'Birds?' Mia asked, startled. 'When were you interested in birds?'

'As a teenager. I belonged to the Field Naturalists Club for a while.'

'I destroyed my bird books,' Jake said, remembering. 'I cut the pictures out and stuck all the bird images on the windows and walls of our bedroom and chucked all the information. Dad was furious with me. They weren't cheap books.'

'And I sold the theatre books,' John said.

The brothers looked at each other across the table.

'And then there are people, wherever you go, asking the same questions,' Jake continued. 'Like, *what's it like being a twin?*'

'Isn't that a fair question?' she asked, baffled.

'Well, what's it like *not* being a twin?' he shot back at her.

'I dunno. It's all I've known.'

'Same for us. It's all we've known.'

'Fair enough…'

John: 'Another annoying comment is, *You two really look alike, d'you know that?* As if we haven't figured it out in ten years of sharing a bedroom and twenty years sharing a house, or whatever!'

Jake: 'Here's a beauty: *Is it trippy having someone else on the planet who looks exactly like you?*'

'Isn't it?' Mia asked nervously.

John: 'It's all we know, honey. And actually it's maddening. Having people constantly confuse you for someone else and then give up trying to figure out who's who. They'd say, 'Which one are you?' Or they'd call us 'Jake-John' or 'John-Jake' and not bother to figure it out. Exit individuality.'

'So you probably don't like that name for my bear,' she grimaced.

Jake shook his head slowly; John said, 'Nope' in a definite tone of voice.

'Okay. Paddington it is!'

Jake raised his fork, a piece of broccoli on its tines. 'Here's a clanger: *Can your parents tell you apart?*'

'Surely!' Mia exclaimed.

'Mum, always,' Jake said. There was a note of something in his voice…

John looked up. 'Dad too!'

'True,' Jake agreed. 'Here's another one: *'Do you fight?'*'

John, answering the question with feeling: 'My oath. It was the only way we could assert a sense of identity and avoid just blending into each other.'

Jake: 'Always having to share birthdays. Never feeling special – that it's just about you.'

John: 'Always having to share *everything*: bedroom, same toys because there was no point buying doubles of everything.'

Jake: 'Then there were questions like, *'Do you feel each other's pain?'* And, *'What's your twin thinking right now?'*'

'Oh. My psychic connection question,' Mia said guilty.

Jake nodded. 'The answers are no and no: we don't feel each other's pain and we don't know each other's thoughts.'

'Not in the 'I can tell you exactly what he's thinking, word-for-word right now' sense,' John intervened, 'but we do often have a sense of what the other is thinking or feeling. And we do finish each other's sentences.'

'You said that the other night,' she remembered. 'So when John had to have stitches in his knee for that go-kart accident, you didn't feel anything.'

'No. Not even in here,' Jake said melodramatically, hand to heart. 'I thought it was funny watching him ram into the tree – couldn't stop laughing, in fact. And then I was envious of all the attention and presents he got.'

John snorted. 'Yeah. Didn't miss the injection or the stitches, though, did you? Here's another one: *'Lucky you! You must never be lonely!'*'

Mia waited, not trusting herself to say anything.

They were both watching her.

'So...' she said cautiously. 'I suppose you didn't see it like that... even though you had someone there all the time...'

They exchanged looks, rolling their eyes.

'Well, I *was* lonely a lot of the time!' she protested. 'I was seriously lonely. I would have loved a twin. Or a sister. Or a brother. Someone – anyone!'

'You *think* you would have,' Jake murmured.

'We didn't count each other,' John explained. 'To me, Jake was part of me, so I wanted a friend who *wasn't* me. Someone else. Someone who had the same interests as me instead of someone who just looked like me.'

'That part was no big deal, though,' Jake cut in. 'We were put in different classrooms pretty young and then when we went to high school we were in different schools, so it wasn't a problem for long. He had his friends, I had mine.'

'That's true. The older we got, the more we developed our own interests. It got easier.'

'Kind of,' Jake said. 'The comparisons have never stopped.'

'No,' John agreed. 'Mum and Dad approved of my vocation and thought Jake was making stupid decisions. Acting! Theatre! Unreliable. Risky... They were right, of course.' He drained his glass.

'But they loved me,' Jake grinned. 'They thought the sun shone out of my bum.'

The old edginess returned with that comment. It was as if the air suddenly grew cooler.

'You see?' John said to Mia. 'Constant competition, even now.'

'It's nerve-wracking,' she said. 'I'm always afraid I'm going to say the wrong thing.'

Jake laughed. 'Oh no! *You* won't say the wrong thing.'

John rose. 'Shall we go?' He waited for them and then led the way to the counter, pulling out his wallet. Jake was bringing his out too, but John waved it away. 'Our shout,' he said.

'Well, thanks,' Jake said. 'That's very good of you.'

Even that exchange seemed to be tinged with something, but what? Mia gave up on them and concentrated on putting her jacket on. Jake grabbed the loose arm end of it and helped her. He settled the jacket around her shoulders and straightened the collar, his hands on the fabric for a little longer than necessary.

'Thank you,' she said, turning to face him, feeling his fingers trailing through her hair and falling away.

He nodded. Smiled a tight smile.

John stepped forward and between them, putting an arm around Mia. 'Let's go.'

21

John had left to go cycling when Mia woke up. She felt dry in the mouth. She lay there for a moment, curled on her side then moved and winced – her breasts felt sore. Tender.

Pregnancy test!

She sat up quickly, opening the drawer beside her. Hurried to the loo, reading the instructions as she went. She peed on the stick and waited, apprehensive and confident at the same time.

Two lines. It was positive!

The thrill of delight was unleashed: that little scrap of reined-in hope leapt from somewhere deep inside her, flinging its arms out and singing a song. She beamed at herself in the bathroom mirror. Scraggly morning hair, bed-crumpled face, flowery flannel PJs, and a beatific smile.

Jake was making coffee when she arrived in the kitchen. It smelt good. She greeted him, hoping that her joy would not be too obvious, concealing it in movement as she made toast and opened fridge and cupboards and fed Bitsy.

'So you're back at work today? Or back in the course?' he asked conversationally.

'Back in the course for a half-day. They're three to four hour classes, two on Wednesday and one on Thursday. Then I'm back across the hallway at my desk.' She sighed. 'What are you going to do?'

'Might go into the city and explore,' he said.

She glanced up at the smudgy grey skies. 'Looks like rain. I hope it doesn't spoil your day.'

He shrugged. 'English boy. Used to it.'

'Of course...'

Jake handed her a cup.

'Thanks. Just a tad of milk and no sugar?'

'Yes. Was that right?'

'That's right. Good memory.' Once she'd said that, she couldn't remember when she'd have told him how she had her coffee... But she was getting more and more fuddled lately. Pregnancy brain, perhaps!

'John's and my lives might be a bit all over the place right now,' Jake said, 'but you look pretty happy. Are you?' He sounded genuinely interested.

The smile radiated out of her in reply. 'I am,' she glowed. 'John and I were a bit stuck before he went to Europe but things have been much better since he got back.' She refrained from saying anything about the little stick now sitting in the drawer in her ensuite.

Jake nodded, almost gravely.

'And I finally got my act together and enrolled in this counselling course that I've been talking about for ages!' she burbled on. 'It makes such a difference when you stop procrastinating, doesn't it?'

He nodded again. Swished the last bit of coffee in his cup and drank. He looked depressed, she thought. Maybe the part of him that was still grieving giving up on his acting career? She wished she could make it better. When you were happy, you wanted others to be happy too.

Bitsy gave a short bark from the living room and she looked out the kitchen window. John was wheeling his bike back up the drive. That was a quick one.

'I gather you're not a cyclist,' she said to Jake as her toast popped up.

'I'm a slack bastard,' he replied. 'Never exercise.' He was leaning back in the chair, arms crossed behind his head. 'Other than with women. I do like plenty of exercise with women.'

She laughed. Of course! Promiscuous Jake with his many girlfriends...

She found it hard to believe, though, looking at him. There was something incongruent...

They could hear muffled noises in the garage as John parked his bike and something fell down.

'Your reputation has preceded you,' she told Jake with a grin. 'I guess that's a hazard of the industry. It must be very easy to feel attracted to someone you're acting opposite as a lover.'

'Very easy,' he confirmed. 'But it doesn't just happen on stage. I can fall in love almost anywhere.'

Was he bragging? She gave another short laugh and began to spread her toast, then stopped, a queasy feeling rising in her stomach.

John came into the kitchen, looking from one to the other as he usually did. Mia put her knife down.

'Good to see you doing your thing,' Jake said in mock admiration. 'You're an inspiration, bro.'

John removed an imaginary hat, waved it in the air, and dropped into a sweeping bow. 'May just a droplet of my magnificence land on you, dear brother –'

Mia bolted. She left her husband in his odd, dramatic moment and rushed into the ensuite, banging the door shut behind her. She made it in time – pouring a nasty little stream of vomit into the toilet bowl. Talk about on schedule. Well, they'd guess now.

She sat back on her heels and wondered what this would mean for her agreement with Reynald. If she was really going to be having a baby, she'd want to leave work for longer than three or six months; she'd want to be a full-time mum. Sheryl's confession about being back at work next May returned to memory. How disappointing. Her images of them walking prams side-by-side and joining mothers' groups together broke apart; her images of Talia crawling around her own baby while she and Sheryl chatted and chopped up pieces of apple and banana disintegrated. It seemed that life never gave you a completely full cup; there was always a leak somewhere.

She sighed and got to her feet. Rinsed out her mouth. When she returned to the kitchen the boys were deep in conversation about their crowdfunding campaign. Melissa, she gathered, had emailed a long marketing plan during the night and they were sitting together reading from the screen and discussing it as they ate breakfast. Neither one noticed her return. Neither one commented on her hasty exit. John was already familiar with her digestive and eliminatory issues – he'd probably just put it down to that. And it would be rude for Jake to comment so she could let go the little flush of embarrassment she'd brought back with her. But could she do toast? She contemplated the butter and then pushed it away. Dry toast today. Just vegemite.

There was no opportunity to say anything to John but she had to tell someone, so on her way to work she called Sheryl, who answered immediately.

'So?'

'Positive.'

A little squeal of delight from the other end of the phone. Mia smiled. So good to share the joy!

'You'll have to do it again,' Sheryl instructed her. 'To be one hundred per cent sure. Get one of the other types of tests for a comparison. Have you told John?'

'Not yet. It's awkward… with Jake there.'

'I can imagine.'

For a moment Mia had the feeling Sheryl was about to say something else, and then she said, 'Well, I'll let you get to work. Pop in here tonight for a chat? So happy for you!'

'I'm not sure what we're doing tonight yet,' Mia said, 'but if I can, I will.'

'Of course. Hosting comes first. Actually, Alec and I would love to have you all over for dinner. Maybe you can suggest that for tonight?'

'I will,' she promised.

But that morning, when they paused for their break, Mia found herself standing with her apple near a noticeboard for the ACCAT students. There was a sign on the board with a headshot that she found familiar. She moved closer to read it.

'*Professional Development Opportunity!*' the headline read. *'Join experienced therapist, Bernard McFafe, to explore the relevance of the Hero's Journey to your clients or your own life experiences.'* It was him! From the conference! She recognised the handsome, weathered face. She read on. *'Join Bernard right here at ACCAT on Thursday evenings 6-9 pm to learn about this ancient mythical structure, and gain insights into your own life choices and challenges. Four weeks of intriguing information – a unique opportunity.'*

Mia checked the date. It was starting tonight. Could she? Could she take on another course at the same time as beginning her official course? And while pregnant? And with a guest?

'*Special opportunity for ACCAT students now! Time-sensitive price! This pilot program is on offer at half-price before release to the general public as a self-paced course.'*

That decided it. The price was very acceptable, and it was only one evening a week for four weeks. Surely she could manage that!

Her fellow students were moving back into the classroom. Reynald had been teaching them a unit on active listening and now they were about to be dropped into the deep end and 'counsel' each other! She paused by his desk.

'That course Bernard McFafe is offering…'

Reynald looked up.

'There's no assessment or anything, is there?'

'No. It counts as PD for qualified counsellors but you can do it purely for personal interest.'

'I think I will.'

'I'll be there myself,' he said.

Mia took her seat in a fluster of surprise at the thought of being co-students with her boss and teacher!

At lunchtime she texted Sheryl an apology and rang John to let him know she wouldn't be home for dinner.

'That's fine,' he said. 'We'll just keep working.'

'All work and no play...' she warned.

'You want us to play without you?'

'No. But you are doing a lot of 'business''

'I've picked up some tickets to a show on Saturday night. I thought Jake might like to see some theatre while he's here.'

'Good idea. What is it?'

'A comedy. I figured the laugh would do us all good.'

'Perfect. Sheryl wants us all over for dinner – maybe on Friday night?'

'That might be pushing it. We have to be up early on Saturday and then we'll be out late Saturday night...'

'Okay. Maybe an early meal on Sunday. And Mum and Dad are going to want to meet Jake some time, too.'

'Sure...' he said, in that non-committal tone of voice.

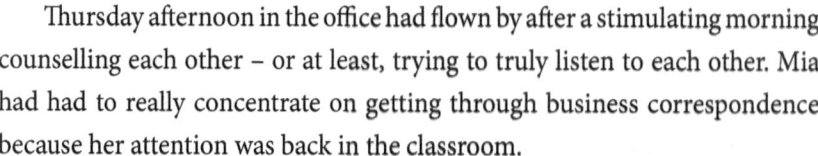

Thursday afternoon in the office had flown by after a stimulating morning counselling each other – or at least, trying to truly listen to each other. Mia had had to really concentrate on getting through business correspondence because her attention was back in the classroom.

She'd been sobered by Reynald's definition of true listening; she could remember plenty of times when she had done the complete opposite of what he described, and had instead cut people off, rushed ahead of them, analysed them, moralised and preached, judged, threatened, blamed, grilled them, been sarcastic, hadn't really paid attention – she could tick every box on the 'Do Not' list. Communication was a minefield!

They'd paired up to practise. Her partner was the young man, Blake, and he was quite good at making her feel heard but when she tried to return the favour she found herself continually butting in with questions and commenting on what he was saying rather than just listening. So when Susan gave her a long instruction about preparing travel itineraries for Paula and Reynald's upcoming trip to the States, and to also begin some research on what other coaching organisations were offering, Mia practised her active listening.

'Didn't I just say that?' Susan asked, frowning, when Mia had finished parroting the instructions almost word for word.

'Um. Yes. I'm onto it.' Mia turned away quickly, hoping that Reynald had not overheard her fumbled attempt at better listening.

He had. He was standing right there, a twinkle in his eyes as he held back a smile. 'It's really best suited for when someone has a problem, an emotional issue,' he said gravely.

'Yes. I...'

He gave her a reassuring little nod. 'I know you know.' And walked on.

She had ordered double lunch for herself and Reynald so they'd have something to eat at their desks that evening before Bernard's course began. She couldn't help wondering, as she sat there munching her pasta salad, if she'd been a huge fool in taking this on as well right now. She already had homework to do from the counselling course – lots of reading and a first assignment. It was probably an insane time to take on another course as well! But she couldn't drop out now: she'd already paid.

People were gathering in the foyer area near reception. Chewing, she saw Bernard arrive and greet them, then walk on toward a classroom, briefcase in hand. Mia watched the small knot of waiting participants grow as more people arrived, some of whom she recognised as counsellors and therapists who came to ACCAT from time to time for meetings and personal development.

Behind her, Reynald emerged from his office. He came to stand by her desk, wiping his mouth with a napkin. Mia swallowed her last mouthful and dropped the greasy take-away container into her bin, and they headed out to join the others. She hovered in the crowd for a moment then realised she needed to pee – again. She made a dash, arriving at the classroom just as he was formally welcoming their guest presenter.

The same tanned, weathered face, thoughtful eyes, the two deep lines on either side of his mouth that were there whether he smiled or not, the rimless specs in his top pocket. She remembered his comment to her at the cocktails night: *You are not in the wrong life.* She'd felt so *seen*. For some reason, right now she didn't want to be seen or remembered; she wanted to disappear into the group. She moved quickly along the side wall to the back of the room and slipped into a seat.

Reynald was introducing Bernard as an experienced therapist who had originally studied anthropology, which was how he'd come across the work of Joseph Campbell, the man who had first documented 'the Hero's Journey'. Having found the principles so useful in his work with his clients, Bernard had decided to develop this course for self-study, so that anyone could more consciously understand and direct their own life path. Of course, he *was* doing them all out of clients…! The group laughed, Bernard smiled, and Reynald finished his intro: they were all very privileged to be experiencing this sneak preview with the creator of the program before it was launched as an online training.

Everyone clapped and Reynald settled his bulk into a chair on the side of the room. Bernard began.

'We all love stories,' he said, speaking with an energy that was instantly completely captivating. 'They're wired into us from way back. Our ancestors sat around fires in caves listening to stories of the hunt and of the gods and of their ancestors. From childhood we've listened to stories about our families and ourselves and our world.' He was roaming around the room; she could see the light in his eyes as he talked about this favourite subject.

'These stories give us our sense of identity. They determine what we seek in life – and what we settle for. They teach us what we need to know to operate in our families and society – and often things that it would be better not to know… we take on other people's ideas, other people's perceptions of us that limit or challenge us. But all of these things become part of our story, of who we perceive ourselves to be.'

He picked up a sheaf of papers from the desk and began to move around the room, handing them out.

'The Hero's Journey is not someone's good idea. It's a pattern that has been observed, a set of principles about how life operates. Most people out there,' waving a hand in the direction of the windows, 'are living quite unconsciously. They're reacting to events and people. Few have any deliberate goals or intentions for their lives. Even fewer recognise that they are or can be the architect of their story. And fewer still realise that there are principles governing their lives that are immutable; you can't change them – no one can. You can only work with them – so long as you know what they are. If you do, you are able to live a more conscious, empowered life; if you don't, it's easy to feel like a victim.'

He returned to the front and leaned against the desk.

'I've given you a list of some of these principles – we're going to work through them together. We're also going to go on a rather marvellous adventure. We're going to look at your lives as if they were the lives of characters in a book or film. Filmmakers and writers often use the Hero's Journey in the design of their characters and stories; very few' – he sketched quotation marks in the air – 'ordinary people' do so. You're about to.'

He walked to the whiteboard and drew two stick figures, a small one and a large one. Next to the small one he wrote 'Character-you'; next to the large one he wrote 'God-You'. He pointed to the large one.

'As of right now, you are 'God'. If you would put aside any beliefs you have about God for the moment and just flow with this working concept… You are going to step out of your shoes as the *actor* in your life and become the *architect*, the writer, the director, the designer of your life. You're going to step back from being personally attached to your lives, from being 'in them', and look at your lives through the lens of a god that has total power to give 'actor-you' whatever experiences will most serve her or him in growing. You are no longer *in* your life at the effect of events; while in this class, you are looking on from the outside. You are the creator, designer, architect, director.'

Bernard paused, surveying them.

'We're going to use the structure of The Hero's Journey to identify your character arc, which is the process a character goes through in learning his or her lessons. Any questions so far?'

'It sounds intriguing,' a woman said. 'So I'm not Frankie anymore; I'm the-creator-of-Frankie?'

'That's right. You're the designer of Frankie's life. You're going to start observing Frankie's journey to date and see what you can learn from that, and then you're going to consider what life experiences would best serve her going forward.'

A stream of images ran through Mia's mind: being born after a sister who had died aged three days; being raised by anxious parents; being lonely; envying her friends' families; falling in love with boys who weren't interested in her; falling into office work because she didn't know what she wanted to do; escaping home to travel around Europe; meeting John and being swept off her feet; having him pursue her back to Australia; marrying him in a crazy, unexpected ceremony, just the two of them with a couple of friends they'd met at a party as witnesses; feeling proud as a new Mrs, and then lonely again, and bored; meeting Sheryl through work; watching Alec patiently court Sheryl; changing admin jobs because she was never happy; the dawning desire for a more fulfilling career and a child; watching Sheryl come from behind and beat her to the finish line as a mother...

Bernard waved the sheet in the air. 'There are some principles from literature and film that apply to our actual lives. For example, the principle of conflict.'

Mia looked at her sheet.

1. Conflict. There is no story, no growth, without conflict. Your character, whether fictional or real, needs conflict in order to grow and develop.

Bernard went back to the whiteboard and wrote *1. CONFLICT.* He turned back to face them.

'We might want to avoid conflict but it's essential. It's required. It's part of the instruction manual for a human being on earth. If you were writing a novel or a film, you would aim to give your characters as much trouble as you possibly could. You'd aim to say 'no' to your characters, to hold back what they want, to drive them into a corner so they have to grow. You'd ask, 'what is the worst thing that can happen to this character?' and then you'd deliver it. The best films and books are the ones where the conflict appears to be unsolvable. Anyone like the sound of that for your actual life?'

There was a laughing rejection of this proposal.

He grinned. 'Well, some of you might be getting off more lightly than that right now but we're going to consider what your personal objectives are and, given that, what kind of conflict you actually *need* to facilitate growth. By the way, this conflict can be inner or outer: it can be an inner struggle with a poor self-image or a bad temper or a learning difficulty or laziness, or an outer struggle with another person or institution or even with the climate.

'All right. Next principle.'

Mia looked again at her sheet.

2. Polarity. The entire universe is constructed around the principle of polarity.

'Light and dark, up and down, in and out, male and female, hot and cold, life and death, energy and matter, rich and poor... you won't find anything in the universe that doesn't exist in polarity,' Bernard said. 'Even our computers operate on a binary 'on-off' system. Magnetism and electricity reveal positive and negative charges with a force being conducted between them. Our bodies and brains are polarised – we've got a left and right hemisphere in the brain, for instance. We've even got this right-wrong, good-bad duality in our thinking.'

He wrote *2. POLARITY* on the board.

'Every story, and every life, begins with a single focus, a purpose. But as soon as you choose a single thought or character, a protagonist, you have automatically generated its polar opposite, a contrary concept or antagonistic character, and the possibility of movement, conflict, interaction between them.

'If you're writing a story about the quality of trust, the possibility of suspicion immediately arises. We need that suspicion in order to test and challenge the concept of trust. If your story-character wants something, there must be someone or some force preventing that.'

He returned to the board and wrote 3. *REVERSALS*, and then drew a yin/yang symbol. When he turned back to face them Mia was struck by how much he came alive talking about this stuff. She wondered if becoming a counsellor would make her come to life in that way – admin certainly didn't do it for her.

'Nothing stays polarised forever,' Bernard said, pacing. 'Eventually what was dark becomes light and vice versa; one state flips to its other polarity, either gradually or quickly, suddenly. They can be temporary, brief reversals or major turning points. Good stories have a number of reversals: a reversal of fortune, a shift in power – the underdog stands up to the bully, the successful person experiences a setback... As viewers watching these films we're intrigued: how is the protagonist going to deal with it? In romance stories we observe the attraction of opposites – our polarity dynamic; then we observe reversals: attraction becomes repulsion, or vice versa. Who's experienced this in your relationships?'

Of course! Mia gave her hand a little wave, thinking of her and John's 'oppositeness': his neat, organised, conservative character and her chaotic, flamboyant muddle... And he was going through a reversal now! She reflected on this, fascinated. And, of course, he and Jake were classic opposites too – they were the proverbial 'odd couple'.

'Now, when one character reverses polarity,' Bernard continued, 'the laws require a reciprocal movement from the character or force at the opposite end of the pole.'

It was true: John was changing, and that was making their whole relationship change. *She* was the one reminding him about being careful with money, and things like that! And the same dynamic was at work with her and Sheryl: as soon as she, Mia, became pregnant and wanted to be home, nesting, Sheryl wanted to go back to work and conquer the world. Or perhaps she had become pregnant because Sheryl was already moving out of that space? This got spooky.

'The pendulum is always swinging toward the point of balance,' Bernard said. 'Any character that begins at one extreme is ripe for the process of polarity reversal. However, it's a strong rule of drama and in life that people remain true to their basic natures. If they've changed, they'll change back. The leopard,' he began, and someone from the group finished:

'Doesn't change its spots...'

'Exactly. We might experiment with the other polarity but we remain true to our essence, although perhaps in a less extreme position.'

'Does that mean people can't make real growth, lasting change?' someone asked.

'No, we can grow, but it means we have a strong instinct to preserve what is truly, deeply 'us'. Someone who loves to dance might put it aside because they think they 'should', but that itchiness to move their feet will always be there; they'll always be looking for an opportunity to express it.'

Bernard returned to the board and wrote 4. *RECOGNITION*.

'The words 'protagonist' and 'antagonist' contain the root 'agon', which refers to agony, pain. The Greek god Agon represented this force of struggle and conflict. 'Agon' also means 'judgement', the ability to evaluate and make a decision. In Greek theatre the agon was often a formal debate between two characters in which their contrasting views are judged by a chorus. We see this in courtroom dramas today.

'In the ancient world there was also a 'recognition scene' where a disguised identity is revealed – masked superheroes are unveiled, the king comes out of hiding, long-lost lovers are united, the tyrant realises he is about to execute his own child. King Oedipus unwittingly kills his father and marries his mother, and then blinds himself when he realises what he's done. The moment of unmasking can be catastrophic but it also offers the opportunity for emotional honesty and acceptance.'

Bernard added to the list on the board: 5. *CATHARSIS*.

'These moments of insight are cathartic: both reader or viewer and character experience a release of pent-up emotion and, usually, a breakthrough. It's similar to a body ridding itself of toxins and impurities.

This, of course, is the outcome of therapy: the moment where the client sees his or her life in a new light and reorganises priorities and belief systems and behaviour.' He saluted them. 'This is the good, important work that you people do.

'We're going to look, now, at the stages of the Hero's Journey, and then I want you to start considering all of this information in the context of your own lives. Over the next four weeks we'll look at your 'Ordinary World', your 'Call to Action', your allies and mentors and enemies – your antagonists; and the various trials you've experienced. And I'll invite you to consider, from the God-you perspective, what lessons and experiences will most serve Character-you, given what you want to achieve and how you need to grow.'

He scanned the room, looking from one to the other, and his gaze came to rest on Mia. 'The solutions to both story problems and life problems have a certain elegance to them, a beauty. We finally own and value what has been disowned; we understand what was unclear; we trust the path and our instincts and heart, and that trust enables us to keep moving forward.'

She knew he'd recognised her. So no more hiding. She wondered if he was remembering their conversation; it certainly seemed as if he'd made that comment directly to her.

She wanted to stop at the break to say hello but there were already a few people talking to him and waiting to talk to him and she was busting for a pee. She ran out, bladder pressing, mind whirling with thoughts of polarity and reversals and recognition…

22

Mia was very tired on Friday. She slept through her alarm and felt too nauseous for breakfast so she just rushed off to work with a coffee. That was probably not a good idea for her baby, so she'd have to get her act together. Fortunately Reynald was out all day and she was able to work quietly and methodically through her tasks, stopping often for a loo visit and hoping no one was counting her trips.

Their real estate agent emailed both she and John during the day to ask how the cleaning of the apartment was going. Were they ready to advertise for tenants? A mild panic seized her – they'd forgotten all about it after that first semi-clean the weekend they went to inspect and had found the blood-spattered tomahawk in the wardrobe. The news that Jake was coming had totally wiped it from their minds – even from John's, which was unusual because he hated either of their properties sitting empty for more than a few days.

She texted him:

Better finish cleaning the flat this weekend, eh?

But there was no reply. Saturday would be out while the guys mowed lawns so it would have to be Sunday. She sighed.

When she arrived home on Friday night she was so tired that she sat on the sofa with her eyes closed and Bitsy on her lap, without the energy to walk the dog or prepare dinner or even get as far as the bedroom to have a nap. The boys were out, or at least there was no sign or sound of them. She let herself fall sideways, pulling the new throw rug over her body from the back of the sofa, and drifting into sleep. Bitsy snuggled against her stomach.

She woke some time later at the sound of the key in the lock and footsteps, something being put down with a little thud, movement through the house. Mia opened her eyes and saw John sitting on the nearby armchair, watching her. She blinked, dragging hair out of her eyes.

'Good sleep?' he asked.

'Mm… I was pooped.' She pulled herself up on one elbow as Jake came into the room, and then she realised it was Jake sitting watching her, and John in the doorway.

'I picked up some pizza. Too knackered to cook,' he said. He was looking from one of them to the other, a wariness in his eyes.

'Thanks.' She sat up properly. 'Did you see my email about Cooney Avenue?'

'Yes.'

'We'll have to do it this Sunday.'

'I was making plans,' he began.

'We can't go another week without getting it advertised.' The shoe felt like it was on the wrong foot. Usually it was him lecturing her about practical stuff like this!

'Yeah.' He was avoiding Jake's eye. Maybe he felt uncomfortable about being landed gentry when his brother was a pauper. 'Come and eat, you two.' John withdrew to the kitchen and began to open cupboards and cutlery drawers. Mia gently pushed the warm Bitsy bundle out of her way and stood up. And felt herself fading, weakening; a darkness was spreading over her vision… She wobbled and Jake said, 'Whoah!' and rushed close and grabbed her arms, holding her up for a moment before gently helping her to sit.

'You okay?' he asked, concern in his voice.

She opened her eyes slowly. He was kneeling opposite her, still holding onto her arms with two steady hands, looking up at her with his beautiful hazel eyes.

'You two coming?' John called from the kitchen, and then was there in the doorway again, and there was a note of irritation in his voice when he asked, 'What's up?'

'Mia looked like she was about to faint,' Jake said. 'Are you okay now?' he asked her again.

'Yes. I think I just got up too quickly.' She was feeling more normal: her vision had cleared and everything around her had taken its old solid shape, and her legs no longer felt as if they were dissolving under her.

'Good.' He released her arms slowly and stood up.

'Something to eat will help, honey.' John was there beside her now, almost pushing Jake out of the way as he moved close to help her up and walk with her to the dining table.

'I'm all right,' she said. 'How embarrassing... I never faint!'

The pizza did help. She felt strength returning as she ate.

'You stay there,' Jake said when they'd finished. He collected their plates. 'I'll wash.'

'You've already figured out where everything goes,' she said, watching him open the cupboard under the sink and bring out detergent.

'I've been finding my way around while you two have been out working and studying.'

Mia turned to John. 'I've hardly heard anything about your massage course yet. How's it going?'

He shrugged. 'Good. Easy.'

'Even the anatomy and physiology stuff?' Jake asked from the sink.

'Yeah. Fine.' John stacked the empty pizza boxes.

'It's so unlike you, John,' Jake said over the sound of running water. 'I'm staggered.'

'What? That I'm showing an interest in massage?'

'Yes. It just doesn't fit the accountant personality.'

'I've been really surprised too,' Mia agreed.

'You both know I'm deliberately exploring new things since Dad died,' John said. He sounded angry. He took the boxes into the laundry, dropping them into the recycling tub and tripping over something on his way back. He swore.

Jake turned the taps off and took the tea towel off the hook inside the cupboard.

'I'll dry,' Mia said.

But John was already taking the tea towel from Jake and rubbing the first dish almost aggressively. 'Not all accountants are boring and conservative,' he snapped. 'Sometimes they break the stereotype.'

'You think so?' Jake asked.

The brothers looked at each other. Identical fury, tightly controlled.

'Movie tonight?' Mia interrupted. She was getting really sick of all this sibling rivalry stuff.

'Sure,' John said immediately, passing her the plate and taking another wet one from the rack.

'Why not?' Jake agreed. He was standing with his back to the stove, arms folded, watching John dry the dishes.

They gathered in the living room, she and John on the sofa, Jake in the armchair. John held her close, almost as if he were marking his territory. She felt uncomfortable with Jake there, alone in the other chair, deliberately looking away at the screen. This tension between them was so unpleasant – and awful timing. She still hadn't been able to tell John that she was pregnant. There just hadn't been a suitable moment. Jake surely wouldn't come with them to clean the apartment on Sunday, so perhaps she'd do it then. Not ideal, but this wasn't about romance.

The boys left early on Saturday morning and Mia gave herself the luxury of a long sleep-in. She could have gone to Cooney Avenue by herself to clean but she had all that homework to do. And anyway, she still felt queasy.

It was almost eleven when she settled at the kitchen table with her textbook and laptop and began to read about the social and historical origins of counselling and the major counselling theories. She'd heard of Freud, of course – who hadn't? And terms like the ego and id and the unconscious, but she knew very little about them. Her own self-help reading had been popular books about believing in yourself and going after your dreams that Sheryl had given her. Maybe the books had helped, since she was now doing it!

The kitchen clock kept up its steady ticking as she sat there reading, sipping chai tea, and eating apples. She seemed to be hugely hungry for apples today, apples with peanut butter... She read, putting teaspoonfuls of nut butter onto slices of apple and eating so automatically that she felt alarmed when she looked into the jar and saw how far the level had gone down.

She returned the jar to the pantry. It had begun to rain. Mia thought about the brothers out there cutting grass in the wet. They wouldn't want to stop because this was their designated day but she knew that if it rained more heavily, they'd have to give it up.

She settled back to her reading in the warm, cosy kitchen. It was interesting. There seemed to be something of value in every theoretical approach. She wondered how she'd go sitting in front of clients and helping them to sort out their problems. She supposed that eventually she'd be good at it...

After a late lunch and a nap, she turned to Bernard's homework. Their task for the first week was to watch movies and observe the Hero's Journey pattern: the character's 'ordinary world', or comfort zone; the event that presented a 'call to action', a challenge of some kind; the various characters who showed up to play roles as mentors and allies and enemies; the various trials along the road; the big climactic struggle; the conquest – or apparent conquest, because often there would be a 'false victory' and then the hero would be plunged back into an even worse darkness, a real life-and-death battle, before finally conquering all and returning home with the insights to create an improved world.

There was also a sheet of questions and tasks. She began to scan through them.

1. Identify your Ordinary World, now and in the past.

Well, that was easy: Life with John. Working at ACCAT. Her friendship with Sheryl. Her slightly strained relationship with her parents. School years…

2. What problems and conflicts have you experienced in the past and what are you experiencing now? (Consider both inner problems and outer problems.) What challenges? What is uncomfortable or frustrating you? What would you like changed? What do you dream about or hope for? What secrets do you keep? These problems and conflicts are your 'Call to Adventure': your invitation to grow. They point to aspects of yourself that need to mature or be developed or balanced in some way.

She considered. Problems in the past: being lonely and wanting a special friend – which was why she had kept leaping into inappropriate relationships – not exactly a very inspiring growth… Wanting to feel special, given her mother's constant preoccupation with the dead Rita. That was ongoing; it was like a nagging toothache. John's pursuit of her had made her feel extraordinarily special; it had tipped the scales onto the 'marry him' side. But now that she knew he'd been at least equally running away from his twin brother, the shine had come off that event and the part of her that wanted to feel special had begun to niggle her again…

Recent problems were: wanting freedom from her stuck relationship with John and freedom from the boringness of her job at ACCAT. She smiled with pleasure at the realisation that she could tick both of those boxes – she was no longer stuck in either one.

So what was uncomfortable or frustrating her now? The tension between the brothers. Not yet having told John that they were pregnant. Wondering how she was going to stay enthusiastic and committed to her job when she just wanted to give it the flick, study counselling and be a mother – she did not want to disappoint Reynald.

Changing career and becoming a mother were her hopes and dreams. And the pregnancy was her secret.

Nick flashed into mind.

Well, there was that secret too. She had not yet said anything to John about him. Should she? Did she need to? It didn't seem to matter anymore. And nothing had really happened. She could surely just let that go…

She looked at the next question.

3. What are your strengths and weaknesses? What's your 'Achilles heel', your 'fatal flaw', your 'psychic wound'? What is the 'agon' in your life?

Strengths… Why was it always so difficult to acknowledge your strengths? She and Sheryl had made a pact that they would not brush away each other's compliments – that was mainly Sheryl's way of helping Mia to accept compliments. Sheryl had a pretty robust self-image; it was Mia who tended to run herself down. So, strengths?

She gazed at John's father's painting of the window scene that was hanging on the wall opposite where she sat. She loved this picture. She loved the details in the people. They were so carefully drawn, as if the artist really cared about the people he was painting. Caring. *She* cared about people. She was interested in them and did her best to help others, when she could… There was a word for understanding others…? Empathy! She wrote it down, then went back to gazing at the painting as she tried to summon more strengths. Doing her best at work – did that count? It sounded so weak. What would Sheryl say? 'You're very generous, a giver.' Was she? Should she put that? She loved colour and beauty, but not enough to be an artist or interior designer, other than their home… A friend had once described her as innocent and trusting. That was true, but was it a strength or a weakness?

She sighed and considered the other list. Weaknesses. The words for this list practically leapt out of her: blame, as John had pointed out the other night; being self-absorbed, as Sheryl had said; envy, of almost anyone who had something or some quality she wanted. She remembered those last couple of years when things with John had become so flat and she'd found herself noticing every decent-looking man and wondering if life would be better with him... There was a biblical commandment about this one: 'Thou shalt not covet'. Guilty...

Passivity – waiting for things to land in her lap. All right, so she was getting a tiny bit better at that now, but she had spent far too much of her life waiting for a rescuer, a knight on a white horse...

Too sensitive. Too idealistic. Temperamental. Impatient. A glutton, at times... She felt herself sinking, burdened by this list of negative traits. So was each of these things 'an invitation to grow'? This probing, delving sort of stuff was uncomfortable, but if she was going to be a counsellor...

She looked at the fourth question.

4. We are all striving for wholeness and greater power (in the sense of the capacity to influence or direct our own behaviour). What, in your heart of hearts, do you feel that you most need to learn or master? Is it the ability to ask for what you want or to apologise or to communicate love or affection? Is it a willingness to listen to others? Is it the courage to say no, to hold your boundaries, or to change something you are doing? Is it patience or the ability to keep going when you want to give up? What is your greatest fear? It, too, holds the key to your growth.

In her heart of hearts... She knew what she wanted in her bladder. Mia abandoned the homework for a pee. As she sat there, she pondered. What did she most need to learn or master? All the things in the previous list: patience, to not blame, to not be envious... She supposed she should express those as positives instead of negatives. What was the opposite of envy? Satisfaction? To be happy with what she had... But what if it wasn't enough? It was fair enough to want more. So maybe she was really being called to be more involved in creating that 'more', rather than passively waiting for it. Yes...

She flushed and returned to her notebook. Not blaming meant taking responsibility, which was another way of saying the same thing. She sensed that this self-knowledge *would* call for action. You couldn't wallow in traits you didn't want; you had to do something about them...

What was her greatest fear?

The image of Rita's tiny, perfect face came to mind. The time she'd overheard her mother say to Auntie Ann, 'All the joy went out of life when she died...' This was her fear: that she was not sufficiently loveable or worthy in herself, because what mother would say that *all* the joy went out of life when she had a lively, active child playing in the next room? Mia couldn't remember what her aunt had said in reply. She had been too hurt by her mother's words to hear anything else.

Noises outside told her that the ute had just pulled into the driveway. She could hear the slamming of car doors and muffled voices.

It's common for the hero to 'Refuse the Call', she read. It's normal to feel wary about taking on a new challenge and leaving one's comfort zone, but as this call comes direct from the heart, we refuse it at our peril. The outcome of taking the Hero's Journey is a deeper understanding of oneself, greater character strength, and greater skills and abilities. The character arc is the inner journey a character takes in the process of transformation. This transformation takes the character in the direction of opposite traits and often requires sweeping change.

As you look at these lists of traits, consider them from the perspective of 'God-you' rather than 'Character-you': What experiences would 'God-you' give 'Character-you' in order to learn your lessons and grow in the ways you need to grow?

She imagined shrinking Mia and sitting her on the kitchen table. Little-character-Mia sat there, legs stretched out on the red-and-white check cloth, leaning back with straight arms, hands on the table behind her, and looking up at God-Mia...

She was smiling, amused, wondering what challenges she would set for mini-Mia to learn her lessons when the brothers came inside, tired and sweaty from their day mowing lawns.

23

J ake knocked on their bedroom door when they were dressing for the show that night. 'Got a shirt I can borrow?' he asked through the door.

John was buttoning up the new paisley print shirt he'd bought. He glanced at Mia. She shrugged and went into the ensuite, dress on but unzipped, one foot in fishnet stockings and the other delicate piece of black netting trailing behind her. She was wearing the new dress, the special one they had bought together, which was perhaps slightly over-dressing but hey, when else was she likely to wear it?

She heard the low rumble of voices in the bedroom as she put the toilet lid down and sat on it to ease the tights up her legs. Straightened up and smiled in the mirror at the effect, smoothing the dress over her hips. Mascara. Lippie. A little bit of blush... They were still moving hangers around and talking in there. How long did it take for a guy to choose a shirt?

When she emerged, both men stopped talking abruptly and looked at her. John gave a wolf whistle. 'Looking very hot, honey,' he said.

Jake raised his brows a little, muttered, 'Stunning,' and walked out.

He was wearing John's only pink shirt, a shirt she'd bought him years ago in an attempt to loosen up the stiff accountant's wardrobe, and through that, the stiff accountant's character... He'd hardly ever worn it. Typical of the actor-bro to choose that one. But, looking at John now in his paisley shirt, there was no doubt that the loosening was in full swing. The only thing out had been her timing – or the fact that the change had had to come from within him instead of from her.

The show was on at the Sumner Theatre. John drove them in the Commodore, Jake sitting silent in the back. As they joined the throngs moving into the brightly lit, open foyer, Mia's smile of excitement was irrepressible. ('Childlike,' she thought, thinking of the lists of traits. But was that a strength or a weakness?) She moved between the brothers, sliding one arm around John's back and linking arms with Jake on her other side. 'This is fun!'

She attracted a few interested looks and smiles as they walked in together, she in her stunning new dress between identical men, both looking handsome in their pink and paisley shirts. John still hadn't lost all of that extra heaviness he'd brought back from Europe, despite the renewed cycling. Jake was as slim as John had been, which was interesting, considering that he lived with stodgy food all the time. Perhaps twins had different metabolisms. She felt comfortable with both of them, as if they'd always all been close. So far tonight they hadn't started arguing, which was a relief.

'I'm going to get you a programme,' she declared to Jake, breaking loose at the sight of a woman standing on a little platform and waving a programme above her head.

The show was *Much Ado About Nothing*. She'd been surprised that John had booked tickets for Shakespeare, but he'd told her that it had received good reviews and was apparently funny. It proved to be better than she had expected.

During interval John went to join the crush at the bar while she and Jake stood in the foyer, gazing at the chatting crowd around them.

'I hated Shakespeare at school,' she said. 'But this is quite good! I actually understand everything.'

'That's because the actors know what they're doing,' he said. 'Shakespeare was never meant to be read or studied; it was supposed to be performed and watched.'

'Really?' It was so much fun having an actor in the family!

'Yes.' He glanced in the direction of the bar. 'Interesting choice, though. I didn't think John was into Shakespeare.'

'I imagine he chose it for you!' Mia said. She had brought the programme out with them to read it in better light. She loved looking at the pictures of the actors and reading their bios. It was the romance of theatre. She kept glancing at Jake, wondering if he was feeling enlivened being here, in his milieu, albeit in another country. 'You must be enjoying this,' she bubbled.

'Doesn't everyone love the theatre?'

'I do! John and I don't go nearly often enough.'

There were so many people standing around them that she could barely hold the programme at a decent angle to read it. 'Nominated for awards, a box office hit, critical acclaim… I suppose that doesn't sound glamorous to you, but to little old me… Hey, what's a reper – repor – how do you even say that?'

They were standing opposite each other. He glanced down at the programme, and realising that he wouldn't be able to see upside down, she began to move around beside him, finger pointing to the spot, but he was already saying, 'Repertory theatre. It's a company that has a repertoire of shows that they alternate or rotate.'

'Ah. Of course! Thanks.' Mia looked toward the bar. 'He's taking a while.'

'Jake!'

They both turned toward the voice. A woman in a close-fitting black dress was walking toward them, a big smile on her red lips, strawberry-blonde hair piled up on her head while long tendrils curled on either side of her face. Diamonds flashed from her ears and neck and wrist and fingers. Or perhaps diamante; Mia could never tell.

'Darling!' The woman leaned in to kiss Jake, who was looking surprised, almost alarmed.

One of his exes, Mia thought in amusement. Perhaps he had so many of them he'd forgotten this one's name. 'Mia,' she said, extending a hand toward the woman to help him out.

'Katarina,' the woman replied. A Russian name but an English accent. 'What are you doing down under, Jakey? I wish I'd known! We've got a show starting in three days and one of the leads has just broken his ankle! I could suggest you.'

'I'm only here for a couple of weeks,' he began.

'Come *on*, darling. That's not the Jake I know! When have you ever let your plans get in the way of a show?' She looked at Mia properly for the first time. 'Or is this gorgeous woman your excuse? A woman would be the only excuse you'd have for not accepting a job...'

'Oh, no,' Mia laughed. 'I'm his sister-in-law. You two have been in shows together?'

Katarina flashed a conspiratorial look at Jake. 'What haven't we been in together?' she asked, raising her brows suggestively. 'A show, a bed, a bath, a pool of mud, a shark tank –'

'A shark tank!' Mia exclaimed. 'Tell me more!'

Jake was looking uncomfortable. 'Come on, Katarina! Don't shock my sister-in-law!'

'Oh, I've been busting to be shocked,' Mia laughed. 'Go on – tell all!'

A bell began to ding, inconveniently indicating that interval was almost over.

'Where *is* John?' she asked, frowning as she scanned the foyer. 'We won't have time for our drinks!'

'You mean your twin brother?' Katarina asked, also looking around. 'Mia is married to the twin? I'd love to meet him!'

'He's coming,' Jake said, nodding in the direction of the bar at John, who was weaving his way toward them with two glasses of champagne and a water for Mia. Everyone else was slowly moving back into the auditorium.

'That was some queue!' Mia exclaimed as he joined them and passed them their drinks. 'Thanks, honey.'

Katarina put her sparkling hands on her hips and gazed from one brother to the other. 'Jakey,' she announced, 'you were not lying. Identical twins. My God! He could pass for you any day.'

John smiled politely. 'And this is...?'

'Katarina,' Jake said. 'We've performed together.'

'And the rest,' Katarina winked. She leaned in to kiss John on the cheek. 'So lovely to meet you, darling! You are the spit of your brother – but I know you know that. If you ever want a career in theatre you'll be able to just step into his shoes. Especially since he seems to have stepped out of them! Nobody knows where you've been these last ages!' she declared to Jake. 'You know you missed an amazing opportunity –'

The bells chimed again and the lights began to dim.

'We'd better go in!' John said. 'Very nice to meet you, Katarina.'

'And you.' She looked again from one to the other, almost curiously, then said to Jake, 'Seriously, darling. You missed a great opportunity. I was ringing you and texting you and… Where were you?'

John took Mia by the arm. 'Let's leave them to finish that conversation,' he said, guiding her back into the auditorium, and putting his barely-touched champagne down as they went.

She turned and waved a farewell to Katarina. Jake was looking so uncomfortable beside her. Mia wondered what the opportunity was that he had missed.

'I bought chocolate,' John said. 'Hazelnut.' He put her in front of him so that she could move through the doorway first. Jake was still out there, captivated by Katarina – or captured. It had looked more like the latter, which was odd.

'Isn't she gorgeous?' Mia said over her shoulder. 'So glam.'

'Who?'

'Katarina, of course.' They reached their row. 'I wonder why Jake didn't look happier about seeing her.'

'It probably didn't finish well. You know how his relationships often go.'

Mia began to excuse herself as she edged past seated patrons on her way toward their seats. When they'd sat, she said, 'But she looked happy enough to see him.'

John shrugged. 'Who knows what goes on in that thespian world? It's probably very complicated.' He took the bar of chocolate out of his jacket pocket and tore it open. Broke a few pieces and offered them to her.

The lights were dimming and the orchestra was playing. Mia glanced back toward the exit. Still no sign of Jake. 'He'd better hurry or they'll shut him out.'

John was breathing evenly, eyes straight ahead, jaw set.

'You okay?' she asked.

'Bit of a headache.'

'Oh. Baby...' She reached out and touched the side of his face gently, running her fingers down his stubbled jawline. 'Better relax this tension, then. Maybe the chocolate will help – magnesium.'

He nodded, giving a small smile.

There was a movement in their row and they saw Jake edging his way toward them. The lights came up on stage as he took his seat.

John's headache had grown worse by the end of the show so they left as soon as it was over. Mia was never in a hurry to leave a theatre – she always hoped for a glimpse of one of the performers. It was another expression of her childlikeness, she reflected, scanning the foyer as they walked out. Quite silly. She only read magazines about actors and the royal family when she came across them in waiting rooms at the doctor or dentist – they made the reader as sticky-beaky as the paparazzi, and she didn't like to think of herself that way. But there was something so interesting about people who exposed themselves to others on the screen or stage. You did kind of feel as if you knew that person, even though they were only acting a role. Perhaps watching them in private moments made you feel as if you were somehow related and had a right to know more about their lives... even though those private moments were not genuine, just scripted moments in a play or film. Bizarre.

She glanced at Jake as they exited into the cool night air. Even he seemed happy to leave quickly. Perhaps he didn't want to run into Katarina again? He'd said it was tiredness after the day mowing and then the show, which was fair enough.

John didn't tease Jake about Katarina on the way home; he was frowning under the weight of his headache. Mia tried the odd comment about the show – after all, it had been interesting and would be good to discuss, but neither responded with more than a monosyllable, and conversation died out.

At home John swallowed some tablets; Jake said goodnight and disappeared into the guest room; Mia took off the sexy dress and fishnet stockings slowly, wondering when she would next have the chance to dress up like this. John was already in bed when she climbed in beside him. He was lying on his side, the heel of his hand pressing against his forehead. She leaned close to kiss him on the temple and sat for a moment, stroking his hair. He murmured appreciatively. She felt a little frustrated by this turn of events. Tonight was the first night since Jake had arrived that she had felt like making love. Her self-consciousness about him being under their roof was finally fading. And plus, it could have been a good time to tell John their news…

Oh well. She gave him another kiss then slid down into the bed, spooning him. He murmured again, and covered her hand with his warm one.

She was wide awake. There wasn't a cell of her being that wanted to go to sleep. She thought about Jake down the hallway and wondered what it would be like to make love to him… How bizarre that would be! Making love to someone who looked so like your husband but wasn't… She smiled in the dark, feeling a little shocked that she was even thinking this. She would never do that – no way! But it was an interesting question. She'd heard of twins swapping dates and their partners never guessing. But had anyone swapped beds without their partner guessing?

John was breathing steadily now, asleep. Mia rolled onto her back and gazed up at the ceiling. Why had Jake been so uncomfortable meeting Katarina? The glamorous actress had seemed completely delighted to be running into him. And what was that about the opportunity he had missed? He'd seemed to be more troubled about seeing Katarina than losing an acting opportunity, which just didn't make sense if that was his great passion.

A sudden queasiness in her stomach made her freeze. It was not pregnancy-nausea; it was a realisation that had begun creeping through her in the wake of those last thoughts.

Jake was not Jake. John was not John. They had swapped.

She lay there on her back, mouth dry, breath caught in her chest, horrified.

She replayed the last month, and all the little moments that had jarred came rushing forward into her memory. John's greyer hair. That he was heavier and still hadn't lost much of the extra weight. That he ate more potatoes, which John would never do... The scar on his knee that wasn't there... That he dealt better with alcohol since he'd come back from England. The smoke on his breath after that night at the pub – her John, who never smoked and thought it was a filthy habit! The extraordinary change of career. Avoiding conversations with Alec, when the two of them had always talked about finance and business. The flat screen TV. The new expensive dress he had bought her. That he was messier than he'd ever been. His new clothes – the paisley shirt. That he'd never noticed how much weight she had lost...

She sat up in bed, gasping, appalled.

The conversation with the director at that show they'd gone to. The gardening. The massage course. The better sex...

And then there was 'Jake', who didn't strike her as a promiscuous spendthrift. 'Jake' who had known she wanted a throw rug, and known what colour to buy. 'Jake' who had been able to read the theatre programme upside-down, an accountant's trait from all the times they had to talk clients through their finances from the opposite side of the table... 'Jake', who was not comfortable about meeting his ex-lover and co-performer, Katarina... Bitsy going nuts over him...

Was she an idiot or what?

John – Jake! – rolled over in bed toward her. 'All right?' he asked muzzily, putting a hand on her thigh.

'No, *Jake*,' she said, shoving his hand away and throwing the covers off her legs. 'No. I am *not* all right.'

He sat up suddenly, and winced, putting a hand to the side of his head, as if to stop it spinning.

'You are Jake, aren't you?' she asked, standing beside the bed in the cold. 'Don't lie to me.' She snapped on her bedside lamp to see him better.

The expression in his eyes was troubled. Guilty. He didn't have to speak.

She snatched her robe from the back of the chair and began pacing as she forced her arms into the sleeves. 'I can't believe it! I'm *horrified*. Whose idea was it? Why did you do this to me?'

He swallowed. 'Mia...'

'Don't give me any shit! I can't believe – you two have been lying to me for months! You!' She twirled around to face him, speechless. 'I thought... so many things didn't fit but I just never...' She threw her hands in the air and then whirled on her heel and began pacing again, furious.

'Sssh,' he hushed.

'What! You want me to be quiet! You want me to not wake up my own husband!' She tore open the bedroom door and strode down the hall to the guest room. Jake was hurrying out of bed behind her as she opened the door to the guest room and slipped inside. She closed the door behind her.

John was sleeping; he hadn't heard them. She stood just inside the room, her back to the door, looking at him.

This was her husband of ten years. This man, lying here, fast asleep, was her actual husband. A husband who had... given her away! Swapped places with his brother for some, for some... words failed her.

She moved to his side and shook him by the shoulder roughly. He jerked awake, eyes snapping open in alarm. Saw her. Relief flooded his face. He smiled. That beautiful smile.

'You bastard!' she spat.

24

Jake spoke from the other side of the door. 'Mia –'

'Stay out!' she snapped. 'I am speaking to my husband.'

John was sitting up, his grogginess falling away. The smile had disappeared too. He looked very serious and very sad. 'You know.' It was a statement.

'Why did you do it? *How* could you do it?' she repeated, standing a little away in the impeccably neat room, arms crossed, as if to hold herself together.

'Don't you remember, Mia? Things between us were dying. Flat. Stale. I felt useless – nothing was working. I didn't like my job. You didn't really want me anymore... And then, going home by myself for Dad's... I felt hurt, sad that you didn't come with me. I hadn't realised how much that bothered me until I was heading over there. It made sense for you to stay back when we were discussing it here, but on the flight and then arriving at Mum's... that one question, 'How's Mia?' He looked away for a moment, and then back at her with a deep sigh. 'It just... the distance between us felt so...' He broke off, and the unnamed word hovered there between them, ungraspable.

She felt a pang listening to him. A pang of guilt as she remembered how delighted she had been that he was leaving, how she had thrilled at her freedom... What had gone wrong between them? Or had it just never been right?

He picked up his tale. 'You remember I told you Jake and I had a really good conversation after the funeral?'

She gave a short nod.

'We talked about the old man's life. His regrets. How he'd had this gift and had kept putting it aside, minimising it, doing what he should instead of what he wanted... And I realised I was doing that, too. I was doing the daily grind and not really enjoying it. Doing the drill at Buxton and managing our property and finances... and dying inside. I was on automatic. I started to wonder what else there was to me – that maybe I had some gift or ability *I* wasn't using, and would I ever find it doing the same old thing all the time?'

She wet her lips. Remembered those dry years when the routine had taken over and the highlight of the week was a movie on the couch on a Saturday night.

'Jake had always had fun.' He sighed. 'Well, that's what it looked like to me. He'd taken risks, had adventures. I didn't want his life, *per se*, but I could tell that he was alive where I felt like a husk... But on his side, I discovered, he was feeling life was empty too. He'd just broken up with someone he really loved – well, truth be told, she dumped him. So he was hurting. Nothing was working for him either. Didn't have the career he wanted. Lonely. Watching his ex-girlfriends partner up with other people. Afraid he was going to grow old on his own... We were envying each other's lives.' He gave a short bitter laugh. 'That was the seed of it. We didn't instantly decide to swap lives. The idea grew...'

Jake knocked on the door.

'Wait!' Mia said. Her voice sounded so harsh.

'I love you, Mia.' The expression in John's eyes was earnest, almost desperate. 'I loved you then but I felt I was no good for you – that I wasn't what you wanted anymore. And I knew I was suffocating at Buxton. I knew I had to get out of there but I had no idea where to go next, what to do. I was just afraid of dying at my desk like Dad. I wanted a taste of Jake's freedom so I could explore. *He* wanted a steady partner. He wanted a home and responsibilities. He has a... 'gift' with women. They've always thrown themselves at him...' A little muscle flickered in his jaw. 'I just had this thought: he'll be what you want. He'll give you the romance I haven't given you. The fun you want. You'll be happier with him... And I... I didn't know what I wanted anymore. I needed some time alone to find out.'

Mia sank to the floor. She sat with her back against the wall, looking at him, imagining the brothers' conversation at the cemetery, by their father's grave... She felt numb.

Jake knocked again. 'Can I come in?'

'No!' they both snapped.

They heard him swear and storm away. A moment later he returned and began pacing up and down the hallway. Bitsy was with him, toenails clattering on the floorboards, excited by this midnight activity.

John pushed the covers away and swung his legs over the side of the bed. He sat on the floor, facing her, back against the bed. 'It was good, at first. Knowing I had this new lease on life, this opportunity for a fresh start. Knowing I'd given you what you wanted.'

'How do you know what I wanted?' she muttered. *But he had...*

'Well, I... It was stupid of me, all right! I know that now. It seemed like the right thing to do at the time – for all of us. But the more I thought about it... *Giving* you to Jake! My God, what a fool I was.' He was looking at her with desperation in his eyes. 'As if he hasn't already taken enough of what was mine! And this time I *gave* him my most precious...' Tears were brimming.

Mia swallowed. Her throat was so dry.

'Watching him plunder our savings.' John shook his head grimly. 'My first idea was to meet him at the airport and just swap back. So you'd never know...'

She gaped at him.

'I'd sorted out all of his problems for him, like we'd agreed,' John charged on. 'But he wouldn't do it. He wouldn't go back to his old life.' He stopped, seeing her expression. His face fell.

She was a churning riot of feelings. Lose this man who had made her feel so loved, so womanly, so attractive? Who had brought fun back into her life?

John was gazing at her, riveted to the spot, the tears welling in his eyes now. 'You're in love with him,' he whispered.

Mia drew her knees up. Wrapped her arms around them. Looked at him through her own tears.

For a moment, neither spoke.

'It's the honeymoon period,' John said, in a voice that cracked. 'Jake doesn't know how to do long-term relationships.'

She brushed at the tears that were falling from her cheek.

'I didn't want to live a lie anymore – all the stuff we had to learn to step into each other's lives…' He shook his head. 'It was insane. That was what planted the seed of doubt. It felt so false.'

She echoed him in disbelief. 'It felt so false!' Gave a short almost hysterical laugh. 'How *could* you!'

'I meant well, Mia. You have to understand that. I was trying to solve all of our problems. You wanted children. I can't –' That muscle flickered in his jaw again. 'I had the test before I left. Couldn't bring myself to tell you. Jake has kids all over frigging Europe, he's so fertile.'

Mia's thoughts ran straight to the seed that was growing inside her right now. *Kids all over frigging Europe…*

'But the more I thought about it the more I regretted what I'd done. It was all rebounding on me…'

'On *you*! You gave me away like I was… some… toy! You told him – you prepared him to just… act your life! I get it now,' she said with a toss of her head. 'Jake the actor! He's just been acting, all this time.'

'I'm coming in,' Jake threatened from outside.

'Mia. Please. I want a second chance with you.' John made to move closer.

Mia shook her head, recoiling, biting her lip.

He sat back again, face white. He looked very tired. When he spoke, he sounded old. Resigned. 'He's not just acting. Jake missed a pretty good role being out here. I learnt about it by accident. I was using that to turn him around – to try to turn him around… I didn't expect him to be prepared to commit to you… I guess all along, at the back of my mind, I thought it would just be temporary. He would tire of all this,' John waved a hand around the room, 'suburbia. Humdrum. He'd want his freedom back. He'd want a back door. Really, Mia. It's just going to be a question of time. He won't be able to do this forever. I know him.'

The bedroom door burst open and Jake stood there. He looked as ravaged as them. His gaze rushed from one to the other.

Bitsy scampered straight across the room and leapt into Mia's lap. She lifted the dog up to her chest, cuddling her, burying her wet face in the warm hairy body.

'So it's all out,' Jake said. He sat heavily on the floor at the foot of the bed.

Neither John nor Mia spoke. The three of them sat in silence.

'I don't know what John's told you,' Jake said at last. 'But you've got to hear my side of it too.'

She raised her tear-stained face to him.

'This wasn't just some game, Mia,' he said.

Another pair of beautiful hazel eyes looking at her intently. She felt as if her heart was broken.

'I really wanted a new life. I wanted a committed relationship. I wanted a job where I could stick with something and succeed at it instead of continually being passed over... I didn't know if it would work but I felt it was worth a chance. John had always said good things about you and when I got here I... liked you. I liked being a husband. I started to really love you.'

She made an involuntary sound, almost a whimper.

'John left you,' Jake said. 'He gave you up. I –'

Mia stood up in a rush, spilling Bitsy from her lap. 'Stop it! Both of you. I can't believe this. This lying. This deceit. This –' She cast around for words. 'I'm horrified. I feel sick. I can't hear any more tonight. I'm going to bed – *not*,' she said with emphasis, 'not to our – to the – I'm going to sleep on the couch. We'll talk tomorrow, if I can bear to ever talk to either of you ever again.'

25

She was throbbing, pulsing with heat, tension, upset, shock, disbelief… Bitsy scampered at her feet as she moved down the hallway to the linen cupboard, pulled out blankets, walked into the lounge room and closed the doors firmly behind her. There was the flat screen TV, false-John's big purchase. There was the blue throw rug, false-Jake's gift. She wanted to chuck something at the TV, rip the rug to shreds. She stood staring, trembling.

She'd been *given away*. Her husband had swapped places with his brother, a brother he'd barely told her about. He'd withheld that 'twin' information all those years – saving up for a gig like this? Surely not. But he'd decided he wanted to be free and so he would just piss off without saying a word to her, and stick someone in his place so she'd never know. Christ! What a jerk. *What an arsehole.*

She went to the couch, savagely ripping the throw rug off the back of it and letting it fall to the ground. Stared at the TV, fighting with three-year-old Mia who wanted to smash it. Stood there, arms folded, shaking.

She'd wanted to be free too! They could have talked about it and changed things deliberately, consciously, like adults, instead of all this cloak-and-dagger creeping around and secrets!

'*Then why didn't you?*' that fucking little voice asked her quietly.

Shut up! she snapped.

'*You could have talked to him about how things were going. You had lots of opportunities. You can't just blame him.*'

But he fucking well swapped places, she argued. *That is far worse. That is massive deception!*

She was shivering now, with cold, with stress. She went to sit on the couch. Wrapped one of the blankets around her. Sat with crossed legs, like a little brown teepee, steaming, brooding.

Bitsy leapt up beside her and began turning in circles before lying down and looking up at her, nose on her paws.

Her mind wouldn't stop churning. She remembered John's emails: 'I'm coming back a changed man.' 'I'll be different.' Bloody hell. When had he decided? Which one of those messages had been the turning point? They must have talked about it, planned it for weeks! How else had Jake known everything about her? Known where everything was in the house? It was a stunning heist! The two of them, cunning thieves planning their treachery together, putting their bad relationship aside so they could pull one over her!

She shifted restlessly on the couch. Why had she fallen for it? Was she really so stupid? Thinking again about all the clues, all the little things Jake had said and done that were so not-John... The fact that John had resigned while he was in the UK, knowing that Jake could never step into those accountant shoes, setting it up for him to 'come back' and work as a frigging gardener. He'd planted seeds in all those email messages from England so she wouldn't suspect. And, of course, she hadn't known he had an identical twin brother! How the fuck was she supposed to guess that the man coming back who'd promised to be different was a fucking twin! If you had no idea of something like that you'd never guess. She wasn't *that* stupid! She'd been deceived. She'd been fooled. She'd been made a fool of...

Mia collapsed sideways, pulling the blankets over her face, burying herself in the couch. She wanted to cry and scream and go to sleep – go unconscious on this horrible mess.

Her feet were cold. She sat up, irritated, to cover her legs with the blanket, and then lay down again. She could feel Bitsy walking around on her legs, then burrowing under the blanket, sneaking her way up higher, the little warm body bumping into her as it went until it reached her chest. 'Oh, Bits,' she murmured, before thoughts of their treachery seized her again.

Them setting it up. Her not expecting it, innocently not expecting any such madness. Jake being identical and her not knowing. Phones – he'd had John's phone and computer, or at least identical ones. Phones say who's ringing; she'd seen Jake's name as an incoming call on John's phone. Little details like that had maintained the status quo. What could possibly make her think it was actually John ringing?

And she'd fallen for it so soundly because she had *wanted* to believe that John had changed and her marriage was alive again. She'd wanted the new John, the tenderness, the attention, the romance, the surprises... She had herself quickly discarded any suspicions. She'd justified, rationalised all those new behaviours because she'd wanted to believe he had really changed.

She remembered the night at dinner when he'd said, *'I haven't made you feel like the beautiful, loved woman you are. I want to change that.'* He'd reached across the table and taken her hand. *'I want you to know how gorgeous you are and how much you mean to me every single day.'* She'd kept those words ever since, turning them over and over in her mind, admiring them, loving them, treasuring them as if they were a precious gift.

My God! Had John told him to say all that? Had John said, 'I've been a shit of a husband lately so the way is clear for you, bro. Just romance her a bit and she'll be putty in your hands!' *Fucking hell.*

She was so torn between anger and grief that she didn't know what she felt. She lay buried on the couch, back to the TV, nursing Bitsy against her belly. She wished she could talk to Sheryl but it was, what? Two a.m.? Three? She lay there, remembered bits of conversation and images battering her.

Picking Jake up from the airport and thinking he was John. Innocently taking him into her bed. Having him touch her, make love to her. *Her husband had planned that!* How must it have felt, for him, standing aside for his rival, the evil brother, to step right into his bed? It made no sense! It was no wonder she had never guessed. He'd hated Jake – that was why he'd left England ten years ago. And then to give his wife, his beloved, to his rival brother? To let the one he despised make love to her! Well, she was clearly no longer his beloved, no matter what he said now. This was the ultimate betrayal.

They were shouting now. She could hear muffled shouting from the guest bedroom. Shouting and thudding noises. Maybe they were fighting. Good. Fuck 'em. She hoped they did some serious damage to each other. Bastards.

Mia woke to the sound of Bitsy whining and scratching at the door. She opened her eyes and saw the back of the couch. The drama of the previous night came rushing back. She felt exhausted. Wiped out. She rolled onto her back and squinted through bleary eyes at the fluorescent digits on the TV: nine-oh-seven a.m. She swallowed, dry-mouthed, dragging herself up.

'All right, Bitsy.' Wrapped herself in one of the blankets. Walked stiffly to the door and yanked it open. The aroma of coffee wafted in. She could hear movement in the kitchen. Bitsy ran to the dog-door in the laundry and shot through; it banged after her.

Jake looked up as she walked into the kitchen. She ignored him. Poked an arm out of the blanket to take a glass from the rack. Turned the tap on. Come to think of it, was it Jake? Maybe it was John. She hadn't looked properly.

'Mia,' he said, taking a step toward her.

She held up a hand to stop him, still drinking. Put the glass back on the sink. 'There's nothing you can say.'

'I know.' He hesitated. 'But –'

She wrapped herself more tightly in the blanket. 'So which one are you?' Her voice was icy, sarcastic.

'Jake,' he said at once. 'John's out riding.'

'Oh. Right.' Figures. The man of reliable habits – until recently... 'So do you actually ride? Or were you always just hanging out in cafés?'

He gave an embarrassed smile. 'Yeah. A bit of both. I actually did start to enjoy it but I'm not up to his standards. I'd ride a bit and then grab a coffee, talk to John about Dad's stuff because early morning was often the best time to connect with him…'

She nodded, mouth closed tight.

'Mia,' he said again. He looked shame-faced. 'I'm sorry. You're right. It seems crazy looking at it now, from this angle. It just seemed so perfect at the time. For all of us.'

She shook her head in disbelief. 'Really? You think I wanted lies? Secrets? Deception? You think I wanted my problems solved for me by the Terrible Twins?'

He swallowed.

'You think I wanted a husband who was pretending, acting the love? All that you said and did – that was crap, wasn't it? You were just acting!'

'I wasn't,' he protested. 'Well, maybe at first. But then I genuinely fell in love with you. I did, Mia.'

'Yeah. Right. And you actually intended to stay around and have kids with me? Have a family? Because you know that was on the agenda, don't you?'

'John told me you wanted kids.'

'And you were actually going to stay for that?' she persisted. 'You were going to give up the girl in every port and settle down to be husband and daddy?'

He nodded. 'I wanted it, Mia. I *want* it. I want some steadiness. I've been in too many relationships that broke down. I want to experience a committed, long-term relationship.'

'And here was one, waiting for you – on a platter. You could just step right in…'

'Yes…' He risked a smile, a genuine awed smile. 'It was pretty bloody amazing to step right into a marriage with a beautiful, committed woman instead of courting women I've picked up in a bar or on stage who turn out to be married or barmy…'

Mia remembered the morning she had woken and seen him looking at her in wonder. Now it made sense. She slammed the door on that treacherous memory and said in a hard tone: 'The irony is that *I* wasn't committed when you got back – arrived. I had one foot out the door myself. I was pretty bloody unhappy.'

'I know,' he said. 'John warned me.'

Neither spoke for a moment. Bitsy bounded back into the kitchen and scampered to her food bowl. She sniffed its emptiness and looked up at Mia questioningly.

'I'll do it,' Jake said. He opened the pantry door and took out the dog food.

'I can't believe he didn't give me a chance to say what *I* wanted instead of just riding over the top of me with this crazy plan!' Mia exploded, and in the same moment, Jake said, 'I knew I had to win you over straight away. I knew you wanted to call it quits.'

They both stopped, capturing what the other had said and listening to it in their minds.

'I guess he didn't want to lose you altogether,' Jake said.

She stared at him, open-mouthed. 'What? In what universe was he not losing me by pulling a number like this?'

Jake shrugged unhappily. 'I always felt as if he was keeping a back door open so he could come back if he wanted to. We didn't make a hard and fast plan. We were playing it by ear. He wanted time to find himself; I wanted to let go the fantasies and start doing something serious, something real with my life. A committed relationship. A committed job instead of bits and pieces of stuff… But it was risky; we both knew that. And we didn't know how it would go. We couldn't anticipate everything. So we just agreed to give it a <u>try</u>. And if it didn't work…'

'You'd swap back and I would never know,' she finished.

'That was never the plan,' he objected. 'We didn't do this as a trial.'

'You're contradicting yourself.'

'Look, we didn't dot every 'i'. Some things were unspoken… It was kind of a 'let's see' and kind of for good because he thought you didn't want him any more and I really wanted to kick my old habits. But then John changed his mind, and when he wanted to come back, I wasn't ready to give you up.'

He looked at her steadily. 'You have two men wanting you, Mia.'

'Lucky me,' she said bitterly.

Bitsy barked and they both looked toward the driveway automatically. John was riding into the garage.

'So he booked a flight anyway, to force my hand,' Jake said. 'You have to give it to him. The guy was determined.'

She pressed her lips tightly together and went back to watching Bitsy scarfing her food.

'I thought you loved me,' Jake said suddenly, urgently. 'I thought it was working.'

She looked at him wordlessly, tears pricking her eyes now.

John came into the kitchen, bringing a rush of fresh air with him. A slim figure in riding gear. His eyes went straight to Mia's. Pleading eyes. Remorseful eyes.

She held his gaze, not giving way, the blanket gripped tightly around her.

He glanced at Jake and something passed between them; she had no fucking idea what. Then he looked back at Mia. With a tight jaw, he walked on out of the kitchen and toward the guest room. In the silence that followed they heard him move around in the room, then walk to the bathroom and close the door. The shower began running.

'Mia.' Jake took a step toward her and halted before she could stop him. 'Did you? Did you come to love me?'

Her own traitorous eyes were brimming with tears.

'I don't know what we're going to do,' he said helplessly. 'We both love you. We both want you.'

Outside, a truck trundled down the street. The shower water drummed in the bathroom. Bitsy went nosing around the floor under the kitchen table. Jake stood, arms hanging by his sides, watching her. Mia stood with her back to the sink, wrapped in her blanket, numb.

'That job Katarina mentioned,' he said. 'It was an audition for a lead in a movie. I turned it down to stay here with you. Biggest break of my career to date, and I turned it down.'

'You had the biggest acting job of your career to date already happening,' she snapped.

'I know it can't mean much to you, but –'

'Oh, sure! I get it! You were about to get that lucky break you've always dreamed of and make it big, and instead, you opted to stay here in suburbia with little wifey Mia.'

He sighed. Plunged his hands into his pockets. 'You're right. Coming here *was* the biggest acting job of my life. I had to step into John's shoes exactly. I had to convince you that I was him and that he had changed. I had to learn my lines.' He spoke harshly, and began to pace around the kitchen. 'I had to memorise where everything was in this house – the coffee, the tea, the toilet paper, the shoe polish. He drew me a plan. He made me learn the names of your friends, your work colleagues. I had to avoid Alec because he would guess. Learn how to solve some of your basic computer problems. I had notes from him in my phone – a crib sheet, for God's sake! He gave me maps of all the places you go – which shopping centres, which restaurants, which cafés… where your parents live and a frigging floor plan of their house! He took me cycling around London to get my fitness up. I had to learn how he cooked those two fucking dishes he makes, and pretend I didn't know anything else. I had to toe his line about what to spend money on.'

'You didn't do a very good job of that,' she cut in, fascinated and repulsed at the same time.

He shrugged. The shower water turned off.

'I had to pay the bills and rent –'

'With *our* money. So it was a pretty good acting job – you were being bloody well paid!'

'Yes,' he agreed. 'It was a good job. It was a fucking trip seeing the amount of money you two have in your bank balance! That there was always money still there at the end of the month. You wouldn't believe how much I reined myself in!' He laughed again; then grew sober when she glared at him. 'Don't you worry – John was watching every cent I spent from England. He was a fucking pain in the butt, breathing down my neck, cramping my style.'

She opened her mouth to object and he stopped her. 'I know. It was fair enough. But I could also see that the two of you were so busy saving money and being careful that you were having no fun. I wanted to liven things up! Treat you a bit.' He looked at her seriously. 'Of course I was acting in the beginning, Mia. But then I really did come to love you. You've got to know that.'

The bathroom door opened and they heard John walking to the guest room.

'Mia?' Jake said again, in a low, urgent voice.

'I just...' she shook her head. 'I'm just staggered...' That queasy feeling was starting again in her stomach. 'Getting dressed,' she muttered. She hurried to the master bedroom, past the open door to the guest room, not looking in, even when John called, 'Mia!' Closed the door to the bedroom, closed the door to the ensuite, leaned over the toilet bowl just in time...

When her stomach had emptied she sat on the floor for a bit. Stood up wearily and went to find some clothes, any clothes. Locked herself in the ensuite to shower and change. A pale, hollow-cheeked Mia stared at her from the mirror. She looked at her naked body and her hands instinctively went to her belly, her womb... She was supposed to be feeling deeply happy right now, nurtured by a proud husband, learning about the tiny pinprick of life, of cells that were multiplying inside her forming a child... not reeling from the shock of the century, the rug of security pulled out from under her, not knowing who to trust or what to do...

When she returned to the kitchen, wet tendrils of hair dripping around her neck and shoulders, Jake had left.

'He's taken Bitsy for a walk,' John said, 'so we can talk. Coffee?'

'Is there anything to say?' she asked, arms crossed. She kept wanting to fold her arms in front of her chest. Protect her heart... 'Or perhaps you have some more nasty surprises for me?'

He sighed. 'Mia. Please. I know how awful this is but it's done now. We have to move forward.'

She raised her brows at him. 'You've had a couple of months to get used to the idea, to make your evil plans and suck me in. I'm still in shock.'

'I'm sorry,' he said humbly. 'You're right.' He poured her a coffee, with the exact amount of milk she liked. Handed her the cup. Drew a chair away from the table for her.

She took the cup and sat down.

'You've lost weight,' he said.

She looked up at him quickly. He gave her a wan smile and sat opposite.

'I noticed as soon as I saw you at the airport, but of course I couldn't say.'

She nodded, stirring her coffee. So the real John *would* notice something like that...

'You look great. I felt sad when I saw how good you were looking. Flourishing without me...'

She bit her lip. Glanced up. Those beautiful hazel eyes regarding her so despondently. She hardened her heart. 'You told him everything about me. Coached him to step into my life, like I was just some character in a play.'

The pained expression on his face deepened. 'I meant well, Mia. I was trying to make you happy and sort myself out...'

'Why didn't you just talk to me about everything?'

'I know. I should have. It was just that strange day at the cemetery. Talking about Dad after his funeral. Talking about his life and what he'd given up, and I just knew we were drowning together, you and me. We were headed for divorce and I didn't want to lose you but I also knew it wasn't working. I didn't look far enough ahead. When Jake said he envied me and caught me in that precise moment envying him, it was like – it was like a sign... The idea came to both of us in the same moment. We laughed at it. It seemed like such a ridiculous thing to do. But it caught hold of us. It just grew.'

'Pull one over Mia,' she said bitterly. 'She doesn't know I've got a twin! She'll never guess.'

'Jake has always been God's gift to women,' John said roughly. 'I knew he'd make you feel special and loved. He's had girls falling for him since school years! It's even there in our names – our parents set us up, for Christ's sake! 'Jake, the rake' – the promiscuous, immoral one, and me, John, the –

what? Nothing. Just common, ordinary John.'

'Oh no, you've got a slogan of your own,' Mia said coldly. 'Yours is 'John the con'.'

He flinched at that. Took it in the chest. 'All right, I'm a cad. But I meant well...'

'How do you figure that?' she snapped. She was suddenly ravenously hungry. She stood up abruptly and went to the bread bin. Put two slices into the toaster.

'I was giving you what I thought you wanted!' he protested, also rising. 'A man who would love you and take care of you. I knew he'd be good to you, Mia. I wasn't confident that he would stick it out but he seemed willing to and I knew that if you felt loved you'd be happy and it had a chance. And it's true, at the back of my mind I wondered if this would just be a way of stopping us from breaking up while I had a chance to figure myself out...'

She shook her head, turning away from him to lean on the bench. The heat from the toaster warmed her face. 'You told him all sorts of private things about me, didn't you?' she said. 'That I have – toilet problems...' Jake had known about that, she realised now. He'd never commented on her long visits in the loo, although unlike the discreet John, he had commented when she farted... 'You probably even told him what I like in bed!'

'I didn't tell him what you liked! I told you – he's good at that. He would figure it out.' A little pause, during which her toast popped up. 'I told him what you *didn't* like.'

She looked at him over her shoulder.

'I warned him that you're not into kinky stuff, sex toys...'

She turned back to the bench and began to scrape a thin layer of butter onto her toast. 'How could you! How could you tell this brother you didn't even like all that intimate stuff about me?'

'He's my identical twin,' John said helplessly. 'Even when I hate him there's a part of me that's close to him, that trusts him.'

'Why haven't I ever heard about that part before? I still can't believe you never told me you had an identical twin!'

'I was trying to wipe him out.'

'This person who's so close to you.'

'You don't understand!' He sounded impatient. 'It's complicated. It's a complicated relationship. A love-hate...'

'Like ours.'

She took her plate of toast to the table, sat and looked him in the eye. 'Honestly. When you first came to Australia, when you followed me here, dying of love for me... How much of that was true and how much of it was just you running away from Jake?'

'They were both true,' he said at once, evenly. 'I was chasing you because I *was* in love with you, Mia. *And* I was taking the opportunity to get away from Jake and constantly living in his shadow.'

She bit a mouthful and chewed, hardly tasting what she was eating. He waited, watching her. 'I was thinking of leaving you when you went to England,' she said.

'I know.' He looked down at his hands and she realised with a little jolt that his wedding ring was gone. There was a faint line where it had been. Jake was wearing his ring. 'I knew I couldn't give you a child and that you were unhappy,' John said. 'I was thinking I should surrender – let you go and be free to meet another man and have a family. But...'

'We could have done IVF,' she said. 'Or adopted.' But even as she said that she knew that she would never have wanted to pass up this thrilling experience of having a child growing inside her. And as she remembered her pregnancy, the fact that he had known he was sterile was just now beginning to land; that he had stepped aside to let his fertile brother give her what she wanted...

'But you didn't love me anymore,' he said quietly. 'Why would you want to go through all the stress and expense of IVF with a man you didn't love?'

It was unsettling, put like that – almost brutal. This conversation was the beginning of all the backed-up, overdue conversations they should have had. But where before it was just a case of a worn-out marriage, now things were complicated by the Jake-factor. She would now have two men to leave, not just one. The thought created a physical pain in her chest.

'Anyway,' he added, 'I needed some time and space to find myself; figure out what *I* wanted.'

She could barely taste the toast; she was just obeying the growl in her stomach.

He sat still, watching her eat. Then he asked, as if reluctant to hear the answer, 'Are you pregnant?'

Mia met his eyes.

He let out a breath, the air escaping slowly, deflating him. 'Does Jake know?'

She shook her head.

'Why not?'

'I just found out. Last Wednesday. Just after you arrived.'

'Jesus.'

Key in the front door and Jake was entering. Bitsy clattered into the kitchen, dashing to sniff Mia and then John and then Mia and then Jake, tail wagging, eyes bright and happy.

'Traitor,' Mia said to her. 'You never told me who was who.'

Bitsy gave a short bark and wagged her tail again.

Jake came to sit at the table with them. He looked from one to the other. Mia was avoiding John's eye; the fact of her pregnancy hung in the air between them. She also didn't want to meet Jake's eye... She picked up her second piece of toast and bit into it, looking at the table, the red and white checked cloth, the crumbs, the pen mark...

'When did Mum figure it out?' Jake asked into the silence.

'As soon as I got back from dropping you at the airport.'

'Shit.'

'There's no fooling her.'

'We never could.'

Not the way they could fool *her*, Mia thought resentfully.

'What did she say?' Jake sounded intrigued.

'Nothing.'

'Pretended nothing had changed?' Jake asked. 'Christ!'

'No. She asked *why*. I mean no judgement. She was proud of us.'

'Proud of you!' Mia exploded. 'What kind of a sick mother do you two have!'

'Not for deceiving you,' John said at once.

'Then what?' Jake asked, also baffled.

'You, for taking some responsibility, stepping into a committed relationship,' John said. 'Me, for letting go responsibility and giving myself a chance to…' His voice trailed off.

'Well fuck me dead,' Jake marvelled.

'When you and I made such a deal of Dad's art she said it was like she woke up out of a sleep. All that crying was about keeping him small, holding him back. He'd wanted to leave his job years ago, did you know that?'

Jake nodded. 'Mum stopped him.'

'She was afraid of the loss of security. But I suppose you know all that.'

'Just that she stopped him. I got that much out of Dad but he wouldn't say more and Mum never said anything.'

John made a little sound of surprise. He'd always assumed that Jake and his mother were close, another reason for resenting his brother. Mia put the last piece of toast in her mouth and sat back, chewing. Her arms automatically crossed again.

'After Mum stopped Dad resigning he got depressed.'

'Yeah,' Jake said. 'That was when we were at school.'

Mia had heard this part of the story too. Their critical, impatient mother and their silent, withdrawn, depressed father.

'Yes,' John said. 'But did you know she felt guilty? I didn't.'

Jake shook his head slowly.

'Once she'd stopped him leaving she felt trapped by his sacrifice. But she was too scared to undo it. She didn't think he had it in him to bring in an income as an artist. That was when he began to paint more,' John told Mia. 'He'd always sketched. But he started to paint.'

Her gaze flickered across to the painting on the wall. It was gaining even more depth as she learnt more about the artist.

John turned back to Jake. 'Mum reckons she'd always known he was good but she wanted him to prove to her that they'd be all right if he did what he wanted – that he would get out there and find a more creative job or sell his work, and they'd continue in the manner to which she had become accustomed...'

Jake whistled. 'You got all that out of her?'

'I thought she talked to you.'

'Not like that. Not about that stuff.'

Mia looked from one to the other: John's expression was one of surprise; Jake was expressionless, flat.

'Dad didn't give her any sign that he would do anything but hobby painting, and that riled her. She wanted him to be the man and not let her talk him out of what he wanted to do. Instead, he just played the victim; turned quiet and passive and she got more and more sarcastic and critical and couldn't stop herself. She lost respect for both of them. That's why she was proud of us. Because we were doing something about what we wanted.'

'What about what *I* wanted?' Mia asked, standing so abruptly that she bumped the table and Bitsy skittered away. 'That story about your parents is all very interesting but you've done to me exactly what your mother did to your father: shut me out. Treat me like a pawn that you can just – move around on some chess board!'

She crossed her arms again, the tight feeling rising from her belly to her chest to her throat. 'I'm going to Sheryl's. I'll leave you two chums to plot your next move.'

26

There was a Corvette parked in the street outside Sheryl's place. Mia climbed out of her car, contemplating it. Bitsy jumped out after her and went to pee on the nature strip at the foot of the plum tree.

She hadn't even rung to warn Sheryl that she was coming. She'd been so caught up in her own dramas, crying on the way over, shouting at John, blubbering at Jake, that she hadn't stopped to consider if this might not be a good time to drop in unexpectedly. That self-absorption... She stood on the grass indecisively, looking from the sports car to the overnight bag on the passenger seat of her car, and then thought: Alec! The sports car driver might be visiting Alec, not Sheryl. And went to ring the doorbell.

Alec answered, with Talia in his arms. Bitsy trotted straight in past him. There was a delicious aroma of something in the air – some sort of pastry.

'Mia!' He gave her a smile and a kiss, and then looked at her more closely. 'Are you okay?'

She shook her head, sniffing back more tears.

Alec glanced up the hallway toward the dining room. 'Sheryl's in a meeting with Lucy –' and just then they heard Sheryl say, 'Hey, Bits! Nice of you to drop in...'

'I'll come back later...' Mia reached out a finger to touch Talia's pink cheek. The infant looked at her soberly. She had also been crying. She gave a little hiccup.

There was movement up the hallway and Sheryl looked out of the dining room. 'Hey, Mia! I'm caught up at the mo with Luce. We're checking out this big takeover, crazy old us, but it's looking good.' She was walking toward them, chatting happily, blonde ringlets bobbing around her shoulders. 'You're welcome to join us – Luce brought the most scrumptious quichey thing for brunch – but you might be a bit bored.' She stopped, registering the expressions on Mia's and Alec's faces. 'What's happened?'

Mia dashed at a tear that was falling down her face. 'Just a bombshell. Go back to your meeting – I'll come back later.'

'*Just* a bombshell?' Sheryl turned and headed back up the hall, calling, 'Luce! Can you do that errand you need to do now and we'll finish later? Got a bit of an emergency.' She disappeared into the dining room.

'I feel awful,' Mia said.

Alec passed Talia to her. 'Have some baby magic.' He closed the front door and added, 'I gather some congratulations are in order... Everything okay in that department?'

She nodded and shrugged a 'sort of' and brushed at another tear. Rested her lips on Talia's warm, soft hair.

'Come on in,' Alec said. 'They've been at it for a couple of hours – they're due a break.'

There were computers and paperwork at one end of the dining room table and a spread of quiche and salads at the other end. Lucy, a skinny, delicate-looking woman with streaks of purple hair and bright red lips, was packing things into a big leather bag that had an abundance of zips and buckles and saying, 'We definitely need to get clear on the discrepancy between those two sets of figures.'

'I'll come back later,' Mia said. 'I don't want to interrupt you. You look really busy –'

Sheryl waved a hand, brushing her objection aside. 'We're done for now. It's all good.' Turning to Lucy, she said, 'The thing that worries me is the staffing issue. I mean, three entertainment managers in the past twelve months – what's that all about?'

Mia hesitated, rocking Talia. She could see Bitsy still nosing for crumbs under the table.

'Yeah. Management problems or ridiculous workload? I'm punting the latter.' Lucy slung the heavy bag over her shoulder and headed toward the door. 'Hope it's okay, whatever it is,' she said to Mia in passing. Her smile was genuine.

'Luce is pure gold,' Sheryl declared as soon as she had gone. 'So don't worry about butting in, for God's sake. She's the most understanding person on the planet, as well as being hard as nails in business and as strong as an ox. Seriously – the clichés all apply. Now sit and tell all.'

Alec arrived with a clean plate and cutlery for Mia. 'Shall I leave the two of you?'

'A male point of view might help,' Mia said.

Did they exchange a glance? It looked like it.

'Boy trouble?' Sheryl asked as they sat. 'Those brothers fighting again?'

'Worse.' Mia settled Talia onto her lap. 'They swapped.'

'Oh my God,' Sheryl said. She looked at Alec. 'You were right.'

Startled, Mia looked at him too. 'You guessed?'

'That night you came over for dinner when Jacinta and Paul were here?' Sheryl said. 'Alec just sensed something not right about John.'

'I knew he was different,' Mia said, almost defensively, 'but...' What a fool she had been, not having picked it up when she was living with the man! Alec had only seen him for a couple of hours and he'd figured it out.

'I wouldn't say I *knew* they'd swapped,' Alec corrected, pouring Mia a glass of water, 'but that puzzle piece about John having an identical twin made me wonder.'

'We invited you over for dinner on Thursday night so we could check them out,' Sheryl confessed. 'You know, the night you couldn't come?'

Mia's brow furrowed for a moment. 'Oh. When I started the course.'

'We were going to put them through some tests – subtly – and tell you if they failed.'

'People can snap when a parent dies or they have a shock,' Alec said. 'It's not a strange thing to decide to make big changes, so I wasn't suspicious of him leaving his job. It was just… who he was… he just seemed too different.'

'That's what a career in human relations will do for you,' Sheryl said with a glance at Alec. 'Makes you good at observing people. Right, hun?' Without waiting for an answer she turned back to Mia. 'So what are you going to do?'

'I don't know,' Mia said. 'I'm still in shock.'

'I don't blame you. My God. What a pair of jerks.'

'I know,' Mia said, and the tears began to flow again. 'How could they do that to me? I feel… violated…'

'Did you do that second pregnancy test?'

'Not yet.'

'I've got one here. One of those 95% accurate, do-it-any-time-of-day ones. I think you should be certain.'

'I'm pretty sure. I've been throwing up. Nauseous. Sore boobs. Tired.'

Sheryl's brow was furrowed as she considered this. 'So you really don't want to be single right now. But which one of them do you love?'

Talia began to whimper and squirm. Mia jiggled her a bit, then moved the little body up to her shoulder and patted her back. 'I don't know how to answer that.'

'Seriously? It was crap with John for ages. You've seemed so much happier again since bro arrived.'

'I know. I was… falling in love with Jake, I guess. But seeing John again… I'm so mad with him for lying and holding out on me for so long about Jake! I'm *furious*. But he was coming home to talk Jake into swapping back…'

'Holy fuck,' said Sheryl. 'So you feel like he really loves you.'

'I know he does.'

'But do you love him? That's more important, right now.'

'I'm confused. I don't know. Part of me does, but…'

Mia's phone rang. She leaned down to her bag, nestling Talia's head between her neck and shoulder while she fished out her phone. It was John. 'Speak of the devil.' She switched her phone off and dropped it back into her bag. 'He's a good man, apart from this mad, stupid idea. I can't believe he did it – it's so out of character!'

'That's what a shock will do to you.' Alec reached out for Talia. 'Here. Let me take her so you can have something to eat.'

She shook her head. 'I don't think I can eat yet. I'm still churning.'

'Would you have him back if he'd had an affair?' Sheryl asked. 'It's kind of similar.'

Mia thought of Melissa. 'He might even have done that. There was an old girlfriend in the UK. I haven't asked.' Nick came back to mind...

'But whether he has slept with someone or not, he's still betrayed you,' Sheryl said bluntly. 'How can you stay with such a – someone who's lied to you like that?'

'I don't know that I can,' she agreed. 'But so has Jake. They both lied to me. That's what's so crazy about all this! John did it out of love, he reckons – giving me what I wanted: romance, a man who could have a baby –'

'*He* can't?' Sheryl interrupted.

'Apparently not. I hadn't known.'

'Do they both know you're pregnant now?'

'John does.'

'Which John?'

'The real one.'

'Stop interrupting,' Alec said gently.

'Sorry.' Sheryl zipped her lips together with the tip of her finger. And then exclaimed, 'My God! How does John feel now?'

Alec shook his head in mock despair; there was laughter in his eyes.

'Shocked,' Mia said. 'I haven't had a chance to tell Jake.' Talia was whimpering again, more loudly. 'It doesn't look like I have the touch today.'

'Here,' Sheryl held out her arms. 'She's due for a feed.'

Mia handed Talia over and Sheryl settled the child at her breast. This was all ahead for Mia, with her baby, Jake's baby. Which of them would be the father, if any? Would she just walk away from both of them – make them pay for their deceitfulness?

'What was I saying?' she asked, leaning her elbow on the table, resting the side of her face in her hand. 'Pregnancy brain...'

'About them both lying to you,' Alec prompted. 'John to give you what he thought you wanted...'

'And Jake, of course, pretending to be John and playing along. But he did – hit the spot. Oh God, that sounds terrible! But the fact is that he tricked me... lovingly. That's what's so weird about this. So unsettling. It's not just your husband cheating on you with another woman. That's so black-and-white: "You cheated? Okay, it's over." This is... complicated.'

'He *has* cheated on you,' Sheryl said. 'Only not with another woman.'

'But even an affair isn't necessarily black-and-white,' Alec said. 'And it doesn't always mean the end of love.'

'No. I guess...' Mia fell silent and they sat watching Talia and listening to her sucking and snuffling.

'Jake's had lots of lovers, hasn't he?' Sheryl asked, looking up.

'Apparently.'

'Is he still with anyone? I would bloody well hope not, but...'

'I gather not. Someone had split up with him just before the funeral, John reckons. That was one of the factors, for him – for doing this.'

'But how do you know he'd stay faithful to you?' Sheryl asked. 'If he's that kind of guy...'

Mia shrugged. 'I don't. I don't know him at all. I mean, what is it? Six, eight weeks?'

'Exactly. He might fall right back into the old habits.'

'He said he wanted to be in a committed relationship. That's why he took it on. He reckons he wants to stay with me. He even gave up a really big role to stay here, with me.'

'But he *is* a flirt,' Sheryl stated. 'He's flirted with me, you should know.'

Mia looked at her in surprise.

'Just flirting,' Sheryl reassured. 'Nothing inappropriate. But it might just be a question of time.'

'Great,' Mia said flatly. 'So I've got one boring, predictable, real husband who gives me away and then suddenly loves me desperately and will do anything to have me back, and one fun, romantic, pretend husband who lies to be with me and might, at any moment, nick off or start having affairs.'

'I think you should rethink 'boring',' Sheryl said. 'It's not exactly boring to do what John's done. And it's definitely not predictable. It's pretty exciting, in a way. Well, unpredictable-exciting.'

Osho, Mia thought. She tried to remember the saying Nick had quoted… Something about needing unpredictability for a relationship to remain alive…? 'So one more point to John,' she said with a wry expression. 'Although that's a pretty sick way of doing it.'

'Pros and cons, that's what you need to do.' Sheryl interrupted her business-like recommendation to very tenderly shift her daughter slightly; Talia had stopped feeding and was snoozing against her breast.

'And if it comes out balanced, what then?'

'All live together?' Sheryl suggested. 'Isn't there some religion that does that?'

'No way! And I can't see them living together in a fit.'

'So what are your options? Leave both of them; stay with John; stay with Jake; all live together – I know you don't like that one, but it's literally an option.'

'Jake needs to know about the baby,' Alec said.

'I know. I haven't been withholding on purpose.' Mia sighed. She leaned forward and cut herself a slice of quiche.

'You love them both. You're pissed off with them both. You've got a baby coming. It's a pretty wild situation.' Sheryl moved the bowl of salad closer.

'Tell me about it,' Mia said with feeling. She took a forkful of quiche. Asparagus and salmon… It was delicious.

'This is a little reminiscent of Jacob from the Bible,' Alec mused. 'You know the story? He cheats his older brother of his birthright.'

'Whoah!' Sheryl exclaimed, putting Talia on her shoulder and rubbing her back. 'Your Jake even has the right name.'

'Except that in this case his older brother proposed the swindle,' Mia pointed out. And then wondered about that. John had said the idea had occurred to them both, almost simultaneously.

'Maybe it's more like the story of the prodigal son,' Alec said. 'But which is the prodigal? John recklessly gives you away – and his wealth. What did they agree about that, by the way? And then wants to come back, if you'll forgive him and have him back, you being the Almighty in this situation. Or is the prodigal son Jake, who keeps living recklessly, and then lands on his feet when the 'good son,' John, gives everything to him? It's no wonder John is feeling angry that the wasteful son has walked straight into heaven... Again, you're the Almighty here: you have the power to decide who stays, who gets what...'

'I don't feel very mighty. Or very forgiving.'

'Nor would I!' Sheryl tapped on the table with long crimson nails. 'But come back to the money. What did they agree about finances?'

'I don't know,' Mia said. 'Jake was drawing on our account but apparently John was too. There's been money going to the UK every week... I thought it was for the charity. Maybe it was... I don't know that side of it yet. But Jake reckons John was watching everything he spent. Makes sense of the fight they had on the phone a few weeks ago after he bought the TV. I can just imagine how John would have freaked!'

'There's a financial aspect to this arrangement that John would definitely have been keeping track of,' Alec said. 'Once Jake had lived with you for twelve months, he'd have a legal right to your assets. So there would have been a use-by on the arrangement for John. If it wasn't working he'd have pulled the plug before then. There's no way he'd have forgotten about that little detail, being an accountant. Whereas whichever one of them you choose, you'll get 50% of the assets. If you opt to leave, maybe more.'

'You'll have the baby you wanted and security and eventually a new career,' Sheryl said. 'There's just the issue of the men to sort out...'

Mia stayed at Sheryl's for the night. She was installed in the guest room and given a stack of books about pregnancy (and the pregnancy test) to occupy her when Lucy returned. The test was positive. She lay on the bed in the pretty white room with its startling abstract prints on the wall and big window looking onto a secluded Japanese garden, reading, visualising the tiny pin-prick of life growing within her, and wondering what to do. Anger, sadness and confusion lapped at her as she read, occasionally swamping her in a wave of grief or despair or fury. Her phone buzzed multiple times – calls and text messages from both of them. She ignored them all.

27

Sheryl had said she should call in sick but Mia headed off to work in the morning. Her face was pale when she looked at herself in the mirror of the Ladies' bathroom. She gave a too-bright smile to the other women coming in to use the loo. When Reynald stopped by her desk with a list of requests he didn't manage to get past the third one before he looked at her more closely and said, 'Into my office.'

She began to disconnect her laptop to bring it with her – such a bloody nuisance compared to carrying a notepad! – and he said, 'Leave that.'

He stood by the door as she passed in and then closed it behind her. Pointed to the armchair and sat in the other one beside her instead of at his desk. His thick fingers lay on the armrest. Gold wedding ring. His father's old watch... 'Talk to me,' he said gently. 'What's up?'

Mia swallowed. How much to say? She'd hold back about being pregnant – that was a risky revelation. She looked into his face. The kind blue eyes. Licked her lips. 'I've got... there's kind of a mad thing happening in my life at the moment...'

He nodded, waiting.

'I... You remember John going overseas for his father's funeral? Well... things weren't great for us at the time. I was even thinking of leaving...'

His phone rang. He glanced at it, frowning.

'You get that,' she said at once.

He moved to his desk and answered it, promising to ring back in ten, and then told reception to hold his calls and put his mobile on silent.

She picked up her tale. 'And then he came back... really different. His father's death had got to him... He decided to change everything: his job, how he did life. Only...'

Someone knocked and the door opened. Susan stood there. She looked at them both. 'Paula,' she began.

'I'll be ten minutes,' Reynald said.

Susan withdrew after another searching look at Mia. Reynald walked to his door, stuck the 'Do Not Disturb' sign on the handle, and locked it. He sat back in the armchair.

'Carry on.'

She would have to spit it out – he was a busy man. 'It turns out that he has an identical twin brother,' she said in a rush. 'I hadn't known – I just knew he had a brother. And they swapped. They were both feeling unhappy and they felt like the other one had a better life. So they swapped. John stayed there and Jake came here to be John. I know! It sounds crazy. It *is* crazy...' She trailed off. It was absurd. It was bizarre. It was insane.

'It's unique,' Reynald acknowledged. 'I haven't come across this one in forty years as a therapist...' He shifted his weight in the chair, watching her, waiting.

'I just found out,' she said. 'On Saturday night. Just figured it out. And now...' Her eyes were brimming again. She dashed at the tears impatiently. Why was she crying so much? It made more sense for her to be angry! But perhaps that was pregnancy hormones screwing with her... She sniffed and he reached for the box of tissues on the coffee table and handed it to her. She wiped her eyes and nose. 'I just don't know what to do. They both say they love me, both want to be with me. But who would do something like that to someone! It's so horrible. I feel so... violated...'

Reynald nodded again. 'You've given yourself one massive problem,' he said, and she looked at him, puzzled.

'God-you.'

Oh. He was talking about Bernard's course. The Hero's Journey. She'd forgotten about that…

'It must feel huge. Overwhelming. Confusing. This needs more than ten minutes, Mia.'

She sniffed again. Blew her nose.

'In fact, I want you to go home. Take a couple of days. Or perhaps not home – they're both there?'

She nodded. 'I stayed at a friend's last night.'

'Good. You need a bit of space. Do you write? Journal?'

'Not for ages.'

'Then start. Do some journalling. I've got a meeting I can't put off starting any minute but we'll find a good counsellor who can support you through this. Meanwhile, do some writing about how you're feeling, what you want. Don't censor yourself. Just let it all pour out of you.'

She was pressing a damp, balled-up tissue to her mouth. He reached across and covered her knee with his big, broad hand. 'You'll be fine, Mia. You've got two men who love you, a friend helping you out, and we'll find that counsellor for you.'

She nodded, voiceless.

'It's not for nothing they say relationships are the key to self-realisation,' Reynald mused. 'They show us our strengths and our weaknesses.' He passed her the box of tissues again and she plucked another few out. 'You've written yourself a doozy of a conflict, Mia, and, at the same time, a phenomenal opportunity.'

The tears were flowing again. 'It gets worse,' she blurted. 'I'm pregnant too.'

There was a little silence. 'Do you know which…?'

'Jake, the brother.'

'Who do you want?'

'I don't know,' she said miserably. 'John's a good man and he's stable and trustworthy and – well, up until this he was! But it was just flat for ages… Jake's fun, romantic… I thought I'd lucked out: the good, reliable husband who had shaken off his boring old habits… I thought I finally had it all.'

'The good boy and the bad boy in one, eh?' Reynald smiled. 'Oh well, welcome back to the land of the mere mortal. None of us gets it all. We need the gap, the missingness, to have a challenge, a growth opportunity.' He gave her knee a pat. 'You'll sort it out.'

'Can *you* counsel me?' she asked.

'I'd love to,' he said. 'It's intriguing. But I can't be your boss, your teacher and your therapist. It would be considered a conflict of interest.'

She gave him a watery smile. 'Well, thanks for listening. It's a bit of a perk having a boss who's also a therapist.'

'I just wish I had more time.' He was frowning, one broad hand rubbing his jaw. 'I suppose this pregnancy will unravel our plans... You'll be able to keep studying if you want to, but you might not want to keep working as well... I might have to do without you, eh?'

'I'm sorry,' she said in a small voice.

He made a little exclamatory noise. 'Oh, don't be sorry! You're a young woman. You've got to do what's right for you.' He sat back, rubbing his jaw again, thoughtful. 'Yes... Take a couple of days. Do some writing. See if you can take a leaf out of Bernard's book and view all this from a distance, from that God-you perspective. There *is* the violation aspect, and you're right to feel angry and hurt about how they've treated you. Absolutely. You don't want to minimise that. But the strange and wonderful thing about this is that they both love you... And the fact is that there's a grand opportunity inside every apparent catastrophe. I wouldn't speak to most clients like this, but you signed up for the course so I'm assuming you're able to hear it. If you can just keep hold of that thought – that there's something positive in this for you – then you won't drown in it.'

'All right,' she said, catching onto the rope he'd thrown her. It was just a piece of string really, but it was something.

They stood up.

'I'll talk to Susan,' he said. And the face he made showed that he knew exactly how she felt about the Dragon Lady.

Bitsy greeted Mia ecstatically when she arrived back at Sheryl's. She knelt to scratch her pup's tummy and then went in search of her friend. Sheryl was tapping away at her computer and at the same time rocking Talia in a bouncer with her foot. She looked up when Mia entered.

'Good. Time off. You need it.' She finished what she was typing and swivelled in her chair. 'Did you tell Reynald?'

'Yes.'

'What did he say?'

'To take a couple of days and do some journaling.'

'He's a good man. The boys have both rung, by the way. Said they couldn't get through to you. Wondering if you're okay.'

'What did you say?'

'That you're devastated and depressed and you need some space.'

Mia sat on the floor next to Talia, who gave her a stunning smile and gurgled. She took the tiny hand in hers, and Tali's fingers closed immediately around her thumb.

'All right, girl,' Sheryl commanded. 'Go start that journalling. I'm going to finish what I'm doing here and then we'll go out for lunch. Somewhere expensive. My treat. Fuck 'em! They're not going to get you down.'

Mia felt as if she was about to laugh and cry at the same time. Sheryl was a treasure. It was like Reynald had said: she would be okay; there were too many people who cared about her.

She had picked up a notebook on her way back from work. She lay on the impeccable bed in the pure white room and began to write. The words poured out of her.

How does someone DO something like that?! I can't imagine what got into them, what made them think they'd get away with it. It's too insane for words… What must they have been thinking of me, to imagine that they could pull this over me? That I'm stupid or really unobservant or not worth honesty?

Okay, I didn't recognise that John was really Jake. I sort of did, but I didn't listen to my intuition, stupid me. Goes to show how much I wanted things to be different and how much I loved being made to feel special... Plus I was feeling guilty about Nick. Aaaaghhh!!!! This is so crap. I feel like shit. I wish they'd never had that conversation. I wish they'd never come up with such a stupid plan... But then I wouldn't be pregnant now... John and I would probably be talking divorce. Because he's right, why start planning on adopting or IVF if your marriage is up shit creek? There'd be no point. So I'd be single, looking for someone to start all over again. I'd be years away from having a baby... Unless I adopted on my own or looked for a donor, but I don't think I could have done that... Shit. Crap. This is so fucked. Why is it that I'm not enough for my own parents or for my own husband? My parents stay obsessed with a dead first child and my husband gives me away... That is so fucked. And then he tries to tell me he did it for love! Christ. I don't know what to think of that... Reynald was nice. I can't remember all that stuff from Bernard's class except his picture of the God-me and the Character-me and some of the points, like conflict and polarity and OMG – 'recognition'!!! Well, I've just had the frigging recognition scene. Talk about a dramatic unveiling... So now what? I suppose I should be thinking about my lesson in this. What did he say? Our lessons come out of our weaknesses, or something like that... I suppose my weakness is this dream of the ideal man. 'Mr Right'. I've always compared John with my idea of what Mr Right would be like: a combination of both of them – and Nick, to be honest. He'd have Nick's body and dangerousness and Jake's romance and fun and John's friendship and stability. Although that's gone out of the window, in a way. You can't exactly call a man who pulls a gig like this 'stable'... So maybe he really is different now? And maybe Jake is a ticking bomb... He was flirting with that redhead the first day he started gardening... with that woman at Sheryl's dinner party the other night – Jasmine, or whatever her name was. Even with Sheryl. So maybe John's right and it's only a question of time. And Nick, well, he was upfront at least. He told me he didn't do commitment. So I guess there's no perfect man out there. I suppose that's my big fantasy... Even Alec. He's a gorgeous person. So devoted to Sheryl and Talia, so patient, successful, rich...

But not so good looking. Not that looks should matter... I am so just crapping on here. What's the time? 11.45. Sheryl will call me for lunch soon but I think really I should go home and have it out with the boys. I've got to tell Jake I'm pregnant. I don't want John to tell him first. What the fuck am I going to do about all this???

She began to doodle a yin-yang symbol, and more thoughts tumbled out. What was it that Bernard had said about each trait eventually flipping into its opposite? It was true: John's reliability had, over the years, become boring predictability, which had eventually flipped into unpredictability... Jake's playfulness had given way to years of promiscuity, and that had flipped into a desire for the opposite, for commitment and steadiness. But Bernard had also said that people didn't change their essential nature... Eventually the flirtiness might lead him right back into affairs... Relationships were often tested when couples had children. What if she threw John out and Jake turned into one of those men who disappears and leaves the woman at home to raise the child while he's out partying...? She couldn't say he wouldn't do that – she didn't know him well enough. And what she did know was troubling.

Mia rolled onto her back and stared at the ceiling.

Was it possible for people to really change? Was it possible for relationships to change? Was there any chance of John being different if they got back together? He'd left Buxton, at least, but he wouldn't want to garden. Surely. And would he want to raise his brother's child?

She felt reluctant to let Jake go. But another part of her was reluctant to push John away. Another part wanted to tell them both to fuck off while she raised this child on her own. Another part fantasised meeting the perfect man who would – oh fuck, there she went again. Looking for Mr Right. Geez.

Sheryl knocked on the door. 'Lunch?' she asked, looking in.

'I think I should go home and talk to the two arseholes,' Mia said, sitting up.

'It's good to hear your spirit coming back,' Sheryl said approvingly. 'I did want to treat you, though.'

'I know. Can I take a rain check? I want to tell Jake before John does.'

'Fair enough.' Sheryl came to sit on the bed beside her. 'I've been reading another good book. It talks about the 'Law of Lesser Pissers'. Heard of it?'

Mia smilingly shook her head.

'It means you've got to look after yourself first. Always piss other people off before you piss yourself off because other people come and go in your life but *you're* permanent… The old 'put your life jacket on before you help anyone else' advice. So don't get tied up in knots about what those two want; you figure out what *you* want because if you're not happy, you've got nothing to give anyone else anyway.'

'You know what's screwed about that?' Mia replied after a moment.

'What?'

'It's exactly what they did to me.'

Sheryl smacked the side of her head. 'Shit. You're right.'

Mia covered her face with both hands in another horrible moment of realisation. 'Me going to your party in that tarty dress? That was me trying out another side of myself. And that was exactly what the boys were doing. I just saw it that second. Fuck.'

'Fuck,' said Sheryl.

They simultaneously fell back on the bed and stared up at the ceiling.

28

The boys were shouting when she arrived at the back door. She hesitated, listening.

'You think you can pick up where you left off? We had an agreement! It's working for me – for once something is working for me! Honour your side of the frigging agreement!'

Jake. Mia stood with eyes closed, a knot in her stomach.

'That is *crap*! We said we'd play it by ear. We agreed that it had to work for both of us.'

John. But what about her? What about making sure it worked for her?

'*And* Mia,' he said, as if he'd just heard her.

'Mia loves me now,' Jake said angrily. 'Suck it up, bro. I'm giving her what she wants.'

'For how long, Jake? Come on. You'll get restless. What's with the audition in Sydney this weekend? It's already starting.'

What audition? He hadn't said anything to her. Mia raked a hand through her hair. Looked at Bitsy, sniffing at the bottom of the door. She'd bark any minute now.

'You want her back?' Jake said. 'All right! See if *you* can make her this happy. Let her choose!'

'Of course she has to choose,' John said wearily. 'There's no other option.'

Silence. A door being slammed. Bitsy gave that bark. Mia opened the door.

John was sitting at the kitchen table, head in his hands. He glanced up as she entered. Aside from looking exhausted he didn't have any black eyes or bruises, and the kitchen looked okay – they hadn't trashed it in the process of a wild fist fight…

'Hi,' he said.

'Hi.' Mia hesitated, shoulder bag and overnight bag in hand. She should have gone out for lunch with Sheryl first – she was ravenous again and there was probably nothing in the fridge. She'd been intending to shop yesterday, before they went to Cooney Avenue…

'Have you said anything to Jake?' she asked.

'What about?'

She made a face. Pointed at her stomach.

'Oh. No.'

Another little silence.

'How are you?' he asked. 'Have you decided anything?'

'No,' she said to the latter. How to answer the former? 'I still feel like shit. Betrayed. Hurt. Confused.'

He nodded a little. Looked away, at the floor. Reached down to pat Bitsy. Then up at her again. 'I don't know what to say, Mia. How to fix this.'

'Well,' she said, and she could hear a coldness in her voice. 'First things first. I need to speak to my second husband.'

John flinched. She was rubbing his face in it but he set all this up in the first place! He could just bloody well suck it up! Which was what Jake had said… Jake, who was equally guilty and hadn't thought to say, 'let's ask Mia what she wants'; John had said that.

'Have you cleaned up at Cooney Avenue yet?' he asked, sounding tired.

'No. I was going to suggest we do it today.'

'I'll go.' He stood up slowly, as if he had the weight of the world on his shoulders. 'You tell Jake. But let me – I want to talk to you. Please. When I get back.'

She nodded. She'd dropped the overnight bag; her arms were folding in front of her chest again.

'Is the key still…?' he began.

'On the hook.'

'Okay.' He sighed. Hesitated, as if he wanted to move close and kiss her goodbye as he always had before leaving. Instead, he walked to the laundry for cleaning supplies, arms hanging by his sides.

Mia picked up her overnight bag and moved slowly through the house. Past the guest room, door open, immaculate bed… into the master bedroom. Jake was lying on the bed, arms crossed behind his head, staring at the ceiling. He sat up as soon as he heard her enter.

'Hey.'

She didn't answer. Put the bag down by the chest of drawers. Looked at him.

John mark two. Same beautiful hazel eyes. Same worried expression. She remembered the night she'd picked him up from the airport, and how he'd made love to her for hours. She remembered the excursion to buy her a sexy dress. She remembered the candlelit dinner. Standing by Talia's crib together. The morning he'd been looking at her like that…

But he'd agreed to pretend he was her husband. He hadn't told her he was auditioning again – if that was true. He had women throughout Europe, just like Nick – children too, apparently. Was he even capable of being loyal? Could he stick around for years, being a father to a toddler, a school kid, a young adult? Could he be a breadwinner, if the magic account John had supplied dried up?

She sighed and sat on the bed. He moved closer, taking her hand. She should pull away – not let him touch her. She should keep to herself. She should protect herself against these two frauds. She should bar the way to her heart…

'Mia.'

What was there to say? Nothing. They were all at an impasse. The only thing to be said was her news.

'There's something I have to tell you,' she said. 'It's crap timing but there's nothing we can do about that now.'

He was massaging her hand with his thumb, rotating it slowly and deeply across the back of her hand, relaxing some of the tension she was feeling...

Stop delaying. Just say it. 'I'm pregnant,' she blurted.

The thumb stopped moving.

She scanned his face, trying to read his expression. Was that little frown a frown of consternation? He was smiling too. Was it a genuinely happy smile?

'That's wonderful,' he said. He lifted her hand to his lips and kissed it. Moved even closer, leaning in as if to kiss her on the mouth.

She pulled back.

He hesitated. 'Aren't you happy?'

'About being pregnant? Of course! You know I've wanted this. But right now... with things as they are...'

'It's not as confusing as it looks,' he said. 'I love you. You love me – I'm pretty sure about that. John left you. We're about to have a baby. The facts are clear. We need to sort out some practical stuff, but –'

She stopped him. 'It's not that simple.'

'Why not? People complicate things too much. We don't need to do that.'

'You *both* tricked me. That's not the basis for a respectful, trusting relationship. How do I know I can trust you? How do I know you'll stick around? You say you're committed now but will it last? What if some... Katarina... comes out of the woodwork? What if you fall in love with someone else – some actress! I gather you've got an audition, so you are going back into acting.'

A shadow crossed his face. 'John told you?'

'I overheard you arguing. But see? More secrets. When were you going to tell me that?'

'I just heard about it... Yes, I've still got the bug. I don't think I could give up acting forever. It's in my blood... But I'm not about to live a crazy, unstable actor's life anymore – I'm done with that. I want regular income. I want to be able to build something.'

'Like what?' she asked, annoyed. 'You're already jumping around from gardening to massage. And now you're thinking of starting down the acting road again. What are you going to do that will be stable?'

'The gardening was always going to be temporary; that is not my thing. Massage, yes. I had a bit of a massage business in the UK. I've been doing it for years. I'm qualified over there, but they don't recognise my quals over here so I have to do the training again. It's a pest but I was prepared for that. It's the sort of work I can do alongside some theatre or screen work – flexible.'

'Right,' she said, jaw locking.

'Come on, you can't see me in a desk job, can you!'

'How would I know?' she asked coldly. 'I hardly know you.'

'Yes, you do. The crap John told you about me is all true. But I *am* changing. I gave up on the old life because I want a change. And look, there are other things actors can do that are more stable. Ads – they pay well. Teaching drama. Recording audio books. Theatre sports and games for corporate team building – hosting costumed dinner parties and murder mysteries. There are even jobs role-playing sick or injured people for medical students – that kind of thing. I was starting to look into it in England just before John came back.'

She gave a curt nod.

'I'll keep the gardening going until I've got my massage qualifications here or until I get some decent acting work, and then I'll let that go. And there's the charity, too. And Dad's artwork. Selling the prints, hawking them around to shops. I can do that.'

'What about the other women? The other children you've got in Europe?'

'Europe! He's exaggerating. One child in Italy. One child in England.'

'Still! Fuck. That's two children. Do you have anything to do with them?'

'I see the kid in England occasionally. Not the one in Italy.'

'How old are they? How are things with the mothers? What happened?'

Jake sighed. 'You want all my skeletons?'

'Of course!'

'Okay. The kid in England is twelve. She – his mother – was a student I met at uni when I was all of twenty. She was eighteen. We were in love but stupid. Immature. She wanted to keep the baby and I knew I didn't have it in me to be the steady partner. I wanted that acting career. She chose to keep it, to single parent. Didn't want to know about me at first but I kept coming back to see them – his name's Harry – and bit by bit she defrosted. For a few years there I was onto a good thing.' He grinned. 'I'd come by, see them, have a bit of a roll in the hay with Angie, head off again. She'd finally come to accept me as I was and wasn't holding out for the big reunion anymore. But one year I came to visit and I wasn't allowed to stay the night. There was a new man on the scene. They got married a few years ago and he's great. A good dad to Harry. But now I just see the kid once or twice a year. Send him birthday and Christmas presents. He calls me Jake and the other guy 'dad'...'

Mia felt glad there'd been a happy ending for this Angie and her son. 'What about the other one?' It was good to know this stuff – to feel as if she was coming out of the dark.

'That was a bit more dramatic. I had an affair with a married woman while I was on holiday in Italy. She got pregnant and wanted to keep the kid but she wasn't leaving the husband. He's some big deal businessman – very rich. They own vineyards, export wine... She wanted to keep me on the side too but I wasn't allowed to see the kid. She was afraid I'd make the kid hate her father and it would all come out. I wouldn't accept her terms.'

'So a daughter...'

'Yes. Sophia. She's eight.'

'And the father has never guessed?'

'Apparently not.'

Mia twisted the wedding ring around her finger. 'And that's all?'

'That's all. A couple of abortions and a miscarriage along the way –'

She looked at him quickly, horrified.

'It happens!' he protested.

'What about those women?'

'Tina was relieved about the miscarriage. She'd just accepted a role and couldn't afford to be pregnant. She was a rising star,' he said cynically. 'Joanne aborted without telling me. Liz was a fucking nightmare, the crazy bitch. She had some, I don't know, some mental illness going on. She was all over the place – loving me, hating me, wanting me, rejecting me, saying she was keeping the baby and then aborting. She nearly died in the process. She's in a psychiatric hospital now. Her parents got involved. It was dire… They forbade me from ever seeing her again.'

Ye gods. Well, John hadn't been lying about his brother's escapades… 'Did you love her – any of them?'

'I loved all of them,' he said. 'Especially Liz, fool that I am.'

She nodded. *All of them…* So she was just another in a long line… For John, she was almost the only one. Aside from that Melissa person. And he was virtually the only one in her life, apart from a few misfitting boyfriends – and Jake, John's brother, God's gift to women, who understood the art of love.

He picked up her hand again, and again, she did not resist. 'Don't you see, Mia? There's hope for us. I can do this.'

She was thinking of John now. Seeing the pleading expression in his eyes, his resignation as he walked out to clean the apartment. 'I just don't know…' she said.

He looked at her stomach. 'May I?'

She pressed her lips together. If that hand rested on her belly… She nodded. His fingers touched down lightly on her shirt, just beside her navel… the palm of his hand settled right across the middle of her belly. She caught her breath. His hand was warm, gentle.

'Hello in there,' he said softly. Then he looked up at her. 'I will love you, Mia, and the baby. I will stick around.'

'If I give you a second chance, I should give one to John too,' she said, surprising herself.

Jake stiffened. He leaned in to kiss her belly and then sat up. 'Yes. You should. You've got to make a good decision. I'll be gone next weekend, so there's your chance.' He threw his hands up in the air in a gesture of surrender. 'I'll let go, Mia. No pressure. You decide what's right for you, but I want to stay in this child's life. I want to get to know at least one of my children. I want to experience being a father.'

She bit her lip. Mr Right was talking. How could John, who'd always been so staid, win her back when he had this charmer to compete with?

'But right now,' Jake said. 'I'm moving out of this room. I'll stay in the lounge. You should have your bedroom back, with neither of us blackguards in it.'

'I was going to go back to Sheryl's.'

'Oh. Well, you can if you want to, I guess. But you might get back here and only find bones. And gristle. If you want any chance of a husband and father for your kid, you should probably hang around.'

'I don't want a child-husband,' she said. 'I want a man.'

He winced. 'Touché. Do whatever you damn well want, lady.'

She wanted lunch. She was ready to eat a horse. She left him emptying the few things he'd bought from wardrobe and went into the kitchen to see what she could cobble together out of the fridge and pantry.

Mia was napping when John got back. She vaguely heard noises in the house and then became conscious of someone nearby, watching her. Opened her eyes and saw John standing in the doorway.

'Sorry. Did I wake you?'

She shook her head, lifting herself onto one elbow.

'I've cleaned the place,' he said. 'They left a bit of a mess, didn't they?'

'Understatement of all time. Did you see the axe – tomahawk, or whatever?'

'Yeah. Crazy. Anyway, we can advertise the place again. Just need to replace the venetian blinds and get some people in to look at the mould and get the carpets cleaned. I'll sort it all out this afternoon.'

'Thank you.'

He nodded. Stayed there, leaning against the doorpost.

'Where's Jake?' she asked.

He shrugged, his face tightening. 'Did you talk? Tell him?'

'Yes.'

'How did he take it?'

'He's happy. Wants to stay. He wants to be a father.'

John nodded again. 'He hasn't had much of a chance so far – with the others.'

'So I heard.'

'He told you?'

'Yes.' She sat up, rubbing her face, smoothing her hair back. 'What about you? Do you want to be a father?'

He looked surprised. 'Of course. I thought you knew that.'

'Well…' She made a gesture of uncertainty. 'You didn't seem excited about it before you left – or even when we started trying…'

He shifted his weight and she wanted to be cordial and invite him in to sit on the bed but somehow… 'To begin with I was worried we might have twins,' he said. 'Knowing what that's like I felt wary… And then, when we'd been trying for a while, I was worried that I couldn't give you a kid. And then I knew I couldn't and I was worried about that – what we were going to do, if we could afford IVF… And then I was telling myself it might all be over; you seemed to have completely lost interest in me. And then Dad got sick…'

'Okay, I get the picture. But…' She pushed the covers back and climbed out of bed. 'But what about you? Had you lost interest in me? It certainly looked like it.'

'No!' he said at once, shocked.

'But…' she frowned, standing there, arms folding. 'You didn't act like you were interested in me. You were just working, riding your bike, watching TV… It didn't look like you were interested in me at all.'

'I know. I'm shit at that… romantic stuff. It's why Jake is probably going to win you.'

'This isn't a contest,' she said, 'and I'm not some prize.' But that was what it felt like… And wasn't that what she had just thought when she was talking to Jake? *How could John, who'd always been so staid, win her back when he had this charmer to compete with?*

'You know what I mean,' he said. 'He's better at courting women. I'm crap at it.'

'Then get your fucking act together,' she snapped. *So what was she doing now? Encouraging him to see it as a contest? Stupid!*

He looked taken aback.

'Seriously, John,' she exclaimed. 'What do you think I was trying to do, right up until I dropped you at the airport?'

'What?' he asked, baffled.

'Communicate with you! Draw you out. Be closer. Have some fun...'

'I'm very bad at that,' he said soberly.

'So get better at it. Whether it's me or someone else, if you want your relationships to work you've got to work at them!'

She could hear Sheryl in her mind: *Go, girl! You tell those badasses!*

He hesitated and then moved toward her in a little rush and wrapped his arms around her, his lips seeking hers. She turned her face to the side, hands on his chest, pushing him away.

'What?' he asked, with a note of such pain in his voice that she felt it in her chest. He dropped his arms and stepped back.

'Too fast,' she said. 'I don't trust you anymore, John. You can't just – do that! You've got to start slowly, by talking to me, not –' she nearly said 'raping me', but that was extreme. And what the hell was she doing giving him instructions for winning her over! This was insane. She needed her head examined.

'Sorry,' he said. 'I just... I miss you so much.'

That hard feeling invaded her heart again. 'So much that you gave me away.'

The despair in his eyes softened and dissolved the hardness in her heart like some powerful acid-eating chemical, but before she could speak he had turned away. A moment later she heard the front door close behind him.

29

The house without John and Jake in it felt very different – almost as if there were ghosts hovering, trying to catch her attention as she drifted from one empty room to the next. A few of Jake's (John's?) clothes were now draped over the back of an armchair in the living room. He'd arrived six weeks ago wearing John's clothes and carrying more of them in John's suitcase – that was another clue she had missed at the time: his struggle fitting into John's pants. Then John had arrived a few days ago wearing Jake's clothes and carrying Jake's tatty old backpack. She expected that they would now wear their own.

She wandered into the guest room and opened the wardrobe door. There was hardly anything hanging up. A few pairs of jeans and some jumpers and T-shirts that she assumed were Jake's lay folded on the shelves. John hadn't travelled with much gear at all – hoping to swap back and move straight into his own bedroom, she supposed. Well, he had his whole wardrobe to choose from again, although he'd have very little use for the crisp white shirts and sharp suits while he was sitting around without a job… She wondered what he was going to do now. Whatever came of them, of their relationship, he also had the issue of work to resolve. And would he stay here, in Australia, if they separated? Or would he go back to the UK?

She returned to her room and put some fresh clothes into her overnight bag. Staying here tonight with the two of them vying for her love and commitment was not appealing…

She left her bag by the door and made herself a hot drink, then sat with it at the dining table. Saw her text books and thought, I should study. Dragged them closer and flicked through them but couldn't concentrate. She wondered what Freud would say about this situation... what Jung would say... What would a therapist advise? And then heard Bernard: *'No one will do that for you.'* No. She couldn't expect anyone else to deliver the answer for her; she'd have to sort her way through this horrible mess by herself. What else had he said? Something last Thursday at the course about how the solutions to both story problems and life problems were always elegant or beautiful. Seriously? There would be an elegant or beautiful solution to this disaster? She shook her head in disbelief. Someone was going to be hurt.

She finished her drink and went to rinse out her cup and write a note to let the boys know that she was at Sheryl's, and then heard their voices outside. When they came inside she wanted to ask Jake where he'd been but held back. Now that she knew who he was – a womaniser, promiscuous, a spendthrift, fickle – she felt as if she wanted to keep track of him, check up on him... Where could he have been? It wasn't as if he knew many people in Australia... But if she was going to turn him away, she shouldn't care what he was doing. And if she was going to build a relationship with him, she couldn't keep checking on him; she had to trust...

'All sorted,' John said briefly. 'I'll call Phillip tomorrow and let him know we're nearly ready to place the ad.'

'Thank you,' she said.

'You talking about that rental property?' Jake asked, looking from one to the other.

There was a stiff and uncomfortable silence. Impasse. Deadlock. The elephant in the kitchen was their future, their relationships, their finances, who got what, who lived where.... And she, Mia, was caught between the brothers. She was both the prize and the challenge, the gauntlet...

'I'm going back to Sheryl's,' she said, standing up. 'You two... don't kill each other.'

Her phone rang and she scooped it off the table. *Mum.*

'Hello darling,' Glenys said into her ear. 'Dad and I are just around the corner. We had lunch with the Bakers. We're going to drop in, all right, dear? We haven't seen you for a while and I wanted to… say something to you… I hope it's not inconvenient – we won't stay long.'

'Of course,' Mia said automatically. 'See you soon.'

'Who was that?' John asked, as she was putting her phone down.

'Mum and Dad. They're coming over.'

'Now?'

'I – it's so unusual for them to drop in like this. She caught me unawares. Fuck! Why didn't I think to say it wasn't a good time or we weren't in or –?'

'It'll be fine,' Jake said easily. 'But who are we each going to be?'

'Who we are,' John said curtly.

'It's probably best,' Mia agreed. 'Too complicated otherwise.'

Jake shrugged, nodded, but was scowling.

'I haven't even told them you were coming over,' she said, looking at John. And then said, flustered, 'I mean, you!' turning to Jake. 'They don't even know you have a twin either,' looking at John again. 'Oh my God!'

'You sure you couldn't have put them off?' John said in irritation.

'Of course! But I was so surprised. They hardly ever drop in here; you know that. And Mum said she needed to talk to me…'

'Do they know?'

'That I'm pregnant? No.'

'How far away are they? Maybe he can piss off for a while,' jerking his head in Jake's direction.

'Thanks!' Jake said. 'No, I'll hang around.'

'She said they were just around the corner.'

'The show must go on,' Jake said with a grin. 'Welcome to my world!'

'Right.' Mia folded her arms and glared at him.

'I mean my vocational world,' he said at once. 'I don't mean my life with you.'

'Except that you *were* acting!'

'Only at the beginning; I told you that.'

'It was such a polished performance that I never guessed,' she said coldly.

'Not so polished. I nearly said John when I should have said Jake a few times. Lucky our names start with the same letter – in fact, I did say John once. You caught me out.'

John was sitting at the kitchen table, drumming on it with his fingers. He stopped and looked up at her.

'I managed to get away with it,' Jake continued, 'but there were quite a few times when I was skating on thin ice. Like when you'd ask me computer questions. I had no frigging clue. I had to text John for answers.'

Mia stared at him, fascinated against her will. She glanced at John; he was glowering at the salt and pepper shakers.

'We had an agreement: phone on vibrate so I could check in about anything I needed to know at any time. Although there was one night you didn't answer,' Jake said to his brother, an impertinent gleam in his eye. 'One time when it would have been late at night, and you didn't answer. Must have been busy… doing something…'

Mia looked at John. A deep flush was starting up from his neck.

'I was asleep,' he snapped. 'Of course!'

'Yeah. Right,' Jake soothed. He raised his brows at Mia.

She wanted to throw something at them both – hit them! Punch them! If this was just a joke to them –

'And then in the restaurant the night you got here, *you* nearly blew it,' Jake continued to John. 'Pretending to be me and nearly giving away the fact that I was a masseur back home. That would have been too coincidental.' He mimed John choking on his food.

'I wish I *had* given it away,' John said darkly. 'I wish I'd bloody well…' he trailed off.

'Why didn't you?' Mia asked.

'Still wanting to talk Jake into just going home without you knowing,' he said. He was slumping in the chair, miserable. 'I know,' he said, before she could lash him. 'I just wanted to undo my idiocy.' He sighed.

The doorbell rang. Mia started.

'So who's who?' Jake asked.

'*I'm John,*' John said firmly. He stood up, squared his shoulders, and walked to the front door.

They listened as he greeted his in-laws and then said, 'By the way, we've got a surprise visitor. My brother Jake is here from the UK.... Yes, very unexpected...'

Glenys's and Lionel's voices murmured something in response.

'Yes...' Pleasant agreement from John, and then, in the tone of voice of someone just remembering something, 'Oh! Have I ever told you he's my twin? ... Yes... identical, in fact. Yes!' Laughter.

So funny. Mia looked at Jake who was grinning. He caught her frown and wiped his grin so quickly that she was impressed.

Their footsteps were approaching. Lionel's voice: 'Well. What an unexpected...' And then they were entering the kitchen and her parents were regarding Jake with polite surprise, and there were smiles and shaking hands and condolences on the death of their father and enquiries about the health of their mother and comments about how talented their father was and how they loved the little picture of the child...

Lionel sat at the kitchen table with the brothers and John engaged him in conversation about fishing, his pet interest; a subtle message to Jake that he had a long-term relationship with this man that Jake could not possibly replicate. Mia stood with her back to the sink, watching them, waiting for the kettle to boil, while her mother stood in front of 'the window painting', examining it more closely.

'It's very good,' she said at last, joining Mia at the bench as she poured tea and coffee.

'You wanted to say something to me, Mum?'

'Oh, darling...' Glenys glanced at the men. 'Not now, perhaps. With so many people here...'

'It's only one more than usual,' Mia said. 'And he's like John in so many ways it's hardly any different.' That was stretching the truth, but since Jake had already played the son-in-law role, it seemed apt.

'Yes, perhaps. But... Here, let me take those.' Glenys took the first two cups to the table and came back for the next two. Mia carried the milk and sugar and her own cup, and returned to the pantry for a packet of biscuits and the fudge that Jake – John – had brought over from the UK.

Her father was now asking Jake about his life, what he did for a crust, and out came the tale about acting and what a tough gig it was but so fulfilling that he could never give it up completely... And then they were on about the charity and how inspiring it was to provide a service that would honour the 'late-blooming artist'. She noticed that both boys sparked up as they spoke about this, and how they wanted to create a national prize and set up a gallery and create a crowdfunding campaign. And how they'd produced prints of their father's work and already had a steady trickle of income coming in via the website they'd set up to sell them.

'You're a bit of a late-blooming artist yourself, Mum,' Mia said. 'Working on the radio show.'

'Really? Do you think so? I wouldn't have thought that was anything very artistic.'

'It's almost like acting – don't you think, Jake? And you came to it later in life.'

'Mm,' Jake said, in a noncommittal tone.

The conversation meandered for a little longer. John stood up at one point to show off the tea towel with his father's artwork on it. After he'd put it away, he came back to the table via Mia's chair, standing behind her with both hands on her shoulders, stroking the skin of her neck and rubbing her shoulders. The husband demonstrating his rights. She'd have pushed him away if it weren't for her parents sitting there; after a few moments she began to relax and enjoy his touch – and to avoid Jake's eye, because she could feel him watching... and simmering.

'Have you seen the new TV?' Jake asked. 'My brother splurged!'

'Goodness,' said Glenys. And they all rose to go and see.

Was that his way of breaking them up, Mia wondered, as John gave her shoulder a last, gentle squeeze before moving into the living room with the others. She remembered about Jake's clothes on the armchair as they entered and felt a little flush of anxiety as she wondered what her parents would make of this untidiness and poor show of hospitality. Surely the guest's possessions should be in the guest room! But her mother's attention was drawn to the throw rug.

'Oh, you bought one! This is lovely,' she said, fingering the blue knotted fabric. 'Where did you find it?'

'Actually Joh-Jake brought it from England as a thank you gift for us having him. It suits the room so well, don't you think?'

'Perfectly,' her mother said. 'It's a wonderful match with the cushions.'

'I thought so too,' she said.

The brothers were studiously avoiding her gaze.

Glenys came to stand beside Mia in the doorway. She took her daughter's arm in a conspiratorial fashion and drew her back into the kitchen. 'I wanted to give you this,' she said, leading Mia to her handbag and opening it. 'After you visited that day, I was thinking about what you said and I went back through our photograph albums and found this snap. I thought it might mean something to you.'

She was holding a neatly folded brown paper bag.

Mia opened the bag and tipped a small square photo into her hand. A picture of her mother, young, radiant, with a blanketed baby in her arms and another, older woman, sitting close beside her, also smiling.

'That's Gran!' she said in surprise. Her grandmother had died when she was young and there were hardly any pictures of her.

'Yes,' Glenys said. 'On one of her good days.'

'And that's… Rita?'

'No, dear; it's you.'

Mia studied the picture. She was just a bundle in her mother's arms, impossible to identify. But the joy on her mother's face was unmistakeable; it was not the expression of a woman lost in grief. She flipped the picture over and there, in Glenys's neat handwriting, slightly faded, was her birth date.

'I wanted you to have this,' her mother said, 'because you're right. I was often neglectful and over-protective – I know you think that of me, and you're right. But I did love you very much, and I think this photograph captures that.'

Mia held the picture to her heart for a moment, and then wrapped her arms around her mother. Both sets of eyes were extra bright when they pulled away. Her mother immediately declared that they'd probably outstayed their welcome for a surprise visit and they would get going now, but it was nice to meet Jake and they hoped he had a lovely holiday in Australia.

As they moved toward the front door, she added in a low voice to Mia: 'They're so very alike! My goodness! One could easily confuse them.'

'Jake wants to stay,' Mia said. And was uncertain why she had revealed this. To prepare the way if he stepped into the son-in-law shoes?

'The three of you living together?' her mother asked, taken aback.

'I don't know about that,' Mia replied with an uncomfortable laugh.

'Just as well. You wouldn't want to hop into bed with the wrong one, would you!'

A joke. Her mother had cracked a joke. Mia looked at her in amazement – and horror. Surely she hadn't guessed?

She and John waved them off and stood in the driveway as they drove away. Bitsy was squatting on the nature strip, looking at her eagerly, and she realised that she hadn't yet taken her dog for a walk. 'I'm going back to Sheryl's for the night,' she said. 'Quick walk first?'

John accepted immediately. Jake looked as if he had reservations about this development when she walked through the kitchen for the leash, but Mia wasn't justifying anything to anyone. She was still on a mission to fill in all the gaps of the last couple of months.

As she and John headed off down the street, she began abruptly. 'So you left to find yourself. Did you? What did you find? And what were you doing over there all that time?'

'Easiest question first,' John said. 'Jake had just finished a gig and had nothing else on offer, and of course no partner, so I didn't need to do as much of his life as he was doing of mine. I stayed at Mum's because Jake's place is a dive. I drove Mum's car unless she needed it because his is a bomb. So aside from helping out at his mate's pizza joint, I didn't get too involved in his life – I was just sorting out some of his financial issues and breaking up an affair.'

'Breaking up an affair?' Mia felt herself go on 'alert' at this. Yet more romantic entanglements for Jake...

'He had a thing going on with the wife of a theatre director. He'd been trying to finish it for months and kept falling back in... I took her out for dinner and then broke it off. Gruelling for him, easy for me.'

'Wow. Talk about brothers with benefits!'

John gave a tired smile. They were walking side-by-side, her arm outstretched with the leash, both of them absently gazing at their feet and the pavement ahead. She'd been watching his shoes hitting the ground, each foot pointing outward slightly as they always did – as Jake's did too...

'What did she say? How did you know what to say to her?'

'She was upset but not too much; knew the fling had a use-by date. I gather she's worse than Jake – always having affairs with the actors. They suspect the husband knows and isn't too bothered; maybe has his own extra action on the side... Anyway, I sorted the finances and the relationship and cooked pizzas and even gave a massage...'

'What?' she stopped walking in surprise, feeling a jerk on the lead when Bitsy tried to keep going.

'He was supposed to call around and cancel everyone before he flew out but he forgot about this one person. She texted that she was on her way so I raced over to Jake's and gave her a massage.'

'You don't know how to do that!'

'I was taking a risk, trying something new,' John said evenly. 'Remember, I was looking for what else I might want to do other than work at Buxton.'

'You'd never become a masseur!' Just the thought of him leaning over a naked body, spreading oil on a stranger's skin, working their muscles... was bizarre.

'No,' he agreed. 'It's not for me, although I did quite enjoy it that once. And you seemed to enjoy the shoulder rub I gave you just now.'

She decided not to respond to that comment; she wanted to delve further into the other bit. 'So the conservative accountant was kicking up his heels.'

They'd reached the corner where she turned right for the park or left to return home. He looked at her questioningly and she indicated left.

'Seeing Dad's pictures really shook me up,' he said. 'There he was, a bored shipping clerk all his life with this amazing talent going unrecognised… If he hadn't been painting he'd have died even younger, we reckon. And maybe he'd have lived a whole lot longer if he'd left that job earlier. Anyway, I knew I was suffocating at Buxton and Dad's death made me wonder if there was more to me too. Not an artist – I don't have any illusions about that. But something… So this was a great opportunity to kick the traces and see what else I might want to do… find out if I have any other abilities lying dormant.'

'And do you?' she asked. She was being pushy, almost trying to hurt him, to hit back… Of course he didn't have hidden talents! She'd lived with him for ten years; she would know.

'Not that I'm aware of,' he said. His jaw tightened, and she felt a little pang at her cruelty and his sense of loss.

They walked in silence for a while, and then she said, 'I haven't had a parent die, of course, so I don't know what that's like. But Rita… that affected me for years…'

He seemed to appreciate this small concession, this toe in the water of understanding, stepping immediately into the space she had made. 'Jake and I were both very affected by Dad's death, although differently. For me, it brought up a desire to get out of my box and question everything, to challenge myself with new experiences. For Jake, it brought up his feelings of failure; he felt he wasn't achieving anything of any significance.'

She pondered this. 'So what else did you try that was new?'

'Not all that much. I was pretty busy working on the charity idea and getting prints made of Dad's artwork and helping Mum get ready to move. And by the time the dust settled on all of that I was starting to kick myself about leaving you. I had an actual panic attack about it.' He looked at her for a moment.

She met those hazel eyes. Not desperate now, not trying to get her back; just resigned, quiet, sad. She looked away. Focused on Bitsy.

'When we first talked seriously about doing this,' John said, 'I wanted to come up with a plan. A rock-solid written agreement – a contract. Jake said, 'Where have plans got you so far? Bored. Stuck. In a rut. Let's play it by ear.' In a mad moment I agreed. It made sense. I'd decided that I needed to take more risks, be free and spontaneous instead of always thinking ahead. Get a taste of his recklessness. He wanted a taste of my orderliness, believe it or not. He wanted commitment and responsibility. Although, of course, flying across the world to Australia and into the challenge of a new relationship that he had to rescue was also a big adventure.' John elbowed her suddenly and said with a comical expression, 'You wanted me to be more surprising. Well? Does swapping with Jake count?'

'How can you joke about it?' she asked, meeting his humour with severity.

'I'm not, Mia. I'm serious. I've shown you that I can break the mould, which is what you wanted.'

That was true. And while he'd been trying new behaviours with John, she'd tried one at Sheryl's party. She pushed that memory aside. 'You said you went to Paris.'

'Just for a weekend.' He hesitated and then said, 'And if I'm going to come clean about everything, you might as well know that I went with Mel.'

'Mel?'

'Melissa. My old flame.'

That put a different light on things.

'But we didn't sleep together.'

She regarded him sceptically.

John dug his hands into his pockets. 'I know you might not believe me but we didn't. I couldn't do it. I was attracted to her again and she was available but when it came down to it...' His voice trailed away. 'We kissed and mucked around but I just couldn't do it. At the time I didn't understand why. Later, after I'd decided to come back, I realised it was because I still wanted you.'

Mia would have dug her hands into her pockets if she had any. And she couldn't fold her arms because she was holding the leash. She walked with her chest open, one arm swinging at her side, feeling touched and vulnerable.

'Mel has two kids and I didn't want to get caught up in that. If I was going to have kids I wanted them with you. And I guess it didn't feel clean since I knew I wanted to be back with you... But at the time I thought it was just conservative, careful old me, too old-fashioned and unadventurous to take a risk. You go all the way across the world and you give yourself permission to be anything and do anything, and then you find that you've brought your old self with you and you're still shocking at first dates and you just want to be loyal and play by the rules...'

Hearing that, she felt a rush of affection for the old, honest, caring John, and felt like hugging him, but held back, afraid of leading him on when she wasn't yet sure where she wanted to go.

'So there you have it,' he sighed. 'I couldn't step into Jake's shoes. And I'm warning you that I don't think he can change who he is either.'

'But he's already shown that he can,' she demurred, 'at least to some degree. And he gave up that big role.'

'*Audition* for a role,' John corrected. 'There was no guarantee he'd get it. And he's heading off to jump right back into that world this weekend. He hadn't told you that up front, had he?'

'Sit!' she commanded Bitsy. They were at the kerb opposite their home, ready to cross back.

'Mia,' he said, and she detected a note of the old urgency in his voice again. He took hold of her arm, but gently. 'Mia, please. You've got every reason and every right to never want to see me again – I know that. And I'll accept it if that's what you decide. But please understand that I was trying to become a better me, and I was trying to give you what you wanted. I know I was a boring old sod for ages and I'm not going to ever be as exciting as Jake, but I do love you and I want to make it work. Please give me another chance. Don't throw the baby out with the bathwater.'

She grimaced at the expression, and he realised and said, 'You know what I mean. We have had good times together. And I will,' he swallowed, 'I will love and look after this baby with you.'

Jake was standing at the living room window. She could see a shadow, a slight movement… Mia looked at John, whose hand was still on her arm, gentle but firm.

'Thank you,' she said. 'I will keep that in mind.'

30

'How's it going?' Sheryl asked, before Mia had even stepped inside. 'We've been thinking about you and talking about this all day. It's epic! How did Jake take the news?'

'He seemed pretty happy about it. They're both promising undying commitment.'

'Jesus! All right, Bitsy! Hello, I love you, too.' She knelt down in the hallway to ruffle Bitsy's ears.

'Mum and Dad just dropped in,' Mia added.

Sheryl stopped ruffling and stood up with Bitsy in her arms. 'How did *that* go?'

'Okay. We just told them Jake had made a surprise visit.'

'The real Jake?'

'Yes. They were both themselves.'

'This is so… it's a real mind-fuck, isn't it?'

'Tell me about it.'

Alec was cooking – a rich, meaty smell pervaded the house. When they sat around the table, Bitsy on the rug and Talia asleep upstairs, their conversation continued to circle the issue, sniffing it and poking at it and making it roll over so they could see its tender underbelly.

'The more I think about it, the crazier I feel,' Mia said. 'Stay with Jake? Stay with John? Go out on my own? I can see the pros and cons of each one and they're so balanced, I can't see a clear path ahead. It's driving me nuts.'

'Okay,' Sheryl said, forking a piece of roast pumpkin. 'Give 'em to us.'

'Well, stay with John: I know him, he's loyal – up until this, anyway... He's reliable. He loves me. He's changing now, out of that stuck place he was in, which is encouraging. But... will it last? And do *I* love him? When he left I was bored, restless, looking for an out... That's my memory of our relationship.'

'He might be quite different if you give him a chance,' Alec said. 'He's just given you a pretty huge demonstration of change – in values and character.'

'Yeah...' Mia toyed with her food. 'He said that too. But I just can't imagine how we could ever recover from a betrayal like this.'

'Maybe it's not a betrayal. Maybe it just looks like that.'

'Are you siding with the boys?' Sheryl demanded.

'No!' He looked at her in surprise. 'It's just that there was a good intention mixed into all that madness. It's quite impressive, at one level.'

Mia made a face. 'I suppose...'

'And he's walked away from that stultifying job. So things might change in the direction you've been wanting.'

'If I go back with him.'

'Yes. But even if you don't, it's not stuck anymore. You've got room to move now.'

'Move where?' Sheryl asked. 'In with Jake? Out on her own?'

'I mean they're not so locked into the old roles they were playing.'

She elbowed him. 'I'm just joshing. I'm the comic relief.'

'I know you're talking sense,' Mia told Alec, 'but...'

She remembered Bernard's comment to her after the conference: *'You're not in the wrong life,'* That *was* how she viewed things – that her perfect life was unfolding somewhere else, without her, because she had screwed up in some way, and if she could just get her act together she'd pull it back over here or she'd step into it over there, and things would come good...

'The problem is the fantasies we have about marriage, the Hollywoodisation of it.' Alec leaned back in his chair and scanned the room, then gave up. 'I'm reading a great book at the moment about marriage; I thought it was down here. I'll find it and show you.'

'The one by Mr Bottom?' Sheryl asked.

'*Botton*,' he corrected, smiling. 'Alain de Botton. It's about how we used to think we were ready for marriage when we had the funds or the property or the qualifications, and then that was all seen as too mercenary and the focus became romantic – you're ready when you *feel* ready, when you *feel* this is the right person for you; and now the realisation is dawning that we're all flawed and marriages are all going to be unhappy and disappointing at times, so there's no point being deluded or getting frustrated about it – just see the hard times as part of the journey, as tests and opportunities instead of failures.'

The Hero's Journey, Mia mused. 'So you think I should take it less personally. Is that what you're saying?'

'I think John is genuinely working through some of his issues, and his stuff happens to dovetail with yours because that's how marriage works. Your weaknesses hook up.'

'Which weaknesses?' Sheryl asked him. 'Mia is a sweetie, through and through.'

Mia made a face. 'I can answer that. We're both procrastinators and we both look for safety. He was staying at Buxton where it was secure instead of finding a company that inspired him, and I was taking forever to decide about starting a counselling course. And he was resentful of Jake and I was resentful of Rita. It is kind of interesting that we ended up together.'

'*And* you were both thinking that the grass was greener...' Sheryl added. 'But Jake is very opposite, so how does he fit into it?'

'He's like the other side of me,' Mia said. 'The all-over-the-place side of me that hasn't succeeded at anything yet.'

'Oh, honey, that's not true.'

Mia looked at her.

'Okay, so you don't own your own company – but you wouldn't want to, if I know you!'

'No, but I haven't done anything else yet either, have I? Just drift from job to job since I left school, not even doing work that I particularly enjoy. And let my marriage just drift along until I was bored to death...'

'Maybe your thing is going to be counselling and mothering. It's all probably ahead of you.'

'I hope so.'

'But geez, what a charming model,' Sheryl said, reaching past Mia to prod Alec. 'Marriages of weakness?'

Alec shrugged. 'That's the reality. Unhappiness is in the design of the thing and it's self-defeating to be upset about it. We just have to deal with the stuff it brings up. Anyway, we can't say that we have a strong relationship until it's been tested, so from one perspective your relationship with John might just be evolving into a more mature form.'

'I guess...' Mia said. 'But why do some of us get these huge issues and other people have really smooth-sailing relationships? You two, for instance.'

'Alec and me, babe,' Sheryl contradicted, 'we're still at the innocent stage – give us a few years and we'll be sure to be fighting and resentful and all that juicy stuff. I'm not the most patient person in the world, as you know. Alec is bound to get sick of me once he stops being so googoo-eyed...'

'And I always wonder if Sheryl will eventually wake up that there's someone much more attractive and fun out there than me,' he said.

They both looked at him.

'You see?' There was a slight pinkness to his bald pate. 'We all feel inadequate about something or other. And marriage flushes out those inadequacies so that we'll deal with them.'

Sheryl blew him a kiss. 'You've got my key, hun.'

He smiled, warmth in his eyes, and proffered the dish of roast vegetables.

Mia speared another few pieces. 'Thanks. This is delicious.'

'Okay, so that's the pros and cons of John,' Sheryl pronounced, forking a spud. 'What about Jake?'

Jake. Mia took a moment to cut a piece of meat and then put her cutlery down. 'More romantic. Better at making me feel like a beautiful, desired woman... But will he sustain that? His track record isn't inspiring... And he's useless with money. I can see him draining our resources and not bringing much in – he hasn't been very financially successful. And he's all over the place work-wise.'

'But he wants to stay with you?' Alec's food was still barely touched. He was the ideal man in so many ways – how many blokes would show such a genuine interest in relationships and what made them work?

'He's saying that. And yet we don't know each other at all! We're, like, eight weeks into a relationship!'

'And a pregnancy,' Sheryl put in. 'Have you seen an obstetrician yet?'

'No.'

'Mine is great. I'll give you her details if you like.'

'Okay. Thanks.'

'Third option,' Sheryl continued. 'Going your own way: pros and cons.'

'Well, I'd be free of all this complexity and madness and the deceit,' Mia said. 'Free to meet someone new and start again. But would they be any better, since everyone is disappointing?' with a hat tip to Alec. 'And I'd be a single mum, and that probably makes meeting someone else complicated. And, really, I'll never escape those two – I'll still have to relate with Jake because he's the dad, and John... I don't know. If I left him and I'm always going to be caught up with Jake now, he might just think that's all too hard and not want anything else to do with me, or he might hang around too. Can you imagine starting a new relationship with two men attached?'

'Two identical men,' Sheryl added. She grinned. 'I would so love to be a fly on the wall when you introduced them to the new guy.'

'Oh my God.' Mia covered her face with her hands. 'Don't. I can't bear it.'

There was a whimper through the intercom system.

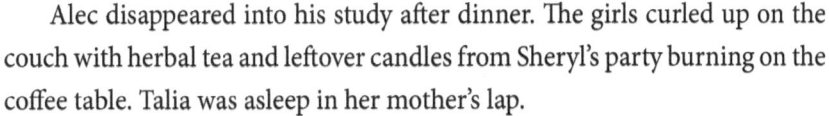

Alec disappeared into his study after dinner. The girls curled up on the couch with herbal tea and leftover candles from Sheryl's party burning on the coffee table. Talia was asleep in her mother's lap.

'What was that about Alec having your key?' Mia asked, transfixed by the infant's peaceful face.

'To my chastity belt,' Sheryl said. 'Private joke.'

Mia smiled.

Sheryl was stroking her daughter's head tenderly. 'We humans are funny mixed-up people, aren't we? Here I am: loving this, loving having Tahls and watching her grow, but also restless, bored, wanting to be back at work driving my biz. And you: torn between wanting security and romance. Which, by the way, is so true for everyone.'

'Mmm,' Mia murmured. Alec was playing music in his office – an acoustic guitar track. It was lovely: relaxing and stimulating at the same time, complex and yet simple. She wondered what the boys were doing at home. Not fighting, she hoped. Surely they got sick of fighting.

'I was watching a sex therapist giving a TED talk today,' Sheryl said. 'She was saying that you have to have some distance to keep the spark in your marriage; too much familiarity is the death knell.'

'I guess that's why I thought things were working for me and John when he came back – except that it was Jake.'

'Yeah…'

Mia thought about Nick. There was no doubt that a stable marriage killed eroticism – or could, if you didn't manage things better.

'So you haven't slept with either of them since John arrived?'

'Shared the bed with Jake but no sex since John arrived. I felt self-conscious with his so-called brother in the house. But maybe it was my intuition talking. Can you imagine how weird it would have felt for John – being shown into the guest room while his brother went into the master with me?' Mia shook her head at the memory.

'Very screwy.'

'But Jake's going to Sydney this weekend. Did I tell you that? He's got An Audition.'

Sheryl gave a dramatic gasp. 'So it begins…'

'Who knows? But it means I'll be alone with John.'

'You can always stay here.'

'No. We need to talk. But thanks.'

'How do you feel about that?'

'Mixed.'

They sat in silence again for a while, listening to the guitar music, watching Talia and the candles.

'We've got a new person on staff who's Indian,' Sheryl said. 'Luce reckons she's in an arranged marriage. That's a whole other ball game, isn't it? Not marrying for love but because you think you'll be suited, and then just making it work.'

'Almost like me and Jake,' Mia said. 'Except that only one of us knew it was an arranged marriage.'

'Huh!' Sheryl exclaimed in agreement. 'Geez, I don't envy you, babe. It's a tricky situation.'

Mia thought about the matchmaking example. What would that be like? If she and Jake did stay together, it really would be like an arranged marriage. John's disappointed eyes came to mind. Was Alec right? Had they needed this betrayal to 'evolve their relationship into something greater'? Would things be better if she got back with him? She sighed.

'Don't think about it too much,' Sheryl advised. 'You'll do your head in.'

'That happened a while ago.'

Sheryl's hair was particularly golden in the candlelight. She made a very pretty picture, her glossy curls hanging on either side of her face as she gazed at her baby.

'You know I was going to get a colour through my hair while he was overseas,' Mia said, 'only I never got around to it. Brown is so boring.'

'Your hair is lovely.'

'It's boring. Brown, shoulder length – I reckon I'd feel better about myself with a new look.'

'As better as you thought you'd feel with a new man?' Sheryl asked.

Mia slept in on Tuesday morning, obeying Reynald's dictum that she stay away for a couple of days. When she joined Sheryl in the bright kitchen for a late breakfast, she learnt that they had an appointment at two that afternoon.

'Where? What for?' she asked, eyeing the spread of fruit and the tub of vanilla yoghurt.

'My hairdresser. To give you a colour.'

'I thought that was putting my power outside of me,' Mia objected. 'Isn't that what you said last night?'

'Only when you're doing it unconsciously,' Sheryl said. 'Eat up, kiddo. My treat but we've got to bleach you first.'

Mia opted for a mahogany fringe and the result was fantastic. Glancing at herself periodically in the rear view mirror on the way home, she was delighted. Okay, she was not doing anything particularly unique – just joining the hordes of women who were dying their hair now, as her mother would be sure to point out – and it wasn't an outrageous colour, but she still felt delighted.

John and Jake were sitting at the kitchen table when she arrived home. John did a double take when she paused in the doorway, and Jake whistled.

'Just felt like something new,' she said, breezing past them to the bedroom.

When she'd unpacked, she wandered back to the kitchen and discovered that Jake was learning his script for the audition and John was working on their father's website. They seemed quite busy and comfortable together there – as if they hadn't missed her at all.

'Doing some good sales,' John said as she filled the kettle. 'Mel's found an art student who's packing and posting the orders for us, and she reckons we're going to need a bigger storage venue than her spare room soon.'

'She's been looking after all of that?'

'Remember I told you she stayed close to Mum and Dad? She wanted to help.'

'Tell Mia about the patron,' Jake said, without taking his eyes from the script.

John swivelled in his seat. 'Mel has also landed a very wealthy individual with an interest in the arts who looks like being the patron of our charity – or at least a significant donor. So we are all systems go to get this show on the road.' He was glowing.

'Wow,' she said. 'That's great. But won't you – one of you, at least – need to be over there?'

John glanced at Jake, who looked up from his script in the same moment to meet his brother's eyes.

'Not all the time,' John said. 'Not with the magic of the internet. But there will be some functions we'll need to be there for. We'd relocate the whole thing over here but that probably won't be possible now that it's set up in the UK. But there are late-blooming artists in Australia too, so maybe we'll get someone else to manage it over there and we'll manage it over here.'

'*We'll manage it over here.*' What did that mean? That they were both planning to stay?

The kettle clicked off. She poured herself a cup of liquorice tea. 'You two want anything?'

They both declined, indicating their mugs. She pulled up a chair between them, nursing her cup, and looked at John's screen. He scrolled through the gallery of their father's paintings and sketches for her to see. Each one was listed with a title and a price in pounds. There were lots, all impressive. Then he tabbed over to the website for the charity, which was also being developed. *The John Hartington Sr Foundation For Late-Blooming Artists.* There was a picture on the home page of their father sitting at his easel – a snap Jake had taken a few years ago when visiting his parents. The rest of the site was still in placeholder text. When she had commented admiringly, he tabbed to another site.

'What's this?' she asked, looking at the 'under construction' message.

He pointed to the URL. She leaned closer, reading it. 'j&jfinancials4artists. com,' then sat back and stared at him. 'Seriously? This is another new business?'

'Got to replace my Buxton income somehow,' John said. 'Selling Dad's artwork is mostly passive income – not much for us to do since we'll get someone else to handle the marketing, and the charity might take a while to build, so meanwhile...' He stretched his arms wide above his head and rotated his shoulders, easing kinks. 'I'm clear now that numbers *are* my thing – not that I thought anything like gardening or massage would be. I just needed a more interesting focus.'

Mia turned to Jake. 'And you're in on this too? J *and* J?'

He nodded. 'Brand new plan. I'll find the struggling artistes and John will show them how to manage their money. He cleaned up my mess so...'

She couldn't help admiring them. This was men for you: no agonising. If there was nothing you could do about something, you got on with something else. She should take a leaf out of their book.

Jake touched her mahogany fringe that evening when they were in the kitchen cooking and John was hunting for something in the garage.

'I like this,' he said. He caught her by the wrist, drawing her closer. 'I miss you.'

Mia put a hand on his chest, locking the distance between them. 'I can't.'

For a moment he stood there, gazing at her, a smile crinkling the corners of his eyes; the sort of smile that melted her, welcomed her, whether it came from John or from Jake.

There was a bang in the garage, and a muttered curse. She broke away. 'Really. I can't.'

Jake's hand fell to his side and they remained where they stood, empty space between them, something sizzling on the stove, some sort of groovy techno-music playing in the background.

John appeared in the doorway, frowning. 'Mia, what have you done with my old archive boxes?'

She flushed, a memory of Jake-as-John authorising their demise. 'The more-than-seven-years ones have been destroyed.'

'Without asking me!' he exclaimed.

She put her hands on her hips and gave him a look.

John turned on his heel and left.

Jake said, 'Oops.'

31

When Mia arrived at ACCAT on Wednesday morning for the counselling course, Susan was talking to Paula in the foyer; they both smiled at her absently and kept on with their conversation, and she walked past them toward the classrooms feeling relief that Reynald did not appear to have revealed any of her crisis to them. Naturally he would keep his therapist's oath of confidentiality but if her inability to work affected the company, that would become a conflict of interest for him. Still, maternity leave was a long way off yet, and she should be fine to go back to her desk after class tomorrow morning – she was feeling less shocked now, and keeping busy would help her push the issues to the back of her mind where, hopefully, a wiser part of her brain would sort out what she should do. She remembered how John and Jake had stayed productive over the last couple of days instead of indulging their upset. If they could do it, she could do it.

Reynald looked up when she entered the classroom; he studied her face closely. There were other students arriving and chatting, so he didn't say anything aloud but his eyes asked how she was. She paused by his desk and said, 'I'm okay. Nothing is resolved but I'm feeling better. And I did do some journalling.'

'Good,' he said. 'Let's have a chat later.' He indicated her hair. 'Snazzy.'

The class spent the morning discussing Carl Rogers' humanistic therapy, talking about the importance of empathy, congruence, unconditional positive regard and no judgement when listening to the client's issues… Well,

Reynald certainly had that one down pat; he hadn't even blinked when she told him her husband had swapped places with his brother and she was now in love with the brother and pregnant to him but also not sure she wanted to lose her husband. What had he said? *'It's unique.'*

She was on the phone at lunchtime with Sheryl's obstetrician, looking at dates for an appointment, when she realised that Monday was John's birthday. Usually she was conscious of its approach and would spend a few weeks thinking about presents since it wasn't easy to buy for him, but with everything that had been happening she had completely forgotten about it. This time it was John's *and* Jake's birthday. Would she even bother with gifts? If she did, she faced the issue their parents had dealt with: how to find two different gifts that were completely equal in value so as not to communicate any favouritism? This problem hovered at the back of her mind, along with the choice she was going to have to make.

At the end of the day she held the door open for Reynald, who had his laptop under one arm and a pile of books in the other.

'Thanks,' he said, as he passed through. 'Did the journalling help?'

'I think so. It was good to get my feelings out.'

'Any insights?'

She nodded.

'Good. Let's find you that therapist.' He indicated his office and she walked through the admin area after him, enjoying the sense of being a visitor. Staff who were packing up to go greeted her as she passed. Nice as everyone was, she wouldn't miss filing or scheduling meetings or taking dictation or preparing travel itineraries or writing minutes...

Reynald put his things on the desk and woke his computer up. He was momentarily distracted by an abundance of emails popping in with their distinctive little sound – the cost of spending a day away from his desk. She didn't envy him the over-time she was sure he was about to begin.

'Our homework to have a counselling session and write up our reflections on it,' she said suddenly; 'I won't have to share what's happening with the others, will I?'

'Not at all. You'll be asked to share about your experience of the process, and how it felt to be counselled, rather than reveal the details of what you discussed.' He brought up a list of counsellors and began to explain their different specialties.

On Thursday evening The Hero's Journey Group met again. Tired as she was, Mia was glad that she'd be arriving late home tonight. John and Jake had been busy working on their businesses the previous night, but even with their preoccupation and the space they were studiously giving her, there had still been a feeling of pressure, of something hanging over her: the need to make a life-changing decision that affected her and both of them – and an unborn child.

She settled into her seat. There were twelve steps written up on the board and on a handout: the twelve stages of the Hero's Journey. Bernard leapt straight into leading the group through them. As she listened, Mia found herself applying the stages to John's journey. She was struck by how closely they fitted.

The first stage, the Ordinary World, was limited awareness of a problem. That was all the years during which he'd had his head in the sand, not wanting to change or deal with anything.

The second stage, the Call to Adventure, was arriving in England for his father's death and discovering his father's talents, and the questions this brought up for him about his own life. He'd also been churning over the fact that he couldn't have children, and what that meant for his relationship with her.

The third stage was Refusal, the reluctance to change. She could imagine him tussling with himself – should he stay at Buxton and cash in on the long service shares or take a risk and do something new? Should he suggest IVF or adoption or just give up?

The fourth stage was Meeting with the Mentor. Who was that? Who had helped him overcome his reluctance to change? Was it possibly Jake? Was that when the idea had emerged that they swap?

'The hero needs outside help,' Bernard said, sitting on the edge of the desk, one leg swinging a little. 'It can be a wise person or simply serendipity – running into a stranger who tells you exactly what you need to hear.'

Or a brother who is equally frustrated and just that little bit more of a risk-taker, who pushes you over the edge...

The fifth stage, Crossing the Threshold, was committing to change. She thought back to the emails John had sent her from England. At some point he had made a decision. He'd warned her: 'I'm coming back a changed man...' Was that before or after he and Jake had decided to swap?

The sixth stage was experimenting with change; it was a period of Tests when Allies and Enemies emerged. This was when he had started to prepare Jake for his role as John. The enemies had become allies.

She was suddenly struck by the memory of a phone call during which she'd sensed something odd. Had she been talking to Jake, thinking it was John? Had they actually been testing her – testing her ability to hear Jake's voice and assume it was John? She shook her head in amazement at their cheek, at their sheer bloody impertinence! No doubt, if she had recognised that the voice wasn't John's, they would have laughed it off as a joke and nothing would have come of it. John would have returned home. As it was, the joke was on her...

She forced herself to concentrate on what Bernard was saying.

The seventh stage was preparing for big change. Its name, 'Approach to the Inmost Cave', was almost too literal. John had prepared Jake to enter her cave: her home and her body...

The eighth stage was attempting the change. This was where John's Ordeal was to follow through, to wave Jake off at the airport and return home to his mother while his brother went through the ordeal of avoiding recognition and winning her over.

The ninth stage was the consequences of the attempt. It was called 'The

Reward', but the reward could be a false victory, as in John's case, because he had realised that freedom was not what he wanted. He'd regretted what he had done. And her victory had been false too. Her husband hadn't really changed; he'd been an imposter. She'd been cuckolded, in a way.

There was a knot in her stomach.

The tenth stage, the Road Back, was rededication to change. This was literal for John – he had bought a plane ticket home. He had realised that while he did want a more fulfilling life, he wanted it with her. He wanted to find a job that he would enjoy that would utilise his skills and he wanted to transform his relationship rather than running away from it.

The eleventh stage was called 'Resurrection'. It was a final attempt at big change, and that was exactly what had happened. John had tried to get Jake to swap back so that he could grow for real: find a more fulfilling job and renegotiate his relationship with her, even if that meant IVF or adoption. He was trying to resurrect himself now. He was trying to rise from the ashes of his error.

She swallowed. Her choice, her response, would determine if he could complete the twelfth stage: Return with the Elixir, the magic potion. His success was in her hands.

'A good journey leaves us with an elixir that changes us,' Bernard was saying, as he paced across the front of the room. 'It makes us more aware, more alive, more human, more whole.'

'Can you give us some examples of an 'elixir'?' a tall woman with very straight, honey-coloured hair asked.

'Wisdom,' Bernard said at once; 'or just experience. Money. Love. Peace.' He was ticking them off on his fingers. 'Fame, power, success, health, knowledge – or a wild adventure. In books and films the elixir is sometimes an actual substance, a treasure, for instance, but the real elixir is always insight and growth – inner change and learning rather than a physical treasure. It might be the ability to speak up or take more responsibility for your life, or learning that love is a skill to be practised, not a passion that invades you.'

'So a good journey means implementing change in your daily life and using the lessons of the adventure to heal your wounds,' Reynald contributed, from his seat at the back of the room.

Bernard nodded. 'Then the circle of the Hero's Journey is complete.'

This was the elegance he had referred to last week.

'You've probably been connecting these stages to periods and experiences in your own life as we've worked through the list,' he continued. 'I'd like you to now begin to put those connections in writing. We go through many cycles of the Hero's Journey in our lives, so you can work on a cycle from your youth or a cycle that's current. Just stick with one cycle until you've seen the whole process. If you're working on a current cycle it won't be complete, so look at the stages that are still ahead through the eyes of God-you. What does Character-you need to experience in order to grow?'

There was a murmuring of voices and the rustle of pages as participants settled to write. Raising his voice a little to be heard over the top of the noise, Bernard added, 'Bear in mind that the *hero* must do the work. The hero, Character-you, begins with a set of flaws that set up the whole journey, and he or she must make the decision to grow at that fifth stage; it can't be someone else pushing you into something – it's got to be your decision. Also at the end of the cycle, you, the hero, must take the final actions that prove mastery of your problem.'

Mia let out a little breath of relief. So, in that case, it wasn't all resting on her. Whatever she chose, John would have to deal with it and turn it to good in his life. She wasn't responsible for his journey, only hers.

But as she began to fill in the first few stages of her journey, she realised that she already knew the answers to the questions that were driving her, and they were very unsettling.

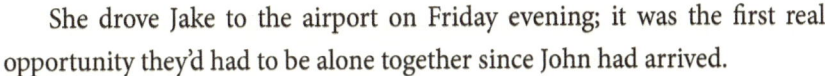

She drove Jake to the airport on Friday evening; it was the first real opportunity they'd had to be alone together since John had arrived.

'So were you going to tell me about this audition?' she asked, as they headed into a magnificent sunset. There was a slightly sulky, resentful edge to her voice.

'Of course,' he said at once. 'I only heard about it last weekend, which is when everything blew up, so I was waiting for a less tense moment.'

'How did you hear about it? I didn't think you had any theatre contacts out here. Or was it through that Katarina?'

'My agent in the UK. He was the only one who knew I was coming here, although he didn't know all the details of the arrangement with John.'

The traffic was horrendous. They were barely crawling now, as they approached the freeway.

'What about that role you gave up, or the audition for it, or whatever?'

Jake shot her a quick glance. 'It was an audition for a lead in a film. Not a big one: a low-budget B-movie but it was a start. My agent knew I was going to be in Australia and not really available for a few months but this opportunity was too good for him to not let me know about it.'

'That must have hurt, letting it go past,' she said, and then thought: active listening! She'd done it, and without even trying!

'Yep.' He was looking out the side window now. In the next moment they spoke simultaneously. He said, 'That's why I told you my friend –' and she asked, 'What do you mean 'a few months'?' She indicated for him to go first, and he said, 'The night I was late home and went to the pub? That was when I found out about the audition and realised I was going to have to let it go. I was shattered. I had to go out for a long walk to get my head right, so I could be with you without turning violent.'

'You said a good friend had died – suicided,' she remembered.

'Yeah. It felt like the death of my dream.'

'But I thought you'd decided to put the dream aside.'

He sighed. 'How do you ever do that with something you love? I was telling myself I *should* put the dream aside – the fantasy; that's how I was beginning to see it. But I couldn't totally let go. I've realised, ironically, that in putting it aside I was doing the very thing Dad did: doing what I 'should' instead of what was in my heart.'

'But you'd followed your dreams already, and they hadn't worked out.'

His jaw tightened a little. 'I know. But that doesn't mean to give up. I just needed a more solid back-up plan.'

'Which you have now, working with John.'

He raised his brows in an expression of utter surprise. 'Who woulda ever guessed?'

They were finally on the freeway, although still moving slowly.

'You were going to ask me something,' Jake said. 'Something about months.'

'Oh. Yes. What did you mean by telling your agent you wouldn't be available 'for a few months'? Weren't you making the commitment to be here forever? Or were you just toying with us?' That resentful tone was edging back into her voice.

'I was taking myself out of circulation for a few months while we found out how things were going to go... with the new arrangement. There were no guarantees for anyone. You might have caught me out at the airport, like one of those trained sniffer dogs.'

'You smelt like John,' she said curtly.

'I was wearing his aftershave.'

'And his clothes.'

'All of it,' he conceded. 'Even the tight little shoes. It's a miracle I didn't get thrombosis – travelling in his too-small clothes.'

'And then? After the first few months?' she prompted.

'Well, I was doing my best to *be* John, step into his shoes, etcetera. I was drilling myself all the way over from the UK: 'I am John, I am John...' But we both knew I couldn't do that long-term. I'd have to be myself. And we knew that – John said you were frustrated with his conservatism and you'd appreciate a livelier partner, which is how I naturally am... and what John was promising to be. So I was trying to pull off a balance of genuine me plus old-John-changing-into-new-John, and gradually let the John-act go and just be me...'

She couldn't help admiring the challenge he had dealt with so well, but wasn't about to say so. Instead, she said, 'Until you decided to go back home after those few months.'

'No,' he said. 'My point is that after the first few months, when I was fully me again, I knew I'd probably start looking for some acting gigs again. I wasn't deciding that consciously at the time because I was genuinely trying to kick the habit, but something deep inside me knew I wouldn't be able to completely let it go.'

They were finally moving more quickly now. Mia was squinting against the harsh orange-white light of the setting sun; she flicked her visor down and could still see white circles for a while.

'You said this – living with me – was the biggest acting job of your life. But that wasn't enough?'

'Geez, Mia!' he exclaimed. 'What do you mean 'not enough'? It *was* the biggest acting job of my life but not satisfying for an actor the way being in the limelight is. That's a whole different ball game.'

'You wanted applause,' she said coolly. 'And of course, this audience had no idea there was a show going on.'

'Yes,' he said simply. 'An actor thrives on recognition. It's in our make-up. But that doesn't mean I didn't want to be with you. I wanted to be with you *and* I wanted to be me and to act again.'

You wanted it all, she thought. *Just like me.* She wanted the 'good' twin – the reliable, sensible, caring twin, *and* the 'bad' twin – the spontaneous, fun, irresponsible twin. She wanted a man who combined all those traits. Was that possible? Was it possible to have it all in one relationship? Jake wanted the freedom to follow his dreams *and* have a steady partner and build a family. There was nothing wrong with that, although striking the balance would be more difficult with a wife and child to support. When it was just him, he could live off scraps and work at his mate's pizza shop to make ends meet, but with a family…

'What about your side of it?' he asked. 'What made you realise?'

She told him about all those little moments that had rung faint bells, those moments when her intuition had tugged at her skirt and she had shaken it off, saying, 'Don't bother me. I'm busy with my new infatuation...'

'There were quite a few times when I thought I'd blown it,' he said. 'Like that scar. Neither John nor I had even thought of that. I was sure you'd guess then. And the food, having to stick with foods he liked and not being able to eat and drink what I liked when you were around. If you ever got into the ute I'd be praying that you didn't open the ash tray and discover all the snack bar wrappings I'd squished in there...' He was grinning. He gave her arm a little push. 'Go on. Smile. There's a funny side to all this...'

'Yeah. For an audience at the movies,' she said tightly. But she was holding her smile in. She wouldn't laugh! That would be making a mockery of the mockery they had made of her...

'You've got to have a sense of humour, Mia,' he persisted. 'If you take it too seriously you'll make yourself sick, and you can't do that. Especially now.' He reached out a hand and laid it gently on her belly. Her insides flipped at his touch. She wanted to cover his hand with hers and keep it there. She wanted to disappear all the craziness and muddle and go back to the happiness of the last few weeks. She wanted to combine the two of them into one, so she could have both of them. She wanted to take the barricades down and settle into being a contented pregnant wife with a husband who cherished her... She gripped the wheel with both hands.

'I've been thinking,' he said, taking his hand away slowly, 'about all the good things that have come out of this for each of us. More fitness for me, for one.'

'You were hiding out in cafés!' she retorted.

'Some of the time. But I was cycling a hell of a lot more than I ever had before. And enjoying it, I have to confess. And I have lost a few kilos, you know.' He carried on with his list. 'I'm grateful for you – for experiencing an ordinary, everyday, committed relationship. No drama. Just every morning waking up next to a beautiful, intelligent woman who wanted me to be there. That's been magic.'

She looked at him quickly. It sounded as if he was saying goodbye.

'And the financial stability,' he continued. 'Not having to worry about money for the first time in my life. Honestly, it's been great. And an eye-opener. It's made me want more of all that. I can completely understand how John had a new appreciation for everything he had once he stepped away from it.'

They were nearing the freeway exit to the airport.

'And there was good stuff for John in all of this. He got to reconnect with Mum, which he wanted. And the opportunity to step out of the grind and all the old expectations, and have a fresh start.'

She drove, listening, quiet.

'What about you, Mia?' Jake asked. 'What's been good about it for you? Other than the buzz of knowing that two men want you...'

'You know.' She could feel tears, just at the perimeter of her awareness.

'Tell me,' he said gently. 'I want to hear it from you. Before I go.'

'Go where?' she asked, engulfed by a sudden fear of loss.

'To Sydney, of course.'

Was that all? Was he coming back? Perhaps this was her last chance... They were crawling again, edging closer to the airport in the midst of the Friday night leaving-Melbourne traffic.

'Feeling more loved,' she said. It was true. There were benefits for all of them in what had happened. 'More special. Going out to shows with you instead of just staying home. How you made love to me...' Her voice trailed away.

After a moment he put his hand on her thigh. 'Thank you for telling me. I'm glad.'

Her mind was chattering: *Are you leaving for good? Are you coming back? This is your child in here!*

'I really don't know what you, what we should do,' he said. 'If we do part ways, I want you to know how grateful I am. I can't fight John for you – he's got the longer claim. I do want to stick around for the kid and I'd like to stay with you but I don't know if it's possible.'

He was giving up. Giving up on her. Walking away from her as he had done with so many others, just as John had predicted.

There were signs ahead of them: this way for three-minute drop-off and that way for short-term parking.

'Just the drop-off,' he said. 'It'll be late by the time you get home. Just drop me off.'

And John would be waiting for her, eager to begin their first weekend alone together since he had left for England three and a half months ago. There was a band of tension around her head, and a slight churning in her belly.

She pulled up and instead of jumping out he turned toward her. 'Forget about me this weekend. Have a wonderful time with John and when I get back, on Monday, we'll talk about it all then.'

So he was coming back.

He leaned forward and kissed her lightly, and then properly, pulling her close until the only thing between them was the bloody gearstick and console.

She must have looked desolate when he sat back because he reached out with one hand to touch the tears at the corner of her eye and said, 'We've all got to trust something bigger than us. To trust that it's going to work out.'

She bit her lip. Nodded.

'Come clean with John about Mr Tall, Dark and Handsome. All right?'

She looked at him, puzzled.

'The hunk at the show.'

Oh. Nick. She flushed and Jake smiled. 'Yes. Him.'

'Nothing happened,' she said. Not in the conventional sense, anyway.

'Something happened in here.' He touched her breast.

She captured his hand. 'I'm going to miss you.'

'Who says I'm going?' he said at once. 'It ain't over till the fat lady sings.'

She smiled, relief flooding. She wanted to say that she couldn't imagine John winning her back, not physically, not intimately, but at the same time she was thinking, he might have done this weird, stupid thing but I still care about him. And he wanted to start a family too... Oh God!

As if he knew what she was thinking, Jake said, 'Maybe you'll just have to keep both of us. The Mormons do it.' And then he was climbing out of the car and she was climbing out on her side and saying, 'Polygamy? No way!'

And he was grinning at her as he took his overnight bag out of the boot and saying, 'Polyamory. Why bother paying wedding license fees a second time? No one would know.'

And she was half-gasping and half-laughing and he came over and gave her a long close hug, despite the fact that they'd been parked there for more than three minutes, and said, 'Think about it.'

And she said, 'How did you get to be such a good lover?' which was her awkward way of saying that John was a staid lover and he would want to make love this weekend and it wouldn't be as good and –

And he said, 'Women. It's women who showed me. You show him.' One last gentle kiss, a beautiful smile, and he was walking away. Erect, feet slightly turned out, overnight bag on one shoulder.

32

John had waited up for her. He was sitting in an armchair listening to one of their Leonard Cohen CDs. He looked up as she entered, an unfathomable expression in his eyes.

Mia sank onto the couch, avoiding his eye. Bitsy immediately leapt onto it beside her. She scooped the dog into her lap for a cuddle, and let the gravelly voice and stirring music wash over her.

'There is a crack, a crack, in everything,
That's how the light gets in...'

They sat there for a while, not speaking, just listening, breathing. She thought of that last kiss in the car before Jake left for Sydney. She remembered John taking her arm in the street and promising his love and his commitment to his brother's child. She felt the madness of their current circumstances again, like a slap in the face – that her husband would give her away and then come back! That he was now sleeping in the guest room. That she had slept, unknowingly, with his brother, and fallen in love with him. That she now loved two men, despite their flaws and deception. That she had no fucking idea what to do.

She thought about John's journey and wondered what he was going to do. What was his 'elixir'? It couldn't be getting her back because the point was not physical treasure, and anyway, he couldn't control her decisions and, as the hero of his story, he had to take the decisive action. Was his decisive action breaking the mould? Was his elixir escaping stuckness and now starting new businesses that were more fulfilling? Or was it simply knowing himself more clearly now? If those things were so, he was already completing his cycle, but what was it where she was concerned?

'Talk to me, Mia,' John said suddenly. 'What are you thinking? What are you feeling? What's going on for you?'

His questions hung in the air. She heard them again in her mind: *What are you thinking? What are you feeling? What's going on for you?*

She sighed. 'Thinking... about everything that's happened. Feeling torn...'

Her question, the one that had launched her Hero's Journey, was 'Who and Where is my Mr Right?' She'd been so sure that it couldn't be John that night when she waved him off for England. Things between them had been so flat for so long. But her question was changing. It had evolved into: 'Does Mr Right exist? Is there any such person?' After all, both of these brothers had only parts of what she wanted. Combined, they would come pretty close... Jake's suggestion as he was leaving flashed back into mind: polyamory. He had actually suggested that they all live together – a *mènage á trois*! He must be mad...

But the question that had begun stirring once she'd woken up to what was happening now sat like a lump in her stomach, waiting to be digested. Was it actually possible to genuinely love several men at once? Did love only happen serially, a new love beginning when an old love had ended, or could a person love more than one man at once? And if you did, how did you manage that? And what if those loves were different – physical attraction for one man and mental stimulation with another, or simply caring or fun or a spiritual connection – did that justify it? Did it mean you could keep them all because they satisfied different parts of you? Osho would probably say yes...

John had been sitting with his elbow on the armrest, chin propped against the curled fingers of one hand, staring down at the floor. Now he lifted his head toward her. 'I know the whole idea was stupid, Mia, but I honestly didn't think he would want to stay. I thought I was just buying some time...'

'Fuck you!' she said, grabbing a cushion and hurling it at him, anger rising again at his decision to secretly meet his needs without giving her a chance to do the same. They could have agreed to a trial separation! There'd been no need for all this cloak-and-dagger stuff!

He instinctively ducked the cushion, and she sensed him scooping it off the floor as she drew her knees up and wrapped her arms around them, churning. Churning. *Because as soon as John had departed the country – even before that – she had been looking for her alternative.* A faint image of Nick floated into mind. His hands on her. Her response. She flushed, thinking of the old saying, *'Point one finger at someone else and you have three fingers pointing back at yourself...'*

'I'm sorry, Mia,' John said, but he didn't sound sorry. She looked up.

He was sitting on the edge of his chair, looking at her intently. 'I know it was wrong and unfair but you can't punish me forever; you did gain. You got to feel loved and special again, I know you did. But – no, wait. That doesn't mean he's the only one who can give you that. He was coming in fresh – he didn't have our history and all the old disappointments and patterns. He's so confident with women. He –' John swallowed. He glanced away with an impatient movement, and then turned back to her. 'I know I haven't exactly been what you've wanted but I *want* to be, Mia. I want to make it work. There isn't anyone better out there,' he jerked a hand toward the street. 'No one's perfect. Jake certainly isn't. We're all struggling. I just want to make it work.'

'But you did give me away,' she said softly. 'And he did win my heart.'

'How? What did he do?' John asked, almost wildly. 'Was it so much better than when we met on the boat and fell in love? Was it really so much better than that?'

With that question all the pieces of her memory and feelings rearranged themselves; she could feel them shifting and swapping places, changing weight... A true note rang through his words: she couldn't compare her first happy weeks with Jake to the desert she'd been experiencing with John; she had to compare them to her first happy weeks with John... And she had to consider the desert against the possibility of Jake's inability to commit. The scales had to be perfectly balanced.

'I knew Jake would romance you... make you feel special... loved,' he said slowly, as if it cost him a great deal to let each word pass his lips. 'I just want to do that for you too. I don't want you to compare how we were this last year or so with that... honeymoon period with Jake.'

'But we can't undo that,' she said. 'I can't pretend that I don't now have him on my mind or...' she hesitated, then plunged in, 'or in my body.'

'I know. That's my punishment,' he said miserably. 'You have to realise that.'

'Every heart, to love will come...' Leonard sang.

'So you want to romance me?' she said.

He frowned.

'Because I don't think I can just jump into bed with you tonight.'

He gave a little nod-shake of his head, as if he were saying, yes, I know that and no, of course you can't. And then he looked straight at her again and said, 'Why not? We don't have to make love. Just lie together.'

'No.' She was frowning and wondering why she felt so cross and resistant. Was it because he might actually get to her, might actually resurrect the love and then the problem would be even worse? She had been like a desert hungry for rain when Jake had arrived; it had been easy for him to win her. Just the merest bit of attention, of tenderness, and she had been his; John now had the odds stacked against him but he wanted to get back into the ring and what if, in his determination to prove his love, what if he did resurrect buried feelings?

'There was one morning you rang me,' she said, backing away from that train of thought. 'Was that you or Jake?'

'The day you made that strange comment about evolution?' he asked.

Had she? She thought back.

'Something about Mum's generation and their inhibitions.'

That rang a faint bell. 'I think so.'

He looked a little sick. 'Jake. I was... there. Mia, do we have to –?'

'Go back over every detail? Some things, yes.' So it had been Jake. They had been testing her. Fuck.

'I'm sorry,' he said again, and sounded it.

They were both guilty. What had Jake said? They'd been in the garage... *I haven't been learning my lines for nothing.* He'd been speaking literally and she'd had no idea. But much as she wanted to throw stones, she'd been deceitful too. It might only be a little bit compared to their huge act, but it was still deceit. She had hidden her desire for other men and then held back what had happened with Nick from her husband – both of them.

'You should know,' she said abruptly, 'that while you were off in Paris with that Melissa, I had my own little...' What? How would you describe what had happened with Nick? It was way too embarrassing.

'But nothing happened with me and Mel,' he said. 'I told you that.'

'Well, nothing nearly happened with me, too.'

'Nearly nothing?'

'Both.'

'I'm confused.'

'It was a guy I met at Sheryl's party. He... got to me. Not at first – at first I thought he was an arrogant prick, but...' Shit. How did you say this? Maybe she didn't have to. Maybe she shouldn't even have begun.

'So you...?' John prompted. He looked troubled.

'We didn't sleep together,' she said. 'It was just a bit of a pash on their love seat.' That made her sound like a teenager. She wished she had never opened her mouth about this. Bloody honesty gene!

'Because you didn't want to?'

Mia shifted on the couch restlessly, bumping Bitsy, who stirred and then settled again. 'My body wanted to,' she said, 'but I wasn't sure. Too bloody inhibited myself, I suppose.' She sounded irritated.

John smiled his beautiful smile. 'We're a pair,' he said. He stood up and held out a hand toward her. 'Come to bed with me. I promise to be inhibited.'

A smile tweaked at her face in response. She hesitated, battling demons, then stood up slowly, unseating Bitsy again, and took his hand. With great tenderness, John led her into the bedroom.

Mia woke to the morning call of birds. There were arms around her; they must have slept in this cuddled-together position all night. John had kept his promise and not tried anything intimate; he'd just held her after they'd climbed into bed, he in his shorts, she in her nightie, both feeling almost shy when they finally lay facing each other. He'd gazed at her with his beautiful hazel eyes, stroking her hair, the other arm resting in the dip of her waist, hand firmly against her back. They hadn't spoken, other than when he had said, simply, 'Thank you.'

It had taken them both a while to fall asleep. Finally she had turned and he had nestled close, spooning her, his breath stirring the hair on the top of her head, one arm across her breasts, his hand lightly cupping her face. He had slept first, the sleep of the contented. She had lain there listening to him breathe, her head almost bursting with the intensity of her need for a clear answer.

She thought back to that last class with Bernard, revisiting the thing that had kicked off this Hero's Journey for her: her desire to be free of the imperfect man and to find the perfect man. How childish that sounded in the cold light of consciousness. Now she doubted that such a man existed. Those first two classes with Bernard had planted the seed in her mind that the perfect partner was the man who pushed her to grow, not the one who climbed out of a gift-wrapped box with all the right looks and qualities. If she was right, then maybe John *was* perfect for her. By frustrating her, he gave her the opportunity to take responsibility for what she wanted out of her marriage rather than living passively and resentfully, waiting for the world to change for her. Perhaps her God-self was asking her Character-self to grow up...

Besides, looking at it from his point of view and from Jake's point of view, what made her such a catch? She had average looks, wasn't successful in some inspiring vocation, didn't have any stunning abilities, often burnt the dinner and lost her keys, had destroyed many a romantic evening by taking a too-long visit to the loo... She was not that special.

John made a little sound, a murmuring waking-up sound. He kissed the back of her neck and as he moved, she became aware of his erection pressing against her.

'Morning,' he said.

'Good morning.' She rotated to face him and he smiled with such happiness that she felt touched.

'I watched a TED talk on the way home in the plane,' he said, stroking the side of her face. 'A sex therapist. It was very good – about how to keep the spark alive in your marriage. And about affairs, why they happen.'

'Sheryl must have seen the same one. She was telling me about it too. So why do affairs happen?'

'Because comfortable love is the enemy of eroticism. You need space from each other, and surprises, to keep the spark alive.'

Unpredictability, Mia thought. 'Well, we've had space,' she said. 'But someone else filled it – and brought the surprises.'

'I know,' John said evenly. 'But we can keep looking for ways of keeping the spark alive. Like talking about our fantasies. I know you have them – things you don't tell me. What if you did? And maybe I could do some of that...'

This was a turn-around for the books. She made a face, wary.

'*I* set up the space and the surprise, remember that,' he added. 'It must mean I'm not as boring as you always thought.' He let his hand roam down her back, drawing her close with a purposefulness that she hadn't experienced from him in a long time. She felt an unexpected response from her body, a warmth, a ripple between them. He felt it too. She saw it in his eyes. They had marvelled over the years at this shared psychic ability to feel a connection between them that wasn't yet physical. It was still there; the connection wasn't dead. He leaned closer and kissed her lightly. She let him.

She let him.

She let him kiss her.

She let him back into the hidden depths of her.

At some point she let her passivity go and began to respond with an intensity of her own. The memory of Jake melted away and she was fully present with John, aroused and responding to him and giving him hell for what he'd put her through, showing him that she was not to be toyed with, that she was a strong, passionate woman with love to give who wanted to be loved and relished and cherished and she wasn't going to stand for a second-best life anymore. When they finally fell apart, panting, the bed in disarray, he said, 'Well, if that was the outcome of me swapping with Jake, I'd do it all over again.'

She laughed and he rolled closer and kissed her and said, 'We've been too serious, you and me. If there's something I can thank my brother for, it's pushing me to lighten up and take a risk.'

'Oh really?' she said, wrapping one bare leg around him. 'Well for your information, he has suggested that we all live together. The three of us.'

'No way,' John said at once. 'I'm not sharing my wife.'

'You already have,' she said tartly, pushing him away.

He pulled her back. 'Are you seriously considering it?'

'If I am, it's your fault!'

'Fuck.' He rolled onto his back and stared at the ceiling.

'Can't share?' she asked. She was part-teasing, part… what? *Was* she serious?

'You know how it's been with us,' he said, almost angrily. 'Jake's taken so much that was mine – toys that he'd play with and then break and discard, Mum and Dad's attention. Now you…'

'You gave –'

'All right,' he conceded irritably. 'I gave you to him. It was stupid. But he's not the sharing type; he's the taking type.'

'How do you know? He's the one who suggested it.'

'But are you really –?'

'I don't know,' she said. 'All I know is we have a bizarre situation. Your brother's child is growing in here,' touching her belly, 'and I love both of you.

What are we going to do with those jigsaw pieces?'

In the shower, watching him floss with the thoroughness she remembered, she quoted, "Life is not a problem to be solved; it is a mystery to be lived."

He turned around, still working the floss through his teeth, a questioning expression on his face.

'Osho,' she said. She felt, somehow, lighter, clearer. There wasn't a final full stop – there wouldn't be until they all died. There was just a new decision and a new set of consequences. You lived through that lot until it was time for the next new decision. You could never fully know anyone, or even yourself, so you just kept going, kept responding to what life threw up. The important thing was to not blame someone else for something she'd had a share in creating. Jake had said that to her: 'It takes two to tango...' There was even a famous cartoon about it – Pogo: 'We have met the enemy and he is us.'

John was bending over the sink, gargling and spitting. He turned back to face her as she turned off the taps in the shower and stepped out and reached for her towel. He looked very serious. 'Jake won't hang around for the baby. Look at his track record.'

'He hung around after he lost that huge acting opportunity.'

'But it's all starting again.'

'Maybe I won't need him to be there all the time.'

'What are you saying?'

She wrapped the towel around her body, feeling drips falling onto her bare shoulders from her wet hair. What was she saying? She held back the words that had been on the tip of her tongue and instead, said, 'Just that I'm actually grateful to you. It was stupid and cruel – and unnecessary if we'd just been able to be honest with each other and keep that spark alive. But we weren't, and it's true, your crazy idea has given each of us something we wanted. Jake knows that too. So I'm grateful for what it's given me.' One hand strayed to her belly, to the life busily multiplying in there. 'Maybe we can figure this out, the three of us, so we each get more of what we want.'

She went grocery shopping without John so that she could look for birthday presents as well. Was stuck. Absolutely baffled. Rang Sheryl for ideas and sat in a café until her fascinated friend arrived with Talia in a sling to help her look and hear the update in person.

'Oh. My. God!' Sheryl's eyes were wide. She threw back her head and laughed. 'Think of the fun you three could have! Can you imagine? Going out with both of them together and totally freaking people out! Or having the boys take turns as hubby – I mean, no one would know!'

'But it's a ridiculous idea. It would go wrong in a heartbeat. They'd be jealous of each other and how would I decide who I was sleeping with? It's insane!'

'Yes, but it's worth a bash. They both love you; you love both of them; they both want to raise the kid.'

Mia spooned the heart off the top of her latté. 'Do you think people take life too seriously?'

'Absolutely. Osho's all over that.'

'I know.' She licked her spoon.

'And isn't enlightenment just about lightening up?'

'Is it?'

'Sure! There's all sorts of spiritual high fallutingness but bottom line, God's got to have a fabulous sense of humour. You three have probably given Him a great old laugh.'

Mia smiled.

33

She and John didn't speak much on Sunday. Mia had assignments to complete and John was working on his businesses. So they sat at the kitchen table together for most of the day, writing and researching. Took Bitsy for a walk and held hands as they used to.

On Sunday night John wanted to pick Jake up from the airport on his own, so Mia waited at home, wondering what they would be saying to each other. But she felt very, very tired, and fell asleep before they arrived home.

On Monday morning when she woke up, the other side of the bed was cool and empty. She found Jake sitting on the kitchen steps eating a bowl of muesli and gazing at the garden. John was out riding.

'How was the audition?' she asked.

'Good, thanks,' he said. But nothing else. His tone was quiet and thoughtful.

She opened the fridge and poured herself a glass of orange juice, then remembered. 'Happy birthday.'

He smiled. 'Thanks.' Proffered his cheek when she came close to give him a kiss.

Unspoken conversations drifted between them, light motes of dust briefly visible in a shaft of sunlight, questions and expression of feelings. It seemed that they were both unable to voice any of it.

Bitsy barked and moments later John entered in his cycling gear, his hairline sweaty; instantly, he looked from one of them to the other.

This was not going to be easy, Mia thought. 'Happy birthday,' she said, moving toward him to give an identical cheek-kiss.

He looked surprised. 'I'd completely forgotten.'

'I have some things for you both. Are we all home tonight?'

They would be, and so they left it at that. Jake prepared to leave for his massage course and continue learning what he already knew; Mia dressed for work, reflecting gratefully that she hadn't felt nauseous this morning or, come to think of it, the last few days; John went to have a shower.

They cooked together that evening, one dish each, negotiating their way around each other in the kitchen with almost excessive courtesy. John had a recipe book open and a frown on his face as he tackled a brand new dish. Jake was making a mess on his part of the bench as he chopped an abundance of vegetables then threw them into a pot, tasting as he went, a glass of red wine within reach. Mia hid in the pantry, working in secret on a birthday cake, the blender periodically drowning out the music Jake was playing. Bitsy nosed around the floor, seeking dropped crumbs; she was particularly successful around Jake's feet.

Mia delivered her cake into the oven and then made a salad and set the table with their best crockery and candles. John had always sat in one particular seat, a position that Jake had clearly been instructed to adopt when he arrived. When the brothers' true identities had first been revealed she had noticed John reclaiming his seat, but in the last couple of days he seemed to have either surrendered that right or decided that it didn't matter anymore.

John brought a plate of carefully shaped and fried salmon patties to the table; Jake followed him with a steaming pot. 'It was going to be vegetable soup,' he said, 'but it's evolved into a stew.'

'That would be the soup-stew you made when I stayed at your place?' John said, pouring two glasses of non-alcoholic wine.

'Not exactly. No dish I ever make comes out the same.'

'Well, it smells delicious.' Mia settled into a seat and took the drink John was holding out to her. She waited for the brothers to sit and then raised her glass, saying, 'Happy birthday, you two.'

They responded with thanks, and in the clinking that followed Jake said, 'To Mia, for being a good sport with two pretty cracked guys,' and John said, 'To resolution and forgiveness...'

Conversation from there meandered around their day, what each had done, John's progress on one of the websites... Finally Mia couldn't stand it anymore. She put her cutlery down and said, 'So what are we going to do?' Jake took a deep breath, as if fortifying himself. John wiped his mouth with a napkin and leaned back in his seat. They both looked at her.

'It's not just up to me,' she said. 'I think we each need to say what we want. This fiasco came about partly because John and I didn't do that, so he and I need to at least say what we want. And I think you do too,' looking at Jake. She almost added, 'You can't just keep giving up and walking away from things,' but decided not to.

'All right.' John pushed his plate a little further in from the edge of the table. 'You both know what I want. I want to stay here as your husband, Mia. I want to keep building the businesses we've started. And I'm happy to...' glancing at Jake, 'raise the child with Mia.'

Mia, whose face was usually an open book, kept her feelings to herself. She turned to Jake.

Jake pushed his plate in. He typically had no problem expressing himself, and if he had anything uncomfortable to say, he often said it with such a winning smile that the sting in his words was diluted, but tonight he was quiet, sober. He picked up his glass of wine and then put it back down again. 'I want to stay here as your husband, too, Mia, and be a father to my kid. I want to carry on with massage and work with John on the businesses and pick up some acting work wherever I can. But fuck the gardening.'

Mia and John laughed at that, and then they all grew still again because the problem now sat, clearly defined, at the table with them. The brothers focused their attention on her.

Mia moistened her lips. She took a sip of her drink and looked from one pair of hazel eyes to the other. Both sets watching her, gentle and deep. Both men waiting, hanging out for her decision.

'You know that I feel very confronted and torn and I've been agonising about this ever since…' A stream of images darted through her mind. 'I thought I was out of love with you, John, but I've seen the possibility of bringing that love back to life.' John didn't dare to smile; his accountant-gene was too strong to count his chickens before they'd hatched, but she saw a little change of colour in his skin, the pinkness of pleasure. Jake was very still, his thoughtful expression etched in granite.

'Jake,' she said, 'you came out here and completed your mission admirably. You did bring me back to life.' Now John's careful smile was freezing and Jake had taken a breath. 'But, of course, I don't really know you. We're almost strangers to each other.' She noticed, for the first time, that neither man was wearing the wedding band. She wondered where it was.

'And yet there's a baby coming. It will be your child, and I know you want to father it, and the last thing I'd want to do is to keep that from you. But…' she looked down at the white cloth, at her empty plate with its remainder of sauce and crumbs and shreds of salad. 'But I think you'll want to keep travelling and taking opportunities that turn up and I don't want to do this on my own. And I know John would stick around.'

Jake made a move, as if he was about to interrupt, and seeing she wasn't finished, he closed his mouth again, shoulders sagging. John had sat up a little.

'There's another thing,' she said, 'if there's anything I've learnt through all of this, it's that my idea of marriage has needed to grow up. I put too much expectation on you guys. I wanted you both to just know what I wanted and deliver it. To give me everything I wanted – the romance, the stability, the fun, the depth… without really taking much responsibility for those things myself. I didn't come out and ask for what I wanted or co-create it with you.' She was looking at John now. 'I mean, I did say what I wanted but I was complaining more than taking responsibility; I just got frustrated when I didn't get the response I wanted instead of persisting or getting better at asking. So,' she paused, conscious that she was about to step off the edge of a cliff. 'So I suppose the thing I most want is to be in a marriage with someone who wants to create it with me consciously. I want to be married to a man who wants to deliberately create a really fulfilling relationship and family.'

John and Jake both shifted in their seats at that, looking up, leaning forward.

'What if that's both of us?' Jake asked.

'We can't all live together!' John objected at once. 'That would be a recipe for disaster.'

'Why?' Jake asked. 'Families are pretty mixed-up these days. With all the LGBT people coming out of the woodwork, and the same-sex marriages...'

'You and I would never –'

'But that's what Mia is saying,' Jake said. 'She wants to know if we're up for working through issues and creating a conscious marriage.'

'She said '*a* man,' John pointed out.

'That's a detail,' Jake said.

John looked at Mia. 'Is that right?'

Mia took another breath. She felt a little shaky. 'None of us knows how it would work, just as you two didn't know if Jake coming out here would work, but it might be worth a risk.'

John made a little noise, a little exclamation of disgust or disagreement or something, and she rushed on. 'I can't choose between you. I can't reject Jake outright even though I've only known him for a couple of months, and I can't reject you, John. Don't you see? I think we need to set it up as best we can and trust.' *Trust the path and our instincts and heart...*

'Set it up as best we can!' He rose, his chair almost crashing behind him, and strode into the kitchen. They heard water running in the sink.

Jake stood up. 'John!'

'I'm coming back,' they heard him mutter. He returned with a pitcher of water and poured them each a glass. Sat and drank. Set his glass back down.

'I don't want to share my wife,' he had said to Mia the other day. 'You already have,' she'd replied.

'I think we need a new house,' Mia said calmly, although she didn't feel calm. 'With a bedroom each. And a nursery. I think you'll both be going back to England now and then on business, and to see your mum, and Jake might end up meeting someone else – really,' she said, stopping him, 'be realistic. You won't want half a wife. Neither of you will. But I can't choose, so to me this is just the next step. We play it by ear. It will be a test, like any marriage, but without making forever promises that we can't keep.'

'My God,' John said. He turned to Jake. 'I could clobber you for suggesting we just 'play it by ear'! For stopping me from thinking things through as I usually would!'

Mia reached out a hand to each one of them, a restraining hand on John's wrist at first, but then she clasped hands with both of them, one on each side of her. 'Do you have a better idea?'

'Yes,' John said, through gritted teeth.

'An idea that works for each one of us?'

She saw him struggling with himself, the muscles in his jaw working.

'What will people say?' he said at last. 'Two men living with you –'

'Identical at that,' Jake grinned. 'It could be fun.'

'You remember what you said about us being so conservative,' Mia said. 'Well, here's our chance…'

'To what? Say 'fuck you' to society?'

'It doesn't have to be a 'fuck you'. It can be a…'

'A 'check this out',' Jake suggested. 'Three consenting adults living together and raising a child together. There are plenty of open marriages nowadays; it doesn't need to be so weird.'

'Oh, it'll be considered weird, all right,' John said grimly.

'But we're not accountable to society. We don't have to fit in with society's taboos.'

'Just because you're a bohemian,' John muttered.

'Do you have a better idea?' Mia asked again.

'I can't share you like that – living together and taking turns in the bedroom with you! I know myself. It would drive me insane. I couldn't do it.'

'I don't know that I can either,' she admitted. She released their hands and hers trailed back toward her on the cloth, then off the edge of the table into her lap.

'Then what are you saying?'

'Just that I can't choose. I love you both.' It was the first time she'd said it aloud.

John looked a little sick. Jake stared across the room at their father's painting. For a long time, no one spoke. Then Jake sighed.

'All right,' he said. 'I'm the wild card here. I do want to stick around but I don't want to destroy...' He looked at John. 'You win, bro. I'll move out. But I'd like to immigrate so I can get to know the kid. I'll be Uncle Jake.' He sighed again, drank some of his wine.

Mia felt as if she was sinking. She held onto herself. *Trust...*

John said nothing; she sensed that he was prepared to accept his brother's withdrawal, not daring to say anything that might jeopardise his success. Jake was the one with the tight jaw now, and she was pulsing. She felt hot. She could feel her own heart beating.

'Fuck it, no!' Jake said suddenly, standing up. 'I wanted to commit and I was serious about that. We set this up and we should bear the consequences of it. We can take turns living with Mia if we can't manage being together.'

She was breathing again, very shallowly, her mouth dry. It was such a crazy idea. It would probably never work! John and Jake would continually fight and she would never be able to choose who she was sleeping with and it was probably a very morally questionable idea and –

'Who gets called 'daddy'?' John asked.

No one spoke for a moment. Jake slowly sat down again.

'We've got seven months to figure that one out,' Mia said. She barely dared to look at John. This was insane, but if a healthy marriage needed space and surprises, then maybe...

The oven alarm rang shrilly and they all reacted.

'Stay here,' she said, and went to get the birthday cake. It was quiet at the dining table. She took the baking dish out of the oven, breathing in the warm delicious scent. She could hear a very low rumble of voices. She strained to hear as she poured cream and sugar into a small saucepan, but couldn't make out what they were saying. She'd forgotten to buy candles. Pregnancy brain again, she supposed. But they wouldn't want candles. She remembered John telling her that Jake had always blown his candles out before he'd had a chance, and then laughed and blown his own out as well, before John could. It was one of those sore spots from their childhood. She could just imagine Jake doing that, now that she was getting to know him. He had a cheeky trait that would have driven the serious, sensible John mad – and yet been good for him.

John came in with the dirty dishes and she glanced at him, but he said nothing. Jake followed with the serving dishes and half-empty pot of stew.

'I thought I told you boys to stay in there.'

They headed back out and she poured the sauce over her cake. Grabbed the two envelopes she'd hidden in the tea towels drawer and took everything in, singing Happy Birthday, although her voice, alone in the room, trailed out before the song was finished.

'Thank you,' John said formally, as he usually did.

'Is that sticky date pudding?' Jake asked.

'I think you both like it.' She set it on the table between them and passed them the envelopes; they both thanked her and slit them open while she cut slices for everyone.

Jake drew out a theatre subscription. He beamed and came over to hug his thanks.

'There's something else in there,' she said.

John was pulling it out of his envelope: a little obstetrician's appointment card.

'Our first ultrasound,' she said. 'I was hoping you'd both come.'

Jake had found his appointment card and was now reading the theatre subscription details more closely. He looked up. 'It's for two.'

'I want to go with you,' she said. Would he realise that she'd bought the subscription as an unspoken message to him to stick around?

John was frowning at the note in his envelope. 'In the garage'?' he asked.

She smiled a 'better go see', smile, and he rose, and she followed him, and Jake came after her while Bitsy tumbled along at their feet.

There was a new bike in the garage. Pink. With a jazzy pink helmet hanging from the handlebars. John looked at her.

'You've always wanted me to go riding with you,' she said. 'I might not be able to for much longer but...'

The smile that burst open on his face was so heart-warming that tears welled in her eyes.

When they'd washed the dishes Mia found a deck of playing cards in the box of games and set it down on the table. 'If we're going to do this, we're going to have to get on with each other.'

'You know he doesn't play fair, don't you?' Jake said, picking the cards up.

'Of course I play fair!' John retorted. 'I also play to win.'

Jake raised his hands in surrender. 'I rest my case.'

'He would distract and try to stop the game early and if he couldn't, he'd sulk and run to mummy,' John told Mia.

'I was a resourceful kid,' Jake explained, shuffling the cards.

'Are you two going to squabble all the time?' she asked.

'Yes,' they both said.

'Suck it up,' Jake added.

'If you want both of us...' John pointed out. 'And actually Mia's not unlike you, where games are concerned,' he told Jake. 'She suddenly gets tired when she's losing. Or she suggests we play something else. Strangely enough, I think I married my twin.' He shook his head at the revelation. 'You two are pretty similar, whereas Mia and I... You know what they say about opposites.'

It was interesting watching this veiled challenge, as if John had surrendered and yet never would. Which was exactly how he was: quiet and unobtrusive, but decisive and persistent and very focused.

Jake was smiling thoughtfully as he looked at his hand. 'You've been given a second chance, bro. I wouldn't blow it, if I were you.'

'What did you do about passports?' Mia asked.

'We swapped them. Why?'

'Just wondering. Will you sponsor Jake to immigrate?'

'If I have to,' John said. But he reached a foot out under the table and stroked the side of her leg to soften his words.

'Don't worry,' Jake said to Mia. 'I'm used to it. I have a very tough skin.'

'*You* have a tough skin!' John raised his brows. 'I was the one suffering when you teased me and broke my stuff and got me into trouble while everyone thought the sun shone out of your bum.'

'It was only while we were little,' Jake said to Mia. 'Once we were older it was John who got all the accolades – the school prizes and achievements – and me always trailing in last.'

John laid some cards on the table and the other two reviewed their hands.

'Actually I was always pretty envious of John,' Jake continued. 'I didn't want to *be* him – I couldn't stand maths – but I did want his success.'

'You were never envious of me,' John scoffed. 'Not until we had that talk after Dad passed.'

'Yes, I was,' Jake said. 'I hid it well. I'm an actor.'

John looked at him.

'So you came all the way out here, running away from your brother, for no good reason,' Mia said.

'That's hardly true,' John began, and then he saw her point. '*I* was envious of *you*,' he said to Jake. 'Your popularity. How easily you made friends and went through life. How creative and imaginative you were, compared to me.'

'And yet you came up with this wild plan.'

'It was mutual, remember?'

'You suggested it first. And you might not have been feeling special, but despite my best efforts to unseat you, Mia won't let you go.'

'If we're tracking ironies,' Mia said to Jake, 'then there are a few for you as well. You might have felt unsuccessful but you revived a marriage and you committed to me even when you could have had that big break –'

'You suggested the charity and the Financials for Artists business idea,' John interrupted. 'And the frigging annual prize. I'm just the lackey.'

'You've got the brilliant detailed brain that's going to take my ideas and make them work,' Jake said.

'And you've got the sense of humour that will keep us on the rails.' John held out his hand for his brother to shake. 'Truce?'

Watching them, Mia felt a tenderness, as if she was witnessing the coming-together of a pair of warring nations. No doubt it would all go to shit again soon, but they'd had this moment; they'd planted this seed. She and the baby were providing the incentive for them to manage their antipathy towards each other. So she wasn't as unlovable or unworthy as she'd always feared. Whatever happened next, and whatever had happened in the past, was immaterial; everyone had been doing their best, and they would each carry on doing just that.

The End

Epilogue

From: Eliza Hartington
1st October
Subject: Thank you and congratulations
To: John Hartington

Dear John

Thank you for spending so much time with me on the phone explaining how to set up my E-Mail. It must have been a terribly expensive telephone call. Well, we shall save on those expenses now because here I am, E-Mailing you.

Thank you for sharing your news. I'm glad that you and Jake and Mia are sorting out your situation. Congratulations, too, on this latest development. I'm sure you will make a wonderful father.

It's been a dreary autumn so far but the move went well. The packing and removalist company was excellent and I am enjoying my new abode. I have your father's artwork hanging throughout my little unit and the retirement village purchased a print for the foyer. Everyone is very excited about their brush with fame, not the least of whom is me.

Your Mother

From: Eliza Hartington
1st October
Subject: Congratulations on two counts
To: Jake Hartington

Dear Jake

Well! What a development. Strange as this arrangement is, I'm
thrilled that you are finally going to have a hand in raising one of
your children. (Yes, I do know about the other children and hope to
meet them one day.)

But now to the child in question. Congratulations. I'm sure you will
make a wonderful father. In fact, I'd like to come over to Australia
for a holiday and meet this child after he or she is born, and also
get to know my daughter-in-law a little better.

I understand, Jake, that you've been successful in an audition.
Ironic, isn't it, how life often delivers us the thing we want when we
stop seeking it? Your father and I both wanted him to experience
success as an artist, and now he's becoming quite famous, albeit
posthumously. I've heard him mentioned on the radio and read
articles in the press – even the Daily Mail – and so he could have
been, and we could have had, everything we wanted had we only
trusted and taken a risk.

Your Mother

Eliza Hartington
1st October
Congratulations and a request
To: Mia Hartington

Dear Mia

I can imagine how difficult the last few months have been for you. I'm very touched that you have not simply turned my sons out, and also touched by how much they both seem to care for you.

I hope you won't be taken aback if your old mother-in-law asks to come and visit – some time after the baby is born, perhaps? I won't intrude. I won't expect to be accommodated but I would like to see you all, especially now. I'm very excited about this grandchild and would be sad if I were never to meet him or her.

My boys have done their father proud and taught me a lesson too. I'm very grateful.

Best wishes

Eliza

Acknowledgements

This book was triggered by a 'what if?' question, sparked by my daughters Emma and Lesley. It was fun to write but I could never have guessed what would happen in the aftermath of writing it when a new man came into my life, turning everything upside down. I ended up separating from my long-time, much loved partner, Derek Rawson, although I'm very glad that we are still firm friends. I want to salute his great love and generosity in the extraordinary and inspiring way he let me go, and to thank him for 29 rich years as life and business partners. Derek produced the layout of all of my books to date and I hope he will continue to do more into the future. He has also provided much technical support over the years and both created and managed my website – the latest upgrades with our son, Jeremy Strong.

Liliane Grace is the author of two 'personal development novels' for youth, *The Mastery Club - See the Invisible, Hear the Silent, Do the Impossible* (2007 Independent Book Publisher's Award for Youth Fiction), and sequel *The Hidden Order*, as well as two children's picture books in the Champion Series: *The Boy Who Barked* (about Dr John Demartini) and *The Boy Who Found His Pulse* (about Don Tolman). *The Mastery Club*® has been translated into Mandarin and German and gave rise to a program for youth that has been taught in England, Scotland, South Africa, America and Bali. *Quest For Riches*, a new book for teenagers that teaches financial literacy through story, is launching in 2018.

Wanted: Greener Grass is Liliane's first women's fiction. Having written many short stories about adult relationships, she was inspired to try her hand at a novel and particularly wanted to contribute some depth of thought to the arena of romance, hence the categorisation of this book as 'Conscious Chick-Lit'. Liliane is also working on a non-fiction book about affairs and has many other works for youth and adults in process.

https://lilianegrace.com for more information and to download your free 'Hero's Journey' mini e-course.

www.ingramcontent.com/pod-product-compliance
Lightning Source LLC
Chambersburg PA
CBHW031141120726
47905CB00006B/1775